Northern Dawn

Northern Wolf Series
Book Four

Daniel Greene

Sign up for Daniel's spam-free newsletter, The Greene Army, and receive special offers and updates on his new releases. Visit http://www.danielgreenebooks.com/?page_id=7741

For Steve and Mike - thanks for all the fun times at the Lake and the never-ending 'Civil War' adventures we had as kids.

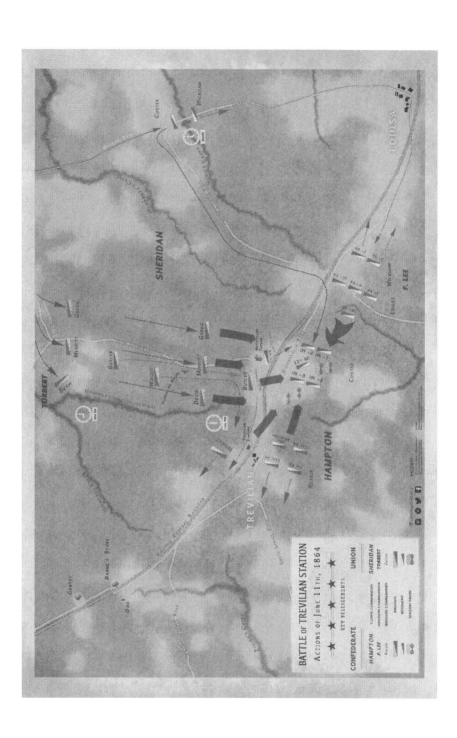

BATTLE of TREVILIAN STATION

ACTIONS of JUNE 11TH, 1864

Chapter 1

Noon, May 28, 1864
North of Haw's Shop, Virginia

Cool wind lapped his cheeks as he galloped in the lead of the 5th Michigan Volunteer Cavalry Regiment's column. His golden locks bounced upon his starred shoulders, soft drums beating his arrival in tune with his horse's strides. Air flipped his wide-brimmed black slouch hat in the front. His horse, Victory, a steady gray gelding, churned each league with healthy endurance muscles flexing and his chest heaving as he put forth continuous effort. Yet it was as if the animal held back, waiting to unleash his true potential at his rider's command.

Union Brigadier General George Armstrong Custer was not alone as he directed his horse toward the sounds of battle. He glanced at the rider on his right. Colonel Russell A. Alger smiled as he kept pace with his commanding officer, his black beard encompassing a handsome face. The two men had been friends since Custer had taken command of the Michigan Brigade. On Custer's other side, his aide, Lieutenant Edward Granger, tried to keep his kepi atop his head as they sped through the Virginia countryside, his eyes gaping on his thinly mustached face.

They raced past a field of green wheat swaying with a breath of wind. A log cabin stood in the distance and a forest of straight pine loomed nearby. The hooves pounded the dusty earth to its own beat. As faintly as a faraway church bell, the sounds of battle rang forth.

So Gregg's got himself into a little scrap? He's lucky to have me at his beck and call. Custer's entire brigade trailed behind him led by the 5th then followed by the 7th, 1st, 6th, and lastly, the 13th Michigan. His men farther to the north had skirmished with rebel cavalry early in the morning, but the rebels had been run off before any battle of consequence could take place. It was all a pity. He had been looking for a chance to bring them to heel. Then he'd received an urgent request from one of Brigadier General David McM. Gregg's aides to travel back to Haw's Shop in support of his division.

The Army of the Potomac's Cavalry Corps had ridden ahead of the main body almost ten miles to spearhead Grant's final and last attempt to outflank Lee's Army of Northern Virginia. Then a decision would have to be made on what the next phase of Grant's campaign would look like. He simply would run out of land to place his army between Lee and Richmond. And everyone in both armies knew it.

The day prior, Custer's men had crossed a pontoon bridge over the Pamunkey River along with the rest of the Cavalry Corps to secure a safe crossing for the slower moving 6th Corps near Hanovertown. The cavalry immediately dispatched scouts to locate the Army of Northern Virginia. With the commotion ahead, apparently Gregg had found more of Lee's army than he would have liked, and Custer could ride to his rescue. It reminded him of Gettysburg.

His small staff sped past an extensive blacksmith's shop with its doors boarded and barred. He noted the absence of gray smoke from a single chimney, twice as broad as one for a house. *Must be Haw's Shop.* A home stood nearby, shuttered and desolate and a reddish-bricked church with a white steeple rested along the other side of the road.

A civilian man in a crimson-stained shirt stood on the steps of the church, watching with his arms folded across his chest. If distant gunfire wasn't a clear indicator of a battle in medias res, homes and churches filled with the wounded sure were. Custer had no doubt that this man would be busy far into the night. The clergyman peered unafraid as Custer and his entourage blurred past.

Cannon fire boomed as they closed in on a Union battery unlimbered beneath a copse of trees. An officer sat atop his horse with field glasses pressed to his eyes. His mount stomped its feet in irritation with every cannon blast, causing the man to try to control the animal with his free hand, and more often than not disrupted his scan of the field. Custer drew Victory to a trot then with a loud, "Whoa." He pulled the animal to a halt. "You did well, Vic," he said, patting the horse's flank. A mist of sweat disappeared into the air, the heat greedily dispersing it.

Brigadier General David McM. Gregg let his field glasses fall around his neck, acknowledging Custer. He was the commander of the 2nd Division of the Cavalry Corps. His long patriarchal dark brown beard centered on his chest below his heart. He was a tall man, as tall as Custer, and his naturally bulging eyes were besieged by stress. "George," he sighed.

Custer flashed him a quick grin beneath a formidable blond mustache. "I came as quick as I could."

Gregg's mouth quivered. "I appreciate your prompt arrival. We've gotten ourselves into a quite a tangle here. If it's not the land, it's the people of this godforsaken state."

"I find this country quite charming," Custer said.

"Then you haven't been here long enough," Gregg said, the sound of perturbation rising in his voice.

Custer steered Victory near the beleaguered division commander. "Rebs found us quick."

"Too quick." Gregg gestured at the forest in irritation. "They were waiting in the woods. Now they have some log works built and are fighting with a stubborn fierceness. There must be at least two divisions, perhaps the whole damn corps. They're hemmed in by a couple of swampy creeks. It would be a true slaughter if we pushed there. Bogged down, our men would be stationary targets. Scarecrows in a field. Perfect for target practice." He turned his head to the side in disgust for the thought. "Davies tried to run them off with a frontal assault but to no avail." His horse sidestepped and danced, and he strained to bring her under control. Smoke choked the air with another volley of cannon fire. "Shot Davies's bloody saber in two."

"I trust the general is unhurt?"

"He's fine. Very excited about the whole endeavor." Gregg appeared to stop short of saying more on the matter but then thought better of it. "I'm lucky Irvin arrived when he did."

Custer recognized the even taller quiet man that sat mounted near Gregg. His men had nicknamed him "Long John" because of his height, and he was David Gregg's first cousin, but most of his peers called him Irvin. His brown beard was shorter than Gregg's yet still longer than most. His limbs were lanky, reminding Custer of a willow tree. A rounded slouch hat graced his head, and beneath the rim, his eyes scanned the terrain, searching for anything to gain advantage over the foe.

Irvin gestured out near the trees and spoke. "They won't push my boys back, but we've spent most of our ammunition." He pointed toward a particular spot shrouded with gun smoke. "Those boys have Enfield rifles. More like mounted infantry. They can reach out and touch us if we're not careful, not to mention they are dug in."

"Who's outfit?" Custer said, squinting at the distant cloud.

Irvin thought for a moment, his words calculated. "South Carolina under Butler, I believe."

"I do not believe I've made his acquaintance."

"Lost a foot at Brandy Station," General Gregg said. "Heard it was a cannonball. Took it clean off."

"Poor chap. Likes to fight then."

"It appears so," Irvin said. "Rosser and the Laurel Brigade are there as well."

Custer's grin widened at the name. Confederate General Thomas Rosser had been Custer's roommate and rabble-rousing confidant at the West Point Military Academy in what seemed like lifetimes ago. He affectionately referred to the man as Tex, and the man was every bit Custer's rival then. He wondered if the man still had the piss and vinegar that he had at The Academy. *Perhaps one day we'll find out, Tex.*

"Merritt's boys already stopped Chambliss from flanking us. I need your brigade here as fast as they can to anchor our left flank before Hampton gets any other ideas. To the west of Enon Church."

Custer removed his field glasses from a hard leather case on his saddle. He wrinkled his nose beneath them, the rotten-egg stench of smoke stinging his nostrils, an odor that a soldier learned to love. Through billows of gray smoke, he could make out a white steeple and building. Thick foliage grew almost right along the church's walls, stretching as far as he could see. He let the glasses drop and eyed the end of Gregg's line.

For the time being, the line was stable, but Gregg was correct in his battlefield assessment. If Hampton really wanted to expose his men to the cannon, a flanking maneuver would succeed, but the attack must take place on foot due to the terrain. The dense forest presented a near impossible obstacle for mounted movements. "Infantry may be better suited for such an adventure."

Gregg shook his head in irritation. "I sent word to Hancock through Sheridan to hurry along the 2nd Corps but haven't heard back yet."

"No need for them. I have an idea." Custer gave a shake of his head and pointed to the left flank. "I'll feed my boys in as they arrive. The 5th should be up in the next thirty minutes. The rest will be close behind."

"Hurry them along, General," Gregg said. "We need you."

Custer smiled and shared a glance with Colonel Alger. "Well, you heard him Russ. Bring your boys up on the double."

***

Less than thirty minutes passed before the 5th had arrived and dismounted, every fourth man taking the reins of his three comrades' horses so the others could fight. The rest of his brigade arrived squadron by squadron on the field behind them. His men were covered with dust, resembling an army of blue-clad ghosts. He placed two of his regiments on either side of Atlee road facing Enon Church. He left the 13th in reserve, ready to call them in to support any stiff resistance they might face. He peered at Alger, observing his dismounted troopers step into a skirmish line.

"Have them form a double-file line, Russ. Shoulder to shoulder. Today we're infantry."

"Infantry, sir?"

"I want any rebs with eyes on us to think they are facing infantry armed with repeating rifles."

Alger gestured at his aide and waved him toward the nearest company of dismounted men. He glanced curiously back at Custer. "You think that'll work?"

"Why not?"

"Cavalry doesn't like to scrap with infantry. So let's give them infantry."

Alger shook his head, watching his men step closer in rank to one another. Their uniforms and high boots may give them away as cavalry, but in the woods with the lingering battle smoke blanketing the trees as if it were an early morning fog, who knew what the rebs would think? When Alger's aide returned, he dismounted and handed his reins to a trooper on foot, intending to walk with his men. He turned and looked at Custer still mounted. "You're staying here?"

Custer gave him a stare like Alger himself was a madman on display at the circus. "You know that's not how I run this brigade."

"But you're still mounted."

"I am." Custer lifted his chin. And he intended to keep it that way. He asked his men to go in harm's way and he wouldn't let them bear that burden alone. He would be a leader they could see and hear, a witness to their bravery as much as they were to his.

Alger shook his head. "Autie, you're already a target. Atop a horse is suicide."

Lieutenant Edward Granger shifted nervously in the saddle next to Custer. The young man's face paled, knowing that his general may ask him to do the same.

Custer lifted his chin. "The men need to see me."

"See you die?" Alger said, looking away in frustration.

"Who said anything about dying?"

"Don't be a fool."

Custer's smile faded. "Fool?" He bent down near his friend. "I am no fool, Russ." He pointed his head shaking. "No man's fool. A general is as much a figurehead as he is a strategist. Men live and die at my command, and they do it willingly, even graciously because they know I would sit atop a mounted horse next to them while they march on foot. I will expose myself to even more danger than they do."

Alger met his eyes. "I understand that."

"These men will fight harder knowing their leader does the same."

"You cannot inspire men from the grave."

Custer smiled again, bearing enough confidence for a dozen men. "I disagree. Look at that Stonewall Jackson fellow or even Stuart. Their legends live on through their men."

"Yet they are not here to see it," Alger spat with disgust.

"They assuredly look down from the heavens above," Custer said. He eyed the skies for a moment before turning back to his friend.

Alger bowed his head to him. "I disagree with your decision."

"Your disapproval is noted, Colonel. Now, let's get these boys into the fight before poor Gregg's heart gives out."

Alger glanced over at Gregg. The division commander still sat atop his horse. He'd relaxed some with the arrival of each of Custer's regiments yet still scanned the field nervously, his tall cousin doing the same with a slight hunch as if he were trying to make himself a smaller target.

Both men represented some of the best commanders the Union could field, but some men were meant to be in the thick of a fight, the American sons of Ares. These men thrived in a brave and noble contest. Men who lived by it and men that would die by it. He had no intention of dying, but he had every intention of putting the enemy to the test.

"The boys want a show," Custer said to Alger. He removed his black hat and trotted in front of Alger's men. He waved his hat as he rode, and the men let up a rousing cheer, fists raised in the air. Hats twirled overhead in response. Voices lifted through the smoke. "Let's show these boys the Wolverines are here to fight!" he shouted. He drove his horse in front of his personal color bearer, Sergeant Mitchell Beloir, and gestured to him with a white glove. "Hand over the flag, Sergeant."

Beloir's mouth opened to protest, but he thought better of it, handing over Custer's personal standard. A red over blue swallow-tailed guidon with crossed white sabers and a list of the battles he'd participated in. He took the flagpole in hand and drifted past across the dirt road and in front of the men of Major James Kidd's 6th Michigan.

The sun shone even brighter as he trotted. Many of the men wore red neckties, inspired by his personal flamboyant style. Their cheers trailed him with love and adulation. He basked in their admiration, hair and flag alike flowing behind him.

He circled his horse around and this time, galloped back to the road, crouching down over his horse. He hefted the flag high and the wind tugged at the standard as it snapped and cracked in the air. He put on a display in horsemanship for his boys, and they loved him for it. He circled back near Alger. "What did you think?" He then handed the flag off to his stunned sergeant, who gave him a silent thanks.

Alger shook his head. "I think you're a madman."

"Madmen win wars." Custer pointed at the brigade band, and they struck up one of his favorite tunes, "Yankee Doodle." "Men always fight better with a battle tune."

Alger shook his head again, laughing. "You're mad."

Custer sucked in air through his nose. "Mad enough to win this war. Move your men along, Alger. It's time to relieve poor Gregg."

His friend drew his sword, pointing it toward the clouds above. "Forward march," he called out. The order echoed down the ranks of his men.

Custer flicked his reins, and his horse followed the double-ranked line of troopers as they marched into the dark dense forest. Victory's hooves thumped the ground. The line of blue-clad troopers staggered as they hit the tree line, not from the enemies' stinging bullets, but from the roughness of the terrain. Snagging roots and vines snared his men's feet. Branches and leaves scratched over faces and jackets, catching one rank to swing back and hit the next man.

More than once he had to bring his horse to a halt to prevent it from trampling the slow-moving soldiers ahead of him. Alger stumbled over a notched root. "Goddamn this wilderness," he cursed and caught himself with a hand against a tree. Custer's eyes ran along the wavering line of blue amongst the green forest. He could barely spot the road and only glimpses of the 6th struggling through the same rough underbrush. He glanced to his left flank. He hoped the 7th would have been able to find a way to squeeze closer to the creek, but a wet lowland forest forced them to slog in murky water up to their ankles, effectively delaying their movement. *Gregg was right. This forest is a godforsaken mess. My boys can hardly keep any semblance of order.*

"Forward, men!" he called out, his words holding more confidence than was warranted.

They pressed onward until the forest ridge became darker before them, almost a natural wall. Smoke hung low among the trees, a rotting egg odor in the accompanying mist. The forest held its breath. A group of his men clambered over a fallen log. A trooper slipped on leaves, tumbling onto his back. His comrades helped him upright by his elbows.

Zippppp! The shot sounded off near Custer, trailing by his head. He pushed his mustache up beneath his nose and sucked in air. *That was close.* He quickly drew his pistol. A ripple of fire crackles exploded along the ridge. The trees were sprayed red as balls and bullets struck his men. A man called out. Another cried for his mother. A few mounds of blue lay left behind the advancing troopers.

"There they are, boys!" Alger called out. "Return the favor! Fire!"

His double-filed line fired back, the rear shooting over the front rank's shoulders at the same time. The men quickly reloaded in only seconds. They stood ready for the command.

"Fire!" shouted a captain. The deadly blaze peppered the enemy line again.

The individual companies of the 5th Michigan repeated the process, and within a minute, they'd unleashed six concentrated volleys on the rebels. They enemy rested silent, clearly overwhelmed by the intensity of such quickly oppressive firepower. A volley went out from the 7th on their left. *Good, those boys are in the fight.* He eyed the enemy's earthen-filled log works ahead. The silence continued to respond to his men's attack. *Perhaps they've run?*

Alger glanced back at him. "You think they ran out of ammunition?"

"I won't have our boys wasting ammunition on target practice." Custer regripped his pistol. He used it to gesture to Granger sitting on a horse next to him. The young man looked about ready to faint, his face ashen with fear, yet his cheeks were still colored with heat. "Get word to Major Walker. Tell him to shift his line forward."

"Yes, sir!" his aide said. He turned his horse, and the forest ahead of them erupted in fire and smoke fit for the depths of hell itself. The Minié balls came for them, seeking their deaths. The bullets buzzed around and through his men, an angry swarm of bees racing to defend their hive with a deadly fury. They struck all around the men. Dozens fell this time.

To Custer's surprise, his horse screamed, rearing on two legs. He leaned forward to stay on the animal, and the mount twisted sideways. He found himself almost weightless. *Don't crush me*, he thought. For a fraction of a second, he thought he might catch himself with his hand. He reached out and he collided with the hard ground. He stretched himself into a roll, throwing leaves and dirt airborne. The beast crashed onto the forest floor next to him, rolling on its back before shifting to his belly. Victory kicked his legs.

Barreling to a stop, Custer popped his head upright. The animal screamed piteously. His men fought on. None had seen their commander go down. Alger raced for him. "Autie!"

Custer puffed air through his mustache. Victory had almost crushed him. It usually wasn't the fall, but the mount landing atop that injured man.

Ramming his sword into the ground, Alger crouched next to him on a single knee. His hands rested on his commander's shoulders. "Are you hit?"

He gave his subordinate a brief shake of his head and spit dirt from his mouth. "They gutted the poor fellow."

Offering him a hand, Alger helped Custer to his feet, brushing off dirt and leaves from his uniform. Victory yawned in terror, foam ringing his mouth, tongue lolling in fear. Custer bent down and scooped up his pistol. He removed leaves from his hair then ran a hand down his uniform. *I will not let you suffer.* He walked calmly to his mount and without hesitation shot him in the head. Smoke drifted from the barrel.

The engagement carried on. Bullets traded back and forth between opposing forces, sounding as if they were in the center of a drum competition.

Custer shook his head, staring at the dead gray beast. It was a true pity to lose such a fine animal.

"Seventh one?" Alger asked, joining him.

Custer eyed him and let out a sigh. "I believe so."

"You're one lucky son of a bitch, Autie."

The dead animal lay there. It had carried out its duty aptly and full of vigor. Yet none of that mattered. It still lay slaughtered despite its noble service. The same could be said for any of his fallen men. It all came down to luck. Another few inches and that bullet would have struck him in the leg. Another foot and it would have pierced his belly. Either shot would have spared the poor animal. Yet here he stood while his horse lay dead. His luck had held once again. "Luck is only a matter of balancing between survival and disaster." Luck was as much as a belief as it was a condition of fate. To believe in one's destiny was a self-fulfilling prophecy.

Alger ducked as a shot struck a tree, cocking his head to the side with a grin. "That one sounded close."

Custer eyed the rebel works. "Let's see how lucky those boys over there are."

Chapter 2

Afternoon, May 28, 1864
Near Haw's Shop, Virginia

Confederate Major General Wade Hampton III sat atop his favorite horse, a burly bay named Butler, near a T-shaped intersection with attending members of his staff. He patted the flank of his horse, who always carried Hampton as if he were an old friend. Together, they had the strength and endurance to overcome anything this war had to offer.

The elevation of Hampton's location gave him probably the best view possible of the ongoing battle despite the overgrown vegetation. He could make out the incoming Federal regiments as they were fed into the fight like lapping waves upon an ocean seawall. Time and time again they would charge forward, building speed like a crashing wave only to turn back, a scattered blue tide of men in clusters.

His enemy seemed as relentless and monolithic as the ocean. He understood that he tangled with more than a single division, and throughout the day, additional brigades of the blue-coated bastards had been fed into the fight. Yet he still held the utmost confidence in his men. They held superior terrain, secured by breastworks and earthen mounds to protect themselves.

He had full faith that his men could fight this battle out until dawn the next day without a break. They were those kind of soldiers. At this point in the struggle for the Southern Nation, those were all that remained. Men who would fight until the bitter end, to the end of days, to the end of the rebellion.

If they had to march to hell and back, they wouldn't complain a lick. Those were his boys.

Even if he itched for a fight, his command's purpose on this field was to avoid one. It was to gather intelligence on their enemy's movements, and as the senior commander of the Army of Northern Virginia's Cavalry Corps, he moved with every bit as much gusto as his predecessor, Major General James E. B. Stuart.

Perhaps even more gusto in some ways. He moved with much less ceremonial flare, embodying a workhorse-like persistence that was his own style of command. He exercised a much greater calculation than his predecessor. Treating the military the same as running a business, he left nothing to luck. Time spent working directly impacted whether or not he ended up in the red at the end of the day.

Although the three divisions of the Army of Northern Virginia's Cavalry Corps reported directly to Robert E. Lee, when in the field together, Hampton led them as the most senior commander in the corps. It was an unusual arrangement that led to confusion in the hierarchy of command as well as a stubborn independence from Lee's kin. He couldn't help but feel Fitz Lee and Rooney Lee were always moving half speed at his request as if they hesitated to follow his lead. For all the greatness in Southern leadership, one trait superseded their brilliance: pride.

He had pride. He was a rich businessman with respectable forefathers. The Virginians had pride. Yet there was a disconnect between the Virginians and literally everyone else as if the Army of Northern Virginia was their very own personal army. The commanders from other states were forced into roles as mere pawns to do their bidding. This attitude lingered underneath every order he gave undermining him, but he gave them anyway for their young nation depended on cooperation and cohesion.

"A rider comes from the front, sir," said Preston Hampton, his son and aide, who was the spitting image of his father at a younger age.

Hampton pressed his single optic telescope back into its compacted case. Hart's battery toward his left lay quiet at the moment. As the day had trudged on, their ammunition dwindled and so did their rate of fire. Now they picked their targets selectively to make each shot count.

The approaching rider was a tall and broad officer on an equally sturdy mount. He walked his horse behind two blue-coated men on foot. He gave one a quick boot in the back and the man stumbled with a curse but kept his feet. "Hurry up, now," the officer said with a sharp Texan accent.

A tinge of a smile crept upon the corners of Hampton's lips, masked by a bushy almost black beard. He recognized the officer as Brigadier General Thomas L. Rosser, commander of the Laurel Brigade. The sun-darkened Texan gave Hampton a quick salute over a thick brow.

He was every inch Hampton's equal in size and stature down to the overflowing beard hanging from his face, albeit he was almost twenty years younger than Hampton. The man could have masqueraded as his younger brother, Frank, or his son, Preston. The thought stung him, for Frank was gone, and the thought of losing his son made the pit of his stomach drop.

Hart's battery unleashed a new fusillade of fire, shelling the center of the Union line and keeping them hunkered down in the trees. Leaves floated down gently upon Union heads after wood splinters and shell fragments showered them with death from above.

The two prisoners balked at the sound, and Rosser spit a glob of tobacco juice on the ground.

"Gener'l."

"General Rosser."

Rosser tongued the tobacco in the corner of his mouth. "I think these boys got something you want to hear."

"That so?" Hampton lifted his chin at the two men standing below.

The two men sitting before him were dirty, sorry-looking men. Both wore blue yellow-trimmed cavalry jackets. One was a corporal, the other a private. The private was missing his hat. Both their faces were covered in black-powder grime.

"'Restled these boys up on their last go around. Didn't get a chance to talk to 'em until them bluebellies went scurrying back to their lines. But they have a mighty story to tell." He urged his horse a step over, pushing the prisoners closer to Hampton. The prisoners let themselves be corralled by the animal. "Go on now. Tell him."

"What unit are you with?" Hampton asked.

The corporal licked his lips, his eyes darting toward the ground and back at Hampton. "17th Pennsylvania under Devin."

"Who's your division commander?"

"Torbert."

Hampton nodded. His instincts were confirmed. It was more than just Gregg's division. He tangled with at least two Union divisions. "Who else?"

"No one."

Rosser kicked the man in the back, and the corporal flinched under the toe of his boot. "Let me remind you about the rope."

Hampton looked questioningly at Rosser, and the subordinate general raised his eyebrows in a bit of mischievous rancor. He tapped the rope on his saddle fondly.

The Union trooper searched the ground for an answer.

"Corporal, I have the power to send you along to prison or leave you in this man's hands." Hampton said with a pause. "Which would you prefer?"

Without pause, the corporal blurted out. "Sixth Corps crossed after us. Second Corps should be here soon."

"Two corps?" Hampton asked. Grant had a way of marching two corps to lead the army so they could support one another. The movement of two corps meant Grant's army was on the move again. His true purpose was revealed.

"That's right, sir."

Hampton eyed Rosser knowingly. "String them up anyway."

Rosser unwound the rope from his saddle loop by loop, a hangman preparing to administer justice. "Which one you want dangling a jig first?"

The Union men raised their palms toward Hampton. The two horses bullied the prisoners from running. "I told you true! I told you true!"

Hampton waved off Rosser with a short wave. "General, you may return to your brigade."

Rosser rewrapped his rope, tying it on his saddle. "Maintain our position?"

Hampton shook his head. "No need. Lee sent us to find the infantry, and it appears that we've found them. We'll get some scouts out in their direction."

Rosser kept his eye. "My boys are dug in like a tick on a fat dog with no paws."

"Another opportunity will present itself." He was sure of that. He turned, looking over his shoulder and motioning toward his aides. "Preston."

His son was a smaller younger version of Wade. Eager. Bold. Far too bold for Hampton's liking, but the boy possessed a warrior's spirit and military life came naturally to him. There was no telling if his business acumen would match that of his father for the war had forced him into his father's adopted trade as a soldier.

The war had changed his son as it did all men. Preston's mustache was thicker, his frame leaner and harder, his eyes stronger. Yet he was still the boy Hampton had carried on his shoulder, hopped on his knee, and taught to hunt. The vestiges of boyhood yet remained, but here stood a man as if Hampton had blinked and his son had turned into an adult before his eyes. *Had I been this bold as a young man?* He shook his head at the thought. He had probably been twice as bold and thrice as foolish.

"Yes, sir," Preston said.

Hampton gestured along his deployed command. "I need you to travel down the line. We are going to disengage, starting from north to south."

"That may leave Wickham hard-pressed by the new arrivals," Rosser said.

Hampton's hard dark eyes glared at the man. "His men can handle it." There was a certain weight to his words as if they were a hammer blow atop a fence post. Rosser averted his eyes at the last minute.

Rosser was well aware of Hampton's dislike of General Wickham of Fitz Lee's Division. The men who knew, knew not to discuss it for fear of facing Hampton's bear-like wrath that came like a sudden onset of a summer storm. He despised Wickham and blamed him for Frank's death at Brandy Station, and nothing could remove the gutty anger that surged in Hampton's belly every time he heard the man's name. Yet he had a war to win and Yankees to best, so he tried to put his distaste for the man away when on the field.

"My boys will depart faster than a hot knife through butter." Rosser gave a quick salute and trotted his horse back toward the front line.

Hampton turned back to Preston. "Go now. Hurry back once the orders have been delivered."

Preston bobbed his head and spurred his horse for the forest. *He'll be fine. He's behind the lines on a task to keep him from harm's way.*

Hampton looked at Hart's battery, gesturing to another aide, Lieutenant Rawlins Lowndes, named after his grandfather, a man of Revolutionary War fame. His family held high rapport in South Carolina's elite society and had been since the states were states. They were wealthy and patriotic, similar to Hampton's line of predecessors. He was a smart man with a thick brown mustache and kind eyes.

"Get them limbered. They go first." He couldn't risk the battery, and if things went to plan, his men would have departed the field before his enemy perceived enough to apply any additional pressure on his line. Lowndes didn't hesitate but turned his horse toward the battery.

Hampton scanned the field. A fight was taking place south of his position toward Wickham's part of the line. A teamster whipped his mules, driving a wagon of wounded away from the front. No matter who was in charge, there was always the butcher's bill to pay, yet he felt good about the day's events.

This had been his first contest exercising command over other divisions since Stuart's untimely departure. It was a tenuous thing as Robert E. Lee had yet to pick Stuart's predecessor despite Hampton's seniority. Leading at the corps level was odd yet familiar to him. It was akin to sprinting along the edge of a cliff without a friend to grab you if you stumbled. Yet even as he ran with no support, he found himself with sound balance.

He had grown used to riding with the young yet unabashedly bold general, who was as flamboyant as he was brave and as dashing as he was tactically sound. And gone in a grave as all young cavaliers descend with the pomp and circumstance of a military march.

He wondered if Stuart would have stuck it out here longer despite Lee's orders. Stuart had never been one to stay in a single place too long, always looking for an opportunity to catch his enemy off guard. Hampton had learned from him. He also learned from his mistakes, and most of those manifested from an inflated ego, an ego contributed to by his success as a young man in command and a code of honor beseeched only by medieval knights. Both expanded his success and fame yet set him up for an equally ugly fall from grace, or in his case, a gallant demise ushering him into the afterlife.

And Hampton was an older gentleman by a soldier's calendar. He had an ego but his was fed by different things: money, status, and family. He would never admit that he didn't love the taste of battle and running one's enemies clear off the field. He only employed more pragmatism about it.

Strike like lightning, only fight on terrain you love, and attack when your enemy is off-balance. If you're going to fight, only ever fight when the odds were stacked in your favor, and if they weren't, fight like the devil until there were none of the bastards left. He would leave nothing to luck for luck was only a fate's whisper in a dice throw from the gods. He didn't have men to fertilize the soil like the Union armies. No. No men to sacrifice. Only the enemy had that luxury, so he played the game with the hand he had been dealt.

He wanted certainty, and that was hard to come by in this war. "Hurry along now!" he shouted to the captain of the battery. "Their day will come."

Chapter 3

Late Afternoon, May 28, 1864
Near Enon Church, Atlee Station Road, Virginia

Less than a mile away, men fought and died the way they do in war. Some called for their mothers. Some were held in the arms of their comrades. Still others were silent, a body falling lifeless to the earth, a soul gone to heaven in the blink of an eye. Some died alone holding their wounds, gasping for breath beneath a hot blazing sun. The 296 men of the 13th Michigan hadn't experienced this day's baptism of fire. Instead, they sat in an uneasy column of fours in a mounted reserve. A general anticipation of battle enveloped them, and the troopers sweated through their shirts and jackets, staining their collars an off-yellow.

Lieutenant Johannes Wolf sat mounted along F Company on the edge of his platoon. As a second lieutenant, his platoon held the rear position in their fifty-three-man company at the tail end of the short column. He rubbed sweat from his brow beneath a wide-brimmed black slouch hat and wiped it on his light-blue pant leg that had a yellow strip running down the side. Halfway to the knee, the stripe disappeared beneath his riding boots. His light-brown beard made him even hotter in the sun, and he itched endlessly day and night. The discomfort was made even worse by the salty sweat saturating through it.

Wolf rested an impatient hand on the handle of his six-shot .44 Colt revolver, the holster flap undone so he could easily draw the weapon at a moment's notice. There seemed little need despite the battle raging in the dense green forests ahead. On his other hip he wore a light army-issued saber, his second sword of the war. This one had yet to be broken in, the grip still too soft and not rough enough for his liking. His Spencer carbine hung off a strap on his back, and a long knife was nestled in the remaining space on his belt.

He squinted at the sky with an uncomfortable malice. *Is it so much to ask for a little cloud cover?* He was taller than most, and it seemed the sun had it out for him since he was closer to its glaring rays. Yet he wasn't the tallest in the platoon. Three men held that distinction, two of which could have been mistaken for grizzly bears, Nelson and Dan, and Sergeant Wilhelm Berles.

The sun ignored his gaze and continued to beat down mercilessly as the men sat exposed in the open road, not a tree in sight to provide them shade. He'd traded in his black jacket for a dark-blue junior officer's shell jacket, which was cut short so as to not constrict the rider and had yellow bars on the shoulders. The lighter color helped relieve a fraction of the sun's heat but not nearly enough. He adjusted in the saddle to accommodate for his leg falling asleep, and he tugged on his knee brace.

The fighting was close enough to know intimately that the brigade's other regiments were in the middle of a fierce struggle. But his men had been ordered to sit and wait for more orders. He leaned to the side on his saddle, trying to obtain a better view of the men engaged, but he could only make out gun smoke and trees, covering the fight like a wet woolen blanket dampening the sound. The only damn thing in sight was the dismounted troopers holding the reins of their comrades' horses. A panicked mount tugged its reins free, and a trooper scrambled after the beast trying to drag the other horses with him.

"Don't suppose we could make much a difference from the road," Wolf said over his shoulder to Sergeant Wilhelm Berles, sitting directly behind him.

The German sergeant's accent was heavy. "Mounted men versus entrenched dismounted men is never a winning endeavor." He was a family friend of Wolf's from Grand Rapids, Michigan, having immigrated with Wolf's father to the United States in the late 1840s when Wolf was a small boy. The voyage was distant in his memory, only fragments that belonged more to his parents' memories than to his own.

Wilhelm was the platoon's rock, having held the unit together on numerous occasions despite losing his son near Gettysburg. Wolf had lost a friend, and his inability to save him he wore around his neck the same as a leaden albatross. Yet Franz was not the only friend he'd lost to the war, not the only man he'd been responsible for and buried in the Virginia soil.

"What are we doing mounted then?" Wolf asked.

"It is not yours to question why, Lieutenant, but only to spur to action and die."

Wolf couldn't tell if there was dark humor hiding somewhere in his voice or if he meant exactly what he said. "Your words are not comforting, Sergeant Berles."

"They were not meant to be."

When the time came, they would do the dirty work of killing as asked and the dirtier work of dying if they must. Both Wolf and Wilhelm would keep their platoon of twenty-three men together and alive. Yet a bit more optimism from his sergeant would have been nice.

Men crawled and stumbled from the woods now, red streaking their faces, hair dampened to their foreheads, blood drenching their blue coats. Two men carried another by the arms and legs. They made for a white wood-planked church that sat fifty yards to the right of Wolf's position. It was quickly becoming a filled-to-capacity field hospital.

Cries came from the church, and they were much worse to the waiting 13th Michigan than any earthly wound. It was as if their voices struck chords of fear to a deadly tune, rattling the men's souls. Wolf's veterans were well acquainted with fear but hid it beneath their gritty exteriors of grizzled beards and emotionless faces.

The brigade band continued to play "Yankee Doodle" over and over again, almost masking the men's cries, but they were unable to overcome the wounded or the battle raging in the woods. Yet they played as if the song itself had the fortitude to overcome their foe.

Private Adams, small in stature and dark in complexion but with an unmatched appetite for chaos and violence veiled by a charming smile and quick wit, gestured at the band. "You think they know anything else?"

"Course they do," grunted his comrade, Private Nelson, a towering trooper well over six and a half feet with the shoulders of a barnyard bull, draped in a bushy beard and a scowl to match.

"That was sarcasm, my big friend."

Nelson grunted his response. "Sounds like complainin'."

Adams shrugged. The two were friends and criminal transplants forced from the 1st Michigan Cavalry. "I don't even like the damn song. Much prefer 'Dixie' to it."

"It don't matter what you like," Nelson said. "Don't matter which song they play as long as they cover up the sound of those men's noisy dying." He spit on the ground with a glare at the church.

A musical voice with an Irish accent floated from the next rank of horsemen. "I wish they would play 'Garryowen' instead. Much better marching and fighting song. Even better drinking song."

Adams gave a quick chuckle. "Anyone understand what he just said?"

Connors's face reddened at his words.

A couple of the troopers laughed, encouraging Adams along, "I'm sure it's a jolly song my fine Irishman."

"Anything sounds better than their dying," Nelson said. A few of the other troopers peered worriedly at the church despite the giant trooper's disdain. Any one of them could be dying inside. Getting their limbs sawed off with less care than a lumberjack gave a tree. Each man knowing full well the reaper could still fetch their souls by the day's end.

"Don't listen to him, lads," Adams said, trying to ease his comrades' worry. "Look at those band fellas, puffing away like a white-laced cherry in a brothel."

This drew a few of their attentions away from the church. Private Joshua Dickson on Adams's left touched the Bible he always carried with him in his pocket. Wolf worried about the two rougher men's influence upon him, but the quiet farmer from Gaylord never complained. Only listening and keeping to himself, always with a Bible in his hand, always reading.

"'Yankee Doodle' is a favorite of Custer's," Private Thomas Powers said with a nod. He was a tall young man with sandy hair from Muskegon. He worked as a sailor on the merchant vessels that sailed over the Great Lakes.

"Pretty sure me mom's cousin once removed wrote that one," Corporal Gary Lowell said. He was a short trooper with an easy smirk beneath his mustache. "Fine tune, I must say." The man was known as a notorious liar, claiming to have founded the rural village of Lowell.

"Bugger your mother's cousin," Nelson said with a scowl. "He didn't write it."

Lowell licked his finger doing the mental math. "Once removed. That's right."

Nelson twisted in his saddle trying to catch a glance of Lowell over a thick shoulder. "He didn't. Now, don't make me do the rebels' work for them and put you in the ground here."

Lowell closed his mouth but couldn't help himself. "Just making talk."

Nelson's lip curled. "No more talk or I'll make ya stop for good."

"Private," Wolf said.

Nelson peered over at him, his eyes angry. Both men had had an arrangement since Yellow Tavern. More of a respect for each other's mission. Wolf kept Nelson in uniform and in the battles where he could do what he was made for, fighting, and Nelson kept his darker skills under control. And for the past few weeks, the arrangement had worked. It was a tenuous agreement, one that teetered on a thin tightrope, but one nonetheless that provided some calm to the violent storm that was Nelson.

"Save your killing for the rebs," Wolf added.

"Suppose I won't need to wait long before Lowell is some crying sack of meat over in that church."

Lowell's smirk disappeared and his cheeks paled. His voice came out at almost a whisper. "Just not right to say that about a fellow trooper."

"Oh, Nelson. Leave the poor boy be. He has a chance yet to survive. Anyone want to make a wager on how long Lowell will last?" Adams asked.

Lowell shook his head. "Just not right." He glanced around looking for men to agree with him.

"No wagers on a man's death," Wilhelm said. "Bad luck for all." His horse shifted uneasily beneath him.

Adams shrugged. "Thought we could at least make a dollar on his untimely demise."

Wilhelm and Wolf glared over, and Adams stared straight ahead with a smirk, having had enough fun at Lowell's expense.

The brigade band continued to play as mercilessly as the battle raging ahead. Brass instruments tooted. Drums beat. The musicians were red-cheeked, sweat pouring down their necks and soaking their collars.

"For men who weren't in the fight, you'd think they'd been at it all day," Adams snarked. He removed his hat and waved it in the air. "Yankee Doodle keep it up! Yankee Doodle Dandy!"

This brought a round of chuckles from the waiting troopers, including Lowell. Even Wilhelm cracked a grin beneath his curled mustache. After Yellow Tavern, Wolf's men who had survived rejoined their company. Captain Peltier had reassigned men from First Lieutenant Wells's command to fill in for the casualties. Wolf knew most of the men but all were men Wells had deemed inept soldiers like John Munn, the overweight company cook; Kent Richards, a depressed schoolteacher who couldn't make out a barn without his glasses; Joshua Dickson, the quiet religious boy. All transfers were approved by their commanding officer, Colonel James F. Moore.

The heavyset colonel sat with an aide behind Enon Church away from his exposed regiment. His horse had a slight bow in its back. He'd added an ostrich plume to his slouch hat and his sword's scabbard glittered in the afternoon sun. With fine riding white lambskin gloves and black polished boots, his blue colonel's jacket appeared clean and immaculate, despite needing to be let out a few inches. The man seemed to be getting even larger regardless of having campaigned for most of the month.

Eyes went skyward as an artillery shell screamed overhead, but a veteran knew it wouldn't land near. Moore, on the other hand, ducked a little. Then after the projectile exploded elsewhere, he sat straighter in his saddle, gazing around as if he hadn't been frightened and the whole shift was an intentionally committed action of an aware and coherent commander.

"Fat bird can't even stand with the regiment," said Adams.

"Stick him on a spit and we could roast him," Nelson grunted.

The platoon chuckled. Even Wolf laughed at this. The colonel had shown his true colors on several occasions, and the men were well aware he was a craven fool but just ambitious enough to get them killed. They looked to Captain Peltier to add a layer between them and the fool, but outranked, the captain could only do so much. But the men understood the ruling laws of the army: to go where they were told and fight when they had to. Moore could only do so much harm from the rear.

The men continued to wait for almost two hours, snickering when the colonel shied from the cannon fire, unable to observe the field of battle from behind the church. Near five o'clock, a courier appeared from headquarters and spoke with Moore.

"Day's fading," Lowell said.

"Might have to fight in the dark," Wolf said. The battle appeared to be dying with the sloping sun. Orders were passed through the ranks of the 13th Michigan, man-to-man.

A lanky rider turned his horse from the platoon ahead of them. First Lieutenant Wells had the air of an aristocrat and the education to match. He held his chin high in the air as he approached like he couldn't stand the stink of the horses or the men who served beneath him.

He had strongly disliked Wolf since their enlistment but had gained respect for him at Gettysburg. In return, a glimmer of tolerance was shown back when Wells had decided to fight rather than run away when facing overwhelming odds. He drew his horse alongside Wolf's. "Lieutenant."

"Wells." Wolf masked his irritation by adjusting his reins.

The lack of return in military honor seemed to irritate the other young man, but he held his tongue in check. "I trust the men from my platoon are doing their part."

"They're doing just fine."

Wells waved to another man in his platoon. The rider walked his horse to them, keeping his head down. "Well, I have one more for you."

"This cannot wait? We're about to march, aren't we?"

Wells sniffled and wiped his hooked nose. "It cannot wait."

"What's your name?" Wolf asked the newcomer.

"Private Benjamin Goffman." He was short in stature with brown curly hair and a thick mustache on his upper lip.

Wells turned away from the trooper. "The information regarding Private Goffman didn't reach me until earlier today, but the colonel has signed off on the shift."

Shift. More like peddling off unwanted soldiers. Wolf suspected the colonel cared little about the matter, and he wondered why Wells wouldn't bother to go to the captain for permission. "What information?"

"Regarding Goffman's background. He has been deemed not up to platoon standards by the rest of the men. He's been accused of thievery and cowardice on several occasions." Wells gulped before continuing. "And Gordon believes he's put a hex on him."

"And you want to give him to me?" Wolf said. The last thing he wanted was a liability in the field. He eyed the short man with suspicious disdain. The trooper held his tongue, but his mouth flattened in anger.

"There is nowhere else for such a man to go." The lieutenant glanced at the rest of Wolf's platoon. "You have a knack for handling men of such caliber."

"I'm going to have to take that as a compliment." Wolf ignored the ignorant fool and scrutinized Goffman, attempting to decipher his worth. Clearly Wells was filled with shit and concealing his true motives. "A hex? You mean like a witch?"

Wells lifted his chin higher, its deep dimple shadowed. "I am an educated man. I would never believe it myself, but Gordon has had a rash on him since we've left camp. I've seen it with my own two eyes. The day before he discovered the rash, he saw that man whispering and wagging his fingers at him around the campfire."

"Sounds like he's been fooling around with the wrong camp girls."

This garnered a fraction of a grin from Goffman.

Wolf eyed him. "Private, did you put a hex on Gordon? Now, answer me true. We got no place for witches in my platoon or any manner of devilry." He glanced back at his men. "Well, devilry that ain't man made. You hex Gordon?"

"I did not."

"Seems that it's his word against Gordon's."

Wells eyed him from the side. "Be that as it may, it is better for morale to have him transferred to your platoon." He composed himself as if the subject was settled. "Very good then." He gestured toward the forest road. "Our boys have them on the run, and we have orders to move about a half mile toward the enemy, finish off any remaining resistance, and cut off any lines of retreat. Should be an easy task." He paused, eyeing the trees with a noble gaze. "Colonel wants us to lead the regiment."

"Really?" Wolf asked. It was an odd request seeing as their company was at the rear of the regiment.

"It took some convincing, but he acquiesced."

"You asked to lead the charge?" Wolf was about as astonished as he was irritated with the man.

Wells almost looked offended. "I did."

"Jesus," Wolf said, shaking his head. "We'll be right behind you."

Wells gave him a stiff nod and trotted to his platoon. Wolf wasn't sad to see the pompous prick leave. The man was ever a headache and irritating to be around. It was no wonder Wolf found the company of his platoon much preferable to his fellow officer.

Wolf regarded Goffman. "You ain't a witch. So what has been done to garner the disapproval of brave Lieutenant Wells?"

Goffman's eyes narrowed and his mouth twisted in discomfort, but he looked Wolf in the eyes when he answered. "I'm a Jew."

Wolf cocked his head. "A Jew? Really?"

"Correct, sir. I'm not ashamed of it either, but I knew enough to keep it to myself. Then the other day, they were all going to church and I abstained. Questions led to me telling them. Most of the boys could care less, but there are always a few that don't like it."

"I see." Wolf eyed him up and down. Goffman glared back, a defiant fire in his eyes. They were the eyes of a fighter. A man that would fight just to prove he could against any opponent. "Can't say I could tell a Jew from any other man. You a coward?"

Goffman's cheek twitched. "I'm no coward."

"You can fight then?"

"I'll fight any man here."

"Even Nelson?"

Goffman scanned the platoon, his eyes narrowing upon the giant trooper. "If need be."

His words made Wolf smile. "Say no more. You may go to the rear of the platoon."

Goffman nodded then spurred his horse away. To be truthful, Wolf had never met a Jewish person. They seemed normal enough. Two arms, two legs. He wouldn't be able to understand why others disliked them so much. To Wolf's end, he supposed he only cared about a few things. Could the man fight, follow orders, and when the time came, kill? And if the answer was yes, he'd take him under his command.

Wolf had considered the soldier in quiet reflection, unsure of what made this man different or more susceptible to thievery and cowardice. He hadn't found some outward defect that would easily tell that he was those things. He supposed what made a man was found in his blood and guts and the courage he could muster in a time of crisis. Time would tell if Wells had adequate cause to mistrust the man, and if Wells's conduct was any indication of his judgement, Wolf doubted there was any due cause for his accusations.

Turning to his men, Wolf said, "You heard Wells. We're leading the regiment forward to support the brigade's attack." He turned and eyed Wilhelm. "The enemy is on the run, so it should be simple: rounding up the poor starving bastards and shipping them off to a proper prison with free room and board."

His words gave the men a few laughs. Every man in the platoon knew he'd been to Libby Prison and escaped, vowing to never return. He never spoke about it as if it were a curse that could be cast upon any man he mentioned it to. So no one brought it up, not a word. Not even Adams. This made him dangerous in their eyes because he was willing to die to avoid capture. Only second to this was the mention of Wolf's notorious enemies, Captain Marshall Payne and his Red Shirts company.

Every man was well-versed in the lore of the infamous Red Shirts, either through experience or stories of their bitter hostility told around the campfire. Wolf's vendetta had become their own, the animosity spreading among them like a disease after Yellow Tavern. A disease that would bring them to risk their lives to defeat their foe. Yet no man was more afflicted by it than Wolf.

Nelson knew. Adams knew. Wilhelm knew. Dan knew. They all knew that if the opportunity came, Wolf would no longer be a lieutenant, but an ambassador of death, his sole purpose to destroy Payne. The other men of the platoon just hoped that they never saw the Red Shirts again and that they could fight a regular old-fashioned war with the rebels without the insanity of an unspoken blood feud.

"He's some fool," Wilhelm said. He leaned closer to Wolf. "Who's the new private?"

"Goffman. A Jew."

"A Jew, huh? And brave Wells doesn't want him?"

"Apparently not, so I said we'd take him. Although I'm not sure we have a choice."

"The army doesn't give many choices."

"They do not."

Wilhelm turned in his saddle and glanced to the rear. After a moment, he spoke again. "He'll fight." He tapped the corner of his eye. "You can always tell if a man will fight by the look of his eyes. There's something there. Something that shows the soul in the eyes."

Wolf nodded, his intuition confirmed by his trusted sergeant. "That's what I thought. A bit on the smaller side, but he told me he would fight any man here."

Wilhelm raised his eyebrows. "Even Nelson?"

"I'm not sure he saw him before he said it."

Wilhelm let out a hearty chuckle.

Wolf's horse stamped a hoof. The bugle call carried forth from the front of the company. "All right, Sergeant, lift that guidon high." Wolf's platoon moved to a walk, following their sister platoon to the front of the 13th Michigan's column. His men walked in six rows of four troopers. Wolf guided them from the front. Behind him were newly made Corporal Dan Poltorak and Corporal Lowell. Each row was anchored by a senior enlisted man. Although permanently held in rank as privates for their criminal behavior, Nelson and Adams had more experience in this war than any of them. Wolf allowed them to operate as de facto corporals saddling on the other ends of two of the rows, never letting a veteran go to waste.

Captain Peltier sat near the front of the company along with Lieutenant Wells, who already had his sword drawn. Peltier raised his hand into the air, his voice stern, "Draw pistols!"

Wolf drew his pistol, metal scraping over leather. His men did the same. If they were going to get mired in heavy timber, sabers wouldn't be effective. Wells lifted his saber over his head. Sunlight flickered off the side of the blade as he twirled it high in the air.

"Boy is way too excited for a round-up action," Wilhelm said.

"He is."

The captain shouted out, "Forward at the trot." The small company surged forward, trotting down the road away from Enon Church. The route quickly enclosed around them, the trees boxing them in as the sounds of battle grew louder. Men scrambled across the road ahead in grays and browns.

"Let's get 'em boys!" Peltier shouted. The company moved to a gallop, and the rebels fled into the trees the same as flushed hares. The company charged ahead. Dust kicked into the air. Amid the dust and smoke, rebel soldiers lingered in the trees on either side of the road, more akin to skittish deer than men. Others bounded over fallen logs, running on foot to the right.

"Don't let any escape!" Wells said. His men whooped and hollered as they charged in a disorganized group into the undergrowth, splitting them into pockets of pursuers.

"He's going the wrong way," Wilhelm said with irritation, his head turning to watch. Horsetails and blue jackets were quickly hidden by green leaves and round tree trunks as Wells's men disappeared.

"Our men are on the left," Wolf said, shaking his head. He cocked his pistol, scanning his men. "They're on their own. Platoon, face left!" His men fanned out on the road, pistols in hands.

The platoon hurried into position, and Wolf shouted down the line, "Forward." They walked their horses into thickets of young saplings overpowered by a canopy of round oaks and maple. Bushes and vines sprouted from every parcel of ground, leaving nothing bare.

Gunshots popped ahead of them. A rough line of rebels peered feverishly around them. They were cornered rats with nowhere to hide. He lined his sight on a dismounted man ahead. The man turned, panic lighting his face like a match in the dead of night.

Dismounted blue-coated troopers from the 5th Michigan came into view as they advanced in haste upon the retreating rebels. "Hurrah! Hurrah!" the advancing 5th echoed as they closed in.

Wolf squinted and the man held up his arms over his head. Rebels up and down the line dropped their weapons and displayed them upside down to their enemies.

"Keep it going," Wolf said. His men marched closer, snaring the dismounted rebels with the double-rank line of Union troopers. Entire companies threw down their arms.

"Didn't even have to fire a shot," Wilhelm said.

"Not today," Wolf said uncocking his pistol. In a loose line, his men marched forward, blocking in the rebel line. Their only purpose now was to block any attempts to flee, more of a visual deterrent than anything else.

A nearby volley went out, similar to a campfire with sappy wood popping repeatedly. The nearest men turned their heads in warning, Wolf among them. Sprinkles of pops snared in return. Wolf locked eyes with Wilhelm. "Jesus, you don't think that's Wells's Platoon?"

A blue rider made a hurried approach. "That's Corporal Frederick!" Goffman said.

Wolf and Wilhelm locked eyes before Wilhelm shouted. "About face!"

Wolf kicked his horse toward the fear-stricken trooper. "Frederick. What happened?"

"Ran into an ambush. Lieutenant's down. We're trapped in pockets."

Wolf shook his head, glaring through the trees. Through the latticework of vegetation, it was impossible to make out man or horse. "Shit." He turned back toward the 5th Michigan men. They wrangled the retreating rebels in the other direction, capturing them in groups and clusters. Smoked hugged the forest as if they were long-lost friends, obscuring trees in their embrace. "We ride to their aid."

Chapter 4

Late Afternoon, May 28, 1864
West of Enon Church, Virginia

"Keep it tight," Wilhelm called to the men. The platoon formed a line on Atlee Station Road, facing the gunfire hidden inside the forest.

Wolf gestured with his pistol, and his men walked their mounts into the overgrown timber. His platoon's formation quickly became unevenly dispersed through the trees, half the time forced to cover their faces and duck their heads through the snagging branches and vibrantly colored, veiny leaves. A riderless horse bolted toward them, zigging and zagging over fallen logs. Jumping in terror, it raced past them. A moment later, a bullet cracked a nearby tree, his men flinching as wood splinters catapulted into the air.

The scent of pungent gun smoke and powder cloaked the air as a gray fog would on a cold summer morning. Sobs of the injured cried out ahead of them. Wolf took his thumb and cocked his pistol. "Quick as we can. Stay close."

"In and out, boys," Wilhelm ordered.

He gave Sarah a slight heel with his spurs and moved a fraction faster. The forest gradually gave way to a creek. The faint murmur of running water accompanied the battle as well as a chime could make itself known in a brigade brass band.

Bursts of flames leapt as rebels fired, opaquely outlined in the smoke. The Union troopers were pinned down. Wounded men lay behind rocks indiscriminately returning fire. A blue-coated body lay face down in the creek. Another man crawled, pulling himself upright with the root of a tall oak. He scrambled away.

Wolf urged his horse into the clearing. He aimed at the silhouette of a man. One, two, three, four shots he let loose in his direction. His men did the same, laying down enough firepower to force the rebels into cover. Now the gunfire exploded in fits and starts as rebels chose between firing and fleeing.

Wolf spurred for a large rock, acting as a shield for a fallen trooper. He turned his horse in a quick circle. "Grab my hand!"

The man, his hat missing, stared up at him with his pistol cocked. "Wolf?" Wells said. He blinked once before he stood, cradling his left arm close to his body. Wolf leaned off his horse and grasped the man, helping him mount behind him. Bullets whipped and snapped through the trees as the rebels recognized it was only a platoon and not a larger force.

"Ride!" Wells urged in his ear.

"Get them out of here!" Wolf called to his men, turning his horse in a circle. His men quickly gathered the wounded. He pointed his pistol in the enemy's direction and fired another shot. "Come on, Sarah!" He tugged her reins, steering her back to the road at a trot.

For a moment, he faced the way he'd come, expecting the rebels to pursue. He only had one bullet left in his pistol. He ground his teeth, scanning the trees. They never should have been in this position. *Nothing can be done now, but save what you can.* The sound of horses crashing through the undergrowth gave way as his men emerged from the woods and onto the dirt road. "Rally here," Wolf ordered his men. They started to congregate in formation.

Shouts came from the rear. Wolf glanced over his shoulder saying a quick prayer that the voices didn't belong to rebel soldiers. Glimpses of blue-coated soldiers turned into two companies of dismounted men from the 5th scrambling on the road. Their captain held a pistol in his hand. "Which way'd those chicken-livered traitors run?" he asked of them.

"There's more of them that way," Wolf said gesturing with his head.

The captain smiled beneath a blond beard, a black hardee hat shading his eyes. "Got them on the run! We've rounded up almost three hundred of 'em."

"The rebs that way want a fight."

"Then let's give it to them! Follow me, boys!" shouted the captain, and he led his repeating-carbine-armed men bounding into the foliage.

Wolf quickly inspected his line. "Where's the captain?" *We can't leave him.* He made eye contact with Wilhelm.

"He fell near the creek," Wells said with a groan.

His men peered at one another. They would have to search for him. A man walked his horse from the trees. Blood ran down his cheek and into his black beard. He stumbled on a root and caught himself on a tree trunk.

Wolf shook his head. "Get him on a horse. We go back."

The battered company trotted along the road. They fell back under the cover of two additional companies of the 13th Michigan. He halted his company near Enon Church, finally allowing himself to holster his pistol. He hopped down from his horse and offered Wells a hand in the dismount.

The tall upper-class lieutenant held his arm, blood seeping from between his fingers, his back hunched.

"Looks bad. Better get you inside. Sawbones will see to ya." Wells only stared at the church as if it threatened him more than the rebels. Wolf glanced at it too. Cries escaped from the doorway. A man in a white apron came out with a bucket and dumped a heap of hacked-off limbs into a pile. The sight made Wolf's belly churn with discomfort.

Wells grimaced, tears in his eyes yet there was anger too. "They bloody well shot me." His eyes scanned his wounded men. "And my men."

"They'll be fine. I think we got most of them." Wolf waved the man forward. "Give me your arm." He took the lieutenant's good arm and lifted him down. Their wounded straggled to the church for treatment. Wells took his cap off and wiped his brow, still clutching his arm close. "I have to thank you."

"Don't. We're all one company. We look out for each other."

Wells winced with a shake of his head, his thought disgusting him. "Your men saved us. Saved me."

"Nobody could have known it was an ambush. The rebs were supposed to be on the run. You would have done the same for us." Wolf eyed him. *Would he?* He had to operate under the assumption Wells would in fact try to save him in a similar situation. He reached out and grasped Wells's other shoulder. "Perhaps next time, we wait for the rest of the regiment."

Wells sucked in air. "Yes, perhaps greater prudence is advised even in victory." He lowered his head and eyes, nodding to himself, the shock of the ambush consuming his every thought. His eyes were lost in the realm of events that never happened, orders never given, words never spoken, and men unavenged.

"Don't dwell on it too long," Wolf said. It felt odd to be giving a peer advice, but it was his to give. He'd lost men and replaying the scenarios never brought them back. All that could be done was to learn and not repeat the same mistake twice. Try to keep his men in one piece and his unit together.

Wells nodded again and gulped, his Adam's apple jiggling with the effort.

"See the surgeon. We'll be here when you're back."

Wells turned away as if he were a bullied schoolboy, his cheek quivering with shame and anger, trudging his way to the church.

Captain Peltier dismounted, slowly following Wells for the church. He stumbled near the doors, falling onto his rear and sitting in the grass. A surgeon's assistant removed Peltier's hat and poked at the wound on his head, taking white bandages and wrapping them round and round.

Wolf remounted, watching the captain with concern. He collected the two platoons. "Anyone too hurt to ride stays here." A trooper turned his horse toward the church. "Everyone stay together until we get orders." He nodded to Sergeant Simpson of Wells's platoon. He was a short veteran with a brown goatee streaked with gray. "You can handle them until we figure out what's going on?"

Simpson spit black tobacco juice on the ground. "I reckon I can just fine."

"Very good."

Colonel Moore pushed his poor overburdened horse near them. The animal had a generally reluctant appearance as if it would only run if it was to get away from Moore. "We got them on the run! The general is very pleased. Well done, lads. Well done." He glared at them as if he expected a rousing

cheer. "Once the regiments are back in saddle, we are to lead the way south."
He peered expectantly at Wolf as if he'd forgotten he was an officer under his
command. "Where is Wells?"

"Wounded."

Moore appeared exceptionally distraught by the idea. "Tell Peltier to ready
his men."

"I will, sir. He's over there."

"Ahh, there he is," Moore pushed his swaybacked mount closer. "Captain.
Prepare your men to ride to Old Cold Harbor."

Peltier looked up at him from the ground, a general air of exhaustion on
his face. He managed a weak reply. "We have some wounded."

Moore's words were as quick as they were dismissive. "Nothing can be
done about it. We are to lead the brigade south. Quite the honor. I will not
have us look haphazard with our task. Prepare to follow D Company when
the call is given."

"Yes, sir." Peltier said with a stiff nod. He let his head fall as if the weight
was too much for his neck.

"Organize your men. They look like a rabble of poor rebels," Moore said
with a dismissive wave. He then moved with his entourage of couriers and
aides along the road leading away from the gunfire.

The company made a loose column of fours under the direction of their
sergeants. Wolf walked his horse over to Peltier. "Sir, can you ride?"

Peltier glanced at Wolf with a grimace. "I can." He let out a sigh and
pushed himself off the ground. Fresh screams echoed from the church like the
call of a man in the throes of torture. The brigade band had ceased playing
and the cries of the wounded gained prevalence over everything else.

"Let me check on Wells," Peltier said. The captain disappeared inside the
church. A surgeon's assistant came out and tossed the lower half of an arm on
the growing mound of bloody limbs. Wolf swallowed bile back down into his
belly. He knew some of those men, and if getting shot into pieces wasn't
torture enough, now a surgeon with a bone-saw hastened the dying process.
If the surgeon didn't kill them, a fever would set in a few days later and finish
the job with a flourish of painful heat and pus.

The company waited in uncomfortable silence. No one spoke or joked; they just waited. Horse's whisked their tails. Men kept to themselves, and the flies bothered both man and beast but found their home on the pink limbs stacked near the wall of the church, piled higher than the ankle-high grass.

The captain reemerged moving slower than a snail in the dirt. Each step took tremendous effort, and Wolf wondered if he'd been shot elsewhere.

Peltier took the reins to his horse and struggled to pull himself atop. He adjusted his hat to the side of his head. "Wells won't be coming."

"Sir?"

Peltier adjusted his reins, the effort appearing strenuous. "He's going to lose that arm."

Wolf shook his head. He had no love for the man, but he wished him no physical harm or death. Having a limb amputated proved a lingering death sentence.

Peltier sucked in a breath. "No one died, but five of our men we're leaving here, and I need a new first lieutenant."

Wolf glanced at the captain. "I can fill that role."

"I don't have much of a choice. You'll act as 1st lieutenant. Sergeant Simpson will lead the other platoon until we can find a replacement."

Wolf nodded slowly. "I can do it."

"I know you can. Suppose you don't have much of a choice. I need you to do it." He pointed at the men. "Get everyone mounted. We don't want to lag behind."

"You heard the captain. Saddle up," Wolf called out. The men watering their horses and tending minor injuries remounted.

"You're only one bullet away from a promotion," Wilhelm said.

"Not all of us." Adams took a slight bow.

"Wouldn't want it anyway. Too much dealing with a bunch of bellyaching babies," Nelson added.

"No, that doesn't apply to all," Wilhelm said.

Wolf joined Peltier. The captain shifted to the center of the small column and gave him a nod, his brow creased in pain. "Give the order, Lieutenant."

"Company, forward march."

F company walked forward.

"Guide left." Wolf shifted to the guide left position, all of the company's movements based on him. In Wolf's mind, nothing had changed. He filled the required role as he was needed. He'd still try to keep them all alive as best he could. Half the time he was making it up as he went along, relying on his experienced sergeant to assist in making sound decisions. The men relied on them both to keep them fed and away from the afterlife.

He knew how the men felt. The entire experience was like being fed into a spinning wheel, one man leading them one moment, the wheel rotated around feeding him out for burial. A new man in his place with every rotation. The causes mattered not. The results were the same whether it be illness, retirement, injury, or death. The wheel of the army rolled on, yet everything continued to change. The wheel turned and Wells disappeared, and Wolf took his place. How long would it be before someone new took his? Would his ride be short? He knew that regardless of the time, it surely wouldn't be without trial and tribulation.

Chapter 5

June 1, 1864
Old Cold Harbor, Virginia

In true army fashion, Wolf's men had had one hell of a go of it over the past two days. After running off Fitz Lee's Division near a small creek along Old Church Road, they'd made haste in their travel to Old Cold Harbor, where they reengaged Fitz Lee's Division along with a few South Carolinian regiments using wooden barricades to bar their path.

Old Cold Harbor was less of a town and more of a small cluster of dwellings surrounding an overlay of intersecting roads roughly six miles from Richmond. Not to be confused with new Cold Harbor. Neither was a harbor in the traditional sense but a refuge from the road, a place to rest for weary travelers. Old Cold Harbor served as a vital junction for Grant to flank Lee's forces. After driving the rebels away from their breastworks with some excellent maneuvering by the 5th Michigan, Sheridan lost his nerve and ordered a withdrawal as it became clear rebel infantry was closing in.

It was the army's version of a tug-of-war. Men would fight and take land, then give it up, only to be ordered to take the same damn town they had occupied only hours before. It wore on the men, resigning them to the numbness of being led by the blind through a forest of foul beasts. Within minutes of departing north of Old Cold Harbor in the darkness of night, Wolf's men were hopping back out of the saddle only to race over ground they'd just taken.

Wolf wondered if the rebel soldiers felt the same way, jerked around by their superiors, forced into a game of give-and-take with the enemy over the same piece of well-trod blood-soaked dirt. Commanders proved to be indecisive about where they wanted their men to die as if they were mere x's on a map, to be drawn and erased wherever the strategists deemed the most critical.

The only peace of mind they received throughout the whole mess was the rebels hadn't retaken the breastworks. Torbert's Division settled in for the night and slept on the ground beneath the captured barricades, manning them from the opposing direction. The rebels had done a pretty darn first-class job too, and Wolf was thankful for that now that he and F Company had found a legitimate use for them.

The rebels had built their wall with wooden carts, cut down trees and brush, chairs and tables to form a makeshift barricade. They'd even gone so far as to pack earth into the barrier, and as the sun awakened over the land, the rebels threatened to take it back. They marched boldly back into the village, this time led by units of infantry and supported by additional artillery as if the cavalry had called upon their brothers to come fight on their behalf.

Buzzzz! Zip! Bullets screamed overhead. Wolf half-laid, half-leaned against the chest-high breastworks. His men lay around him, their carbines gripped in soiled hands. Kent fumbled with the lever of his Spencer. He shoved them back up. Wilhelm fired a shot quickly and crouched back down.

Each man took his turn risking shots from above the protective barrier. *Crack!* Wolf flinched as a bullet struck the wood, burrowing into the log like a starving termite at a wooden banquet, puffing dust and splinters dangerously out the other side.

"They must realize Grant's intent," Wilhelm said over the gunfire. He kept his head low as he dropped metal cartridges into the buttstock of his Spencer carbine. *Click. Click.* It held seven cartridges that were locked into place with a spring in the tube.

"Not sure I know what Grant's intent is," Wolf added with a bit of sarcasm.

"Get us killed most likely," Kent added. The trooper hated every aspect of the army, and generally speaking, a gloomy rain cloud of despair followed the man as if it were a loyal dog. If there was such a concept as bad luck, he embodied every aspect of it. "With my luck, it would be me first."

"If you had your own luck, you'd already be in the ground," Adams chided from his other side. He crept toward the top of the barricade and let loose two shots before slinking back down.

Kent fumbled with his lever again, his glasses slipping down his nose. He shoved them back up. "You don't understand the mockery of it. God will have me suffer through this whole war only to have me catch a cold and die just as the war ends. That's the utter cruelty of the whole pitiful thing. I have to endure time and suffering with you deplorable men before he'll welcome me to heaven."

"Who said he'd let you in?" Nelson called over. "You ain't special."

Kent sighed his eyes downcast. "He speaks the truth. I am a sinful creature and have no golden deeds to my name just like my father before. We are a doomed line of sinners." A bullet knocked shavings of wood off the barricade, sprinkling the woeful man below. He quickly blessed himself with the sign of the cross. Then turned his eyes to the sky. "Just get us done with."

"Jerk that lever like you mean it, trooper. You ain't going to break it," Wolf called over at him. He nudged his carbine over the top of the barricade, peering for an orange burst to aim at down the town street. He squeezed off a shot, flipped out his breach and shot again. Rotating the barrel slightly, he let loose two more then ducked down again.

Kent succeeded in getting his weapon back in firing order. "You haven't been listening, Lieutenant." He half stood to fire a shot yet did so timidly, the gun kicking violently in his hands.

"Keep your head down!" Wilhelm growled at him. He locked the spring tube in his buttstock closed.

Kent dipped his chin to his chest and shuffled back into the dirt. "Sound advice, Sergeant. Even for a poor man such as me."

"Stop your bellyaching!" Nelson called at him. "If you want to die, roll over this way and I'll oblige you. I could use the extra ammunition."

"Prefer living too much. Rather catch a fever," Kent said, shaking his head.

Nelson pointed a finger at him. "Shut your mouth and fight, or hand over your cartridges."

"Keep firing, men!" Wolf shouted down the line.

The gunfire hitting the barricade increased in intensity and the men were forced low into cover. Wolf glanced at his sergeant in concern. "Infantry." The nature of cavalry going against infantry wasn't a new one but was more defined by the accepted tactics of the time period. Every cavalryman was well acquainted with the unsaid rules that they should avoid a scuffle with infantry. The densely packed firepower unleashed by a regiment of a thousand men bunched together was enough to make a well-watered man sober.

An infantry regiment could easily run off a cluster of dismounted cavalrymen unable to withstand the intensity for long. Since the success of Buford's men at Gettysburg, cavalry commanders seemed less hesitant to stand before infantry due to widespread issuance of the repeating Spencer carbine and rifle. Cavalry had the potential to engage with exceedingly rapid firepower but usually lacked the density or manpower to maintain an engagement for long. The idea made most men a bit squeamish and struck them as a foreign affair.

Sergeant Berles waited for the pattering of lead rain upon the barricade to die down and peeked over the lip. He slumped back down. "Lots of infantry. We're going to need more ammunition."

"Check your sardine boxes," Wolf ordered the men around him. They opened pouches on their belts and thumbed through everything they had left.

"Thirty-two," Kent said.

"You fired a shot?" Nelson said.

"I did. You've seen me."

"Jesus, I got fifteen left, Wolfie," Nelson said. He held out an expecting hand and Kent handed him a cluster of cartridges.

"Twelve," Adams added.

"I'll see what I can scrounge up," Wolf said. He leaned his carbine against the barrier. "I'll be back." Crawling down the line, he made his way to Captain Peltier. Balls of lead continued to whistle over the top of the barrier. A volley from the opposing infantry wailed as if it were a gust of wind composed of distant firecrackers. Marked by the booming explosion of cannon, a shell crashed through a house behind them, leaving an oblong hole through the clapboard wall.

He kept moving down the line, keeping his hands in the dirt. He glanced down his platoon and couldn't make out any injured. "Keep shooting," he said to John Munn. The company cook breathed heavily, his pear-shaped body and gray mustache shuddering with the effort. Private Herman Scholtz was next to him, muttering to himself in German.

"Schießen," Wolf urged. Scholtz spoke no English and relied heavily upon Wilhelm and Wolf to follow any orders.

Scholtz spoke rapidly, his mouth running through a list of curse words that Wolf couldn't keep up with. Although born in Germany, Wolf hardly remembered living there. After immigrating to the United States in the late 1840s, his father had all but outlawed the speaking of their native tongue in their home. While he knew German, it was limited, but he recognized it if he heard it. He couldn't write in German if his life depended on it. The trooper held out this carbine in frustration. Wolf took it. He'd had some malfunction of the weapon.

Wolf worked the lever once then twice, finding its movement hindered by a blockage. He flipped the weapon sideways to inspect the breech. A brass casing rested inside, lodged in the extraction tube. He flipped the gun upside down and dug his finger in the hot barrel, the edges burning the pad of his finger. He clawed it loose with a fingertip and then shook the gun again until the casing rattled free. He handed it back to Scholtz. "Schüttel es." He made a shaking motion with his hands. Scholtz nodded.

He continued to crawl along the barrier. Powers nodded to him, the tall young trooper looking exceptionally uncomfortable behind the breastworks. He rotated to the side and fired a shot then hunkered back down. Next to him was Goffman. The Jewish trooper's forage cap almost covered his eyes. He turned and fired his carbine over the barrier. Then Powers would go. Dickson sat on the other side, quietly shooting in intervals. He placed his head to the gun barrel as Wolf crawled past, praying before each shot.

He crawled over the body of an unknown trooper whose head was dented with a bullet wound like he bore the outline of a grim coin in his skull. Another shell screamed overhead. He stopped crawling and covered his head and neck with his hands. The shell popped and he was thankful the boom was muffled.

Reaching Captain Peltier, Wolf moved to a half-kneel on the ground. The black-bearded captain had streaks of gray in his facial hair. His head wavered, and every time he blinked, his cheek shook repeatedly. "Captain. We're going to need more ammunition if we're going to fight all day. There's a lot of infantry over yonder."

Peltier continued to study the opposing infantry from his kneeling position. The white bandage wrapped around his skull turned red as blood seeped from the wound.

"Captain?" Wolf said.

Peltier glanced at him like a jittery sparrow gazing at a hawk. "Lieutenant?"

"We need more ammo."

Peltier grimaced and gingerly rubbed his temple. He closed his eyes and gave his head a quick shake. "Can't focus." He squeezed his eyes shut. "Our orders are to hold."

Wolf put a hand on the captain's shoulder. "I'm telling you we can't hold long without more ammunition or support. Infantry's coming up, right?"

Peltier's jaw shook as he attempted to answer. "I-can't remember."

Wolf gazed around the rattled captain. The regiment had lost their major early in the war to the wasting death and had never replaced him. As the regiment shrank from conflict and illness, he was one of many not replaced. That meant Wolf's next ranking superior was Moore or another company's captain. "Keep your head down, Captain." Peltier nodded blankly.

Wolf crawled on all fours to the next stretch of barricade. D Company laid along the barrier. "Captain Corby? Where's Captain Corby?" Wolf shouted at a trooper. The cavalryman pointed farther down the line and Wolf clambered in that direction.

Captain James Corby was tall for an Irishman. He held his sword in one hand and crouched on the line with his men, urging them on with words of encouragement. He gave Wolf a wide-eyed stare when he arrived. "What'd you want, Lieutenant?"

"F Company, sir."

"It's a goddamn hornet's nest. Better be here to offer me some help."

"It is for us too. We're running low on ammunition. We need more." A bullet cracked the top of the barrier and both men ducked.

Corby scanned over the barricade in anger as if he looked for the culprit to punish. "Don't come over here looking. We're low too."

"Sir, a lot of infantry are coming our way. We won't be able to hold 'em without more."

"More infantry? St. Peter give us strength."

"There, sir." Wolf pointed in the general direction of the most recent rebel regiment to take the field.

Corby stuck his head higher into the air, glaring farther down the line. "Christ almighty." His head jerked backward, and the captain tumbled onto his rear.

Wolf gaped in shock. The man he'd been conversing with one second lay sprawled out in the dirt the next. He'd heard of shitty luck balanced by close calls, but he could only stare.

Corby's arm twitched and he propped himself onto his elbows. "Bloody damn. Bloody hell. Bloody, bloody goddamn." He grabbed his fallen hat and held it in the air for all to see. "Those bastards shot my hat!" He ran a finger through the hole in the cap, wiggling it. "Just got the fellow before we left for campaign. Ruined in a month." He shook his head and flipped it back atop.

"Ammunition, sir."

Corby shook his head. "Not much we can do until the brigade's wagon trains arrive. You can thank Sheridan for that. All that marching back and forth."

"We won't hold." It was a fact. As additional rebel infantry added their weight to the fight and the gunfire waned from the cavalry, eventually courage would grow in rebel bellies, fanning the flames of bravery in their veins. They would charge upon the barricade to enact their violent solution. Then pistols, knives, and swords would do the dirty work, and the sheer weight of their numbers would surely send the 13th to flight. Then it would be a mad dash to avoid capture or death with the Rebel Yell ringing in their ears to send them on their way.

46

"These orders are coming from Grant himself. We hold. Everything you've got."

Wolf gave a terse nod. "It will have to be enough."

Corby clapped his back. "Get to your men, Lieutenant. They need you."

Wolf turned away, scurrying on all fours back toward his section of the line.

He made his way to Wilhelm and gathered his carbine. Wolf rolled onto his knee, keeping his head well below the breastworks. "We aren't getting any more ammo today."

"Figured as much." Wilhelm turned away toward the men. "Make those shots count, boys. Nice and slow now. We have to make it last."

Another volley went out, sounding like a brush fire fed with fresh dry leaves. Bullets hit the barricade and sailed over the top. He leaned forward on the barricade and fired a shot then ducked down. "Peltier isn't right. Those orders came from Captain Corby."

"If something has happened to the captain, that puts you in charge," Wilhelm said.

Wolf shook his head no. "He's still with us."

"But you may be in charge all the same. You remember that. These men depend on it."

"Peltier is still in charge of this company."

Wilhelm leaned closer, pointing at him. "There can be no question. The men need someone to follow. Order must be maintained. With no structure the unit will fall apart. Is the captain incapacitated or not?"

Wolf eyed his sergeant, a man he considered as close as a father. "He is still in charge."

The sergeant's steel-blue eyes held strong, and Wolf clenched his jaw in anger. Wilhelm turned back to the men. "Grab that man's cartridges. Any man injured leave his pouch."

"Move quickly, lads," came a shout from behind them. Wolf turned to see a wall of blue moving toward them like a dark ocean swell of a tsunami. In a solid rank, Union infantry marched down the village streets toward the breastworks. The Stars and Stripes whipped in the air next to the red-outlined white cross of the 6th Corps. Their feet beat the ground in time, and Wolf felt a great joyful relief in his chest.

"Wright's boys are showing up just in time," Wolf said.

"They are."

An infantry captain ordered his men forward. "Company, advance!" The infantry men rushed toward the barricade in a blue tide, clutching their rifles in their hands. In minutes, the 13th was reinforced by two infantry regiments. All up and down the breastworks, infantry piled behind the barricade.

"Ready!"

"Aim!"

"Fire!" barked a captain. A volley ripped from the barricade at the rebels and then another, staggering the exposed enemy soldiers. The infantry captain crouched next to Wolf. "You boys done well holding as long as you did."

"'Bout as fun as painting in the rain."

The captain grinned. "Never is." He clapped Wolf on the shoulder. "You men head to the rear. We got it from here. Almost got the devils pinned. Few days and this bloody madness will be all but over."

Wolf wasn't convinced. The more they fought, the more stubborn their enemy became, but the war would end, and he would be there for it.

"First Platoon and Second Platoon, withdraw!" he called at his men. His men were quick to disengage, and they jogged away from the breastworks. They kept to the side as a regiment of infantry marched down the streets, mostly young men with hardened faces. He wondered how his men appeared to them or if anyone even cared to notice.

F Company met their comrades holding their mounts, and the platoon sergeants took stock of their men. They'd leave two casualties behind, one dead and one wounded. Wolf peered at his men with a sigh. Today could have been a bad day, even an ugly day for the company yet with the arrival of an infantry corps the entire situation was changed.

"For that hot of a fight we held our own," Wolf said to Peltier.

The captain sat atop his horse, his eyes vacant and mumbled, "We did."

"Sir, is everything all right? That wound you took a few days ago bothering you?"

"Head hurts, Lieutenant, but nothing worse than an ache. It will pass." Peltier eyed them. "Our orders are for Old Church."

Wolf walked his mount back to his men. Wilhelm held the wolf's head company flag. They fell into rank behind D Company and they took a slow march back to the Old Church while the infantry battled it out in Old Cold Harbor. Wolf wondered if any of it would make a difference or if it was all just a general's miscalculation on paper. *How long before we are merely erased off the map?* None of it mattered because he would have fight either way.

Chapter 6

Morning, June 6, 1864
Union Cavalry Corps Camp near New Castle Ferry, Virginia

Brigadier General Custer sat behind a small writing desk made from a polished red maple. His pen tip scratched across the paper as he wrote in sharp sweeping penmanship. This was the third sheet of paper he'd use to compose a letter to his beautiful wife, Libbie. They corresponded with one another often and with a lavish tongue. The letters would make a lady blush and a man smirk, but her words were all for him and his for her as the lovers embraced through the written word.

He kept all her letters in his personal wagon that accompanied the baggage train at all times. Every important personal effect he owned was stashed away including his wedding uniform, chapeau hat, long frock dress coat, double-striped trousers, woven belt sash, and dress gloves. Also, there was a small writing desk, a personal gift from Libbie so he could write her from the field, and a saber given to him from by the men of the 5th Michigan. Not to mention the items that made a man civilized and not a mere beast: shaving kit, toothbrush, combs, brushes, and a leather valise.

Words couldn't describe how much he loved that woman, but he fumbled through letters in an attempt to make her understand the depths of his feelings for her. He only had two true loves in his life. The army and Libbie Bacon Custer. Both always seemed to be in a tug-of-war over him, but when Libbie was near, she won every time.

Other men spoke of their wives with such critical disdain, and it baffled him why they'd married in the first place. Sure, there was much fun to be had living as bachelor men do, but if there was no deep love there, then why force the arrangement? In his mind, he settled upon the notion that most people would never experience love the way he and Libbie would with that undying yearning for the other's embrace. It was as if they were tethered together with a rubber band and any distance too far would only bring them crashing back together even faster. He continued to scribble on the sheet.

Cold Harbor has turned into a terrible massacre a few days past. There are rumors that Lincoln will call for Grant's resignation leaving us under the care of the Old Snapping Turtle, George Meade. The enemy finds himself with his back against the wall, yet he remains tenacious and will not go down without an adamant fight.

He paused as he thought. A military camp was adrift with rumors, most false, some with bits of truth. In Custer's mind, Grant was Lincoln's best hope and while the rebels would fight, victory was within their grasp. Yet morale was down after Cold Harbor. He put his pen back to the paper.

7,000 men dead, wounded or missing in a matter of hours and almost everyone wearing blue. Three divisions marched forth in a silver ground fog only to be met with a scythe of rebel lead cutting our men down like a field of wheat. We haven't seen such a slaughter since early in the war.

My boys have gotten an adequate rest over the past few days and it is well earned. The enemy battens down the hatches. Forgive my naval speak. We find ourselves doing the bloodiest and toughest work of any of the brigades in our division, and my boys are the best for it. Torbert knows it and so do the other commanders, probably garnering some envious looks, but glory goes to those that reach out and grasp it. But perhaps I dabble too much in the wars of men, my lady. When not on the field of war, I can only think of your embrace. Your tender touch. If I were with you now, I would kiss every part of you and no part would be unknown to my lips. You are the only object of my desire. All a man could ask for. Being in the field is a struggle without you near. I so long to ride with you again.

Custer set his pen down for a moment and sighed. He imagined her, all of her, in his thoughts. She was a short woman, but it made him feel even more masculine. Everything about her was small and perky, her simper one of a clever woman, one with a sharp tongue. Her lips curved just enough to spark the interest of many suitors like she knew the secret to life, and it was a glorious answer that she could only share.

Her hair was made of divine looping curls like chestnut circlets, her skin the softest shade of pink without a single blemish aside from the birthmark on her inner thigh. He'd nicknamed it Connecticut for its shape and traced it often with the tip of his finger. Her nose, not overbearing nor too small, was the perfect combination for her petite stature. Each piece of her formed a goddess in his eyes.

"Dear God, I miss that woman." He eyed the ceiling of his room sucking in air, trying to calm his heartbeat. Her letters were beyond provocative and raised his hackles, arousing either a need to fight or make love. And with her gone, that left little else but to take his newlywed frustrations out on the rebels.

He kicked his chair back and stood stretching, releasing another heavy breath. "Need a cold shower." He took a hand and pressed it into his cheek. He held up a letter from her. *I look forward to sitting Tomboy for a ride.* He rubbed his brow with heart-pounding intensity. She must realize what she was doing to him. She must.

He inhaled heavily again, glancing at her letter, and shook his head. These kinds of letters could get a man killed, his head elsewhere when he should be focusing on his task on hand. He let the air out from his chest. Love. His feelings were pushed under by the smoky aroma of frying bacon as it drifted up the stairs from the kitchen below, activating a different desire, to eat. He bent down and tried to focus on finishing his letter.

I must bid you adieu for my duty calls to this great nation. Keep a stout heart. Your words give me meaning and purpose more than any uniform ever could. I return your one thousand kisses and add one more so you know that no matter how much you love me, I love you more.
OOO

Your darling boy,
Autie

He nodded at that. She was much better at this, yet he felt that he held his own better than any other man he knew could. He was as much a romantic as he was a fighter.

Sometimes in the field he'd receive batches of her letters. It mattered not. He was glued to the page as her words were majestic poetry. She took the mundane woman's life and made it leap with action, jump with glee, and sing with joyous harmony. Then came the double entendres she'd written throughout each note, words only meant for him. The writings of a lady insinuating unladylike things. Private things were swaddled in the words, daring yet encased with a level of classiness belonging to a woman of her elevated station.

He shook the letter gently to let the ink dry then folded it and placed it in an envelope and stuck the letter inside his breast jacket pocket for mailing. He then took her letter and placed it inside a leather valise where he kept all of her love notes.

A man's voice sounded from below and Custer cocked his head to the side. *Must be time to meet with Sheridan.* He draped his hussar-style jacket over his shoulders. Taking a hand, he brushed off a single star. He tugged the jacket down for a better fit and noticed a button missing along the double-breasted columns of brass. "I thought I told the boy to replace that button." His voice rose to a shout toward the next room. "Johnny!"

The young boy was no older than ten, but nobody really knew his age. He'd shown up in the camp one day and asked Custer if he wanted to see a magic trick, one that required the use of Custer's watch to perform. Custer took him up on the offer and the boy ran off with his watch. Quickly run down by Russell Alger and officers from the 5th Michigan, he questioned the boy as to why he'd done it. It was a sad tale and probably a lie, but Custer cuffed the boy atop the head and employed him on the spot for a dollar a week, meals, and a place to stay.

Now the waif pressed his shirts and laundered his clothes and performed whatever errands the general needed done. The greasy-headed sandy-blond-haired boy ran into the room trying to tuck in his shirt. His hair stuck straight into the air in the back. He had tried to copy the general and the officers by dressing nicely and combing his hair, but some part of him was always out of place. It was endearing to the men, and every officer looked out for him. Big blue eyes peered at Custer. "Gen'ral, sir." His eyes shifted downcast.

"I thought I told you to sew this button on my jacket?"

The boy squinted although the jacket was right in front of him. "That one? I thought you wanted the other one mended."

Custer raised his eyebrows. "Now, Johnny, tell the truth."

The boy squinted a single eye now as if he were taking aim with a gun. "Hmm, you sure you didn't ask Eliza, sir?"

"I did not. I asked a Mr. Johnny Cisco to mend it."

The boy bobbed his head. "I'll make to let Ms. Eliza know." Johnny made to duck out of the door.

"Wait, boy!" Custer said. "When I return, you'll have it mended. Leave Eliza to her chores."

Johnny sighed. "Yes, sir," he said and rolled his eyes.

Custer buttoned the coat halfway and quickly tied his red necktie, a piece of prideful crimson flair that had become a symbol of their brigade.

"Autie, we're going to be late!" came a voice from below.

Now that wasn't the voice of Eliza. It had been over a week since he'd seen his friend. Alger had come down with a feverish spell after Haw's Shop and had been shipped back to Washington to recover. Custer hurriedly ensured his pistol was on his hip and sword on his other side and bounded down the stairs.

"Russell Alger. You're back!" Custer said when he reached the first floor.

The handsome dark-haired and black-bearded colonel grinned. He'd appeared to have lost a few pounds but aside from that was no worse for the wear. "Let me tell you one thing, Autie, don't ever let me get sent to Washington again. The amount of boredom is criminal."

"As are the people."

"Too many chiefs and not enough Indians."

The two men embraced quickly.

Custer released him and with a slap on his back. "You can't tell me you didn't enjoy any company while you were there."

Alger's smiled turned devious. "Autie, please. Not with the lady present. I was sick and in need of care."

Custer eyed Eliza Brown, his servant and a former slave. Her hair was held back with a bandana over the top of her head. Her dress was plain but finely made. It had been a gift from Libbie the last Christmas past. She gave a slight disapproving stare and a nod as she spoke. "Ginnel. Ginnel Sheridan is a'waitin'."

"As always, Eliza, you are correct and keep me on track."

The colored servant nodded emphatically. "That's why I'm here. Make sure you whip those rebs back to Richmond."

Custer belted a quick hoot. "Could never be done without you."

"Now come and get dis bacon and biscuit 'fore it gets cold."

Custer grabbed a biscuit and a handful of bacon. He took a bite. "Crunchy, just the way I like it." He turned toward Alger. "Bacon?"

"Would love some," Alger said with a grin.

The two men grabbed up every last piece and Alger stuffed an extra biscuit in his pocket.

"Hurry now, Ginnel." Eliza shooed them with a hand towel. Custer dodged a swipe and Alger took a towel snap on the rear as they fled for the outside the same as two scolded schoolboys caught thieving a pie.

The two officers stepped outside to a warm day, Alger rubbing his behind. "That woman. I see she's still walking around here like the Queen of Sheba."

Custer laughed at his friend. "She hasn't changed since the day I met her. She has a gift. Don't know where I'd be without her."

"Well, you could tell her to take it easy with the towels."

"You tell her!" Custer gave him a maddening look. "Sometimes I don't know if she's working for me or if I'm following her orders." They shared a chuckle as they mounted their horses.

They traveled to the nearby Williams' home where Sheridan had established his headquarters. Two whole cavalry divisions were camped over the land. They passed sutlers hawking goods, and quartermasters doling out rations, blacksmiths pounding horseshoes, a group of men playing cards, and others bowing their heads in prayer.

"I trust that my boys have been staying in line."

"I think they were too tired to create much of a ruckus."

Alger frowned. "That doesn't sound like them. I'll have to have a talkin' with Magoffin, ruining all the lads' fun." Alger took a bite from a biscuit, swallowing before he continued. "I'll say, it's just grand to be back. That place is a rotten swamp. If you can believe it, it's hotter there than here, and for a man with a fever, nothing is worse."

"Not possible," Custer said with a fair share of sarcasm.

"It's true, but more humid," Alger said with a nod. "Give me a rebel bullet any day over the words of a politician."

"All part of the game, my dear friend."

"Not the part I prefer to play." Horse hooves clopped the ground. "Ahh, wait." He stuffed the biscuit into his mouth before reaching into his jacket and pulling out a letter. "I saw Libbie."

Custer's eyes gleamed with joy at the mention of his love. "You should have said something before." Custer took the letter and pressed it beneath his nose and breathed in deeply in the hope of a faint whiff of his love's scent. A floral aroma tickled his nose like a sweetened feather. *Roses? Lavender? Lilac?* "How is my lady?"

"As lovely as the day you two wed. Lovelier." Alger gave him a respectful nod. "Brought me a sweet cake to help me heal up."

Custer grinned again, inhaling the letter's fragrance. "Lilac." He glanced at Alger. "It even smells of her. Lilac is her favorite flower. You just made me a happy man." He reached out and patted his friend on the shoulder. "The brigade is blessed to have you back so soon."

"Your words are most kind." Alger bowed his head in respect for his friend and commander.

"Men haven't had much rest, but I can feel it. The rebels are almost done. They have to be."

"Do you think even with what's going on in Cold Harbor?"

The news from Cold Harbor made bile rise in his gut in disgust. "Trenches and mud. A labyrinth of breastworks. That's no way to fight a war. Lee must be mad."

"Or desperate."

"There you have it, Russ, desperate."

"Yet he inflicted great casualties with such defenses." Each man rocked with their horses before Alger spoke again. "Perhaps he's on to something."

Custer dismissed him with a wave of his arm. "Reeks of desperation. Men are meant to move and seek tactical advantage, not sit and wait for a shell to explode overhead. Or a bullet to sing his name in death."

"I would tend to agree. But you can't deny, it worked."

Custer dismissed his friend with a wave. "For now. I smell victory as much as the lilac on my letter. We fight more rabble than rebels."

"I'll take your word for it." Alger smiled and popped a piece of bacon into his mouth. As they neared a large affluent beige home, rousing piano music flowed from inside. Tied mounts lined a section of fence, each mount tied to a post.

A trooper standing out front held the Army of the Potomac's Cavalry Corps flag, a blue guidon with white crossed sabers, a large red C overlapping the sabers. Another trooper held Sheridan's personal standard, a white over red guidon with opposing colored stars on each side. Nearby the 1st and 2nd Division flags were planted in the ground.

"Fellows be getting into it already," Alger said.

"Lively, aren't they?"

"Better balls are had out in the field than in the city!"

The men dismounted and tied their horses to a nearby fence post. "Let's go find out what all the fuss is about," Custer said.

Alger gestured for him to go first. "After you, sir."

Custer walked the path and opened the door while removing his black slouch hat. The music escalated in volume. A woman in a light-blue dress played the piano with upper-class skill while the man sitting next to her hammered away on the black and white keys as if the devil himself egged him on. Other men in blue surrounded the piano, clapping in time with the song. More blonde women, clearly related to the piano player, stood with the officers, pleasant smiles on their faces. The sight of the attractive women made Custer yearn for his Libbie even more.

A bushy sideburned general turned with a grin for Custer and Alger. "George! Great to see you!" Brigadier General Alfred Torbert said. He commanded the 1st Cavalry Division. He was an intelligent man, formerly an engineer, but lacked cavalry experience. He depended upon his stout brigade commanders heavily in the field for direction.

Custer gave him a winning smile. "You as well, sir. Grand old time in here."

"Ah, it is. By God, we needed some Southern comfort after the last few days."

"Amen to that, sir," Custer said.

"A wonder to look at these fine ladies," Alger added. He grinned, eyeing each lady around the room. He bowed slightly to a nearby lady. "The name is Russ and to whom do I have the pleasure of speaking with?"

"Sarah Williams."

"Such a beautiful name," Alger said. The woman let out an entertained titter. "Have you ever been to Washington, my lady?"

Custer left his friend to his charms and glanced over the room. Brigadier General David McM. Gregg was there with a smile on his bearded cheeks, hands clasped behind his back, as he rocked to the music. His tall cousin loomed nearby, towering a head over the other officers. Near them was Brigadier General Wesley Merritt, a short fellow with an equally short mustache and hard calculating eyes. He was accompanied by Colonel Thomas Devin, who had a thick mustache, a broad jaw, and a bayonet for a nose, and fiercely pointed eyes to match. He'd earned his name as "Old War Horse" for his expertise in the field. Brigadier General Henry E. Davies stood near the bar cart fixing himself a drink. The former lawyer stirred the drink with a pinky finger and took a sip beneath a mustache that curled downward as much as his worried eyes did above. He had a new saber on his hip, and it clanged into the cart as he turned. He was a holdover from Kilpatrick's command. While Custer was wary of the man, he was a competent commander. Other officers lined the edge of the room, regimental commanders standing intermixed with their brigade superiors.

To no one's surprise, the rotund Colonel Moore of the 13th Michigan had already arrived. Any joy disappeared from Custer's lips. Moore stood near the piano with a grand smile on his face. The presence of a pistol on his hip surprised Custer. Perhaps he wasn't as dense as Custer had pegged him to be, yet here he was bowing and scraping to the other generals before Custer had even arrived. He wondered what schemes the man worked outside his presence.

Custer moved around the room as the piano picked up its pace, and the officers and ladies clapped faster to the tune. Lanky Captain Alexander Pennington was there. Captain Randol of the combined batteries H&I, 1st U.S. Artillery, stood in attendance, tapping his foot. He had a bushy goatee on his chin. Custer shook hands with Pennington. "Alexander, a true pleasure to be in your company again."

"General, you are a sight for sore eyes. It seems like ages since we last met. Gettysburg?"

"No, can't be," Custer said, brows crossing with visible thought.

"I believe so, sir. They attached us to the 1st Cavalry Division now."

"And the wolverines have missed you every day since."

Pennington blushed with the compliment. "Thank you, General."

"With all these fine gentlemen here, we must be preparing for something of epic proportions."

Alexander nodded with a fond smile. "Rumor has it a glorious raid."

"Really?"

"That's right. We're going to burn Charlottesville."

"Surely we don't need two divisions for that?"

"Yet here we all are," the lanky officer said, spreading his arms wide.

Not all of them though. Brigadier General James Wilson was farther south, and Custer wasn't the least bit disappointed with the distance. His rival and political enemy could lead his men to death somewhere away from Custer. Their feud was long standing and when Grant had taken overall command of the Union forces, Custer had been absorbed into Wilson's command. He had to lobby hard to weasel out from under that blowhard's yoke, and it paid off. Given he was shifted under another infantryman, but a much more manageable commander, Alfred Torbert.

But all eyes in the room settled upon the short officer on the edge of the bench as he continued to bang away on the piano until he finished with a loud - *bang da bang!* Sheridan stood with his hands in the air, acknowledging his musical prowess.

"Hurrah!" Torbert called out.

"Bravo!" a lady cried, clasping her hands together in glee.

Sheridan bowed at the hips. "Encore?"

"Oh yes!" said another lady.

A colored boy in a Union jacket brought Sheridan a glass of whiskey. "Thank you, Freddy." He raised the glass to everyone in the room. "Alas, we have war business to conduct." He took a sip and swallowed it down with a bow. "Thank you, ladies, for all the fun! You are truly worth fighting for. Perhaps we will play again later tonight." He paused taking another drink of the brown liquor. "All right, you gentleman soldiers. Come into the next room." He bowed again then strolled into the dining room of the home.

Alger leaned over. "Quite the showman."

"Gave Stuart a run for his money."

"He did, sir."

Custer grinned. "We did."

The cluster of officers followed the short-in-stature major general, almost a replica of a little bandy-legged Napoleon. The major general patted his breast pocket and removed a finely rolled cigar. One of his aides lit a match and handed it to him. He puffed his cigar alight and rolled out a map of Virginia. He set his glass on one edge to keep it from rolling up.

"Grant's run out of damn space." He puffed his cigar. "There's no more room to squeeze between Lee and Richmond to force a fight on our terms."

"He could reverse course, sir. Shift his men to the right flank?" Gregg said.

"Could but that isn't the stubborn son of bitch's way. Cold Harbor's gone poorly and he's looking for a way out." He tapped a finger farther down the map, south from Richmond. Railroads ran to and from each city on the map. "Petersburg will fall."

"We're headed to Petersburg?" Torbert asked.

Sheridan gave him a knowing frown. "No, Grant's going to Petersburg. He's going to cross here on the James, but he needs us to throw Lee off his trail so he can cross unmolested." The officers nodded around the table. A diversionary raid. Grant had used them before with success. Custer nodded in appreciation. There was always time for a good raid. Ripping through the enemy territory as a hungry hell-born tornado was a morale boost in the newspapers and hindered Lee's essential supply chains.

"What about Richmond?" Torbert asked.

Sheridan gave him an irritated glance. "Grant's decided to starve Richmond by sieging Petersburg. It's the largest supply depot for Lee's army. The second biggest depot for the Army of Northern Virginia. The other three supply depots and stations will be ours, and every piece of track between them. Gordonsville, Lynchburg, and Charlottesville."

"Surely that is better left for our forces in the Shenandoah," Devin said.

Sheridan smiled. "General Hunter routed Grumble Jones Army only a few days past. Rumor has it Grumble perished, leaving them leaderless. Hunter marches with his army toward Charlottesville, and we will come from the east, burning our way through Virginia and making a necktie out of every piece of railroad track we come across."

"Surely Lee will try and stop us," Custer said.

Sheridan grinned around his cigar. "That's exactly what I hope. I hope he'll send that big dumb brute Hampton after us or maybe one of his mouth-breathing kin. That will further free up Grant to cross uninhibited. Hell, maybe he'll send them all. And I'll tell you this. I couldn't give two shits about any of them. It's just another chance to thrash the bastards and I'll take 'em up on that."

The officers smiled as the multiple strategies of the expedition became clearer.

"Our pace is going to be the same as we did before Yellow Tavern." The tip of his cigar flared bright orange at the thought of victory. "Nice and slow. Give that dumb son of a bitch Hampton an easy target." He let the smoke billow from his mouth. "If he's anything like Stuart, he'll bite. If he doesn't, that will make the raid even easier. We burn the entire place until Lee has no choice but to pay attention." Sheridan leaned on the table, hands spread far apart, nodding as he studied the map, eyeing the railroad tracks and roadways.

"Our mounts are pretty exhausted," said Gregg. He was a careful planner, foreseeing as many obstacles as possible before charging forth. One of the better generals still alive in the Union cavalry ranks, he was more of a strategist than a man who led from the front, but the army needed all kinds.

Sheridan eyed him with lack of concern. "We travel light. Three days rations, a hundred rounds a man. We forage everything else we need. We won't go fast, hopefully that will save our mounts." He turned toward Custer. "I trust your great horse killers can keep their mounts in one piece until we're done?"

Custer gave a wicked smirk. His brigade had acquired the reputation of being excellent horse killers, not in a malicious sense, but one of overwork. They were one of the best, if not the best, shock force Sheridan had at his disposal. Sure, some men would argue for other brigades, but his men had built a reputation earned with blood and guts on the field of battle. His regiments required remounts on a regular basis, which the War Department did not appreciate. "We will go easy on the poor beasts."

A round of laughter erupted from the officers. Smoke quickly filled the room with a blueish-gray haze. Confidence brimmed from the officers. There wasn't a smidge of negativity weighing on the men. The war was theirs to win. Their army marched with relative impunity over enemy soil, and while the enemy fought, they felt the tide turning in their favor.

Sheridan's smile was broad and deep, revealing all his teeth. "Very well. Mum is the word, but prepare your men for a raid, boys. We leave with the rising sun."

Chapter 7

Afternoon, June 6, 1864
Union Cavalry Corps Camp near New Castle Ferry, Virginia

Wolf lay beneath a tree using a stiff root as a pillow. Thick leaves shaded him from the sun's heat as he dozed in and out of consciousness. It was damn near as close as one could get to heaven in the military if you could ignore the sound of hooves and men talking as well as the buzzing of insects. Then there was the smell of horse manure that permeated through everything. And the latrine. Best to avoid stretching out near there. If a man could ignore all of that, he had a chance at a respectable snooze.

His proper cavalry shell coat hung from a tree branch above him. It was drying out from the wash he'd given it in a creek. He'd had to take his horse brush to scrub out the white sweat rings. His pants were rolled to his knees, and his socks and boots sat nearby having undergone the same soldierly cleaning treatment.

The day was as close to perfect as he could recall in a long time. It had been the brigade's fifth straight day of rest. Scores of teamsters rolled into the camp in the night, driving light-blue wagons with white canvas buttoned-up covers. Quartermasters then went about resupplying the men, and the men were given bacon and salted beef, coffee and flour, dried fruit and desiccated vegetables, and feed for their mounts.

Munn had cooked up a few batches of his famous flapjacks, and the men ate heartily. Afterwards Wolf settled down next to a tree, placed his hands over a full belly, interlocked his fingers, and took his nap. For hours he lay motionless, drifting in and out of sleep, basking in the comfort of shade.

He felt cool leather tap his foot. "Lieutenant," came Wilhelm's accented voice.

"Are we moving?" Wolf said, eyes still closed.

"Not yet."

"Then why are you waking me?"

"Captain wants to see you."

"Why?"

"Probably be moving soon."

Wolf cracked his eyes. "You could have led with that." He pushed himself into a seated position. He stretched his arms over his head and flexed the scar-tissue-laden skin on his back, a constant nagging reminder of the debt owed to Captain Payne of the Red Shirts. A debt he would pay before the war's end for Wolf's war would not be over until he'd killed the man. He slipped his boots on and stood, his rusty brace creaking with the effort.

He glanced down at the infuriating contraption that kept his knee from buckling when he walked. Faded leather and rusting metal were never meant for the outdoors. He tugged on the leather strap around his thigh pulling it upward.

"It appears the wagon train's arrival had greater purpose than to just feed us."

Wolf draped his jacket over his shoulders, slipping his arms into the warm coat, not bothering to button it. "Fatten us up before we're back into the wilderness."

Wilhelm frowned slightly. "It could be much worse. There could be no wagon train."

"No army does much without one. An army marches on its stomach," Wolf said, patting his belly.

"A man's morale is directly related to his stomach and his leader. One feeds the other." Wilhelm grinned at his own words beneath his curled mustache.

"How would you explain Lee then? His men wear rags and fight with broken-down guns on empty stomachs, yet the war rages on."

Wilhelm frowned. "He never wastes time. Picks quality ground for his men. Hardly ever wastes them. He does many things well."

"How do we win then?"

"Do the same. Everything is harder on a man who doesn't eat well." Wilhelm patted his stomach. "We eat better although not as good as home."

"Not as good as home." Thoughts of his mother's roasted pork danced in his head. Wolf smiled. "If we have to fight, I'd rather do it on a full stomach."

"And that, my boy, is the point. Imagine those poor sons of bitches over yonder starving and staring down the bayonet at the pointy end. Perhaps he carries on out of pride or honor. Perhaps he kills to eat. But he is always close to breaking." Wilhelm tapped his head. "Here. Those things eat away at a man." He grinned again with a glance at Wolf.

"You are chipper today, aren't you?"

Wilhelm patted his stomach. "Well-fed men are happy men."

"Join me while I meet with the captain."

"My pleasure."

They walked through tents until they found Captain Peltier sitting on a log near a campfire despite the heat. He set a mucket over the fire, hooking it on a spit. The small pot was used for boiling coffee, and for the men, coffee was an all-the-time necessity, not just in the morning. Each soldier was issued thirty-six pounds of coffee per year. Often it was the fuel to keep the men going before a fight, after a fight, and sometimes during a fight.

Peltier took a rag and peered inside the pot.

"Make sure it's black as tar," Wolf said.

Peltier didn't look up, bandage still wrapped around his skull. "Never once had a wishy-washy brew." He glanced at them with a smile, a glimpse of his former self showing through. He poured the coffee into two cups and handed one to Wolf and then one to Wilhelm.

Wolf took a sip of the rich dark brew and gave Peltier a slight nod. "Like tar."

Peltier followed suit, pouring some into his cup and slurping the hot liquid. "Battles have been won or lost on this stuff."

"Nothing can beat it," Wilhelm said.

Peltier sighed. "I trust you men are rested up. Blisters mended. Saddle sores healed."

Wolf looked at Wilhelm and answered. "Yes, sir. The men are in high spirits despite our licks. Ready for a scrap at a moment's notice."

Peltier grimaced and squinted his eyes. He glanced warily at the sun. "So bright." He placed his hat back and shaded his eyes. "Been piercing lately and my head has a heavy feel to it."

Both the men nodded. The sun was intense, but no more than usual.

Peltier continued. "Make sure everyone is well-fed tonight. Three days rations, one-hundred rounds of ammunition, any man with a weak mount try to secure another. Otherwise, he's Company Q. I will not take him."

Company Q was the infamous designation for cavalrymen unfit for duty whether he was ill or without a mount. They were often reassigned as infantry or forced to sit out any mounted action until additional horses could be procured from the War Department. Peltier didn't want to abandon men in the field.

"Are we preparing for action?" Wolf asked. It was a simple question, but any information was better than nothing at all.

Peltier nodded, pained by the movement. "We are. A raid west."

"Railroads must tremble before us," Wolf said.

"Rumors abound but my guess is Charlottesville. Everything along that way is part of the Southern war effort."

Wilhelm took a sip of coffee before he spoke. "We expecting any resistance?"

Peltier shrugged and drank some of his coffee. "Any more than normal? No. There are enemy forces near Charlottesville, but our two divisions will prove superior in numbers." He shook his head softly. "That blow to the head. Everything's foggy, you understand?"

"Should you see the surgeon?" Wolf asked.

Peltier grinned. "What's he going to do? Can't amputate my head."

"I mean, he could, but not sure how'd you fare," Wolf said in jest.

Peltier waved him off. "I appreciate your concern, Lieutenant, but I'm fine. Maybe not fit as a fiddle, but put me back in the saddle and I'll die a happy man." He sighed and even that looked pained. "Daybreak, we ride."

"The men will be ready."

Peltier gave another nod and sat back down to stare at the flames and sip his coffee.

Wolf and Wilhelm made their way back to their platoon. "Grab Sergeant Simpson and meet me by the wagon train."

Soon after, Wilhelm returned with Sergeant Jesse Simpson. He was much shorter than Wilhelm and had a brown goatee streaked with gray. He reached into his jacket and pulled a plug of tobacco out of a piece of white wrapping paper and bit into the stuff, shoving it into his cheek. "Lieutenant Wolf." He held out the dark brown tobacco plug, and Wolf shook his head. Many of their Southern counterparts chewed tobacco, but Wolf preferred a cigar or a pipe to it. Simpson turned the plug toward Wilhelm who removed his pipe from his jacket and placed some of the tobacco inside, lit a match, and puffed away.

"Captain wants us ready to go by morning. They're saying a hundred rounds per man. Forty in his pouch. I want it doubled."

"For a raid, sir?" Simpson raised his eyebrows. He had grown accustomed to Lieutenant Wells, letting him steer the platoon. He'd acted as a company quartermaster sergeant since their original one mustered out with chronic flux early in the war. He spit a black glob on the ground.

"Every raid I been on, we needed every bullet we had. And then some," Wolf said.

Simpson tongued the tobacco and gave a slight nod. "Can't say I disagree, but the regimental quartermaster knows me. A real miserly fellow that one."

They both looked at Wolf. Wilhelm puffed his pipe. "How do you propose we get more?"

"We make 'em think we got more men than we do."

"The regimental quartermaster knows exactly how many men we have."

"I'm not talking about him."

"You mean the brigade's quartermaster?"

"Exactly. You came from the 7th Michigan originally, right?"

Simpson tongued his tobacco again. "I did."

"Who's the regimental quartermaster?"

"Lieutenant Ogden."

"You know him?"

"Enough."

"Give me your jacket."

***

Thirty minutes later, Wolf stood in front of the brigade's quartermaster. The captain stared at Wolf with narrowly placed scalelike eyes. His chin was as round as a saucer with a great divide down the middle as if it'd been cleaved with an axe. He stood in front of a wagon with U.S. painted on the side of its white canvas surrounded by stacks of crates and boxes. Barrels lined one side of the tent, a board running over them serving as a table. Everything was covered by a canvas tent, preventing exposure to the rain and the sun. "You're new. Which unit are you with?"

"7th Michigan, sir. D Company."

"Why isn't your regimental quartermaster coming with this request? I believe that is Lieutenant Ogden. What happened to him? I see no burial detail, so he must live."

Wolf gulped, wishing that Roberts was still with him. That man could lie his way out of the army. "Sergeant Wilson is ill. In his tent over there. We're going to leave him here to recover."

"Nonsense. I spoke with him not an hour ago."

"Not no more. Seen him doing the Virginia Two-Step. Skin flushed with fever, sweat pouring down his cheeks." Wolf placed his hand over his heart. "I'm only trying to make sure our boys are properly supplied, sir."

"I'm going to speak with him." Troopers bustled behind the quartermaster moving boxes and feed out of wagons.

"Be my guest, sir, but he's incapacitated in his tent." He shook his head. "Doc says he doesn't know if he'll make it."

"Dear God, he's taken with fever."

A man wearing a lieutenant's jacket walked past. "Goddamnit, Sergeant, hurry the hell up!" he shouted in Wolf's direction.

"Hurrying, sir."

"Lieutenant," the quartermaster called lifting a hand to wave him down. "Lieutenant!"

The junior officer kept marching away. He barked orders at a private and carried on. The private stared at the man's back as he passed.

Wolf shook his head. "Lieutenant is getting on me. Anything you could spare for our company. They missed us entirely."

The quartermaster's eyes bulged. "You have no ammunition?"

"No, sir. Over sixty men and we'll be doing plenty of saber work without bullets."

"Goddamnit!" the quartermaster cursed. "Private." He grabbed a young man detailed to him. "Get this sergeant a dozen boxes of carbine ammunition and pistol ammunition, caps and the like. Hurry now, on the double." The young man nodded hurrying toward a cluster of crates.

"I got some boys to help carry," Wolf said. "Leave your men to their regular work."

The quartermaster gave a brief smile. "As you wish, Sergeant. Follow Thompson."

By nightfall, the company's wagon was filled with double the ammunition originally allocated. Wolf had traded back hats and coats with Simpson. Each man had his pouch and saddle bags stuffed with over eighty rounds and anything extra went in the company wagon. The men were happy, and Peltier gave Wolf an extra smile. "Where'd you find all this?"

"The brigade's quartermaster was happy to help us out."

"I find that hard to believe," Peltier said.

"Handed it right over."

Peltier stared for a moment, eyes questioning the truth of Wolf's words. "I don't want to know. Just be ready in the morning."

"We're ready, sir." Wolf said with a smile and took a seat next to a fire.

Chapter 8

The sun had yet to breach the night when the bugle call for boots and saddles sounded throughout the camp. The men bounded upright from a dead sleep. It was similar to waking the dead, but there was excitement among them as well.

The raid promised some great destruction and ravaging of the Virginia countryside. Wolf and his men took pleasure in a good raid, and if he had to be honest, his men were well-suited for it. The initial sounds of men prepping their mounts for march drifted from the encampment.

Wolf took his time refolding his blanket so the crusted sweat wouldn't irritate his horse. He made sure the blanket was folded to six-folds of thickness with no loose ends in front. He slid the blanket from the front to back to ensure the horse's hair wasn't brushed up, which would cause unnecessary irritation and potential injury to his mount. He draped the saddle over Sarah, straightening the girth and stirrups as well as his saddle bags.

Then he circled to the other side to make sure everything was untangled and level. On the way back to the side he would mount from, he hooked Sarah's tail through the crupper, ensuring all the tail hair was cleared through the loop. Then he made sure the girth strap was tight on Sarah's belly and not wrinkling her skin. He waited a moment before securing the strap through the girth ring, again ensuring she wasn't pushing out her belly to resist him.

Then he secured the surcingle belt buckle right behind the girth. He patted her flank when he was finished. "Thanks, girl." She stomped a hoof in response, forcing flies airborne.

He double-checked the rest of his belongings on her. There was a rope wound and hooked to the saddle with his picket pin. His saddle bags held his currycomb, brush, extra ammunition, and extra horseshoes. Then he fit all the rations he could in his haversack. The rest he'd eaten the night before. His socks, shirt, and drawers were rolled into his bedroll on the cantle of his saddle and his greatcoat on the front. He had another non-issued sack holding his plate and silverware along with a cup, crackers, a sewing kit, and the remaining piece of his father's sash. He also had a feed bag with two days of forage for Sarah. He quickly checked his carbine and his pistol.

After he had finished, Wilhelm offered him a cup of coffee, and they both sipped theirs as the men prepared to depart. "Men look good," Wilhelm said.

"Rest suited us just fine."

"Ja, it did."

"Ja."

F Company of the 13th Michigan was mounted in twenty minutes, coinciding with the rising sun. It peeked over the eastern horizon, first by leaking rays of light and then revealing itself with a blaze. Heat came rapidly with its rise.

"Gonna be a hot one," Adams said.

"I burn easy," Kent muttered, scratching at his neck.

"Fuck the sun," Nelson said. Then as if he remembered Kent's statement, he said. "And quit whining."

"I wasn't whining. I was sharing my discomfort for all to endure."

Nelson was about to let the man have it, but Wilhelm called out first. "Ranks of four, lads." The platoon hurried to obey, and they stacked in front of 2nd Platoon.

Wolf walked his horse passed the other platoon. The men looked worn yet well rested. He nodded to Sergeant Simpson, who was acting as platoon leader. Five days had done them well. He found the captain between the two platoons.

"Lieutenant. The 13th is falling in behind the 5th Michigan. Gregg's Division is leading the way," Peltier said.

"Do we need to send out scouts?"

"No, we are falling near the center rear of the column. Not much to worry about there."

"A relaxing raid."

"Ha!" Peltier said. "Who's heard of such a thing?"

"In my experience, there's no such thing," Wolf said.

They waited, knowing somewhere ahead the regiments and squadrons of cavalryman marched, but their company's time had yet to come. "It's good to have you with us," Peltier said, his words laced with greater meaning. He meant it was good to have Wolf rather than Wells if he had to take one of the two junior officers.

"We have a fine body of men."

"Agreed. You men had us worried at the beginning of the war." Peltier gestured out. "I think even Moore has been surprised by us."

"Wish we could say the same about him."

Peltier grimaced. "He's been peddling hard for a promotion. If we are successful, maybe he will get what he desires."

The thought of the colonel acquiring command of more men made Wolf feel a touch ill. However, if it got them a commander with a spine, it would be better for the men of the 13th and that had to count for something.

"Our men will perform either way. You can count on us. As long as we are above ground."

"You should have been a preacher, Lieutenant. Your words inspire a morbid hope."

"We're soldiers. That's all we have." Wolf shrugged his shoulders. "Can never say what tomorrow holds." Both the men shared a laugh at the thought of Wolf preaching to a congregation of willing patrons.

The only man who Wolf actually thought should be a preacher had been killed near Yellow Tavern by Captain Payne. And a man didn't get much holier than Zachariah Shugart. The Quaker abolitionist had forsaken his vow of pacification in order to fight for the freedom of the colored people, and he paid for his convictions with his life.

An hour passed and the sun rose in the sky like a slow-sailing gull gaining altitude. Company D moved to a walk and Peltier gave Wolf a nod with a grimace. "Company, forward march!"

They moved at a walk, hooves plodding the dry ground.

"An officer's voice," Peltier said to him with a shake of his head. "Never thought you'd make an officer with your leg 'n all." Wolf stayed near the captain. The company didn't need a guide so early in the march, only needed to follow the men ahead.

"I'll take that as a compliment, sir."

"I meant no harm. It's just men surprise you. Catch you off guard. Some men that are supposed to be bred for it couldn't lead a man to a latrine. While others that are born to the lowest common factor have the spark."

"More bad luck than anything else."

Peltier chuckled, pulling his hat lower over his eyes. "One man's bad luck is another's gain."

"Suppose it could be. Or he brings that bad luck to all his men."

"That is possible. Sometimes the bad luck is what defines us. The bad times." He glanced at Wolf. "A man that continues to fight even when he knows he's lost sends a message."

"Too dumb to quit? Hope them rebs ain't like that."

"Me as well. Perhaps we need to be the ones to never quit. This country deserves as much."

"Well, I ain't going to quit on you, Captain."

"I know that much."

***

At four miles per hour, the column marched north toward New Castle Ferry.

Rumors always followed an army like a murder of crows tailing a feathered deer while it bled out. Grant had chosen to withdraw, and the cavalry would secure important crossing points along the rivers. Other rumors buzzed quietly through the ranks. Fitz Lee's Cavalry Division was ripping through Maryland, gallivanting like Stuart used to do, and they would stop him. They would ride far and wide and pressure Richmond from the west. They were going to protect Washington from certain assault. The thing with rumors was most were nonsense, but if you looked hard enough, something could be seen.

"What do you think, Wilhelm?" Wolf asked.

The German sergeant reached up and twisted the curl in his mustache as he thought. "We aren't going anywhere in a hurry. If we were trying to stop Fitz, we'd be doing a scheiße job."

"I hear we're going to surrender. Grant's running back to Washington with his tail between his legs," Kent said with a nod.

"We ain't going to surrender," Adams added.

"We sure could. Been nothing but a slaughter, and the rebs ain't giving up."

"We aren't going to surrender," Wolf assured him. The thought of folding when they'd already sacrificed so much disgusted him.

"We could. What if Lincoln loses the election in November?" Kent said. "One of those Peace Democrats gets in the office. War will end then, and we would be trespassing on sovereign soil."

The 1864 presidential election was only a few months away. Wolf had never considered that Lincoln might lose, especially with the majority of his opponents in open rebellion. "You don't think Lincoln would lose?"

"It's possible," Wilhelm said. "We live in a country where a man may voice his opinion by casting a ballot. Not all men want to be at war. I, in fact, do not wish to be at war, but the situation dictates that I keep this country whole."

"Bunch of cowards," Nelson said. "Rumor has it Little Mac was going to run against Lincoln."

"The only thing worse than him running the army would be him running the country!" Wolf said. The men around him laughed, but it added a sliver of worry to the march.

Goffman pulled out a paper. "See here. They're meeting today in Baltimore." He held it out. "Despite some doubt about Lincoln's ability to win the war, it appears that the Republican delegates will select him to run for a second term. With the dropout of Salmon P. Chase due to a loss of support in Ohio and Lincoln's endorsement as the Republican candidate, the second only wartime election will commence."

"Wonder how good his chances will be when the papers catch word of the slaughter at Cold Harbor. Probably the end of Grant," Kent added. "All he's done is gotten more men killed faster. At least Little Mac spread it out, same with Hooker. Knew when to run too."

"We've been giving as good as we've got," Wolf said.

"Doesn't matter, Lieutenant," Goffman said. The troopers turned to look at him. "All that matters is how the public sees it. If it looks like we are losing even if we aren't, the public will vote him out. This war has cost us all very much. I stand with our cause, but if the public loses their belly for the fight, they will let their voices be known through the election."

Wolf nodded. His words rang true even if he didn't want to hear them. During the Kilpatrick-Dahlgren raid, Wolf found himself at the forefront of the public relation's war in the papers with the secret orders to assassinate Confederate President Jefferson Davis. Even though he had the orders secretly smuggled north, the Southern papers took the rumor as fact, damaging Lincoln's credibility and negotiating power with the rebels. Without the orders in hand, it became a propaganda war, each side calling the other foul. With the stroke of a pen, a newspaperman beat the drums of war or doused its flames, turning an effort, no matter how noble, to faint wisps of smoke. "Well said. Then we'll have to give them some good news to read in the newspapers."

"All this bloodshed could be for nothing if Lincoln grants the South sovereignty," Wilhelm said. Herman leaned over and spoke softly to Wilhelm in German. Wilhelm nodded as he spoke. "Exactly right, Herman. We've gone this far. May as well see it through to the end."

"Not much of a choice for us," Nelson said. "We're in the army." The troopers laughed scornfully at this. His words were as simple as they were true. They all had obligations based on their enlistments. The general spoke, the colonel directed, the captain ordered, the lieutenant relayed the order, and the sergeant yelled the order. Either way, they all did what they were told.

"Well, I know one thing. We better hope it's Lincoln, or Little Mac will be in charge of the whole sinking ship."

Snorts and huffs came from the men. Little Mac was relatively well-liked while he was in command of the Army of the Potomac, but he'd fallen from favor as the men had progressively better leadership, even going so far as to become a running joke amongst the Michigan Brigade.

The sun still hugged the horizon, a ripe lemon threatening to drop upon them from above. With the sun came the early morning heat, even more threatening because rings of wet sweat formed on their collars and underneath their armpits.

The men continued their slow march north until they came to New Castle Ferry. The engineers had already constructed a pontoon bridge that had been in use for over a week. Wolf still marveled at the bridge built in less than a day. Northern armies had the ability to cross a river anywhere with the construction of the portable bridges.

The bridge had been used in all major campaigns, and the Union had learned to give their men time and space without the enemy present for the most effective use of them. They had learned a lesson in blood at Fredericksburg in 1862 when engineers building a bridge across the Rappahannock River had been massacred by the rebels, the bridges only partially completed. This forced the Union army to use landing craft to secure the position so the bridges could be finished.

Hooves sounded similar to heavy rain as they clopped off the wooden planks lining the bridge. The tops of the bridge were made up of timber decking planks secured to sections of balks along the gunwales then curb-like rails were placed atop the planks. They stretched in sections over the small flat-bottomed, square-ended watercraft lashed to one another yet anchored upstream and also anchored in place to the shore.

The depth of the river mattered not with the bridges. Even the width of the river didn't seem to mean much although shorter crossings were sought after. The width of the Pamunkey River here was no more than twenty-five yards across. A man could swim the river if need be, but when it came to crossing hundreds, thousands, or tens of thousands of men, these bridges became critical, allowing the army to penetrate anywhere along a natural obstacle that the river employed.

A detachment of engineers and pickets sat in the woods nearby, smoke rising from their fires. They sipped coffee and observed the cavalry with interest. Less than a week before that, all these same men marched in the other direction. Now they rode north for some unknown purpose. Retreat? Pursuit? Victory or defeat? The engineers looked on with relative apathy. There was always a new bridge to build, and when the war was over, there would be even more to rebuild.

Captain Corby's D Company crossed ahead, and Wolf's men walked their mounts close behind.

"Take it slow!" shouted an engineer. He cupped his hands around his mouth. "You ride this bridge hard, and it will break apart."

Wilhelm leaned over in his saddle. The wolf guidon rested on its pole, no wind to raise the flag, and too slow of a movement to lift it in salute. "Think of it this way. No matter Sheridan's purpose, we're headed closer to home."

"I'll believe it when I lay my eyes on the rapids of the Grand River."

Their hooves thumped the planks, sounding hollow over the river yet muffled by the placement of sand and straw over the surface. Water rushed beneath the small watercraft propping the bridge. Fully bloomed trees lined the other bank.

Adams leaned back. "What's that Caesar saying?"

"Alea iacta est," Goffman said.

Adams turned his head to the side and grinned at the Jewish man. "That one there is smart. Best be careful of him. What's it mean?"

"The die is cast," Goffman said.

"The words he spoke while marching over the Rubicon," Wilhelm added. Herman leaned in and they quickly conversed. "He was with the 13th."

Wolf raised his eyebrows. "Perhaps it's a sign."

Kent frowned. "Or an ominous omen. Caesar was killed after that."

"It was an act that sentenced Caesar and all his men to death for breaking Roman law," Goffman said. "No general could lead his army south of it. By that act, Caesar declared war on the Republic."

"You think that's how the rebs see it? And Caesar Lee is their leader."

"Don't be stupid. They want the freedom to keep their slaves," Nelson added.

They closed on the other side of the small bridge. "Surely the Rubicon is larger than this. Those are mighty serious words for such a shallow ford." The men laughed.

"Besides," Goffman said. "Caesar won his civil war."

Wolf nodded as Sarah's hooves touched the other embankment on the other side. "The die is cast," he said, attempting Caesar's voice.

"Didn't know Caesar was German," Adams said with a smirk.

"How do you know he wasn't?"

Adams shrugged a shoulder. "Can't."

"What's the name of this critical creek?" Wolf asked the men around him.

"It's the Pamunkey River," Wilhelm said.

"Crossing the Pamunkey just doesn't have the same ring to it," Wolf said. The men around him chuckled. Spirits soared high. The sun beat red-hot down on them. Lieutenant Wolf and the 13th Michigan crossed the Pamunkey River, and the Cavalry Corps ventured out to create havoc throughout the rebellious Virginian countryside.

Chapter 9

Afternoon, June 7, 1864
Somewhere north of Hanover Court House, Virginia

Wolf was sure the best place to be in a cavalry column was in the absolute front of the ten-mile-long army. The two divisions moved at a leisurely pace in an attempt to save their mounts, yet a canopy of gritty dust billowed around them like they were a herd of stampeding cattle instead of mounted men. They marched through the irritating clouds, wiping eyes and rubbing noses, sneezing and coughing as they went.

The filth coated everything, trying to bury them as they walked. Every trooper turned a yellowish-tan shade of brown. Not a single inch of the men or horses was left untouched by the stuff, and any semblance of cleanliness afforded to the men while they rested quickly disappeared.

Wolf gritted his teeth and crunched the particularly coarse bits. He tried to spit to the side and found his mouth too dry. He grabbed his canteen, wrapped over his pommel and great coat, unscrewed the top, and took a swig of the lukewarm liquid, swished it around his mouth, and spat it to the side. He spit again, attempting to extract a bristly horsehair that had found its way onto his tongue. He tried to remove it with his fingers only to find another in its place. Unable to find any relief, he hurried to drink some more when a gust of fresh air drove away the dust cloud.

The unrelenting heat only added to the dryness, seeming to suck the moisture from their mouths even faster and sting their eyes with impunity.

Wolf capped his canteen and turned to his men. "Stay hydrated, boys. Sun don't care who it bakes."

Grunts and "yes, sirs" came from his men. They didn't need to be reminded of how hot and dusty it was, but with the drone of hooves stamping the beaten earth, one could lose focus and forget to do essential things until a man was overcome. From the outside it looked easy, but nothing was truly easy in the army, and Wolf did not want to lend his men to Company Q over something as trivial as overheating. He gave Sarah's flank a pat and sweat misted from her sides. "Attagirl."

"Nothing like the Kilpatrick raid," Wilhelm said. He wrinkled his nose over his mustache, trying to stifle an itch.

"Or our actions near Yellow Tavern." The men looked no worse for the wear. They could keep this pace forever. The animals worked hard but not nearly as hard as they were normally pushed.

"This is what all them boys been talking about. The Sheridan March," Adams said with a grin. "Could get used to this."

"Get me a bottle of whiskey and a lass for each knee, and I could do this forever," Nelson said.

"Bacon," Dan said. "And bacon."

Nelson smiled at the other solidly built trooper. "A whole fucking roast pig."

The two men could be mistaken for a team of oxen. They shared a grin thinking about the delicious food.

Could have been a hell of a lot worse. They could be lost. They could be caught in freezing rain. And they could be cut off from command. There was a great sense of safety that came with marching in an eight-thousand-horsemen column, an attitude that they could take on the world. Their enemies should tremble before them even if they advanced at barely quicker than an infantryman's pace.

A man on foot struggled by the line of horses. He had a saddle draped over his shoulder. His clean-shaven face was shaded the color of a ripe strawberry with exertion, sweat pouring down his cheeks leaving small trails of wet dirt over his dust-caked skin. The only action worse than riding mounted in the column was walking dismounted next to it. He kept his head down trying to avoid the men, the dust, the sun, or all of them combined.

"What happened?" Wolf called at him.

The private glanced upward, shading his eyes. "Horse went lame."

"Where'd you leave her?"

"On the side of the road. Had to shoot her."

"Shoot her? That bad?"

"I think she'd have gotten better, but the column is moving, and they wouldn't let me try." He shook his head. "A shame. She was a good girl."

Wolf patted Sarah's flanks again, reassuring her and himself that she wouldn't suffer the same fate despite an order. "They making you walk?"

"Back to Washington or Cold Harbor. Company Q for me if the rebs don't grab me."

"Check with the teamsters. Maybe one can give you a ride."

The young private tipped his hat. "Thanks, Lieutenant."

Within the hour, more men straggled by on foot in a sorry procession toward the baggage train or friendly lines. Sun, bugs, sweat, and horsehair were their lives. They marched past three freshly put-down mounts, the flies already settling in for their meal. Colonel Moore walked his mount back to Peltier, his feathered hat and plump body giving him an especially ridiculous appearance. Men snickered as he passed.

He spoke to the captain, but his voice was loud enough for most men to hear. "You tell your company that there is no overworking their animals. No gallivanting. Any man whose horse goes lame will be marching back on foot!"

"His face is extra red today," Wolf said to Wilhelm.

"He looks like a pig waiting for the spit," Nelson growled. "Maybe God has answered my prayers for a feast."

Adams pulled out a piece of bacon from his saddle bags and flopped it into his mouth.

"I'll take a slice," Nelson said. Adams handed him some and then passed a strip to Wolf. They munched the salted pork, the fat melting in their mouths, the salty flavor sucking any moisture from their tongues.

Without another look, Moore trotted his poor horse back to the head of the 13th Michigan.

Peltier twisted in the saddle. "You heard the colonel. Keep your mounts watered and fed. If they go lame, we shoot them, and you are Company Q."

The men muttered their agreement. No man liked to put a bullet in an animal that he cared for, an animal that carried him into battle and cared for him in return, especially when the horse could be rehabilitated given enough time and rest.

"Great waste of animal flesh," Wilhelm said.

"I agree." Wolf patted Sarah's neck. The prospect was even worse for him; he would surely be captured without a horse, something he vowed to never let happen again. It was his personal code of conduct even if it ended him in the same boat as Captain Yates, a bleached skeleton in a Southern forest.

The column meandered by a modest farmhouse. A woman and two children stood on their porch. The mother kept hawklike eyes upon them, hands on her hips. A few of the men called to her, but she only stared, her mouth twisted with disdain.

"Your heathen friends already took everything we have!" she said, raising a voice that dripped with venom. The little girl clinging to her dress started to cry.

"Not everything," Nelson muttered.

"Quiet in the ranks," Wilhelm said loudly.

"Everything!" she called at them. "Each one of you is worse than the last!"

"We should see if she's hiding anything," Adams said. "You know Southern women. They'll lie out their mouth one way and spit tobacco from the other." Murmurs of agreement came from the troopers.

"Leave her be," Wolf commanded. He would not have any harassment of the civilians under his watch. War matured a man fast.

His men heeded his words without much resistance. It was only the first day of their raid. They still had a couple of days' worth of rations in their bags. Coffee, salted beef or pork, or bacon, flour, and dried fruit and desiccated vegetables. They wouldn't need to forage for anything yet, but rations went quick, and foraging became a necessity in the army if one didn't want to starve.

By the time they stopped for the day, they'd traveled close to fifteen miles.

Over fifty men had made that sullen walk through enemy territory back toward Federal lines. It was a lonely and dangerous trek, each man a potential victim for angry Southerners to round up or hang from a tree. They'd passed through Aylett's Crossroads, Sharon Church, and Brandywine, ending up near the southern part of the Mattaponi River. They set up camp in a fallow field, unplanted and unkept. The men sat around campfires cooking and eating all their rations. It was tradition to eat everything the first day of campaign then forage for everything else as they marched.

"You think we'll cross?" Wolf asked Wilhelm. Munn stood near the fire with Nelson, Adams, and Kent nearby. They waited expectantly with their bowls for the stew the cook had pieced together.

"Nope. We aren't retreating. We're raiding," Wilhelm said. "I say we'll go west. Plenty of track between here and there."

"That's where my boys do their best work," Wolf said. "Make the rebs feel it in their bellies." Waiting a moment, he eyed Private Munn, his stomach growling to remind him how hungry he was. "Munn, how's that stew coming? Enough *desecrated* vegetables?"

The heavyset cook sprinkled something into his pot. "Plenty of dem." The men had combined their rations and let the experienced cook among them whip it together. Although they were used to providing for themselves and cooking their own food, they would relent to anyone with experience. Munn stuck a spoon inside the stew and pulled it out, slurping from it. "Could use a smidge more salt. Who's got any?"

The men peered at one another, searching for a weak link. Kent touched his pack with a protective hand, and every eye in the platoon locked on him.

Adams lifted his chin before asking, "What's in the pack?"

"Give it over," Nelson growled.

Kent's head wavered. "It's my last bit. Can't blame a man for saving some."

"It'll be your last. Give it." Nelson marched over and snatched his pack, handing it to Munn.

Kent sat back down with a glower. "We ain't got no more rations for the remainder of the campaign."

"Quit your crying. You know how we do it. First night feast. Rest of the time, we appropriate our food from the surroundings."

"A man can't be careful?" Kent lamented. "My belly turns something awful if I don't get food in the mornings."

"Careful men are dead men," Nelson said. "And quit your whining."

***

The next morning, the aroma of fresh coffee tickled Wolf's nose in the growing light. He pushed himself awake before the bugler trumpeted out reveille. He buttoned up his lieutenant's coat and puttered his way to the fire. Wilhelm stood straight as a broom, sipping from his cup. Around the fire sat three colored men tending the flames.

Despite the early hour, Wolf felt rested, the rich coffee scent invigorating him. He held out his cup and let the colored man poured the dark brew in it. "Thank you," he spoke softly.

As the sun bowed to the land, colored men, women, and children had caught up with the column. This happened on every march as any slaves brazen enough would congregate and follow the Union troops with the hopes of finding freedom. On embarrassing occasions, it became a race to see who could flee before the rebels the fastest, neither wanting to be caught. With such a tremendous force, safety was all but assured for the former slaves now deemed captured enemy "contraband" by the Union Army.

Wolf liked them around as they provided his men a respite from some of their menial tasks, which the former slaves were happy to do. Playing a part in the war effort meant something to them, and immense thankfulness flowed from their lips. Not all of the soldiers handled them with respect, yet most tolerated them if only because they didn't have to dig the sink.

The abolitionists in the ranks treated them as equals, sharing food and company. The majority of the soldiers viewed them with apathetic indifference. Any man who held negative wishes kept them to himself now as the escaped slaves had become a permanent fixture of camp life.

Only a few men in Wolf's platoon had been with him when Dahlgren had ordered their colored guide hung, witnessing the dastardly event. Wolf would never be a part of such a cruel action again. Bugger the orders and the man who gave them. Yates putting a bullet in Dahlgren didn't bother him so much now. It was as much justice as a colored man could come by in this war.

"How many of you boys came in the night?"

The colored man was short with a crooked smile. He wore a white linen shirt and beige jean-linen pants, both soiled with dirt, ripped and torn. His feet were bare. "Dunno, sir."

"Twenty, thirty?"

"Say 'bout a hundred."

"A hundred?"

"Yes, Genr'l."

Wilhelm and Wolf shared a glance. "I'm a lieutenant, but thanks for helping us out."

The young man grinned happily. "When we's first saw you, couldn't tell if you's was rebs or yanks. But when we saw the flag, that brave stars and stripes, we knew we's a'right." His comrades were taller and broader in shoulder, clothes equally as ragged. One wore a straw hat. Neither held an ounce of fat on their bodies.

Wolf brushed off the shoulders of his jacket. "It's a dusty road we travel." He stared at the men for a moment, before he said, "You men are welcome here."

"I can do lots, sir. Shoe a horse, drive a team, cook, dig, anything. You tell me what needs done and I'll do it."

"We appreciate it, but that is not why are welcome. What's your name?"

"Roody. And dis Charles and Big Ben."

Wolf gave each man a welcoming nod.

"I insist, sir. We want to help," Roody said, nodding vigorously. "Let us help."

Wolf sighed with a nod. "Your help is appreciated. Keep the coffee coming. That's all we need today. My boys will be up soon and need a pep in their step." He nodded toward the company's supply wagon. "There's more in the wagon."

"Be a pleasure, sir." The colored men left for the wagon and rummaged through the back.

After taking a long swig of his coffee, Wolf addressed Wilhelm. "Probably travel farther today than yesterday."

"Odds are. Doesn't seem Sheridan is in too much of a hurry to get wherever we're going."

"No, it doesn't. Can't bellyache too much. It's easy on the horses and the men."

"Yet a blind man could follow us. Easy to anticipate if we aren't careful."

Wolf sipped the hot black liquid. "Maybe that's what he wants. Worked once for us."

"What if the enemy learns from their mistakes?"

"I guess we'll have another fight on our hands."

"I'd prefer to have a rout of them."

As dishonorable as a rout was for the enemy without a fight, if it kept Wolf's men together and alive, he'd take it. "Better them than us." Wolf sipped his coffee.

"No truer words have been spoken."

The bugler emerged from his tent, straightened his shell jacket, pushed his boots together, and stood at attention. He raised the brass bugle to his lips and belted out his tune.

Wolf readied his horse as his men joined him with groggy sleep-yearning eyes. "Coffee's ready, boys," he said as he passed them. The men grunted and groaned as they awoke preparing to march.

He had Sarah watered and saddled before a commotion flared near the fire pit. He hobbled his way over. A cluster of troopers stood around the fire, and Nelson pointed a meaty finger at Roody.

"What did you do, boy?" Nelson said.

"Nut-nutin. Did what the lieutenant asked me to do."

"Did you? The lieutenant asked you to brew all the coffee?"

"He said they's was more in the wagon, so I took it and brewed it."

Nelson spit. "Goddamn imbecile. Should send you back to the plantation."

Wolf shouldered his way forward through the tired troopers. The memory of the hanging boy flashing before his eyes. *No, I am in charge here.* "What happened?"

Adams pointed with his chin. "Our local contraband here has brewed our company's entire ration of coffee."

Wolf let out a sigh. *Shit. The man took my orders literally.* "All right, you heard the bugle call. Boots and saddles." He gently moved men in the direction of their horses.

"Clear out," Wilhelm said as he approached. "Get your mounts ready."

Roody stood head down, rubbing his hands nervously. Wilhelm joined them, peering at Wolf for an explanation.

"He brewed all the coffee."

The sergeant looked away from the contraband. "Damn." A coffee-less command may as well slog their way back home. It was their lifeblood. It gave the men that extra bit of energy in battle or during a march. The men expected it as well as they should. It was a part of their assigned rations. The effect on the morale of the company would be immediate and that included both Wilhelm and Wolf who drank it with every opportunity. There was no wrong time for a cup of the brew.

"We eat all the rations, but we never brew all the coffee."

"Why you eat everything and not the coffee?" Roody asked.

"'Cause the Southerners don't have any coffee to replace it, and I sure as hell ain't drinking sweet potato water or whatever vile concoction they drink as a substitute. But they have plenty of food for us to forage."

Wilhelm shook his head. "No use in getting mad at the boy. He didn't know. He thought he was doing right."

"I know." Wolf viewed the pots bubbling over the fire. "Get as much of it as you can in canteens for the men."

Roody didn't move. He kept his head down and his eyes on the ground.

"Did you hear me?"

"I heard you, sir. You not gonna turn me over to the Johnnies?"

Wolf reached out and touched Roody's shoulder. The young man flinched. "I would never do such a thing. You only did what you thought I asked. That's on me."

Roody's eyes darted up, eager for forgiveness. "Honest?"

"You're safe with us." Wolf glanced over at Wilhelm and he nodded.

"You'll be safe with us. You have my word."

The young man beamed. "Thank you, massa!"

"I am not your master."

Roody's eyes went downcast again. "Sorry, sir."

"Help the men get the coffee in their canteens. We'll be departing soon."

Roody carried a pot trooper to trooper, pouring the coffee into their canteens. The men cursed and complained, but they took as much of the stuff as they could with dirty looks.

"They're going to be cranky tomorrow," Wilhelm said.

"I know. Let's just hope we can find some. Perhaps D Company?"

"Let's hope."

The sounds of "To Saddle" blared out from buglers all over the Michigan Brigade.

"Let's get mounted, boys!" Wolf said, walking back to his horse.

"You heard the Lieutenant. We got another long day of marching!" Wilhelm called out, mounting his horse. He eyed the sky. "Gonna be another hot one."

Chapter 10

Morning, June 8, 1864
Near Mechanicsville behind Lee's lines, Cold Harbor, Virginia

Major General Wade Hampton III took a sip of his morning coffee and peered down at his map. He eyed the pencil marks where he'd sketched the relative positions of the armies. Grant still persisted around Cold Harbor despite Lee's men being dug in deep. Now the Army of the Potomac lobbed shells at the men in the trenches and earthworks, having learned a lesson they'd known since early in the war. Assaulting entrenched men led to unnecessary slaughter. It was like marching regiments in battle formation off a four-hundred-foot cliff.

After Haw's Shop, Hampton had been put into a position of protecting the Army of Northern Virginia's flanks. He also protected critical transportation junctions from marauding cavalry raids. He took a sip of his coffee eyeing the little square representing the Hanover Court House.

Only a week past, he'd been hard in the saddle leading three of Rosser's regiments in support of Rooney Lee. Rooney was one of Robert E. Lee's sons, and while an adequate commander, he'd yet to prove his worth since his release from a Union prison camp.

Rooney had been struggling against his adversaries for days, and it wasn't until Hampton had arrived in support that the situation had stabilized. With his sword in one hand and a pistol in the other, Hampton hammered Union Brigadier General Wilson's command as they tried to disengage. He couldn't count most of his pistol kills because the Yankees were on the run, and he never counted a kill that didn't follow the code of a gentleman soldier.

Over and over he chased the Union horsemen. Even when they put up a stout resistance near a railroad cut, Hampton sniffed out their weakest point and split them in half, taking prisoners and weaponry. Even now, he wasn't sure the cost was worth the reward.

"What do you think, Father?" Preston said. His son studied the map trying to understand its secrets, not realizing his father was attending the map to avoid reviewing his stack of dispatches. After a while his eyes would lose focus, the letters blurring into masses of ink, forcing him to quit. A map was much easier on the eyes and in many ways much more interesting.

Hampton pursed his lips as he thought. "We're in a tight spot."

"Truly?" Preston said, his eyes reading his father. "Lee's won almost every engagement for weeks, repelling Grant at every chance."

"This is true, but Grant tries us furiously without any regard for his men's lives. Even if we kill many more of them than us, they can sustain greater casualties over the long term. Lee's known this from the beginning. Our advantage is time. Theirs is men and material. The longer this goes on, the likelier Lincoln will sue for peace. But only if we have enough men to put together a credible force."

Preston examined the map again."There's nowhere for them to go."

Hampton's eyes ran along the battle lines. Grant had run out of land to continue his southward leapfrog. "Let's hope they go back North and call this campaign to an end."

"Why?"

"Give us a chance to regroup and look credible enough to convince the Northern population that we'll never surrender. Then they can vote that tall ignorant fellow out of the White House."

Preston nodded, rubbing his chin with his fingers. "I see."

He took the opportunity to educate his son. "Not all war is waged on the battlefield. Often the more important struggle is fought in a people's hearts and minds."

His son eyed him questioningly but turned as an officer entered the home, his big frame filling the doorway. Hampton immediately recognized Brigadier General Thomas Rosser. The rugged Texan pushed a colored boy in a Union cavalry jacket inside the room with a large guiding hand.

He gave the newcomer a nod. "General Rosser, I was not expecting you. I trust everything is fine with the Laurel Brigade?"

"Everything's just fine. My men are happier than a bunch of dead pigs in the sun." He pushed a boy forward. "Thought you might want to talk to my friend, Freddy."

Hampton's eyes darted to the colored boy. The boy kept his eyes downcast. Realizing he still had his hat atop his head, he removed his cap and crushed the brim between his fingers.

"What do we have here? Too young to serve. Unless they're more desperate than we realize."

Preston folded his arms over a thick chest. "What an oddity." He stepped around the boy, eyeing him. "You think he can fight?"

"I ain't no soldier, massa," the boy said.

Squinting, Preston continued, "Then I'm sure we have some latrines for him to dig. About as much bloody war as he'll see," he said with a cocky smirk.

Hampton ignored his son's remarks. He still didn't understand the reality of the situation. It was the rebels that toed the line, teetering on the edge of the precipice of defeat. Any small fraction over and they could collapse. They needed every victory, every man, every movement to go their way for a fighting chance. Not just over the war but for their family. They must win this war of brothers.

The war had already bled their entire fortune. If they lost, they would forfeit one of the few assets they had left, their slaves. Without their slaves, he would be forced to sell thousands of acres of land at a decreased valuation. He could only expect a tiny fraction of his pre-war income going forward. It was possible to rent the land, but nothing could possibly provide the same way as over a thousand head of free labor. Nothing. He would be destitute, a mere pauper struggling to feed his family.

It was a grim future the North forged in Hampton's mind, and if Lincoln had his way the change would be swift and decisive, knocking the head off entire generations of hard labor and the Founding Fathers' blood, sweat, and tears. It was an insult to force them to adopt a new way of life now. He simply couldn't afford it. It was as if his people had played a game for hundreds of years only to find out now that the federal government was going to flip the board and cast away the rules. And the new rules would ensure his family for generations to come would sink into financial ruin.

So he hung up his planter's clothes and donned a military uniform like his father and his grandfather had before him, only this time the invader was the government they'd fought to create and protect. Could Lee dredge a victory in similar fashion to George Washington? Could he do it without foreign intervention? It had been done before with smaller forces, less well equipped and poorly led against the most powerful military in the world. If they did that then, surely Lee could finish this war now. Hadn't Washington faced tougher odds with less?

"Leave the lad be, Preston. He's a good boy," Rosser said with a half-smile. "Aren't you, boy?" He smacked his shoulder and the boy's head bobbed up and down, a buoy in a wavy sea.

"What do you have for me?" Hampton asked. Rosser wasn't a man to make a social visit, so surely he had something to say.

"Go on, boy, tell him." The big Texan nudged the boy in the back.

"If it pleases ya, sir." The boy gulped, his eyes darting nervously around the room. "I was with the Yanks." He stared wide-eyed as if he expected them to whip him for his disloyalty.

Hampton glanced at Rosser. The subordinate general cocked his head to the side. "Tell him what you told me, Freddy."

"Yes, massa." He feverishly creased the brim of his hat with calloused fingers. "I's wit General Sheridan before he left."

Hampton perked up at the mention of his most recent rival in blue. "And?"

"I's wit him. I hear all his plans. Gave me dis coat. I ain't no Yank though, but 'tis a nice coat."

Hampton nodded. "Of course you aren't," he said hurriedly. "What were his plans?"

"He's riding out wit two divisions. They goin' west along the North Anna River. I tell you west."

"West?"

He looked at Rosser before eyeing the map. *Two Union cavalry divisions are headed west along the North Anna River. North or south of it? Hmm.* He ran a finger along the blue line representing the river, looking for potential targets of Federal interest. "Is that all?"

"He kept talking 'bout a Gen'l Hunter. Don't know who dat is, but he talked 'bout him a lot. Gonna meet him."

"General Hunter." He looked back at the map of Virginia. "Vaguely recall the man. Must be operating out in the Valley." He snapped his fingers at Preston. "Get me those dispatches." His eyes scoured the armies' positions in relation to one another. *Sheridan couldn't go straight west. He would have already run into us. He'll have to go north then west.*

His son returned with a stack of papers. Hampton flipped through them quickly until he found the document he was looking for. He knew he'd read it, but there were so many to digest on a daily basis. He tossed the paper to the side and ran a hand over the map following the river then took his other hand and tapped the valley. He sighed.

"What is it, Father?" Preston said, not seeing the plan.

Hampton eyed Rosser. "Send the boy out and get him a new jacket. I don't want any of the boys thinking he's a colored soldier." Nodding to the young man, he said, "Thank you, Freddy. You've done a great service to your country today."

Freddy's head bobbed in pleasure. "Yes, sir, massa, sir. Me pleasure."

Rosser showed the boy the door before taking the jacket from his back and returning.

"Sheridan's got two divisions and he's headed west." Hampton shook his head, staring at the map. "He's got to be going to destroy the railroads near Charlottesville and Gordonsville. Blow the bridges there and we are cut off from the Valley. General Hunter's army just routed Grumble Jones's army, leaving the way open." He pushed the dispatch at Rosser and the man picked it up.

William Edmondson "Grumble" Jones. The crotchety man had been shot in the head leading a charge. It was always a risk, but no one ever thought it would truly happen to them. If one had foreknowledge their death was on the horizon, why would they put themselves in danger? How so few of us remain. He glanced at Rosser and then Preston, and for a moment in time, he saw his brother Frank.

Frank's skin was pale, his eyes ringed in the bruised darkness of death. His beard was full but lacking the plump bushiness of vigorous life. They were so much the same yet so different, and now Preston was present and alive next to Frank. His brother faded and only his son remained. While he was saddened by the loss, he was only slightly less sad that it was Frank instead of Preston. His heart may have truly broken if he'd lost Preston at Brandy Station. For he could imagine no love greater than a father has for his son.

"They're hoping to burn down those junctions. Cut off our supplies," Rosser said.

"I'm afraid so," Hampton replied. "Two divisions, which means there's one more hovering near Grant's army." He paused. "We can at least get close to matching Sheridan man for man. We can squeeze out a fair fight if we reach him before he joins with Hunter." He found himself slowly nodding as the plan played out before his eyes. "Yes. We must beat them to the crossing point near Gordonsville." He traced a path over the map with his finger. "They're like a herd of swine."

Rosser grinned, tugging a paper-wrapped tobacco plug from his coat. He dug a pinch off the plug and pressed it inside his cheek, tamping it down with his finger for a tight pack. "A hog hunt? Can't say I've ever been."

"You know me. Always searching for the next game to hunt." Hampton was as prominent of a game hunter as he was a businessman. Now he added soldier to that list of pastimes he'd mastered. His favorite though was hunting. Nothing beat a top-notch hunt, bear being the pinnacle of the hunting game. Danger. Excitement. Thrill. Give him a pack of forty dogs, a thoroughbred, and he'd hunt until the end of his days.

"You use dogs to run 'em. Bay dogs to find 'em, and catch dogs to pin 'em. Hogs move quick when they're going for food, water, or bedding down, but if you know their destination, there's an opportunity to beat them to it." He stared Rosser in the eyes, affirming the man understood. He had a pack of dogs at hand, and the enemy advanced across the land like a herd with a destination in mind.

Sheridan and his two divisions weren't much different except maybe a bit deadlier with the Spencers in their hands. "See here, we go fast and hard toward Gordonsville. We'll save time by traveling the interior south of the North Anna River. We have some of our boys harass them along the way just to make sure they're headed where we think they are. Then we catch them here. Southeast of Gordonsville."

"That'll put them in the spot to attack."

Hampton nodded. Exactly what he had in mind. *I choose the field and invite them to play.* "We can even build some works set along these roads. Even layer them if there's time. As they top one, we move to the next. But all that is about as useful as tits on a bull if we don't win the race to the watering hole."

"Just like hunting," Preston said, a pleased look on his face.

"Just like it." Except here, his opponents meant to kill him and were far deadlier than a grizzly or black bear. For no matter the plans he made, they would most certainly be countered. These were not the same green leaderless men they'd faced during the war's inception; this enemy was as stout as they were smart. But man-to-man even forces. Hampton's smile deepened. Those odds were ones he would take. In this war, he would be crazy not to.

"Rosser, prepare your men." *You're my catch dogs. The ones that will pin them down so they can be killed*, he thought. "Preston, send a rider to Fitz Lee's command. He must hurry behind as quick as he can. We leave as soon as the day turns."

"Been too long since I been on a good hunt," Rosser said.

"I agree. Until a more formidable opponent arises, Sheridan will have to do."

Both men shared a smile.

"Move quick. We have an army to intercept."

Chapter 11

Afternoon of June 8, 1864
South of the Mattaponi River, Virginia

The Army of the Potomac's Cavalry Corps marched a slow meandering pace along the south of the Mattaponi River. Torbert's 1st Division was split. Custer and Devin's commands braved the dust and heat and insidious horsehair of the column while Merritt's Brigade destroyed the railroad for the day.

They passed small tributaries snaking across the land, unremarkable and without name. The land rolled over hills as if they were forgotten grave mounds of ancient peoples. Fields of clover and grain, tobacco and corn broke apart dense vegetation in square plots of land. Yet almost every homestead they marched by had already been stripped clean of any animal, grain, oat, or edible food for the men.

This route had been heavily traversed by both armies through many campaigns, foraging anything they could lay their hands on. Anything not bolted to the ground was fair game for soldiers on the march, and no matter the morality of a man, most were guided by their stomachs.

For Johannes Wolf, this march was near as boring as one could be. The drone of a thousand lazy hoofbeats could lull a man to sleep. Sweat trickled down his back, and his knee rubbed sorely in the mounted position. Munn pulled out a harmonica and Wolf smiled. The company cook blew out a tune. A few of the men sang a bandy tune to his shrill notes, and the march took a slightly less arduous tone.

"I could teach everyone 'Garryowen?'" asked Private Patrick Connors. He had reddish hair and a short orange goatee, and his skin was reddening by the minute, a fine shade of a ripe tomato rather than his normal ghost white.

"What's he building? A church choir? Nelson said.

"Watch out for the priests," Adams said.

"Priests always liked me as a lad," Kent said. The men didn't bother to ask any more questions, assuming the worst for the poor man.

"You lads never sang a song while drinking a pint?" Connors added.

Nelson's voice held a hint of unnatural amusement for him. "Course we have."

"This be one of the best."

"I myself would like to learn," Wolf said.

Connors gave him a nod. "I appreciate your sentiment, Lieutenant. Not hard to learn, but a lot of fun. Perhaps our fellow men are correct. May be better with a pint and a band."

"If it involves a pint, we'll have to wait." He had other ideas for his men. Something had to be done to break up this maddening monotony. His platoon fought the urge to sleep in the saddle. The swirl of dust and horsehair was enough to drive a man insane. Men constantly wiped sweat from their brows and spit grime from their mouths.

Wolf sat tall in his saddle to get a view past Captain Peltier and the company marching ahead of them. "All right, lads. See that road up that way? I need four men to join me for a quick forage." He glanced at Wilhelm. "How about a bit of fun?"

"I'll stay with the men."

"Oh, come on, old man."

"I won't."

"You can lead the next foraging party."

Wilhelm gave him a slight nod. "If that's your order."

"It is. Nobody goes hungry under my watch." Wolf scanned his platoon for volunteers.

Lowell's voice piped up from among the men. "I'll go with ya. I'm an adventurer thru and thru. My mum's grandfather was an adventurer.

Discovered the Great Lakes, he did," Lowell said. "Lived with an Indian tribe for seven years. Made him a chief." The men started to roll their eyes. "Had six wives, every single one a princess. I guess they selected him for his prowess as a hunter and," he paused for a moment, "his prowess in other areas. Called him 'He who has three legs.' Can't say why. Don't ask which one of those princesses I was related too. Don't know. But am sure I got Injun blood in me veins."

A string of jeers rushed forth from the other troopers.

"I'm surprised they didn't name a lake after him."

Curses and a threat from Nelson to cut him down shut the young blowhard's mouth.

In a few minutes, Wolf trotted down the side road with a squad of men at his back. The fresh wind flowed over him again, allowing him to breathe without constraint.

Lowell, Kent, Dan, and Goffman trailed behind him. Their experience kept them focused and prepared for a fight. But they weren't looking for one, only easy pickings for food and if they were lucky, a cool drink. If they were luckier, perhaps a spirit or two.

Wolf led them down a trail that splintered from the main road, spacious enough for two horsemen to ride side-by-side. He figured anything larger than a single-file path meant people would be living in the backwoods. "Pick it up to a trot," he called to them.

"But what about Moore?" Kent asked.

"I don't see him around here."

"His orders are to not tire out our mounts."

"Don't apply here."

They came upon a two-story log cabin with a chimney on either end of the home. Wolf pointed at Kent and Lowell and made a sweeping gesture with his hand. The two troopers circled the property, searching for a way in.

Wolf walked his horse to the front of the home. He nodded to Dan and Goffman, and they dismounted, jogging to the door. Wolf's eyes scanned the windows, watching for movement. No one called out or threatened the men. The men in place, Wolf gave a nod, and Dan lowered his shoulder and forced the door with a crunch. The two disappeared inside.

Lowell gave a short call from the rear of the home. Wolf's hand went to his pistol, and he tugged the reins, walking his horse to the other side. A field had a series of short logs set upright as well as a garden filled with lettuce and short sweet corn. "Good find, Lowell."

The corporal lifted his chin and pushed up his cap with a finger. "I told ya about my great uncle the explorer."

"Thought it was your grandfather?"

"Did I say that? Meant Great-Uncle Oliver Lowell the explorer. But look there, Lieutenant."

Wolf looked out at the row of logs sitting atop flat rocks. A bee buzzed near and he shooed it away. "Those beehives?"

Lowell scratched his cheek. "Yes, sir, they be. My pa's cousin used to keep bees back in the day. Only a couple hives, kept 'em in a basket, but let me tell you, sir. Those hives gave the sweetest honey you've ever tasted. Nothing better. I'm telling you."

A moment later, the door in the back of the house opened and Dan stuck his face outside.

"It's fine, Dan. Continue the search."

"Yes," Dan said and ducked back inside.

Lowell squinted, eyeing the hives. "I have an idea."

Wolf didn't know what to think about the young man's ideas or if they were fantasies. "I dunno, Corporal."

"Now hear me out, Lieutenant. I think I can get some honey."

"You know how to get the honey without bringing them down upon us like a bunch of rebs?"

"Of course. My pa's cousin showed me how."

"Really?"

"Yes, sir." He pointed at a clothesline. Dresses, sheets, and bonnets hung drying in the sun. "There's our answer."

Lowell hopped off his mount. He walked down the clothesline inspecting the dresses, imitating a French aristocrat in a high-end Parisian store. Wolf stayed atop his horse, walking it along curiously watching the corporal's plan unfold.

"You see, Lieutenant, the bees don't want to sting ya, but will fight to the death to defend their hive. So, you have to be covered up." He felt a dress's sleeve on the clothesline then let it drop. "It's in their nature; they can't help themselves. Or something like that." He held out a woman's dress, rubbing the fabric. "Nothing better than a dress to cover up the whole part." He ripped it down. "And a bonnet."

Dan and Goffman emerged from the house, their hands full of bread, chickens, and a bottle of wine. "Yes?" Dan said with a happy grin.

"Very good," Wolf said, but all the men were now focused on their comrade dressing in women's clothing.

Kent shook his head. "I thought I seen everything in the army. Blood, guts, disease, a man's head shot clean off by round shot, but I never thought I'd clap my eyes on a man in a woman's dress. It ain't natural I tell you."

Lowell stood before them in a woman's floral dress, a white bonnet on backwards to cover his face. He still donned his cavalry gloves, and he smiled from underneath. "Whatcha boys think?" He gave a twirl.

"If the rebs caught you now, they wouldn't know whether to shoot ya or kiss you," Wolf said. The men all laughed.

"I'm telling you. Fresh honey is king."

"Thought it was tobacco in these parts?" The men shared a laugh. "Do your work, Corporal." Turning to his other troopers, he said, "Pack up everything you can fit on your mounts."

The men did as he bid but couldn't help but stop to watch Lowell stroll across the field toward the hives. He hiked his dress into his hand, trying to keep his feet. He still stumbled every dozen steps, the bonnet over his face.

"He'll bring a swarm on us," Kent said. "I've seen it before. I kicked a hive as a boy. Over thirty stings. My mother thought I would die. Almost did."

Dan's brow furrowed. "Yes. Bees bad."

"Lieutenant, I have a bad feeling about this," Goffman added.

Wolf eyed Lowell. "Let the poor man try."

"We'll all be sorry men," Kent said. He made a hasty sign of the cross.

Lowell reached the first hive. He slowed his approach, holding his glove-covered hands out in front of him as he sized it up. Taking a sackcloth bag, he calmly whipped it open. He gently removed the shingle covering the top of the first upright log. He shook the bees off the honeycomb and adroitly scraped the honeycomb from the underside of the shingle into the bag. Replacing the shingle, he closed the sack quickly, tied the opening and moved on to the next hive where he repeated the process. After the last log had been robbed, he slung the honeycomb-ladened sack over his shoulder, marching triumphantly back to the other troopers.

"What I tell you?" Lowell called over. "One only got me on the finger." He held it out for them to see. "And I'd say it was a mistake. Truly peaceful little fellows. As long as they know you mean no harm."

Wolf laughed watching the man struggle back in his dress. "Honey for all."

"Precisely, lieutenant. A little faith is all it took." He removed a piece of honeycomb from the shingle, shaking a bee off, and tossed it to Wolf. He popped it into his mouth. The succulent honeycomb turned to sweet goo on his tongue. "Dear God, that's delicious."

"What'd I tell ya?" Lowell said.

"You're right, damn near amazing."

A whirlwind of buzzing sounded in the distance. Wolf squinted at the hives. "Can they all communicate with one another? With buzzes and such?"

"I don't know," Goffman said, eyeing the remaining hives.

Lowell mounted his horse like a victorious gladiator in a dress. He removed his bonnet with a flourish.

"Your dress, Corporal," Wolf said, trying not to smile.

"Anyone hear that?" Kent asked.

Wolf swatted a bee away from his head. Another took its place.

"Dagnabbit!" Lowell said. He felt the back of his neck. "Must've snuck under there. "Damn!" he shouted as he swiped at another bee.

One landed on Wolf's hand, its stinger piercing his skin. "Ouch," he said, shaking his hand. "You sure that bag is closed?"

"As closed as it's going to get."

Lowell held out the bag. Bees crawled out from inside in a maddened fury.

"They're coming out and fit to be tied!" Kent said.

"Dump the damn thing!" Wolf shouted at him.

"I earned it fair." Lowell held out the bag, his own words unconvincing.

Sarah whinnied, tossing her head. Wolf turned her away. "Get rid of it! That's an order!"

Lowell threw the hive and the bag exploded upon impact with the ground. The buzzing roar of a thousand angry bees swarmed the air.

Wolf spurred his mount. "Ride!"

The troopers kicked their horses to a gallop, the bees trailing behind them like angry bullets. They slowed a half-mile from the home. Welts lifted on Wolf's hands and neck where the bees had stuck him with their stingers.

"Halt," Wolf said.

"Damn," Lowell said, swatting at his face and back. He twisted in his saddle, still battling the creatures.

They stood nursing their wounds, staring at a tree branch hanging over the road. Wolf drew his pistol and his men did the same. A life-and-death alarm washed over them. Wolf's eyes scanned the road before them, searching for threats.

A blue-coated man hung from a rope in the tree. He didn't swing or shake. There wasn't enough wind for it. His body simply hung with his weight bowing the branch in the middle. Wolf pushed his horse closer.

Blood ran down his fingers and pooled beneath him. A half-dozen bullet wounds desecrated his torso. A sign hung from over his neck. It read: *Invader.* Lowell stopped rubbing his welts. "What happened?"

"Bushwhackers got him."

"Nobody does anything alone," Wolf ordered. It was as if the very land itself hated them. Assuredly the people residing there did. "You didn't see anyone in the house?"

"No," Dan said.

Wolf turned and looked back down the road. He half wanted to return to the home and burn it to the ground in retribution. He had no proof that they were accomplices in this attack on Federal troops, but they weren't there and now this body was here.

"Cut him down," Wolf ordered.

Dan walked his horse forward and drew a knife from his belt. He quickly sawed through the rope and the dead Union man fell to the ground. "Take that sign off him."

They dug a quick grave near the tree and rode back to the main road, following along the river. Union troopers passed by oblivious to the threat that had taken one of their own. The men rejoined the column and worked their way back to F Company of the 13th Michigan in silence. Despite the goods gained, everything seemed soured by the hanging man whom they knew nothing about. No unit. No horse. Only a soldier who strayed too far from the safety of the army.

Wilhelm eyed them when they returned. Jokes were made about Lowell's dress, but nobody had enough heart to banter. Lowell ripped the dress over his head, discarding it to the ground. "We found a dead trooper in the trees," Wolf said.

"One of ours?"

"No. Didn't know which unit he was with."

"You remember the people here are against us."

"I do."

"You were smart bringing a squad with you."

"Ja." He turned toward his men. "Anyone foraging goes in a group. I don't care how hungry you are." His eyes ran over them. "You shoot anyone who doesn't look right."

Adams smiled, showing teeth. "Wolfie tightening the iron fist."

Nelson only grinned. Being given the order to take out frustration and rage on the civilian population was right up his cruel alley.

Wolf shook his head. "Do not harm the civilians. Just make sure no one is getting the jump on you. These people are not our friends."

They continued to ride, the leisurely merriment of the raid having been lost on Wolf and his men.

Chapter 12

June 9, 1864
Near Hanover Junction, Virginia

"They're like a plague of locusts over the land." The old man shook his head. His coat was dusty and dirty, he wore no hat, and his head had more sunspots than hair. Struggling to keep pace with the mounted men, he hurried next to Hampton.

Hampton listened to the man as they passed by his homestead, but he would do no more than listen. He would send no men to trail the foragers. He had to win the race and prevent the Union raid's intent, not hunt brigands. His men had been moving rapidly in this race since just after midnight. Yet he listened to his words as a man deserved to be heard.

"They took every scrap of food we had. Emptied our larders, our cellar, smokehouse. I had three fine hams down there. Every last chicken. Then when that group passed, another horde of them came on swarming over everything. Made a real mess and took my vegetables. Made some crude jokes about my cucumbers then picked my cherry tree empty! Even the green ones. I hope to god they keel over with a bellyache fit for the devil himself."

Hampton gave an understanding grin, letting the man know that he felt the same way. "I am sorry to hear that, Mr. Hobb. I truly am. This war demands sacrifices of us all."

"Sacrifices?" The mostly bald man sputtered and stumbled over himself as he tried to keep even with Hampton's horse. "Demands? I am telling you; I have nothing. My wife, grandkids, two cousins, their wives, and a dozen slaves. We'll starve." He gestured toward his land. "Took every single horse I own. Even the swaybacked one."

Hampton nodded, trying to sympathize with the man's plight. He had an army to feed, lead, and keep supplied. A task that was becoming increasingly more difficult by the day, and an army couldn't march far on an empty stomach. That kind of army became a disappearing rabble quick. "I am sorry, Mr. Hobb. There isn't much I can do. I barely have enough rations for my men."

Mr. Hobb's shoulders slumped, his breath still ragged as he hurried to keep pace. "I have nothing. I can't fight. I can't feed my family. I appealed to the only man in these parts that could do a damn thing, and he turned me down."

Hampton reached into his pocket and took out a handful of coin. He held out his gloved fist. "Take it."

The man's eyes lit up with the delight of a starving beggar at the prospect of food. "You jest? Don't be cruel, General."

Hampton shook his fist. "I don't jest. Take the money. Should get you through the week."

The coins clinked into his palm. "You're a generous man. A very generous man." Tears welled up in his eyes, circling near the corners.

"Take care, Mr. Hobb." He tipped his hat to the beaten down man. One way or another the war would end soon. The rebels only needed to make a stand before the presidential election in the North. Enough victories would take the wind from Grant's sails and in turn, the North would implode with unrest, turn on itself, and sue for peace. The Army of Northern Virginia only needed to eke out enough wins to create doubt, which would require him squeezing enough from their men to win the war.

Mr. Hobb left the column of gray horsemen, turning back toward his farm. Hampton gave a slight wave of his hand, and Preston appeared at his side. "Yes, General?"

"Find Lieutenant Fickles and William Scott." He gave a grim smile. It was time to unleash his bay dogs so the chase could begin.

***

Hampton's Iron Scout William Scott rode his horse hard, the wind blowing his shoulder-length gray-streaked black hair behind him. The long rifle slung over his back thumped as he galloped. A spare mount kept pace behind him, tied to his saddle. The dust barely had enough time to cling to them as it was kicked into the air, hardly enough to bother the men in the heat.

Another Iron Scout, Dan Tanner, rode next to him with his extra horse. He grinned white beneath a finely trimmed beard, his hand over the top of his black hat.

They'd gone almost twenty miles, and Scott suspected they'd run into the rear Union column within a few more. "Scott!" Tanner called over the sound of the thundering hooves, "My mount."

Scott slowed his horse to a walk, followed a moment later by his companion.

"Damn, Tanner. What's wrong with her?"

Tanner stroked his horse's mane, then patted her neck. The mount favored her left side, her front hoof striking the ground with tepid movements. "Let me take a look." He hopped from his saddle. Moving around the front of the animal, he bent near her front leg and picked it up for a look. "Can't tell, but she won't run."

"Goddamn, lame. You know what to do," Scott said, then spit at the bad luck.

Tanner looked at him, his theatrical face drooping like a pantomime. "I will not. I refuse." He shook his head. "This girl has carried me all over this great state without a tick."

Scott exhaled sharply. *Uncomfortable deeds are best done quick.* "We don't have time for this. Get it done or I will do it for you."

His companion ran a hand along the top of the horse's muzzle, his voice becoming soft and playful. "Don't listen to that mean mountain lion. I would never let him hurt such a fair filly such as yourself." He gave a backward glance at Scott and he scowled back at him.

"You hurry this up. We got work to do and standing around sweet-talking your horse ain't one."

Tanner hushed him, repeatedly stroking the horse's muzzle. "You must be one of those fellows who says goodbye by leaving without saying a word. What do they call that? An Irish goodbye?"

"Don't know about that." Scott's horse moved uneasily beneath him, and he spit again. "But to a horse, yes."

"That a girl." Tanner scratched behind his mount's ear. He walked around and unhitched the saddle and removed the bridle and reins, walking it to his other mount now grazing along the weeds on the side of the road. He saddled his spare and Scott waited impatiently.

"You gonna put her down?"

Tanner glanced back, tightening a strap. "Dear God, man, of course not. This horse will be fine given rest."

"You're going to leave her?"

"Why not? Maybe some poor Company Q will find her. Heal her up. An injury is no reason to end a life."

"It's a horse. That's the main reason to end her life."

"Your methods are uncouth, Mr. Scott. I prefer to give life a chance."

"By dawdling for so long, you've given Yanks a chance at life. We got plenty of work to do."

Tanner swung into the saddle of his spare mount and patted its neck. Then with a flourish of his hand, he said, "We're off."

The two men continued their ride. Scott contemplated the fact he might have to leave Tanner behind. Without a spare horse, there was no way to rest the other horse while they rode. They were one of a half dozen teams of Iron Scouts whose primary mission was to make the lives of the Union troopers miserable: capture, sharpshoot, and create a general havoc among the corps. Anything to make their leisurely travel dangerous, and in the meantime ensure the Union cavalry traveled exactly the direction Hampton thought they were headed.

The Red Shirts were the largest unit conducting harassment operations. Their movements would be more direct, trying to draw companies or regiments into ambushes. They were more numerous, at least a hundred men, and were now led by the slightly less deplorable Lieutenant Fickles instead of Captain Payne.

Scott didn't like either man, but he despised Payne. He was happy to hear the captain was back in South Carolina recuperating from his saber wound he sustained only three weeks past. There was something off about him, as if he were a compass that always pointed twelve degrees off north. The man took too much pleasure in his craft. He prioritized a man's suffering when he did his killing, something that took a twisted heart and a warped mind to enjoy.

Sure, Scott never minded killing a man, hell, he'd done it plenty enough, but he never really took much joy in it either. It was a means to an end. Some men needed killing, so that's what he did. Shooting a man was the same as shooting a deer or a bear, except they looked the same as you. The dirty work came easy, but he didn't live for it.

He scouted better on his own, but he didn't mind riding with the other Iron Scouts. Although Tanner wasn't like the other scouts either. The man had a highfalutin tendency to him. With his fine coats and hats, silk neckties, and gorgeous polished riding boots, his appearance was one of a city gentleman rather than an army scout in the wilds. Spoke like he had money too.

Scott slowed his horse when he smelled smoke. Smoke always meant men. Whether or not they were the men they sought was another question. Yet they were close enough to the column to suspect Union foragers.

A blind man could track the Union army. Hundreds if not thousands of riders had come this way, consistent with what they expected to find which was the rear of the Federal column. The tracks riddling the ground were fresher, the earth darker where it had been dug out more recently.

"You smell that?" Scott asked Tanner.

"Must say I do. Foragers?"

Scott licked his gums, his tongue feeling painfully for tobacco. They almost ached for it, shuddering at the thought of the sweet leaves. Not the effeminate snuff. Snorting it up the nostril seemed ludicrous. Give him a twist or a plug of the stuff and he was as happy as a beaver in a lumberyard. "Could be." They walked their horses farther down the road until they came across a log cabin farmhouse. No smoke billowed from the chimney, yet the scent of burning wood grew more pungent. The scouts dismounted, shifting silently to the trees. He unslung his long rifle and Tanner glided through the foliage in a flanking position to the other side of the home.

Scott stalked through the trees. A campfire came into view through an overabundance of green leaves in flickers of orange and yellow. Men in blue uniforms were seated around the fire, cooking and chatting. He knelt next to a tree and watched them, taking stock of their numbers.

The closest trooper sat hunched with his back to him. Another walked around the edges of the trees, gathering sticks and logs to feed the fire. A third faced Scott's direction, his jaw working as he ate something. Scott's eyes shifted toward the horses. There were four mounts. He let his eyes run over the foliage searching for Tanner.

Only tree trunks, leaves, vines, and ferns filled the space between the vast oaks separated by dogwood, red cedar, thin pines, and shrubs of hazelnut and blackberries. *The fellow with his fine clothes. Shouldn't be hard to find.* His eyes continued to scan for his comrade. A hint of black. *There.*

His comrade stood motionless watching the Union men. *Bloody good spot. Now what to do with these fellows?* He'd need at least one to interrogate. Shoot them in the back? He'd risk losing one then wherever that fellow was. He'd sneak closer. Union horse boys were cowards at heart, only brave in numbers.

He crept closer as a hunter does when tracking an easily spooked deer, the difference being these men couldn't smell him coming from a mile away. His hand moved slowly to his hip. He unfastened his pistol holster then he stalked as close as he dared. He could make out their words.

"Beautiful pace we're keeping," said the man facing Scott.

Slower than a herd of turtles.

The man with his back turned responded. "Aye, it's Sheridan's way. Easy does it. Let those bastards come to us then we whip 'em."

"In the meantime, we take whatever we can from the ever kind Virginia folk," said the man carrying the wood. He dumped the sticks and logs into a pile.

His words made Scott's blood boil. He was a loyal Virginian thru and thru, never a doubt in his mind which side he'd fight for. Not a shred of it. Him, his brother, and his cousin all enlisted right away. Both were gone now.

Neither were killed in action. Nope, that would be the day a Yankee bullet laid low one of the Scott clan. Sickness, an invisible curse to the marching soldier, snuffed out their lives. Made Scott want to spit. Better to be in the wild away from the camps. Camps is where they got it. The camps were always rife with illness. Camp too long in one place and the illness came soon after. They'd shake horribly, fevers setting their skin ablaze. It'd turn your guts inside out until you were too weak to carry yourself to the latrine. One day you'd wake up, and they were dead and gone to their maker. Everything was always safer in the wild.

Slaughtered chickens laid in a pile next to the fire. The man with his back to him plucked them one by one. "These Virginians sure do feed us well."

"They sure do. Better than the army ever does."

Scott swept to the left, shifting to acquire an easier firing position. Never paid to be directly in front of a man with a gun. He inched closer and closer and then skulked into their clearing, a pistol drawn in one hand, a rifle in the other. "You boys mind dropping those pistols?"

The three men stared at him in surprise. He may as well had grown horns and turned into a talking deer. They all three sat motionless. The one man held his hand mid-pluck, feather wavering in a slight breeze.

"You boys deaf and dumb? Put your pistols on the ground."

The Union troopers did as he bade, their sidearms thumping in the grass.

"What's your unit?"

"10th New York," said a trooper with corporal chevrons. Holding out his hands, he took a step closer. "Easy now, we surrendered."

"Little far from the column, ain't ya?"

"Just out gettin' some rations," said the one with the chicken.

"That so. Where's the owner of the house?" he said, gesturing with his chin.

"Dunno. Don't care," said the other trooper. His eyes flickered over Scott's shoulder. *The missing trooper.* Scott tongued his gums hard and spun while moving. The fourth Union horseman aimed at him from the cabin doorway. Scott bladed himself sideways resting his pistol over his other arm. The Union trooper's pistol reported with a bang. Dust and dirt exploded into the air behind Scott.

Bastard missed. He had a split-second choice to make. He could engage the enemy trooper near the cabin who was farther away and hope that the men behind him didn't shoot him in the back, or he could turn around and rapidly unleash on the men behind him, men surely diving for their weapons on the ground. *Tanner, you better be getting ready to unleash the fury.*

He grimaced as he turned around on the three men. It took him a moment to register which one presented the biggest threat. He fired his pistol, smoke and fire exploding from the barrel, at the closest man on his hands and knees, grasping for his gun. The trooper clutched his breast and rolled atop the slain chickens. He arched his back in pain. *One down.*

Gunshots bellowed behind him, and Scott retreated for the trees. He fired once then twice if only to keep the other two men from shooting at him unimpeded. Another pistol shot rang out from the cabin. Scott dove into the foliage, crashing through limbs and leaves alike. The trooper scrambled over the grass for his revolver, and the other ran for his horse. From the ground, Scott aimed his pistol at the man racing for the horses and fired. The Union man screamed as a bullet entered his back, falling into his mount.

The last man near the fire held up his hands. "I yield! I yield!"

Scott rolled to his side and peered from behind a tree. The trooper near the cabin was gone. He leaned to the other side quickly. *Where did he go?* Rapidly, he checked his rear, twisting his head to scan over each shoulder one at a time. Nothing. His breath was stuck in his chest. *Where the hell is this guy?* Then he saw Tanner marching forward with the man at gunpoint.

Scott exhaled and stood, pointing his gun at the man still sitting awestruck by the fire. He made his way through the clearing to the dying man atop the chickens and kicked his revolver out of reach.

"You should have shot that one," he said at Tanner.

"Now that wouldn't have been right. He yielded fair and square."

Scott glared at the trooper. The man had an overgrown mustache and round stubbly cheeks. "I oughta kill him anyway."

The man's eyes gaped like two coalpits. "I surrendered. It wouldn't be right."

"What's not right is you trying to shoot me in the back." He bent down, collecting the men's pistols then shoving them through his belt. Couldn't hurt to have a few more pistols than you needed at any time. Might be able to sell one or two to some of the men back in the division.

"All right, let's get these boys back in the saddle."

"What are you going to do with us?"

"Send you boys down to Andersonville."

***

The Blue Ridge Mountains were a wondrous and beautiful sight to behold even from a distance. They created a faded blue backdrop to emerald rolling hills and lush forests. A gray tint masked the mountains as if a linen sheet ran from ground to sky. Hampton thought for a moment. Perhaps the mountains belonged to Stonewall Jackson; his family had originated near the blue peaks. Jackson had even worn a blue Virginia Military Institute uniform at the First Battle of Manassas.

The war had been so much different then. Abundant hope for a short conflict, men coming with anything and everything they had to fight. Not a lick of uniformity at all, just men coming to serve a noble cause. Things had changed. Hope for a quick war had disappeared as dew on a hot summer morning. In fact, Hampton knew that it was Lee's objective to drag it out as long as possible. To stay in the field as long as possible for the newspapers, politicians, and public opinion to waver and give way before the Southern cause. Then all this land would be free again.

He stood on the front porch of Netherland Tavern, a sturdy two-story building built for the purpose of lodging travelers along the Virginia Central Railroad, the very objective that Sheridan was intent on destroying. Trevilian Station was roughly six-hundred feet from the tavern and serviced passengers from the railroad, a short path running between the two buildings.

Gordonsville Road stretched behind him, traveling roughly the same route as the train tracks only to intersect Fredericksburg Road that ran mostly north. The Poindexter farm was situated about a half-mile away, the road leading to Bibb's Crossroads. Then almost nine miles farther north was the North Anna River, the same river the Yankees followed before they would attempt to cut to Gordonsville Road by way of Fredericksburg Road to travel west to link with Hunter's army. His scouts had confirmed that this was indeed the route they marched for.

The terrain slowly rolled into hills, most were forested, the only gaps in the trees for farm homes and fields of grain, clover, and livestock. Gorgeous country, the kind of land one could fall in love with. Green, lush, plenty of animals to hunt, earth prime for cultivation. When one stood upon his porch in the morning sipping his coffee, he appreciated his true freedom only beholden to God. In all regards, terrible ground for cavalry operations, yet one he was prepared to litter with the Union dead.

He dusted off his uniform, horsehair and dust puffed airborne. "We've won the race." It had been a hard journey. Although he didn't know if it truly was a race if the enemy didn't realize they were in a contest. Soon enough, he'll find us at his front, at his flanks, with a river to his rear, unable to escape. Hampton may be able to destroy two thirds of Sheridan's Corps in a coup-de-grâce.

He squinted as a feral-looking man with a black beard streaked with gray walked his horse into camp, a string of captured Union horsemen at his back. Each one was linked to the last with rope. The lead rider turned into William Scott, probably the best of his Iron Scouts.

"What have you brought me, Mr. Scott?" he called out.

Scott brought his horse to a halt and sniffed before he spoke. "I'd say thirty-one-and-a-half prisoners for interrogation."

Hampton hid his mirth at the odd number. "Thirty-one and a half?"

Scott peered back at the captured men, judging them. "Welllll," he said, his voice wavering as he tried to think of appropriate words. "You see, I knocked one senseless with my pistol butt, and he ain't spoke right sense. I'm sure he'll come out of it, but he's just been babbling along to himself about baking pies. Apparently, apple pie is his favorite. Almost got us caught more than once."

Hampton nodded quietly. "Job well done. They'll be more of them before we're through."

"You can count on it. Anyone bring in more?"

Hampton let out a rough chuckle, sandpaper over wood. "No, they did not. You and Mr. Tanner the very most. George brought in twelve."

"I'd say Lieutenant Fickles owes me a bottle then."

"When he returns, I will send him your way."

Scott gave himself a satisfied nod. "There be at least seven-thousand Yankees, maybe eight-thousand in that column and they're headed this way. Sheridan's leading them. Torbert and Gregg are his division commanders. Don't know where that sorry chap Wilson is. Probably still back with the main army."

"Very good. It's as we expected." Hampton sighed. "You've done well. Report to me later with any details."

Scott spit on the ground with a nod. "Come on, you ugly girls." He tugged a rope and the column of prisoners paraded before the major general with defeated downcast eyes.

Hampton grinned faintly as he thought about that. His first true time head-to-head with Sheridan, he could destroy the man who'd killed Stuart. It could be one hell of an accolade and a morale boost for his men, but he wasn't interested in just the notoriety of destroying the Yankees. He was interested in doing something Stuart could never do: knocking them out of the war.

Chapter 13

June 10, 1864
Near North Fork of the North Anna River, Virginia

Tall oak, cedar, and hickory surrounded by dogwood and laurel covered every foot of available land. If one wanted to venture into the trees for a piss, dense ground cover of honeysuckle, greenbrier, and arrowwood impeded a man's path. Vines with tiny prickers along their stems scratched exposed skin, causing a fierce itch. They threatened to trip a man with every step or snare him in a vegetation trap. Others with thick almost root-like tentacles spread across the land. If the men were unlucky, they'd run into poison ivy. If God really had it out for them, they'd sit on some when they went to relieve themselves.

Yet, the forest wasn't all misery. If the men were lucky, they'd run into a blueberry bush, which could grow as tall as twelve feet, and hope that the berries were ripe enough to eat or risk frequent trips into the forest latrine.

Wolf's company walked by a man sitting on a log. He had no mount, meaning he was the newest recruit in Company Q's footsore brigade. Every day, additional men joined Company Q as they trailed behind the column, but despite the number, only a few straggled in at the end of the day. Where the rest went was subject to the men's imaginations.

The exhausted trooper's coat was unbuttoned, and he had the downtrodden appearance of a defeated man. "You ever seen such a sorry sight?" Wilhelm said.

"No, I haven't."

Wolf kicked his horse toward the side of the road. "You there."

The man looked up. His cheeks were red from the heat. Sweat beaded along his brow. His light mustache hardly filled in. "Yeah?"

"You need some water?" Wolf asked, offering him a canteen.

The man shook his head. "I got some. Feet gave out." He peered down at his boots. "'Bout raw. Not used to walking so much." He stopped speaking and gulped. "Infantry have it rough."

Ain't that the truth, Wolf thought.

The trooper continued, "Think I'll rest for a while."

Wolf eyed the marching cavalry ahead then looked behind. "Anything I can do?"

"You been mighty fair, Lieutenant. Just leave me be. Let me rest. I'll catch up."

Wolf nodded. "Try to stay with the column or you'll risk capture."

The young man nodded vacantly. Wolf turned his horse around and trotted to catch his company. Another rider approached from the other direction and stopped in front of the trooper. He had an angry irritated air about him.

"On your feet, Private. Do you think Uncle Sam pays you to sit? We're at war!"

The young trooper waved the officer away. "I ain't gonna walk no more."

"By God, you will walk. You'll walk to Catmandu if I tell you, you skedaddler. You been nothing but a lazy sack of bones since you came under my command."

The young man didn't budge, studying his hands. "I ain't running from the fight. Me horse is dead. I ain't walking 'nother step 'til I'm ready."

"Get up. That's an order." The officer's horse stepped sideways and tossed its head.

"Can't. I'm not going to march no more 'til I'm ready. Now leave me be."

"I will walk you back myself."

"No, you won't." The young man shook his head at the officer.

The lieutenant peered around in frustration and drew his sword, threatening to flog the trooper with the back end of it.

The trooper stood.

"You will walk. Forward! March!" the lieutenant yelled. He had attracted the eyes of every passing horseman. A few walked by with mild jeers for the officer; most quieted down by their own. Every man saw himself in that trooper's boots. It could easily be any of them marching along, struggling to keep up with the column while hoping they didn't find their way into a rebel prison camp.

"You think he'll flog him?" Adams said. "Been awhile since I seen a flogging. Anyone want to make a wager? Wolfie? Kent?"

"No," Wolf said. He made it a practice to never take a wager from Adams unless he was completely sure of the outcome. Yet he couldn't help but be suspicious that Adams was setting him up for an even bigger and costlier bet in the future.

"I don't have a dollar to my name," Kent said. Frowning, he continued. "I send it all back to my ma. She's sick with the wasting disease."

"Gee, lighten up, Kent," Adams said. "I'd take you up on a dollar bet if you could spare it from your dear old dying mum."

Kent shook his head. "Ma needs her laudanum."

"Anyone else than the downer?" Adams said, eyes darting from man to man as he looked for a man to take the bet.

"I'll take that bet," Lowell said. "My mum's father was a gambler on a riverboat. Name was Merrick the Maverick."

"I bet he was," Adams said with a predatory smile. "I'll bet you five dollars he doesn't flog the man."

"You're on," Lowell said, producing a green bill and waving it in the air. It had an oversized five in the center, United States running along the top, and pictures of Lady Liberty and Alexander Hamilton on either side. All the decorations, unique numbers, and fancy writing on the bill were to prevent counterfeiting on this new legal tender to assist the Federal government finance the war effort. Who knew what it would be worth when the war was over if anything at all?

"You sure, Lowell?" Kent asked. "Sure is a hefty bet. Just think of the things you could do with it. Buy an acre of land or a few months' rent!"

"Quiet, Kent!" Lowell said, trying to see backward as they walked.

All the men turned to watch the showdown between the exhausted private and his commanding officer.

"Walk, damn you!" the officer said voice growing in command.

The trooper shook his head. "If you make me walk any farther, I'll kill meself. I will."

"Nonsense. You're fine." The officer leaned off his horse. "I'm trying to help you. You want to get captured by a bunch of Home Guard, or worse, those Red Shirts?"

"I don't, but I ain't going to walk 'til I'm ready."

"You will," the officer said, pointing his sword.

The private reached to his hip and drew his revolver.

"How dare you draw that in my presence. Holster that weapon, Private!"

The private didn't say a word, but now he had everyone's attention. Men twisted in their saddles, peered over their shoulders, and stood high in their stirrups to watch the action. He shifted the pistol to his temple and squeezed the trigger. The gunshot rocked the column. A horse reared. Men shouted in dismay.

"Did he?" Lowell said, his mouth dropping.

The private lay unmoving in the dirt. The officer held his sword out as if he were going to issue more orders, but his mouth refused to obey, his eyes wider than twelve-pound solid shot balls.

Wolf shared a look with Wilhelm before speaking, "Eyes forward, boys."

"Nothing you've never seen. Keep moving," Wilhelm said.

To witness a comrade killed by an enemy was harrowing, angering, and cruel in a divine way. It was another to watch a fellow trooper do it to themselves. It made every man squirm and uneasy. To have reached a place in his mind where suicide was the answer, it must have been a long hard struggle, one that Wolf couldn't fathom yet understood. It made him wonder what could have been done differently to save the man or if he was a lost cause from the beginning.

"Some men don't have it," Nelson grunted.

"It's true," Adams agreed with a shrug of his shoulders.

"Quiet," Wolf said. "No more talking about it."

"Of course, Lieutenant," Adams said, giving him an understanding nod. "Lowell, I'll be taking that five dollars now."

"What? No."

"The bet was he wouldn't be flogged. He wasn't."

"But the man killed himself."

"He did. Not a bet I would have taken. But the matter is settled."

"You got one black heart, Adams," Lowell said, reaching into his jacket and handing over the bill.

"I told you not to take the bet," Kent said. "That poor man feels about the same as I do. Tired of this war. Damn tired," he mumbled, carrying on in melancholy. "Think about all the things you could have done with that money. Just think. I know what I would have done. Used it to buy me an acre. Build a fine little cabin. Plant some corn. Find me a girl. Buy her a nice ring." His fantasy life died in his eyes at the reality of his situation. "But who am I kidding. No woman would like a man like me. Bad luck follows me around the same way a cat follows a fisherman."

***

Sheridan's column halted and camped where they'd ended the day's march, spread across the land. Custer's brigade shifted southward, away from the main column, down a road Wolf heard one man call Marquis. They bivouacked on Buck Chiles Farm, the only clearing big enough to hold the fifteen-hundred man brigade.

A stream ran along the edge of the property, and the men had their fill of fresh water. As much of the cool water was dumped over dry skin and faces as sloshed in full bellies and canteens. The men were experienced campaigners. Setting up camp to them was accomplished as quick as taking it down. For the men knew the faster they made camp, the sooner they would eat. Hundreds of campfires leaked their smoky tendrils to the sky, filling the air with the rich odor of burning wood. The sun disappeared behind trees on its downward descent while Wolf's men sat around a fire trading gossip.

"One of my old pals in the 1st Michigan said they were attacked by Hampton's men today," Adams said. He took a hand and wiped it through his greasy black hair, the strands sticking into place.

"Aye," Nelson added, staring at the flames.

"Hampton's? No, must be partisans," Lowell said. "We left him in the dust."

"Want to make a wager?" Adams asked, eyes searching for a way to rob the man.

Lowell gulped, his confidence rattled for only a moment. "How could I tell the truth of the matter?"

"I could ask my friend again?" Adams said with a raise of his eyebrows and a shrug of his shoulders.

"Just for you to lie!" Lowell pointed at him and shook his head with narrowed eyes, thinking he'd caught the other man in a lie. "Nope, I won't take it."

"Suit yourself. Can't win that five dollars back if you don't take a chance."

Wilhelm sat near his tent, puffing his pipe, and it released its own pleasant aroma into the air. "I find it hard to believe that two divisions of cavalry are meandering over enemy territory and Confederate high command has no idea where we are."

If Wolf had any understanding of the rebels at all, they were well aware of their movements. "I agree. The enemy must know we march."

"Surely not our destination?" asked Lowell.

Kent stared longingly at the fire as if he debated whether or not to throw himself in. "Hampton probably knows every move we take. Where we march to. Where we shit. Where our families live." He gestured toward the forest. "I bet you he's laying a trap for us as we speak. That would be my luck, walk into one of Hampton's traps. The giant would come barreling down on us, taking us prisoner or worse."

Wolf clenched his jaw. Kent's incessant depressive talk was bad for morale. "Shut your mouth, Kent. Hampton can be beaten." He shared a look with Wilhelm. Not every man in their platoon knew about Franz's death, but surely the mention of the enemy general stung the sergeant. Wilhelm had fought Hampton once and almost killed the enemy general. The next time, Wolf was sure the sergeant would finish the job. The same way Wolf would kill Payne.

Kent nodded sadly. "If I were you, I'd yell at me too." He glanced at Wolf. "Sorry, Lieutenant. Just can't shake the feeling we're in for one hell of a fight."

Wolf licked his lips while considering the value of thrashing the man with his fists, yet he didn't think that would change anything. "Nothing we can't handle. Little Phil knows what he's doing. So does Custer."

Kent sighed as if he battled internally to stay alive. "You're probably right." The long-faced man looked up. "But you know when a man feels his days are numbered." He grimaced then patted his chest. "I feel that in my heart."

"Private, let's stop talking for a while or we're going to have a problem." Wolf angrily removed his jacket.

"No need, Lieutenant. Probably better if I keep me thoughts to myself."

"You're a wise man."

"My mother always says the same thing. Keep my mouth shut if only sadness is going to come out. Suppose my mother is right." Kent nodded knowingly.

"Quit your blathering," Nelson said.

The downtrodden trooper gulped and gave a short nod.

"Have no doubt, men. Lee will not let us raid unchecked," Wolf said. "There will be a fight, but we'll have plenty of time before it happens. We've been at this for a few days now. It will take them a while to come up with a response. The only question is where?"

"But when they do respond, it will be quick," Wilhelm said. "That's Lee's way."

A series of "Ayes" echoed from the men. They understood they could not act with impunity on Southern soil. Those that had survived the war long enough to be considered veterans knew better. The men that had survived Kilpatrick's ill-fated raid appreciated it. It was ingrained in the men that survived Wolf's daring mission near Yellow Tavern. This war had the deadly versatility to take them in any number of ways. As intimately as one knew a lover, he accepted that being a prisoner in a rebel prison camp was one of the slowest and surest ways to die. The only surer and slower way was consumption.

"We'll be ready," Wolf said. "Everyone plays by the same rules here. Don't venture from the command without a partner. Keep your eyes peeled for bushwhackers or otherwise." He let his eyes scan the younger men. "We'll get a fight but on our terms. Not theirs, ya hear?"

"What about the colonel?" asked Kent. "He has a mean eye for bad ground."

Nods came from the men and then a silence. Not the same as Kilpatrick's raid. They were more naive then. These men would be ready, and Wolf would make sure they were up for a fight.

"You don't worry about the colonel. Captain Peltier is sound."

"He ain't right in the head," Adams said.

Wolf eyed him. "I won't let you men down. Me and Wilhelm will look out for your best interest. Just like always."

The men murmured "Ayes" once again. "Now, let's take a bit of the edge off." Wolf went to his tent and pulled out a bottle. "Little O Be Joyful, never hurt." The bottle was passed from man to man. The men bonded over the shared alcohol the same way they shared the burden of soldiering, together.

The night cooled and the flames became welcome. The men shifted closer to the fire. The wolf guidon rustled in the cool breeze, its golden head over the black fabric bright in the firelight. Munn speculated that rain may be coming. The rest of the men talked him down.

One by one they drifted to their bed rolls, and Wolf sat staring at the flames. He took a swig from his bottle, thinking about his dead friend Roberts. "Bastard went before your time." He took the bottle and dumped it out on the fire. The blaze flared high and then died down again. He pissed the flames out and kicked dirt on the rest. Things weren't the same as they once were. Despite being easier, the men were harder, the layers of innocence stripped from them like the skin from Wolf's back. They were veterans, wary to the ways of the cruel world.

Chapter 14

The morning was chilly, dew dripping from blades of grass and clinging to the tips of leaves. Everything was saturated with a dampness that hung in the air. It was the kind of moisture that could stick in a man's chest and kill him before he could fetch his lawyer to settle his will.

Brigadier General Thomas Rosser had tobacco off his plug and in the corner of his mouth before he crawled from his cot. Donning his uniform and hat, he exited his command tent before the first rays of light assaulted the blue mountains like gilded thieves of day.

His men faced west, the most likely direction of Union General Hunter's forces approach. They also acted as a reserve for Hampton's other brigades. He gave his orderly a soft kick with the toe of his boot. "Henry," he said none to softly.

The man scrambled upright, rubbing his blue eyes. Lieutenant Henry Marlow was a humble man. Of middling height and slender frame, he owned a small farm and two slaves. Never questioned an order and never let Rosser down.

"Hurry along."

"Yes, sir," he mumbled, departing to prepare their horses.

His other aide, Lieutenant Robert Lafayette, stood, tossing his gray jacket over his shoulders. He sported a rough beard similar to Rosser and his family owned an exquisite stable near Fredericksburg that produced fine well-bred animals. "Morning, sir."

"Morning, Lafayette. Head over to White's command. Make sure they are well-fed. Mounts watered. I have a feeling we'll be fighting today."

Lafayette eyed the surrounding trees as if the enemy already lurked nearby. "Poor ground for it."

"I'm sure we'll make do."

His aide nodded. "No doubt in my mind." Lafayette took his leave and departed for the regimental commanders of the Laurel Brigade.

Rosser was an early riser. More work was done in the quiet of the morning than during the long hours of the day. Before the dawn cracked was when a soldier got the jump on the enemy. A hunter a sight on his prey. That's when he thought the best, the time before the complications of the day reared up. He mounted and trotted his horse along Gordonsville Road, waving his black hat in the air as he approached General Butler's pickets. "Friendly rider coming up."

They squinted in the morning light, stepping out from behind trees. "Genr'l," they said as he passed.

"Boys." He touched the brim of his hat and continued into Butler's camp. Most of the men were still in tents and bedrolls. A man squatted over a smoldering fire here and there. Butler had the greenest brigade in the Cavalry Corps, almost thirteen-hundred men in three regiments from South Carolina. They'd been conducting local defense of the Carolinas prior to being shifted north. He found Butler's command tent with its flaps closed, no movement inside or out.

"Fancy son of a bitch," he said to himself.

Brigadier General Matthew Butler was a close friend of Rosser. From the outside looking in, they were dissimilar in almost every way. Where Rosser was broad and tall with a domineering look and scowling face, Butler was short and thin with a wispy mustache and neatly cut goatee. Rosser had been two weeks away from graduating West Point before resigning to join the rebellion. Butler had been a lawyer and politician, with no military experience. Rosser had grown up on a farm, hunting, raising livestock, living as country gentry, and earning his sun-darkened tan. Butler had graduated law school before being elected to the South Carolina House of Representatives in 1860 then resigning to fight when the rebellion broke out to serve in the Confederate Army, garnering the pale skin of a man who did his best work indoors. The bugle call of service to one's nation trumpeted from deep within some men's souls. Others took up arms in defense of their homes and kin, no man less noble than the last.

Rosser undid the flaps of Butler's tent and ripped them aside, bowing his head to walk inside.

Butler squinted a single eye, the other still closed. His hair was combed to the side, looking respectable even while he slept, and he wore a white nightgown reminding Rosser of an old maid. "Tom?"

"Jesus Christ our Savior. Would you look at this? You're wearing a dress."

Butler wrinkled his nose and sighed. "It's sleepwear." He sat up on his field cot and rolled his legs to the side, rubbing his eyes. One foot touched the ground, the other leg a mere bald stump at the ankle. "More comfortable that way."

"You city folk. Pampered living." Rosser glanced down at the general's missing foot. "How's the leg?" he said with a touch of empathy for his friend.

"Aches with the change in weather. Did it rain?"

Rosser looked back outside. The camp was beginning to stir in the damp morning. "Can't say it did, but the ground's wet and we got a nice mist clouding over us."

"A warranted reprieve from the indelible heat." Butler slipped on a wooden artificial limb. He tugged the leather straps over his leg and tightened it above his knee. It would act in place of his foot. He grabbed his crutch and stood. "Leg always knows."

"Who would have thought that all it took to know the weather was losing your foot? Might make a farmer out of you yet." Butler threw off his nightgown, and Rosser turned his back to him to give him privacy. "What do you think Hampton's got in store for us today?"

Butler went about changing into his uniform that had been brushed down after their march until it looked almost new. "Damned if I know. I suppose he means to fight. The enemy is before us despite the unfavorable terrain."

Rosser leaned outside the tent and spit tobacco juice. "My boys are ready for a dance with the devil."

"As are mine. I've had my men prepared for it all morning." Butler tapped Rosser on the shoulder, and Rosser raised his eyebrows at him. "That was quick."

"You adapt to doing things different."

"You mean wearing a dress?" Rosser said with a smile.

"Sleepwear, my friend." Butler gave a clever grin. "You don't know what you are missing out on. Cool, free, like sleeping on a cloud made from silk."

"You can keep the dresses, Matthew. I'll stick to my drawers."

"A prudish and rough existence you lead."

"Jesus," Rosser said, spitting. He respected his friend, but his ways he would never understand. "Let's go see what Hampton's got for us."

"Better than being wasted waiting." Butler waved over an aide. "Prep the 4th, 5th, and 6th. Mounted and ready to move out."

"Yes, sir." The aide scurried away in search of the regimental commanders.

The men mounted their horses with their aides and rode for Netherland Tavern.

***

The two generals, along with their aides, trotted down Gordonsville Road, catching glimpses of the Virginia Central Railroad tracks. In a few places the tracks would cross the road only to cross the road again a few hundred feet away. It depended on the terrain.

They passed a train depot, a newly built single-story depot with sides made of rough-hewn tan maple, and soon reached a tavern sitting on the edge of a crossroads and the railroad tracks. The corps's baggage train had been placed only a few hundred feet away, a ring of over a hundred supply wagons and thousands of additional mounts. The drivers had opened their day hovering over campfires, cooking bacon or perhaps a flapjack with any flour they might have. A company from the 7th Georgia guarded the train; they stood around small fires. The rest manned the roads and surrounding areas as pickets.

Hampton's division camped in the locations they had halted for the night. Rosser the farthest west, followed by Butler, then Wright's Brigade. The other division under Fitz Lee was miles to the east, supposedly at Louisa Court House.

Rosser sensed the underlying animosity between Hampton and his technical subordinate by virtue of time in rank, Fitz Lee. When out of contact with another, it was difficult to know if Fitz's tardiness or lethargy was due to the fog of war and operational difficulty or a slight reluctance to obey the burly major general. It took a special man to bind them all together, and now that Stuart was gone, Rosser wondered how they would fare.

The two generals dismounted in front of the tavern, finding Major General Wade Hampton sitting on a hanging swing on the porch. His thick arms were folded over his chest and his head leaned backward, mouth open as he snored, sounding like a frog choking on a June bug. His uniform was layered in dust from the past two days of hard riding. His black boots were almost the same shade of gray as his clothes.

The two generals walked up the short steps. Butler thumped his crutch on the top step extra loud, startling the sleeping general. Hampton's eyes shot open and he blinked with recognition of his two subordinates. He grinned at them from beneath his bushy beard and stood, pressing a hand on his hip to stretch it.

Hampton stifled a yawn with his hand. "Crisp little morning, isn't it?"

"Crisper than a New Englander's heart on judgement day," Rosser said.

This brought a wider smile from the commander.

Butler spoke up. "If I may be so bold, what do you propose we do today?"

Hampton looked at his men then picked up his black slouch hat and placed it on his head. "I propose we fight."

Rosser tongued his chew again, squeezing the molasses-flavored tobacco leaves for all their worth. He spit off the porch.

"Very poor terrain for mobility," Butler said.

Hampton reached out and squeezed Butler's shoulder. "Your boys are better off on foot with their rifles anyway."

"But alas, I am not," Butler said with a chuckle and a heft of his crutch.

Hampton released him. "I don't disagree. This ground is poor. Let's find a better place to kill some Yankees." He turned toward the tavern. "Preston!" he called inside, combining every ounce of his irritation as a father with the order of a commander.

Hampton's son emerged from inside with his jacket open, boot half on, and pistol in hand. Seeing the congregation of rebel officers, he paused, looking around for a threat. "Where are the Yanks that need whippin'?"

Hampton pointed north. "They're that way. Holster that pistol. We aren't under attack."

Preston had the audacity to appear disappointed, and this made the rest of the officers chuckle. Even after all the fighting and dying, this young man still desired a fight.

"Your boy's ready," Rosser said.

"As is the father."

They mounted their horses and trotted along Fredericksburg Road north. They hadn't traveled more than a half-mile, surrounded by dense forest, before the distant cracks of carbines crowed as roosters with the rising sun.

"I got men from the 4th South Carolina posted up here as pickets," Butler said.

Hampton stared fiercely northward, trying to discern the threat.

Rosser spoke first. "I wonder if Little Phil's gotten ahead of himself. Perhaps he knows we're here."

"The impetuous little fool. No, his movements are without any kind of expedience."

A rider galloped down the road from the north, fleeing the fighting.

"That's Captain Mulligan, A Company," Butler said.

The horseman halted. His mount resisted the reins. "Sir, generals," he said with respectful nods to each of them.

"Captain, what's happening up there?" Hampton cut in with a point.

"Looks like we riled up a whole nest of bluebellies. Drove my boys back. At least a regiment or two of the lily-livered bastards."

Rosser spit in irritation. The Yanks were coming in force. *One shouldn't wish too much for a fight because that fight will find you*, he thought. *Sometimes before you were ready.* He eyed Hampton, judging him before he spoke. "Looks like they're coming down in a hurry. That bandy-legged Irishman's ass is itching for a whipping."

"It appears so." Hampton squinted as he judged the threat. "Butler, move your brigade up and engage. Let's see how committed they are." He turned to Rosser. "I need your boys to mount up and shift back to Netherland Tavern. Prepare to lend support." He motioned a courier from Fitz. "William."

The lieutenant hurried his horse beside him. "Yes?"

"Ride to Fitz. Tell him to travel north on Marquis Road. See if he can get around the flank of them."

"Yes, sir!" William said, turning his horse to gallop away.

A company of horsemen galloped down the road. A few of the riders were bloodied. One man held his abdomen with his off hand. The lieutenant pointed backward. "There be a whole damn brigade of the bastards coming this way."

Rosser spit again. "We're going to have a fine dance with the devil today!"

"We are, General. The hogs intend to brush past us." Hampton turned to look at him. "Consolidate the wagon train. They are committing. It's time for us to concentrate our forces as best we can. I want Hart unlimbering this way too."

Rosser nodded. "I'm away then." He looked at Butler. "Don't have all the fun without me now, my friend."

"I would never deny you and your brigade a good old-fashioned Yankee killing."

"You're a good friend!" Rosser turned his horse and galloped back to the Laurel Brigade.

Chapter 15

Early Morning, June 11, 1864
Near Buck Chiles Farm off of Marquis Road, Virginia

Custer had awakened with the rising sun. A cool morning dew dripped from blades of grass and steel alike. A crisp breeze ran through the trees, the first respite from the dust and heat in some time. He doubted it would maintain throughout the day, but for the time being, it was pleasant.

Despite the want to sleep in well past the waking morning light, when on campaign, he appreciated the early morning was when opportunities arose. He was glad he did. He'd already had a report from the 7th Michigan that they had been engaged by elements of Wickham's Brigade. He wasn't too concerned; however, it was somewhat peculiar that the rebels had somehow placed themselves in front of the column. Perhaps he should be more concerned, but the rebels were falling back, which meant they weren't looking for a protracted engagement. He doubted today would bring such an endeavor. Either way, he'd roused the 1st Michigan and shifted them to be in position to support the 7th.

In the distance, carbine fire popped the same as an almost burnt-to-ashes log of pine, faint and soft with the occasional loud crack. Eliza appeared at his side with a mug of steaming coffee. "There ya go, ginnil sir." She gave him a smile.

"You are much too kind to me, Eliza Brown. Much too kind," he said. "Libbie would be most happy to know you're taking such dutiful care of me."

He took a quick sip, trying not to burn his tongue.

"You're trusted to my care, so I make sure you're cared for. You just make sure you take care of them Johnnies out there."

He gave her a pleasant smile and glanced at the sky. "Might be a good day for it. What do you think?"

Her voice cracked like a whip. "Is there ever not a good day to whip a reb?"

He chuckled at the woman's brazen disdain of their opponents and then sipped his coffee. "I must say, my dear. You are most correct." He cocked an ear. The faint popping trended toward nothing. "Must be giving way." He thought for a moment. "It's a bit disparaging that they've somehow appeared ahead of us."

A courier hurried into camp, his bay stamping its hooves heavily. The lieutenant halted near Custer and gave a hasty salute. "General Custer, sir. I come with a message from General Torbert."

Custer eyed the young man. "How is the general this fine morning?"

The aide's horse danced. "He is well, sir. Busy as Merritt and Devin are heavily engaged."

"They are?" He turned and glanced over his shoulder as if he could catch a glimpse of them fighting and somehow had missed it. Only the obscure report of a fleeting skirmish sounded in the distance.

Custer's brigade had been detached from the rest of the division the night before to provide a flanking assault if the opportunity arose. With rebels turning up in front of the column, the appearance of the enemy could scarcely be a coincidence. "How many rebels?"

"At least a brigade."

The rebels may be before us in a formidable force. "Go on."

"Gregg's Division is marching along Fredericksburg Road in support of Torbert. Torbert wants you to travel down a side road." The lieutenant thought for a moment trying to recall the name. "Nunn's Creek Road. Then link with Merritt and Devin and drive off whatever force is to our front."

Custer nodded and took another sip of his coffee. It was fine delicious stuff. Eliza was a master cook and was well-known for her coffee brew. On a regular basis, men inquired about how she brewed the coffee to just the perfect strength but without leaving it tasting as if she'd boiled dirt, something Confederate soldiers did on a regular basis. "Tell him I will move my men in the next hour." He stood, taking another sip of his dark morning brew.

The aide saluted and turned his horse back through the camp. Eliza awaited his word, hovering nearby. "I hate to waste a fine cup of coffee, Eliza, but we must make haste."

She gave him a nod. "You go on ahead and waste it. Just give a whipping to those rebs."

"You know? I think I will." He drank as much of the hot liquid as he could handle and tossed the rest into his campfire then waved Lieutenant Granger forward. "Send for Colonel Moore and Colonel Alger."

***

"We ain't got no fucking coffee," Nelson said, hovering over the campfire with crossed muscled arms. A disgusted scowl spread beneath his bushy beard, indecisive if he was going to spit or yell.

"How's a man to live?" Adams chimed in, tossing dry fuel on their soldierly flames of anger.

Lowell glanced from his plate holding a flapjack. His face was covered in red welts from the encounter with the bees. "Can't eat Munn's famous flapjacks with no goddamn coffee," he said. "Wouldn't taste right."

Wolf agreed with the men. A morning without coffee wasn't a morning at all, more the walk of the dead, especially when night still clung to the land. It was difficult to shake the grogginess of sleep before the sun was up with no coffee in his cup.

"I lived my whole life without a drop," Kent muttered. "Then when I came to the army, I was enthralled by it. Really brought joy to my joyless life. Now I'm back in the dark. No coffee. No pleasure. A bunch of men over yonder waiting to shoot me dead."

"We'll find you some. I promise," Wolf said. He contemplated he might have to thieve some from another company or the brigade itself. His men depended on him not just in battle but in camp too. The only thing keeping his men from open revolt was the plentiful amount of food they'd procured from the forage.

Wilhelm puffed on his pipe as he did every morning. He was fully armed and ready for action, a contemplative look on his face.

"We're going to have to find some coffee," Wolf said to him.

Wilhelm spoke around his pipe. "Aye, we are."

Herman Scholtz said something quickly in German, and Wolf only caught the word coffee. Wilhelm nodded to him and puffed.

"Not sure we can pull one over on the brigade's quartermaster again," Wolf said.

"Probably not wise."

The men of F Company continued to complain about the lack of coffee in their lives and cook. Distant gunfire crackled in the waking hour, and where green men may have been concerned, the veterans knew it was far away. They enjoyed what time they still had in camp by eating while uniformed, horses saddled, and boots on, knowing that a call to action lingered in the air. Wilhelm had seen to that.

Wolf peered over the encampment at the company guidon next to Wilhelm's tent. A light drizzle tapped the leaves above, almost drowning out the sounds of fighting too far away to care about. The thundering hooves perked the men's interest as a rider made his way to Captain Peltier's tent. The captain still wasn't awake yet, his tent flaps closed.

The rider wore a fine shell jacket with yellow piping around the collar and sleeves and a kepi pulled low over his eyes. He made for his tent and hopped from the saddle in a hasty dismount, still holding the reins of his horse. He spoke to Sergeant Simpson before addressing the tent. Wolf watched the man poke his head inside and call out in alarm.

Men from F Company made their way over in fits and starts. Wolf hobbled through them.

"This man is dead!" exclaimed the aide.

Wolf pushed past him. "How?"

"In his sleep apparently." He eyed Wolf's uniform. "Are you in charge here?"

Wolf ignored him for a moment and dipped into the captain's tent. Peltier was dressed in a plain white shirt and white drawers, a blanket covering him to the neck. His face stuck out from the top of the blanket, pale as an early snow made even more apparent by the blackness of his beard. His death was clearly final.

Wolf knelt on the ground next to him, hoping he was wrong. Peltier's eyes were closed, his appearance as peaceful as a sleeping angel. Wolf grabbed his hand; it was cool to the touch. He put his ear near his chest, listening intently. There was no faint sound of an exhale and inhale or the light thump of a beating heart. The men of the company crowded around the opening, their faces looking in.

"What's wrong with the captain?"

"He dead?"

Wolf looked at them. "He's dead." Under his breath he cursed as he tugged the blanket over the captain's head. "Damnit." He pushed himself upright and walked outside.

"Who's in charge?" the aide asked again over the din of the men.

Wilhelm threaded through the crowd. "The captain?"

"He's dead."

Wilhelm frowned and poked his head in the tent. He put a boot into the captain's foot and pressed down hard. "Looks that way."

The men carried on muttering and murmuring amongst themselves.

"You," the aide said. "You're an officer."

Wolf continued to watch Wilhelm for the man's assessment of the captain's death. The sergeant frowned. "Sometimes men die in their sleep."

"Do you have a senior first lieutenant? I have orders for this company."

Wolf turned on him. "No first lieutenant. Just me."

The aide wasted no time. "Your men are to mount and lead the brigade toward Trevilian Station."

"The brigade?"

"Those are Colonel Moore's orders. As soon as you can." Not waiting for a response, the aide turned and remounted his horse.

"Is there going to be a fight?" Wolf called at him.

The aide shrugged. "Who knows? Good luck!" He spurred his horse and galloped off.

The expectant eyes of F Company turned on Wolf. There was some disdain and some mistrust. A few men were just waiting for orders. Wolf scanned them. "You heard him. We have a brigade to lead."

Thirty minutes later, F Company clopped down Nunn's Creek Road toward Gordonsville Road. Wolf rode in the lead guide position of a single-file column, as the way was extremely narrow, resembling more of a footpath or deer trail. Sergeant Simpson led the other platoon. Wolf hadn't had time to digest the fact that he was now in charge of the company. There had been no time to think. Only carry out their orders.

"We're with you," Wilhelm said from behind. "It isn't that much different than leading a platoon. More men. More moving pieces. Simpson and I will fill in wherever we're needed."

Wolf nodded, focused on the rough land ahead. "I've had the equivalent of three promotions in a month, instead of hanging or rotting to death in a prison like I thought." He turned to steal a look at his sergeant.

Wilhelm grinned beneath his curled mustache. "As is war. As I like to say, you're only one shot away from a promotion."

"Isn't that the truth."

They traveled almost four miles, eating up most of an hour's time before Nunn's Creek Road intersected with another much wider main road and they veered westward on it. Here his company was able to shift to riding in fours, allowing his forty-four men enough space to move much quicker. Wolf rode as the front guide, Wilhelm with the first row of troopers right behind him with the guidon. They traveled roughly two miles in this formation before he saw the smoke and campfires in the distance. Wolf raised his fist and his company came to a halt. "Ours?" Wolf asked Wilhelm.

His sergeant shook his head, his hand resting confidently upon the company guidon pole. "Sheridan's wagon train would have had to have traveled fast to beat us here."

Wolf agreed but operating outside the main army created more than a fraction of doubt in his mind. When the column stretched over ten miles long as they marched, friends and foes could be anywhere.

"May be prudent to wait until the rest of the regiment is up," Wilhelm said.

"Or we could create quite a scare," Wolf said with a sniff. And perhaps he could gain the confidence of his men. A swift rout of the enemy may even raise morale more than a hot cup of coffee. Either would do the trick.

Wilhelm nodded slowly. "Much less prudent. However, we haven't been challenged by any pickets." He glanced behind them at the men. "The rest of the regiment isn't far behind if we need support."

"Well, let's give these boys a ride through. If their ours, they'll have one hell of a wake up. If they're rebs, they'll have one hell of a wake up."

The men laughed behind him.

He called over his shoulder. "How about it, boys? How about a bit of fun?"

A few of the men cheered. No grumbles reached his ears. "Draw pistols and sabers, Sergeant."

"You heard the lieutenant. Pistols and sabers!"

Wolf drew his saber and rested it on his shoulder. The sergeants belted out commands and encouragement to the men until they were in place. Birds chirped their morning songs. Wood smoke filled their noses. It was a fine morning for a charge.

"Forward, at the trot!" Wolf shouted.

As one, his company brought their horses to a trot. He let them all find their place before calling out. "To gallop! Ja!" The men moved their mounts faster. "Ja!" Wolf called again. His men picked up the cheer. They whooped at the tops of their lungs, the men gaining energy from the speed of their mounts. The guidon fluttered in the wind, the golden wolf-head biting at the air. A trooper fired his pistol into the sky. Anything to raise the hackles of their enemy. Anything to make them think they were fighting against a thousand men instead of forty-four.

The men in the camp sat up straighter next to their wagons. Two or three turned to stare from the nearest campfire. Others, leaning against wagons, squinted and shaded their eyes to block the rising sun from their view. To them, the charging horsemen were as curious as a circus come to town.

Wolf lifted his saber into the air. "13th!" The men standing near the fires hardly reacted until Wolf's company turned into the camp. The encampment grew in size, revealing dozens of campfires and even more wagons. Most of the wagons were uncovered, some with white linen tops covering the carts. Teams of oxen, horses, and mules were picketed nearby grazing over the lush grass and forest foliage. Campfires from the teamsters and cavalrymen released smoke into the sky.

Men dove to the ground while the others continued to stand, gaping wide-eyed. There weren't too many blue coats among them, one for every dozen. *Perhaps we guessed right.* Then he saw the Confederate flag near the center. "Bloody hell!" Wolf said. "To the flag!" He twirled his saber in the air.

The company pounded their way through the camp, wind whipping, swords flashing, pistols blazing, and havoc followed in their wake. Wolf slashed a man as he ran, and the teamster fell into a tent, causing a shout from inside. Rebels fled into the trees. Spooked horses leapt on their lines. A tent went ablaze, flames leaping to the sky. A rebel pointed a musket at them, and Wilhelm brought him down with an impressive pistol shot between the eyes, resulting in a red mist where he once stood.

They cut back to the road, routing a couple of pickets facing the other direction. Wolf drew his command to a halt. "About face!" His men reversed ranks. He turned his horse to face the camp again. Men scrambled. Horses bolted. A wagon had tipped on its side. A few men jumped atop mounts bareback and galloped into the trees and down the road.

"Back in! Round those boys up!"

Wolf's heart beat like a drum, exhilaration beaming on his face. The attack was as splendid as it was chaos for the enemy. His company burst back through the camp for a second charge. This time he split his platoon one way, and Simpson took the other in a different direction. Wolf rode down a man in a filthy butternut jacket and straw hat, and instead of stabbing him in the back, he tapped him on the head on the way by. "You're mine," Wolf shouted. The man stopped, raising his arms in the air in surrender. "To the flag." The platoon broke into squads and sections of men as they gathered any prisoners to slow to flee.

Captured rebels were led to the center of the camp in fits and starts. Gunfire still puffed from the edges of the encampment. Wolf came to a halt near Wilhelm. "Must be over fifty wagons."

Wilhelm's eyes were fully open, taking in every inch of the camp. "And over a thousand horses. Spare mounts for an entire corps."

"An entire corps?" Wolf said. He pointed at Simpson and called to him. "Get your boys to the other end of the road. Dismounted. Send word if anyone responds."

Wolf set guards around the captured men and the prisoners quickly outnumbered Wolf's small command. F Company began the process of looting whatever they could. Nelson opened a cook pot and peered in, his pistol still trained on the prisoners. "Would you look at this? Even the damn Johnnies have coffee."

"Don't touch that, Yank," said a prisoner, hands in the air.

Nelson regarded the prisoners with scorn. "You ain't in no position to argue." He grabbed a ladle and dipped it into the coffee and slurped the steaming liquid. "Tastes like shit," he said and licked his lips, "but it's coffee." He glared at the rebels. "Which one of you fools made this?"

No one answered him.

"Well, it tastes like shit."

"How'd you know what shit tastes like?" called a prisoner back.

Nelson aimed his pistol at the front rank of captives. "You wanna find out?"

Adams hopped from his horse and took the ladle, drinking some too. "Ahh, the sweet taste of victory."

"They got bacon too! And lots of it," Munn exclaimed from one of the other wagons.

"Bring it on over," Nelson waved.

"Make sure you make some for 2nd Platoon," Wolf commanded.

The men grunted their agreement. Carbine fire carried on near the other edge of camp. The men ignored it as they started again on preparing breakfast while drinking coffee in front of the prisoners. Taking hardtack from the rebels, they tossed the iron-like bread into the coffee pots, letting the boiling brew kill any bugs inside. Then they skimmed the slaughtered pests from the top of the pot, the bread softened and ready to eat.

A rumble of hooves drew their attention back to the road. Captain Corby galloped into the camp at the head of D Company followed in close pursuit by C Company and then by Colonel Moore with his staff. The two additional companies trotted into the camp, and Wolf breathed a sigh of relief. The more support that reinforced them the better.

He spurred Sarah, guiding her next to the pole holding the Confederate flag. It was the battle flag, mostly red. The only Yankee blue was found in the bars forming an X over the red field, white stars lined each arm of the X, numbering 13 total. He reached out, snagging the standard by the corner, and ripped it from its pole. He urged his horse toward Moore.

"Who's in charge here? Who led this foray?" Moore called at Wolf's platoon. The troopers looked in his direction but with little concern or respect and continued eating and guzzling coffee.

Moore looked like a giant strawberry dressed in a blue uniform, struggling to stay mounted. His face flush from the short ride as if it had completely exhausted him. His horse looked terribly uncomfortable with such a heavy man on its back.

Wolf put his horse abreast of Moore. "I did, sir."

Moore blinked as he adjusted to the sight of Wolf. "You? Where is Captain Peltier?"

"He's dead, sir. Died in his sleep."

Moore's puffy round cheeks jiggled with disbelief. "When?"

"Found him this morning before we marched."

"Dear God, I never would have sent a company in the vanguard without proper command elements. You should have notified me."

"Only followed orders."

Moore's lips quivered. "You would do well to address me as sir."

Wolf took a slight bow. "The camp is yours, sir." *Enough respect, you witless pig.* "Looks like the entire Confederate Cavalry Corps's baggage train or damn near close."

Two more companies of the 13th entered the camp at the trot, reinforcing the perimeter. With the sight of every new blue jacket, Wolf relaxed.

"You men took this camp without orders?" Moore said. He gulped as he eyed the magnitude of a company's actions. "You attacked without orders?"

"We were ordered to lead the brigade, sir. The opportunity to capture the enemy's wagon train presented itself, sir." He left out the part where he hadn't even known whose baggage train it was. "So we took it, sir."

The colonel was so blind to his own aggrandizement, he didn't even notice Wolf's false respect. Moore snorted through his nostrils with contempt. "Plausible story from the likes of a man such as yourself."

Wolf reached over and handed him the flag. "The enemy colors are yours."

Moore held the flag with a bit of mirth rising on his pudgy cheeks. Gunfire crackled behind them, and a minute later, troopers from the 5th Michigan galloped into the camp.

Colonel Russell Alger peeled off from the squadron of his men, spurring his horse towards them. "Colonel? The camp is ours?"

"It is, Colonel. The 13th has carried the day," Moore said, triumph dripping from his voice.

Alger grinned broadly beneath his black beard. "Scattered some boys and captured the enemy colors and wagons. Custer will be pleased."

Moore looked down at the red, blue, and white battle flag in his hands again. He stretched the flag skyward for all to bear witness to his greatness. "Yes, my men tore through their camp, an exemplary account for the regiment."

"If those boys be on the run, I want to pursue," Alger said. With a nod to Moore and his staff, he turned his horse back to his regiment. He gave a shout and galloped westward from the camp.

The colonel couldn't take his eyes off his prize. He continued to speak, mesmerized by it. "As much as it pains me," he said, lifting his meaty chin. "Colonel Alger may be correct this time. Keep the camp secure. We shall wait here for further orders."

Wolf regarded him expectantly, waiting for another reprimand.

"You may carry on, Lieutenant. You will lead F Company until we can find a suitable replacement for Peltier," Moore said with a smile for the captured colors.

Wolf turned his horse away with a self-satisfied grin. Nothing like keeping a superior's ego properly stoked to stay in his good graces. He guided his horse back to where his men were gathering with their prisoners.

"What'd the colonel say?" Wilhelm asked.

"I can keep leading the company until a more suitable officer is in place."

"Then we have had a great success this day."

"I'd say so. He didn't have me flogged on the spot." He paused, taking in his men eating and drinking coffee. "What's our status, Sergeant?"

"1st Platoon is all accounted for, no injuries."

"A glorious first action," Wolf said with a disbelieving smirk. All in all, he was pleased. The colors. The camp. He hadn't lost a man in the attack. He laughed to himself, smiling. If all battles were as such, the war would be over quick. Fortune favors the bold.

"Hell of a start as a company commander."

"I'll say."

"If a bit lacking in caution."

Wolf stiffened, waiting for Wilhelm to preach discretion.

"There were more rebels here than we thought. We could have easily been those men sitting captured."

Wolf shook his head, smiles fading for seriousness. "Not me."

"Then we would be prisoner and you'd be dead." Wilhelm moved closer. "Bold action is favorable action, but we had support. We aren't on our own. If those men turned on us in force, our small company would be much smaller."

Wolf eyed his men over his sergeant's shoulder. "I understand your concern but look at all this." He called over to his men. "How's that coffee, boys?"

The men raised their cups to him with smiles on their faces. "Didn't I tell you I'd find you coffee?" Wolf called to them. Cheers went from his men. Their cheers faded as a youthful looking officer galloped down the road awkwardly, his black horse bucking every dozen paces.

"Major Kidd's mount is giving him a fit!" said Wolf. The rider continued into the woods, the horse panicking the entire way. Members of his staff hurried after him.

The men laughed. Wolf reached out and gripped Wilhelm's arm. "We routed the rebs. We got them coffee. Things are going our way. No reason to sing caution when we've already won."

Wilhelm blinked. "We've done well, but the day is young."

"Enjoy your coffee, Sergeant. Maybe enjoy an easy victory for a change."

"There are no easy victories."

"Except today."

"You know better than that." Wilhelm eyed him with wariness then walked back to the platoon.

Chapter 16

Morning, June 11, 1864
Fredericksburg Road, North of Netherland Tavern

The ferocity of the battle raging in the forests to the north initially caught Hampton by surprise. The Union had pressured his men with an intensity he hadn't seen them employ in some time. He hoped this wasn't a new trend. A general wanted his enemies complacent and timid, ripe for flight. Never fighting with fire in their bellies.

He brushed aside the thoughts. It mattered not. Yankees were only ever a few charges away from a rout. He would see to it.

A squadron of Butler's 4th South Carolina boys with their Enfield rifles rushed through the trees to support the 6th South Carolina. They worked best while dismounted, the regiments more akin to mounted infantry than traditional cavalry. His burly bay stamped a hoof as the lines of men disappeared into the shadowy forest.

He faced Merritt's brigade in front and Devin's along his left flank, and there had to be more Union brigades lurking somewhere nearby if these were committing so heartily to the fight. He hadn't chosen this particular ground for a protracted clash, but it would serve its purpose.

Man-made thunder rippled from the left of Butler's line. His eyes scanned the smoky woods searching for a threat. The pressure had grown as the morning progressed and elements of Devin's brigade appeared, blue-coated devils in the cool morning mists. Hampton's men had wisely given ground, falling back to the Poindexter House where he'd placed Hart's Battery.

Rows of apple trees stood uniform against the unruly forest. Tiny white flowers decorated the trees offset by the green leaves, no fruit yet to bear. The land was cleared near the orchard and cut along a ridge until it reached a farmhouse standing on his right.

Hart's battery was unlimbered next to the house, pounding the Union lines through the trees. The battery stabilized the whole affair, raining exploding shot over the advancing Yankees. Metal and wood showered the men from above, leaving the wounded in clusters of blue draped over logs and leaned against tree trunks by their comrades as they leaked into the soil. It would be enough while he waited for Rosser and Fitz Lee's arrival to strengthen their resistance. As long as the field remained even, he had no doubt that his defensive stance could withstand the enemy until the time was right for a vicious counterattack.

The guns boomed, masking a rider speaking with Butler nearby, and the former lawyer removed his hat and slicked his hair back toward the rear of his skull. The courier gave a quick salute and departed back to his command.

"What is it, Matthew?"

"Lieutenant Colonel Aiken has been wounded."

Hampton shook his head with a slight grimace. "How bad?"

"Through the lung," Butler said. "He won't have long."

Another irreplaceable loss for his division. The next in the chain of command would take his place, but there was always an adjustment period, much the same as he had underwent as acting commander of the Cavalry Corps. Every battle took its toll on his officer corps, leaving him fewer men than he started the war with. All that remained were fresh faces and scarred bodies, each one with worn eyes. "He was an exceptional commander, he'll be missed."

Butler nodded gravely. "Sorely missed."

Gunfire blared behind them, not close enough to be a threat, but a concern when the battle lines were in front of them. Saddles creaked as they strained to see back toward his headquarters, Netherland Tavern. Carbine and pistol fire echoed through the trees followed by faint shouts.

Hampton glared at Butler. "What in the hell is that?"

"I do not know, sir. Have they gotten around us?"

"No, they would've had to pass through Fitz or Rosser." Hampton turned his horse. "Somebody in the name of Christ find out what is happening in our rear."

"I'll go!" Preston spun his mount before Hampton could counter the order, galloping down the road and disappearing into the trees. The day was proving to be a greater challenge than he had expected. He peered back toward Netherland Tavern again. The angry crack of gunfire hadn't diminished. For however calm he was able to keep his nerves, it was an ill-gotten sign. Now his son galloped into harm's way. He busied himself with urging a squadron from Wright's Brigade forward into the dense foliage. "Come on, lads."

"They'll flank us," shouted a captain.

"Flank 'em back," Hampton retorted. They rushed toward the left flank which still sounded as if they'd upset a hornet's nest.

Minutes later, Preston came thundering down the road, his hand on his cap as he galloped. He shouted as he closed in. "We got Yanks in our rear!" He brought his horse to a halt. "They're fighting over the baggage train!"

Hampton held up a hand. "Tell it to me slow."

"The Yanks are crawling over our baggage train. I'd have to say at least a regiment, maybe two. Got our boys captured in the center, stealing our wagons."

Hampton sucked in air through his nose before an uncommon anger took him over. His eyes flared with brute violence directed at the men around him. "Damnit all to hell! How on earth did they get behind us? Where's Fitz? Where the hell is that man!" Hampton thundered like a twelve-pound Napoleon smoothbore. *This was our trap. We were set to snare them. Now, they are in our rear? Damnit!* The rage of battle grew in his belly as water over a dam, the kind of frenzy that spewed from him when he was in the thick of a fight, sending men back to God before their time.

Members of his staff glanced away. Butler's horse sidestepped as if Hampton's words hurt its ears. Even Preston's eyes went downcast as if his father threatened to use the rod on him. If only Hampton had the ability to use the rod on Fitz Lee and squeeze some semblance of urgency in the man. He composed himself after a moment.

The situation was beyond dire. The sudden shift in tactical positioning almost disoriented him. *To the front and the rear. Have the hogs ensnared us instead of the other way around?* It was better to not question why, but to accept that this in fact was the current disposition. The Union forces were to his rear, and he risked being enveloped in part or whole by the enemy. If it was only a token force that carried away his baggage train, it was also an utter failure, and his corps would be weakened most likely beyond repair. They would be forced to operate as partisans and guerrillas and cease to be a credible army in the field.

"You're sure, Preston?"

His son paled a hair at being questioned. There was hurt in his eyes. Hampton moved his horse closer, not caring for his feelings. "Boy, you better be for goddamn sakes sure." He reached out and grabbed Preston's coat. "This entire campaign might rest on how sure."

"I spoke with Captain Hines. He said it was Michigan Brigade."

"There's no time for doubt. You're sure?"

Preston nodded feverishly. Despite being a strong young man capable of easily lifting a sack of flour over his shoulder, he cowered before the old grizzly bear. "Yes, Father, I swear it."

Hampton released him. Preston's jacket still crumpled where Hampton had gripped him. His son tugged his jacket straight, embarrassed by the exchange. There was fear there too, but he was afraid to make much of a display of it, his pride rankled by his father's outburst. Hampton reached his hand out again, and Preston shied away from him as a beaten child. He adjusted the young man's collar, smoothing it straight. "You did well riding quick."

Preston blinked back fear, shame, and anger. "Of course, General. I only did as I was bid."

"You did. Well done. Now, let's deal with this threat. We can attack the enemy in detail." He pointed at Butler. "What's your closest unit?"

"The Jeff Davis Legion is in reserve," Butler said blinking. He too thought better of angering Hampton now.

"We have to defend the wagons. I want them to charge whoever is there. Then move the 6th South Carolina and the Philips Legion down the road here to secure your rear." He pointed to his aide, Lowndes. The man moved his horse closer but kept his distance. "Get to Fitz. Tell him to make all due haste. We need his men here now." He turned. "Preston."

His son gulped. There was fear of another tongue-lashing coming his way yet an air of determination about him.

"Get to Rosser. Tell him to hem them in from the east."

The enemy thought to encircle him. *Well, they have another thing coming.*

Chapter 17

Morning, June 11, 1864

Hampton's Wagon Train, Near Trevilian Station, Virginia

Brigadier General Custer trotted onto a crossroads. The Fredericksburg Road ran north, ending near the point at which he stood. Somewhere farther north, Merritt and Devin battled through whatever resistance Hampton could throw at them. It shouldn't take his counterparts long to break through. It would become even easier when Hampton realized he was pinned between forces.

Gordonsville Road intersected Fredericksburg Road, running east to west. On the northeast side of the intersection sat a seemingly lofty two-story tavern. A few hundred yards away rested Trevilian Station, a newly built single-story depot with the sides made of rough-hewn tan maple, but the thing that truly made him smile was the sprawling camp south of the intersection filled with wagons, mounts, and crawling with his beloved troopers. *Dear God, it's Hampton's entire train.*

He peered around the wagon train bivouac. What a prize indeed. Almost four-hundred rebels sat under guard. Over a thousand spare horses, every bit of supply the Confederate Cavalry Corps managed to scrounge together for a campaign, ambulances filled with the sick and wounded, and all of it within his grasp. He reached up and smoothed his mustache in glee.

"I want those guns silenced over that way." He pointed down the road. The rebel guns atop an elevated knoll once facing north were being turned to face the direction of Custer's brigade. The Confederate battery would be a problem as they had excellent vantage on the wagon train camp and the road. Eventually it would have to be dealt with or they would risk being shelled with impunity.

"Tell Pennington to hurry his battery here." Visions of a total rout of rebel forces flashed before him. Shelling the bastards from the rear while Merritt pounded them in the front would leave the rebs little choice but to surrender. And without their baggage train, they couldn't sustain any campaign for long.

"Sir," Lieutenant Farrand Stranahan said. His aide was tall with an admirable mustache that stuck off the corners of his mouth, a smart looking kepi settling atop his head. He was a Vermont man and recently assigned to Custer's staff. "Colonel Moore claims he's captured enough mounts to outfit an entire brigade, thousands of rounds, and enough food for two divisions."

Custer couldn't shake the thought of his good fortune. His luck had won him a great victory again and with little loss. It was almost as if he'd had divine intervention. Alger pursued the fleeing rebels. Kidd rode to support. Moore's men secured the camp perimeter. The newspapers would rejoice at such a heroic victory. "Very good, Lieutenant. Send word to Stagg to hurry the 1st along."

Fitz's men must linger close by, yet they were not here. Soon the rest of his division would arrive, and he would present Sheridan with the most golden of prizes, save for the capture of Hampton himself. Yet the day was young, perhaps he could pull that off too. No one could deny his luck now.

"Granger," he said to another aide. He motioned him closer. "I need you to ride to Alger and tell him to return to me when the time is opportune. I want my forces consolidated until we know what is out there."

"Yes, sir!" Granger kicked his horse and galloped off westward.

A plump officer with a gaggle of staff, extra than was necessary for his position, pushed a struggling mount toward the general. Custer eyed Colonel Moore with relative distaste like the man was the embodiment of a walking bloody flux. He had always been Custer's least favorite regimental commander from the very beginning of his brigade command. While the 13th had developed solidly over time, his respect for Moore had not. He noticed the colonel had added an ostrich plume to his hat, reminding Custer of a decorated Thanksgiving turkey parading as a peacock.

"Colonel Moore."

"General," Moore said with a deplorable smile on his pudgy cheeks. He made a swooping hand gesture as if he were a circus showman in a previous life. "I give you the enemy's baggage train."

Custer eyed the rebel cannon in the distance turning their guns. "Your men did well to capture the camp."

"I must say they followed my every order to a T. Good planning. Took the initiative. Exploited the enemy's weakness. They never saw us coming." He knifed a hand this way and that, describing his flawless battlefield commanding.

Custer doubted every word. *He must have a quality captain under his command.* "When is the last time you spoke with your supporting regiment?" Custer asked.

Moore's mouth shook as he struggled to stop speaking about himself. "I don't know."

"You don't know where the 5th Michigan is? You're not supporting him?"

Moore glanced at his staff in anger. "Where is Alger?" he yelled at a prim and proper captain.

"I don't know, sir. He rode through like a lightning bolt." He looked over his shoulder. "Went down the road there." The captain pointed along Gordonsville Road.

"I know he went that way. I want him back," Custer snapped. "We need to consolidate our forces. We've given the enemy a grievous blow and I intend to keep it." His eye danced toward the rebel battery. In the distance, he made out hazy gunners prepping their artillery piece. *They could cause us some grief before this day is over.*

"I have their flag, General," Moore said, holding up the rebel colors like a prized fabric spun with gold.

Custer nodded, taking it. *I doubt you Colonel Moore had a lick to do with this victory.* "It's a fine take, but I'm going to need your men to take that cannon before it creates too much havoc."

Moore squinted his eyes. "Cannon?"

Fire burst from the cannon's mouth and a shell whistled overhead. Moore almost fell from his saddle. His staff flattened overtop their mounts. Custer could tell from the sound that the projectile wasn't going to be close. They always aimed high for the first few rounds. He supposed it depended on the crew and how fast they readjusted.

"By God, those bastards are firing down on us!" Moore exclaimed, securing himself with his reins.

"When Kidd gets his men up, shift to the depot and start forming a barricade over the road. I want those guns cleared."

Moore blustered, spit forming in the corners of his mouth. "Of course, sir." He pointed at a captain with an alarmed look on his face. "You lead them!"

***

Wolf's men ate as quickly as possible, ravaging the rebel supplies with the expedience of veteran troopers. His first action as a company commander had gone exceptionally well. He'd secured coffee and food for his men at the enemy's expense, and on top of that, no one had been wounded in the attack. As a regiment, they'd crippled the rebel's supply chain, and it wasn't even noon yet.

Wolf drank his coffee a bit faster as an artillery shell screamed overhead. The lull wouldn't last forever, but as long as they had situated themselves next to the rebel prisoners, he doubted they would fire upon their own men. He wouldn't have said he didn't flinch when the shells exploded with earth-shaking booms that sent shockwaves over one's body. A man could never really not flinch. To Wolf, it was the body's involuntary attempt to save itself, but a certain amount of conditioning in war changed that.

"Rebs are hungry for revenge," Lowell said.

"Not as hungry as they're going to be tonight," Munn said. He hefted a sack of flour and tied it to his horse. He patted his horse's rump. "An extra five pounds of flour and bacon, a bag of sweet potatoes, and a sack of onions. We'll be eating good for the rest of the week." The company cook's mount appeared more like he was using it to peddle food stuffs than ride to war.

Sacks and bags dangled from every part of the saddle, overlapping his saddle bags. Every man had hefted everything of value they laid their hands on, tying everything to their mounts.

Nelson eyed the sky. "Bastards would rather destroy their own food than let us have it."

"Cockeyed bastards by the looks of it," Adams said. The cannon boomed again. The shell screamed closer to the camp but struck trees near the other end, shaking limbs and decapitating leaves from branches.

The wagon next to Wolf splintered, leaving a dime-shaped hole. He crouched down. *That shot was close.* His men took cover behind wagons and tents. Wolf peered out. Smoke hung in the woods, surrounding the nearest side of the rebel wagon train bivouac.

Wilhelm knelt next to him, a carbine appearing in his hands in a blink. "Sharpshooters?"

From the trees, snaps and cracks echoed and bullets sang their angry song. "Secesh bastards want their camp back," Wolf said. He eyed his coffee, that delicious black liquid that they'd fought to acquire, and for a fraction of a second, he contemplated ignoring the rebels shooting at him and finishing his drink. But self-preservation won out and he begrudgingly tossed it on the ground.

He grabbed his Spencer carbine from over his right shoulder where the men carried them when not in use. He aimed down the sights. Scanning for movement, flames and smoke burst from behind a tree. He settled his sights there and squeezed the trigger, returning fire. "You want coffee. You drive them off."

His platoon spread out along the perimeter, using wagons as cover and exchanged fire with the rebels in the trees. He spun off the wagon's corner and limped to the next wagon covering Lowell and Nelson. "Lowell, run to the other side of camp and find 2nd Platoon. I want them back. There's plenty of other boys to watch the road."

"I will," Lowell said.

"Hurry."

A bullet twanged as it struck a metal tin cup over the campfire, knocking it into the flames below.

Lowell sprinted through the encampment, his carbine in one hand, his other hand over his hat. A few minutes later, he returned with Simpson's platoon. His men raced for cover. Their carbines quickly added their weight to the fight.

"Where's Captain Corby?" Wolf asked Wilhelm. The entire regiment should have been within the camp, but in the chaos companies had been separated losing communication with each other.

"Don't know."

"We need support."

As if to answer his call, troopers from the 5th Michigan galloped back into the camp from the west in general disarray. Bloodied men held their wounds tight. Horses jumbled together their riders; they held no military formation. The road quickly clogged with riders and wagons as the brigade's teamsters drove the captured wagons away from the front line, which was quickly encroaching upon the encampment. Gunfire crackled from the north near the Netherland Tavern as a battle raged for the guns on the knoll.

"Hold your positions, men. Steady now," Wolf said. The pressure of leadership weighed upon his shoulders. Only minutes before, they'd been sipping coffee and eating the enemy's rations even if the tack was filled with weevils. Knowing the secesh bastards would sit down at the end of a long hard day without a morsel of food in their hungry bellies overshadowed by a hasty retreat was enough to lift even Kent's spirits.

The war had taken an almost easy tone that had quickly disappeared. They lacked clear orders as the rebels showed the semblance of a backbone. "We have to hold until we can liberate our prize." He walked behind a wagon with his back bent, his leg aching beneath his brace. "You want coffee tonight. We hold these rebs back." He knew they needed orders, or they would risk isolation and destruction at the hands of the rebs.

"Wilhelm. Hold here. I'm going to find Moore. Perhaps the rebs do want a fight."

Wilhelm gave a stiff nod. "I'd rather they didn't." He stood tall and fired his carbine one, two, three times before taking cover again, and Wolf clambered atop his horse. "I'll return."

Chapter 18

Late Morning, June 11, 1864
Gordonsville Road, west of Trevilian Station, Virginia

Brigadier General Thomas Rosser held a pistol in one hand, the reins to his mount in the other. A disorganized mob of Union cavalry galloped his way, and Rosser waited as they approached. He licked his lips with anticipation, a wolf finding his prey charging in his direction. His tongue found the tobacco in the side of his cheek and pressed hard, squeezing out flavorful juice.

While he was surprised to run across them, his gut was awash with relief. He had been itching for a fight all morning and was disappointed that Butler was getting to have all the fun. And like most battles, he had found himself in harm's way and didn't regret a second of it. He spit a glob of tobacco juice from his mouth.

He gave a shout to the 35th Virginia Battalion troopers, affectionately nicknamed "The Comanches," around him on the right side of the road. "Seems those Yanks up ahead are lost!"

A chorus of coyote yips and wolf howls loud enough to rival Indian war chants erupted from his men's throats. The 11th Virginia picked up the yell on the left side of the road. They didn't want to miss out on a fight either. He counted on that.

The Yanks couldn't hear him over the thundering of their hooves, yet maybe they could. Perhaps the rebel call to arms pierced their hearts and souls like a canister shot from a dozen paces, shredding their courage and forcing them to bleed out fear.

The lead rider's eyes enlarged into two silver-dollar orbs as the ranks of men grew closer. It was the realization that the rows of rebels deepened with each stride, yet it was too late for him to retreat.

"Let's have some fun!" Rosser shouted and ground a spur into the side of his mount, aimed his pistol, and screamed, "Charge!"

His men surged forward as if they were wild cats chasing brave rabbits. Men gave forth their battle cry. Rosser managed to tongue the tobacco in his cheek extra hard as he galloped, its juices giving him a bit stronger ecstasy buzz in his brain. *Sweet battle, how I missed you*, he thought. He kept his pistol angled high and didn't bother to aim until the Yankees were close.

Pistols coughed smoke around him. He added his weight to the haphazard volley from his men. The trooper across from him swung a saber as he passed, and Rosser ducked his large frame near his mount's neck. He pointed and pulled the trigger as he penetrated the Union ranks. His pistol sang its brash song again and again until it was empty. He shoved it into his belt and drew his secondary revolver to the din of battle.

More of his men forced their way into the Union lines, and the blue troopers began to turn tail. They clearly didn't expect his men, and panic ruled them as a master. "We have them, boys!" Rosser fired his pistol into a Union trooper's back, and he screamed, clutching at the wound while trying to stay in the saddle.

Lieutenant Colonel White wedged his horse near Rosser's. He was a diminutive man with a stringy goatee and gaunt cheeks, a man you may overlook until he stuffed a knife in your belly. He was a veteran of the border wars in Kansas and a true Southern Son. "You want us to run them down?"

Rosser watched them flee, half galloping away in a cloud of dust toward Trevilian Station and the rest scattered among the trees. Horses jumped like deer through the thick forest. "Skittish fellows. Didn't want to fight for long." He glanced at his men reforming. "Well done, boys! Got 'em running."

With pursuit came the greatest victory in captured men and gear, but most importantly, it damaged the enemy's morale. He also knew walking headlong into an even larger force of Yankees could spell disaster and reverse all that was gained. Yet in the distance, the swirl of clashing men danced in a ballet of death. Gunfire cracked like breaking tree branches.

"Hold your men, Colonel."

"Form back up," White called at his regiment. Horsemen guided their horses back into a battle line.

"There's fightin' ahead. Union coming from that way." Rosser tongued the tobacco again, reached into his breast pocket, and removed his plug. He ripped off a hunk of the reddish-brown compacted leaves with his teeth and jammed it into the corner of his mouth with a willing tongue.

In battles like this, he would leave the same wad in until the fighting had passed successfully, piling more and more in until some of his men thought his cheek resembled one of the hot-air balloons the Union army were known to scout the battlefield with from the sky. A hot-air balloon was a most unnatural contraption for battles, but it was something the Union thought they could use to outmaneuver the rebels in the field. Made for proper target practice for the artillery.

"There's an enemy ahead, no doubt." He spit fresh juice. "I'd love to slam right into them but two things. One, they either broke through Butler and arrived that way or they came from Fitz's direction. Neither's good, and we could find ourselves in a pinch if we hit at the wrong point."

"So you want to wait?" White said, tugging at his reins.

"I didn't say that, now did I?" Rosser said in his thick Texas accent.

"No."

Rosser thought back to every battle he'd fought in. "The way I figure it, if those boys are here then our line is in danger of breaking. Don't take a scholar to see that." He spit the sweet juice. "We run these boys right back where they came from and we'll figure it out from there." He paused, licking his lips. "I want the 11th rounding up those boys we just ran off. White, the Comanches are with me. Let's set these Yanks a running!"

They galloped toward Hampton's headquarters, the Laurel brigade, some of Virginia's deadliest horsemen in the field. He could vaguely make out blue-uniformed men swarming over the wagon train near Trevilian Station. He grinned when he saw a blue and red flag with crossed sabers on it. *Fanny, you desperately ambitious fool.* From a distance he thought he might be able to spot the golden-haired dandy.

His friend and rival from West Point, George Armstrong Custer. A real rabble rouser and general delinquent that one. Just the man Rosser would be friends with. Although he would have bested his friend in class rank at West Point had he graduated, the two of them were not exemplary examples of West Point pride. Nothing like the Marble Man, Robert E. Lee, but he would never know. He resigned from The Academy two weeks before graduation and was commissioned in the army of the newly formed Confederacy, while that dandy, Custer, had his court-martial rescinded. Both men found their way into the war's opposing sides. He remembered the day they parted ways right after the war had broken out.

Both young men were all grins and strong handshakes to determine who would give in first, each man knowing that they may face one another in the future. It had been the talk of The Academy as the country barreled toward permanent division, and it appeared to be the best time to be attending West Point. One had an assured chance to lead in the field, except about half the men there would go on to fight on the opposing side.

George Armstrong Custer had short hair then and was clean shaven. They all wore gray cadet uniforms. He always had a mischievous smile that matched Custer's rambunctious demeanor and poor classroom work. They would drink together in the nights and challenge one another to races, wrestling, and feats of strength. The men competed against one another in every event that could be contrived by a young man's mind.

Striving to win every contest with or against your comrades was the nature of The Academy. Little did the young cadets realize that they would be competing against one another in the field using tactics that may have been better left for the last war. Fanny had excelled, perhaps because he hadn't learned a damn thing through all those lectures. Rosser utilized a gritty frontiersman attitude toward fighting and stretched the principles taught to fit his men's needs. And that's exactly why he was here now leading these men. *Let's see what you've learned since we last met.*

"Comanches, these bluebellies have failed to leave out the appropriate pickets. Let's make 'em pay for it," Rosser growled. He spurred his horse and galloped toward the wagon train's camp with a rebel yell.

Chapter 19

Morning, June 11, 1864
Near Trevilian Station, Virginia

Wolf weaved through the nearest wagons and found his horse. He patted her side for a moment to ease her fright at the gunfire and pulled himself on top by the pommel. From the saddle, he had a slightly better view of the encampment.

Union troopers still led captured rebels toward the center of the camp. Elements from the 6th Michigan arrived in companies and squadrons. Companies of the 13th were spread throughout the bivouac. In the chaos, he struggled to make out the different commands.

He scanned the camp for the regimental colors. A bullet whizzed past overtop his head, and he ducked down a few inches. There near the rear of the blue-coated Union troopers, he spied a blue Michigan regimental flag with an eagle in the center and a plump Union officer nearby. *Must be Moore.* He took a heel and pressed it into his horse's flank. "Git up now."

He trotted Sarah toward the rear where he found the unmistakable Colonel Moore on his swaybacked horse. The colonel's staff of at least ten officers and orderlies surrounded him. Wolf was familiar with most of them, a gaggle of geese with about as much military sense. Captain George Harmon, the diminutive sharp-nosed son of a lumber baron from Detroit; Lieutenant Brian Macks, the owner of a well-to-do grocer from Lansing with the body of a laborer, thick hands, and a plain face; Lieutenant Robert Fleming, a close friend of Wells and a college graduate, slender with a drooping brown mustache. All of them were Wolf's peers in name only.

"Sir, Lieutenant Wolf, sir," he said, walking his horse in front of Moore.

Moore frowned in his direction. His gelding moved uneasily beneath him. Hooves darting to the side, it was clearly skittish from the sound of the gunfire and the weight it was forced to bear. Moore's lip raised as he spoke. "What do you want?"

Wolf blinked. "Orders, sir. We are engaged to the south. Plenty of rebs in those trees."

"Plenty of rebs everywhere, Lieutenant. I don't know what you want me to do about it."

"What are our orders?"

"I've been very clear. You are to hold your position while our reinforcements are shifted westward. I don't see why you need me to hand-feed you everything." A Confederate shell screeched like an attacking eagle before popping near the south of the encampment. Moore unnecessarily covered his head with a white-gloved hand. His lip shook. "Get back to your unit."

"Sir, we will not hold forever."

"You will hold as long as I tell you to hold." Moore raised his chin a fraction.

"Yes, of course, sir."

Moore continued on, ignoring him. "When the enemy wagon train is secured, we move west toward the depot." Moore's close-set eyes narrowed. "You shouldn't even be in command."

Wolf thought the same thing about him.

"I have half a mind to give your company to one of my staff here." He glanced at his officers. They looked about as skittish as their commander, a general uneasy demeanor surrounding them. None of them spoke up or asked to take command. Moore eyed all of them quickly. "But alas, I need all these men here with me." He looked at Wolf again, venom and disdain dripping with every word. "Soon enough we will assign an officer in your place that deserves to be there. Now leave me be. We have regimental business to conduct."

"Yes, sir," Wolf said with a snarl. He spun his horse away from the inept colonel. "Goddamn that man. He'll get us all killed." He trotted his horse back across the camp toward his men. He adjusted Sarah's reins to avoid a dismounted trooper leading a captured rebel toward the collection point.

Thunder rolled across the land like a barreling windstorm and Wolf glanced upward first. The sky was a cool slate, not near dark enough for a thunderstorm, yet the sun threatened to break through the cover and cook them all. Then his ears perked up at the yells and whoops of an impending attack. *What now?* He was soon answered as gray and brown clad horsemen poured into the camp from the road.

A company of reserve troopers from the 6th spurred their horses to meet them. Soon the crash of sabers sounded akin to a hundred blacksmiths in a forge combined with drummers snaring out a pistol tune. Dismounted Union troopers ran for cover behind wagons and trees, shooting at the rebels as they blurred by.

Wolf heeled his horse's flanks, dodging through a cluster of running troopers with carbines in hands. "Come on, Sarah!" he called to her. He crossed the center of the encampment, dodging fires, wagons, and men alike. The rebel prisoners stood, trying to steal a look at their allies sweeping into the camp like devils in gray. He should have seen it coming before it happened, but he was too focused on reaching his men. He was too focused on the stupidity of Colonel Moore.

It took only a moment's hope before the prisoners made a break. The nearest ones jumped their guards. A cluster of rebel men tackled a trooper, pummeling him with balled fists and sticks. They wrestled the carbine from his hands. Another rebel wielded a log from a campfire, clubbing a Union man from behind with a spray of embers. Fleeing rebels raced to all corners of the camp, a flock of sheep on the lam. They rushed past Wolf, and he used his horse to keep them at bay.

A towering Confederate with a great blond beard grabbed at Wolf as he passed, his arms large enough to bear-hug a horse to the ground. His comrade threw a rock at Wolf's head. It blurred through the air and pain exploded in Wolf's jaw as it hit him, forcing him to yank Sarah's reins. His vision jostled then turned into bouncing stars. Angry hands leapt for him from below, burying themselves into his waist and shoulders then he was dragged from his horse.

The ground came too fast to do anything but grit his teeth. Everything blurred in a rush. His shoulder was the first part of him to crash into the earth. His eyes refused to focus, and his heart beat the inside of his ribcage in a ragged panic.

A hand grasped for his pistol, fingernails tearing at the leather. Wolf scratched at it with fierce desperation, ripping a finger to pry away its grip. Indistinct angry faces rushed past his vision. A fist hit him in the face. Not the first time he'd been hit, hardly the hardest either. The hand swung for his head again, and he jerked to the side. Breezing by Wolf's head, the knuckles slammed into the ground. The rebel screamed in pain, gripping his wrist.

He blinked getting his bearings, orienting his eyes. A huge foot stomped down near his head. He rolled and a prisoner dove for him. He kicked the man square in the groin, forcing a pig slaughter squeal from his lips.

Wolf rotated on his knee and used a wagon to pull himself to his feet. As soon as he was standing, two hands squeezed his shoulders like a bale of hay about to be tossed. *Ah shit.* He was lifted off his feet and slammed onto his back. Air was forced from his lungs as if he'd taken a sucker punch to the belly.

Gasping for breath, he fended off strong hands. The rebel grasped for his pistol, and Wolf pushed down on the weapon's handle to keep it in his holster. His vision flickered with the rush of a fight. Black spots peppered his vision. His other hand instinctually ran along his belt.

The rebel growled in his face and punched Wolf, rocketing his head off the ground. Wolf's vision clouded in response. His heart beat uncontrollably in his chest, and his hand fell upon the hilt of his long knife. He drew the blade in an underhand grip pushing the knife between them. The weight of the man pierced his own belly. He shot upright with a yell, putting a hand on his stomach. "You bloody Yank!" He looked around, but his comrades scattered on the run. "You bloody Yank!" he shouted again. Wolf flipped the blade around into an overhand hold, jabbing at the man.

The rebel fell back into a wagon, pushed himself straight, and disappeared into the camp, holding his belly. Another man stepped out, grabbing for his knife, and Wolf punched him with his other hand, cracking the fellow's nose. The man tumbled on his rear. He scooted backward and sprung onto his feet into a run.

Chaos reigned as the prisoners made for the mounted men while others held their hands toward the sky, shouting. "Don't shoot here, boys."

"Not us!" More rebels scattered into the trees.

A squadron of blue riders galloped, sabers flashing in the air toward the incoming rebels. Yet more gray horsemen piled into the encampment. The forces intermixed with no clear line of battle. The camp had degraded into a shamble of chaos. Blue and gray mixed together in a deadly pool of capture and be captured. Kill or be killed. Men who once held prisoners were now prisoners themselves. Pockets of blue chased pockets of gray and vice versa.

A rebel horseman in a brown hat and dirty gray coat pointed a pistol at Wolf. His face wrinkled in consternation. "Yield!"

Wolf drew his Colt and the man shot, dirt jumping into the air near Wolf's feet. Smoke puffed from the barrel, and Wolf capped his pistol three times as the rider drew close, not bothering to aim. The rebel yelped and clutched his side, riding past. His horse led him through the camp.

Wolf breathed. *I have to reach my men.* A bugle sounded out the tune to retreat. *Was that for my men? Whose orders were those? Moore's? Custer's?*

He scrambled atop of Sarah. It didn't matter. The camp was being overrun, and his men were in danger of capture. He spurred her back in the direction of his troopers and almost ran into them. Wilhelm had the men ahorse, and they were fighting their way back toward the opposing forest line.

Wolf spun his horse, joining his sergeant.

"What are our orders?" Wilhelm asked, his mustache fluttering.

"We're to hold the camp."

Wilhelm's mouth twisted beneath his curled mustache. "There is no line to hold."

"Eastern edge of camp." Wolf pointed back the direction they'd traversed. "To the fence there. We'll assist any men regrouping on the road."

Wilhelm gave him a quick nod. He approved. Wolf didn't need his approval to give orders, but it sure as hell helped knowing his sergeant was on board. Wilhelm called quickly to the men. "Rally on the road. Dismount with carbines in the trees."

Chapter 20

Morning, June 11, 1864
Near Trevilian Station, Virginia

Custer's jaw dropped as more rebels poured from the road into the camp clearing. He hadn't expected such a strong response so quickly from the rebs. It couldn't be coincidence. *Have they laid a well-planned trap for me near Trevilian Station?*

The sight of the enemy flag made his belly fill with joy and dread. *The goddamn Laurel Brigade.* The command of his friend and rival, Thomas Rosser. Yet he still refused to believe it. The regiment in the lead was particularly partisan in appearance, they wore almost as much stolen blue uniforms as brown and gray. Their standard was a Confederate battle flag with a blue X on a field of red with white stars, reading 35th Virginia Battalion in white lettering. Another squadron of mostly gray troopers rode on their flank, more than enough men to make him nervous.

The rebel horsemen galloped into a company of the 6th Michigan, scattering them like a pile of sawdust in the wind. Then rebels began enveloping the camp as if they were a gray cloud covering the moon in the night.

A large dark-haired man led a squadron directly for Custer's staff, every man still standing flatfooted. "Can't be," he said under his breath. Standing his ground, and impervious to his well-being or danger, he squinted at the rebels swarming through a segment of the 6th. He lost sight of the man as the whole scene quickly degraded into a mass melee. He watched one of his men get shot through the skull, his head kicking backward with a spray of gore. Troopers from the 6th darted for the trees amid the chaos.

The battle sang to him like a Siren from the sea. It lured him closer to her powerful and deadly embrace. Ignoring the battle raging and the bullets sailing his way, he sat even taller in his saddle. He was already a tall man; sitting atop a horse and stretching one's neck seemed like a bad decision, especially within range of an easy pistol shot. Yet he couldn't help himself. He had to be sure if the man was, in fact, his dear friend.

"Git up," he called to his horse, walking closer to the maelstrom of battle. His staff nervously followed without contesting him. He drew his revolver, holding it skyward as he scanned the fight. Like a gray ghost, he caught a glimpse of the black-bearded officer. In a wild rage, the officer emptied his pistol one way and then the other. "Thomas Rosser, you big dumb Texan. Fancy seeing you here."

The men around Custer ducked their heads. Their horses danced nervously as the fighting surged closer like a tornado of blades and bullets. Bullets whistled as they flew around him.

"Sir, orders?" asked Lieutenant Stranahan. He stayed cool under pressure and Custer attributed his calm to having once been a sergeant before being promoted. *The cream always rises to the top.*

Custer wrinkled his nose after losing sight of his rival. He adjusted in the saddle, trying to come by a better look. He pointed at the fighting, thinking he caught a glimpse of his man. Sabers swirled and clanged over and over again as if they tried to turn their swords into horseshoes. The wave of gray grew encroached. The men's eyes were fiery rain buckets, filling with the lust of battle.

"You see that man. Right there. The grizzly riding a horse?" He pointed again. The black-bearded fiend disappeared into the flashing steely mist of the melee.

"Yes, sir?" Stranahan said, a frown forming beneath his bushy mustache.

"That is Thomas Rosser. My best friend from The Academy."

"Yes, sir," his aide said, a confused and startled look on his face.

Another bullet twanged as it passed. Custer didn't move. Something reached up and bit him on the arm. He frowned. It was a searing pain yet nothing to deter his focus still trying to make out his friend in the melee.

"Sir?" Stranahan said.

"What?"

"I think you've been hit." He stared at Custer, his mouth slightly agape. "Look."

"Nonsense," Custer said, ignoring the piddling concerns of his aide. "Sergeant Beloir, hold those colors higher. I want to make sure old Tex knows I'm here."

The color bearer lifted the flag into the air. "Wave it about now. We have pride in our unit." He waved at Stranahan. "Send whatever of the 6th is in reserve in there. Drive them back." He spurred toward his reserve elements still coming along Gordonsville Road.

His other aide, Lieutenant Granger, gaped at him. "Sir, your arm."

Custer felt it now. It stung and refused to stop. The pain wasn't near as bad as he'd been told. He looked down at his right arm. He took his left hand and began to feel the most painful spot. His finger found a hole in his coat and threaded through it.

"Sir, you've been shot."

"Nonsense," he said, but a queasiness filled his belly anyway. His fingertip felt the skin, poking around the edges. Everything was still intact. He showed his bloodless hand to his aide. "See nothing to worry about. Not even a flesh wound."

"Lucky break, sir."

A reserve squadron of the 6th Michigan added their weight to the fight led by Captain Birge. They blunted Rosser's push with metal, horse, and flesh. The fresh spear of blue staggered the screaming men in grays and browns.

Bullets continued to whistle around them. No telling if it was the men in blue or gray that shot in their direction. A Union trooper brought his saber into the shoulder of a rebel, the bone cracking under the blunt trauma. The Union trooper seized as a bullet struck his breast. He dropped his sword and clutched his chest. A horse screamed, rearing on two legs, tossing its rider backward. The man called out before he was trampled under the hooves of other riders. The shod hooves shattered his limbs and his cracked bones. Custer glanced at his color bearer. The flagpole in his hand dipped.

"Higher, Sergeant! We'll show Rosser the men holding him at bay are mine." Custer grinned with delight. There was nothing better than going up against a formidable opponent and having them be your friend. A man whom you knew intimately the ins and outs of his life. A man you had learned how to anticipate. A man he could write to when this was all over, or a man that he would share a drink with while they chatted about the time when who bested who. The same as in The Academy when they would test each other's worthiness with any means of competition from how far one jumped to who climbed the fastest. Today it would be whose men would carry the day. The flagpole thudded as it fell to the ground. It didn't roll, only rested in place, his standard crumpled and lifeless.

"Beloir, what's wrong with you man? I said higher."

"They got me?" Beloir said, holding a hand to the center of his chest. "Can't be, sir."

"What do you mean?"

His personal standard bearer held out a white glove for Custer to inspect. Shock washed over his face, his eyes growing wider and his mouth open. Wet crimson stained the glove as if he'd taken a handful of berries and smashed them into his palm. "I think they've killed me."

"Surgeon!" Custer called back at his staff.

His standard bearer toppled from his horse, joining the fallen flag. Custer jumped down, crouching next to the sergeant. "You'll be fine now, old chap."

"Sorry, General. I stayed up as long as I could."

"You did a fine job. A fine job indeed." Custer grasped his hand, ignoring the blood from his man. The sticky liquid bound their hands together. He turned away calling at his staff. "Surgeon!"

Two men came with a stretcher and laid it next to the fallen sergeant. "Straight to the brigade surgeon with him. No delays," Custer ordered. The privates nodded. Custer helped them hoist Beloir on the cloth stretcher. The two privates picked him up, holding the handles at either end.

"I'm sorry, General, but I think I must go." Beloir grimaced in pain, his complexion much shallower than it had been.

"You'll go nowhere. I'll see you at camp tonight. You've done well." Custer's words made the standard bearer give him a grim smile as he gritted his teeth. "Go!" he yelled at the privates, and they jogged back to his wagon train.

Custer stepped near the fallen flag. It was cut with swallowtails and was half red on top and blue on bottom. A set of crossing white sabers was in the middle, and a list of battle names sewn on the flag. The flag was wrinkled and folded in disarray. He bent down and picked it up. He ran his hand along the cloth, brushing it off. Blood streaked the blue part. He remounted and handed the flagpole to his aide. "Until we find another color bearer."

"It's an honor, sir," Granger said, but after watching the last color bearer dying in the dirt, the lieutenant appeared more nervous than honored.

"You'll be fine. Beloir rode with me for over a year with not even a scratch."

"Of course, sir."

"Can someone find me Alger or Kidd? How far off is Stagg?" he demanded of his staff. His line was stabilizing with Rosser's. Now fire picked up from the north, raising with intensity. "Butler that one-footed bastard. Shift the 13th to face them." He was getting boxed in quickly with nowhere to go.

A chubby colonel with an entourage fit for the president came from the rear, Stranahan riding alongside. "Sir, you were looking for me," Moore said.

His aide glanced away as the colonel spoke, his mustache giving a fierce shake.

Custer largely avoided the colonel. "I was not." Then he saved a glare for his aide.

Another rider joined them. "Lieutenant Snyder, sir, 1st Michigan. The baggage train is blocking the road. We're stuck behind them along with the 7th."

"Get the train out of here. We need support to hold what we have. I need the train moved to the rear."

Moore's face lit up. "Sir, I would be honored to lead such a vital movement."

Custer cocked his head. The colonel was looking for any excuse to remove himself from the front. He wanted to reach out and slap the man, but perhaps he could rid himself of two liabilities at once. "That is a most grand idea. You may lead my baggage train and all of our captured wagons to the rear."

Moore smiled. "It would be an honor." He turned to a captain on his staff. "Captain Harmon, you will command the regiment in my absence."

The small captain held the appearance of a young boy playing soldier. "I will do my best," he squeaked.

Custer had no doubt who the captain would be looking to for tactical leadership, yet somehow, he thought it better than having the coward Moore leading a regiment. "Hurry now. We must make room for the rest of the brigade." He glanced at his aide as Moore turned around, heading back to Gordonsville Road. "I said Alger or Kidd, Lieutenant Stranahan. Not Moore."

"Sorry, sir. He was the only one I could find."

Custer peered back at the fighting. Dismounted rebels from the woods to the west now engaged his men in the camp, stalling any headway that the 6th had made against Rosser.

"Fetch me a rider with a fresh mount."

Granger nodded at him. "I can go, sir."

"No, you carry the flag today." Custer pointed. "You. Snyder."

Snyder drove his horse closer. "Sir?"

"I need you to ride to Sheridan. Tell him we are in Hampton's rear and under pressure. Please send support immediately or advise orders."

The man nodded. Turning his horse, he rode into the woods north.

"Haven't heard a damn thing all morning," Custer muttered. "But our luck holds," he finished with a tepid grin.

Chapter 21

Mid-Morning, June 11, 1864
Near Trevilian Station, Gordonsville Road, Virginia

Colonel James F. Moore of the 13th Michigan trotted his horse beside the elements of Hampton's captured wagon train. It had combined with the brigade's wagons eastward along Gordonsville Road. Each step he took, the farther he got from the battle raging near Trevilian Station, allowing him to relax sliver by sliver. Some men were better suited to lead from the rear and belonged on the major general's headquarters staff. Men such as himself.

Presenting the captured wagon train to Sheridan, he could take full credit for the entire endeavor. After all, it was his men that captured the rebel camp. He could leave out the part about that upstart Lieutenant Wolf leading the charge. None of the battlefield bravado and heroics actually mattered. What mattered was standing alongside the right man when he rose to prominence. Being a sound and true friend to the major general by supporting him with kind words and a friendly ear were the way forward. He'd been working on Kilpatrick before his sudden fall from grace. Now it was Sheridan's turn. Yet Custer always seemed to see through him. Perhaps the Boy General perceived him as a threat. The greatest enemies were once that resembled yourself. More than likely, Custer sifted through all the pleasing and ego stroking to see his true intent. Either way, Moore had appraised Custer and he was not destined for great things. His commanding general was too brash and naive. No, other men would go further, and it would be essential that Moore followed them to the top.

He recognized a guidon of the 1st Michigan. The blue riders split around his command, pressing their way through the thick underbrush along the road. The drivers slowed their approach to accommodate the brigade's rear guard.

"Slowing down. That's not right." Moore raised his voice at a group of passing riders, grizzled and bearded men, veterans of dozens of battles, the very best the brigade had to offer. "Out of the way!" he said with haste. "Make way!"

The troopers eyed him as they passed, neither diverting any farther nor acknowledging his vehement shouts.

A clean-shaven captain with narrow-set eyes, a beak-like nose, and a floppy red necktie finally called at him. "Careful that way, Colonel. We seen rebs in those trees."

They keep getting younger and younger. Never even seen this man before in my life, yet he speaks like an equal. Probably hasn't even seen a lick of combat. Tell me to be careful, Christ. Someone should teach him to tie a tie. He waved his arm ahead as he spoke, "We're going to the rear. Keep the wagons safe."

"Which way's the rear?" the young captain said with a chuckle. Without waiting for a response, the captain led his men around the wagons and westward toward the rest of the brigade.

"This way," Moore muttered to himself. He continued walking along at a slower pace, his staff members around with him. The densely packed trees surrounding the route were pressed close enough together to remind him of a box of cartridges, however not as neatly spaced. Vines scrawled over tree trunks like frozen brown snakes. Fallen scrub oak and pines laid upon their upright brethren as wounded men in battle would. Everything was shaded green as if it were a wall of fauna built to keep them on the road. The Virginia wilderness was enough to suck the soul from a man, steal the life from him at every step. The men had grown used to hating it. Damn terrible ground for cavalry.

They drove against the tide of spread out companies, passing each one. Then the wagons came to a halt. Moore sighed. *Goddamn 1st Michigan.* He spurred his horse to a trot toward the front of the column. "Why've we stopped?"

The teamster in the front wagon straightened on the rear left horse. His wagon had become the Union standard: powder-blue painted exterior, red interior, chocolate red wheels, and lamplighter black paint on anything metal. There was no space for a driver to sit on the wagon, so he would ride a horse at the rear of his team. Although from time to time, one would see a driver sit upon a crate if their load was light so they didn't have to drive from horseback.

The driver was a civilian, and he made over twice as much as an infantry soldier for only driving. He had a piece of grass stuck in the corner of his mouth. "Which way we going, Colonel?"

"To the rear. Carry on."

The man dug a finger up and underneath his brown floppy hat and scratched long and hard. "Which way's that?"

"Down this road."

"Well, as far as I recollect, we came down that path over yonder this morning." He sucked on the piece of grass as he nodded toward it.

Moore eyed the narrow track. He recognized it. A long single-file line on a trail hardly fit to be named a road. The tree canopy engulfed the dusty, heat-baked path with some much-needed shade. It would take a long time for the wagon train to rumble along back to the safety of their old camp.

Alternatively, they could travel by this well-trodden road that ran beside the train tracks and then cut north by more accommodating means. It would be faster; it must be much faster. The quicker he reached Sheridan, the quicker he could take credit for this day's success.

"We go straight east then we will cut north. Stay on Gordonsville Road."

The teamster wrinkled his brow, eyeing the way ahead. "Seems that there were rebs this way earlier."

"Does it?" Moore stared at him, anger bubbling in his belly. The teamster had stubble outlining his face and intelligent eyes. Just enough intelligence to be a problem for a commander. Moore pointed back toward the station. "The rebs are that way."

"Weren't they out skirmishing this morning then?"

And why is this man daring to test me? He's an insignificant wagon driver for Chrissake. "They were, but that has passed. We go this way unless you want to end up in that mess back there."

"I don't reckon I would, but I think we should go on down the old path. Seems safer."

"Nobody is asking for your opinion, *teamster*," Lieutenant Macks said angrily at the driver. "Mind your place."

Moore nodded to his subordinate pleasantly. Macks was as dependable as he was loyal. Maybe he'd continue to employ him after he was promoted. The man laundered Moore's clothes, holding them to an exceptional standard. "We go straight. Your commanding officer is giving you a direct order."

"Custer be my commanding officer."

Macks drove his horse near the teamster. "You insolent prick." He reached for the driver, and the driver shifted out of the way, holding out a hand. "I only state the obvious."

"Who do you think put me in charge to lead this baggage train to safety? Custer."

The teamster nodded. "Yes, sir. I'll carry on forward." But his words lacked any real respect. He flicked his whip over the backs of his horse team. "Come on now," he called at them in a pleading voice counter to any kind of command as if he wanted the animals to choose the way forward.

Moore let the infuriating man lead his wagon followed by the next and the next. Each one rolled past, wheels turning, whips flicking the air like hissing snakes. With no brakes on the wagons, they were slow to start and slow to come to a halt. "Insolent bastards. How dare they question my orders."

He walked his horse next to a wagon, contemplating a way to assert his authority back over the teamster. "Flogging is a bit extreme. However, disobeying orders."

"Would you like me to place him under arrest, sir?" Macks asked.

Moore waved off his aide, wavering his head as he thought. It all depended on how he wrote the report. *We were in a battle when the man questioned my explicit orders. Men's lives were on the line.* In the scales of his mind, the argument shifted. *Perhaps it's better if I let it go. You won't have time for that when you are on Sheridan's staff.*

He grinned at the thought, looking down at Custer, that golden-haired fool. It was only a matter of time before he got himself killed. If Moore had Sheridan's ear, perhaps the brigade would fall into his capable hands. His grin widened. Moore's Legendary Michigan Brigade. The best of the Army of the Potomac's Cavalry Corps.

He imagined himself on parade out in front of the White House. Old Abe Lincoln in his back suit and tall top hat watching Moore ride past. Medals hanging from his chest, so many they would clink against one another as he rode. Giving Lincoln a salute. The president nodding his thanks on behalf of a grateful nation. It would be a wondrous thing. Articles would be printed in the newspapers of his grand victories.

But the war would end. One way or another. Moore really couldn't care less who was the victor. He wanted to win, but if the Union didn't or if they signed a peace treaty, it mattered little to him. Either way there would be plenty of opportunities for a man such as himself. He was well-known and well-liked by the other officers, Custer excluded. Many of these men would go into politics and a favorable impression in the press would drastically increase the chances of getting elected. He imagined himself living for part of the year in Washington, D.C., rubbing elbows with the rich and famous from around the country, making decisions for the well-being of lesser citizens. The benefits were a thousandfold, but with great gains came an abundance of work. He thought for a moment. Perhaps an appointment would be better. Then there would be no need to compete in an election.

What I need is a position that I can acquire through network and goodwill alone. The president's cabinet? There would be a ton of drudgery there especially if the North didn't win the war. *Hmm. Ambassador?* Now that was a position he saw himself filling. He smiled as he thought about it. With lavish dinner parties at palaces and haciendas, it was more of being an entertainer than any real craft. *Perhaps somewhere down in South America? Or better yet, France?* Frankly it didn't matter much as long as the status and the money was real enough, and the social functions exciting enough. The negotiations would be second nature to him. Socializing was his forte, and if he didn't understand the language, who cared? He could eat and drink with the best of them. They'd learn to speak his tongue before long.

A faint sound pulled him away from his thoughts of fame and glory and riches. It was the call of a pack of wolves, primal and skin tingling. He peered into the forest. Lush and vibrant green growth stared back. The clops of horses, mules, and oxen continued with the creaking of wagon wheels as they rounded repeatedly. He shook off the shrill sound of animals until the wagon train came to a begrudging stop.

He glanced at Macks. "That insolent son of a bitch. Go deal with him."

Macks gave a broad grin, his plain face filling with malice. "It would be a pleasure. Should I beat him for disobeying orders?"

"No, just get him moving by any means necessary."

Macks spurred his horse, turning into a fleeting cloud of dust.

A young waif drove a carriage and a colored servant girl sat next to him. Unlike most of the wagons in the train, this was a covered buggy and had once been a symbol of a wealthy man's status in society. Formerly, it had been painted a rich black and polished to shine in the sun with leather-covered seats and hanging shades. Now, the paint was chipped and the shine worn away. It was dilapidated and leaned to the right. Trunks and bags hung from the back as if the owners carried everything they owned. Behind that was Custer's personal baggage wagon.

The colored servant gave Moore a haughty glance and he recognized her with a glare of disgust. That godforsaken slave woman Eliza Brown was never far from Custer's belongings, keeping an eye on everything and ensuring the general was well-fed. She was around so much that Moore and others thought that perhaps Libbie wasn't enough to sate the general's appetite for women, so maybe he used the guise of hired help to conceal his sinful deeds. No one could prove it, but that colored woman had the loyalty of an impassioned lover.

That godforsaken teamster. I should have ordered Macks to beat him. When you let them grow in disobedience, they are harder to beat back into line.

Galloping riders in gray thundered past, whooping like a native war party. Moore gaped at them his jaw to his chest. He locked eyes with a nearby wagon driver seated in the rear of his team. "Do something. Shoot them," he said to the driver.

"I ain't got no gun. I'm a civilian."

"You do something," Eliza chided him. The damn presumptuousness of that colored woman combined with the rebels froze him in place as if he'd grown roots. The colored woman dug around behind her, removing a pistol. "You get down, Johnny," she demanded of the boy. The young boy scrambled from the carriage and disappeared into the trees.

Moore's mouth shook. A few members of his staff drew pistols, heads darting around in panic. They faintly called to him in the background, but he'd lost all ability to hear them. Another platoon of rebel riders pounded down the other side of the wagons. A driver fell from his team, a bullet having punched his breast with grim and bloody detriment. His team bolted for the trees.

Eliza had a pistol. *Where had she found that?* She held it with two hands and fired. A horseman toppled off his mount and rolled into the trees. His staff fired around him. Fleming spurred his horse into the trees in one direction. The other men followed, spurs raking their mounts. Moore could only sit atop his horse, turned into a statue of indecisive fear.

"Someone's got to get word to the general!" Eliza said.

Moore stared in a daze. His mind couldn't function under such stress. His eyes were unable to focus, his vision crowding itself around the edges. Rebels weren't supposed to come from this way. They were all in the other direction. That meant that Custer, no more than a couple miles away, was surrounded. His rear was flanked. The situation must be even more dire than he thought.

A few teamsters attempted to turn around. Their wagons and horses struggled to turn without running into one another. This led to a jam of yelling men and nervous working beasts. A wagon tipped into the trees. Animals screamed in panic as they toppled down, kicking their legs. A man cried, pinned beneath a wagon. Moore scanned the chaotic train of blue wagons then the mishmash of captured rebel wagons for a way out. Only woods surrounded him. His hand never once went to the pistol on his hip. *Safety. I must reach safety.*

"I'm riding for Sheridan," he said to the driver of a wagon. He didn't bother to look to see if he acknowledged him.

Eliza half stood, pistol in her hands, and shouted at him. "You're going to leave us? What about the general?" She fired her pistol again and the hammer clicked, the gun empty. She tossed it in the back of the carriage.

"Someone will get him word. Stand your ground. I will return with reinforcements," he said with about as much emotion as a telegraph machine. He spurred his horse into the woods.

Her voice, laced with venom, trailed after him. "Coward!" But he was too far away to decide if she was calling him a coward or someone else. *Must be someone else. I am riding for help.*

Limbs scratched at his face. Gunshots blared from the wagon train. *I must reach safety first then we will send men to rescue the train. Nothing can be done if I am captured. Yes, it is the best course of action. Really the only action. Evade capture.*

He was so composed with his own internal thoughts he didn't catch sight of the branch swinging in his direction. It caught him right in the belly, knocking the wind out of him and unseating him like being struck with a lance in a jousting tournament. He fell onto his back, the ground sending shuddering pain through his body as if he'd been the bell and the limb an angry monk sent to ring him.

Trying to catch his breath, he rubbed his leg where his sword and scabbard broke his fall. He let out a whimper, his belly trembling with pain. Gunfire and hoots still engulfed the wagon train as if they were beset by a wild gray fog. His mount bolted through the trees, jumping high over a log.

He pushed himself to his side, and his breath came back to him in fits and starts. "See you in hell, you mangy beast!" he called after it. He never liked the dumb animal anyway. It always gave him a queer look every time he climbed in the saddle as if it were annoyed with him. *It's a godforsaken beast of burden. Could they even think?* He used the young branches of a tree to pull himself upright. One snapped, and he fell back on his rear. He shook his head, exasperated with the tree's insolence and hooked his arm around the trunk. This time he was able to stand.

His sword lay nearby, bent in half at a 90-degree angle. He unbelted the unwieldy item and tossed it to the side. "I'll get a new one," he said aloud.

The forest all looked the same. He knew if he was on this side of the road, then he faced north. He needed to head that way and hopefully find Sheridan's headquarters. Probably better on foot. Anyway, it was easier to hide.

He wiped the leaves and dirt from his uniform then reached for his pistol. It was still on his hip. His thick fingers fumbled with his holster and unfastened the securing strap. His hand caressed the smoothness of the handle. That flamboyant dumbass Custer was always harping about wearing arms. For the first time, Moore had a moment of nervous comfort, washing over him with its touch.

A wheezy voice stopped him before he even took a step in that direction. "Now what do we have here?" A hammer cocked and Moore dared a glance down the barrel of a pistol.

A shabby-looking man pointed it at him. His clothes were little better than rags. His big toe stuck out from a hole in his shoe. His coat was torn and frayed along the edges. His shirt was held together by worn out white-linen fabric and soiled with countless stains. "I'll be takin' that pistol from your hip that you unlatched so nice." The rebel reached over and tugged out the revolver. "Looks like I bagged myself a proud little piggy." The rebel let out a wheezy cackle of a dying train engine.

"I am Colonel James Moore of the 13th Michigan. I demand to be taken to your commanding officer."

His captor ignored him. "Hey, Stuart," the man called over. "Got myself a colonel."

New men on horses steered toward them. They turned into rebels wearing faded gray coats, their pistols held in the air, their mounts skinny and on the verge of collapse.

"Well I'll be damned. A full bird himself," said the lead rebel with a thick brown snarled beard grown long in an attempt to cover his harelip.

"Wants to be taken to our leader."

"I demand it as granted to me by the rules of war," Moore asserted, but every word required even greater false bravado and courage. *Stay brave. You are a man granted status by the virtue of your fine breeding.* His lip wouldn't obey him and assumed a slight tremor.

"Rules of war. What's that?" said one. "I only answer to God." He nodded fiercely. "And he has blessed the South with his most righteous cause."

"I demand safe conduct as dictated to prisoners of high rank. Gentleman."

"There be seven things the Lord hates: prideful eyes, a serpent's tongue, hands that shed the blood of the innocent, a wicked heart, feet that make haste to run to evil, a false witness who breathes out lies, and one who sows discord among brothers. The way I see it, you're every single one and deserve neither mercy nor respect by virtue of the Lord."

Moore gulped and found his throat parched and dry.

"I say we put the fat little pig on a spit and roast him," said the closest rider.

The three men laughed, and Colonel James F. Moore pissed himself.

***

Brigadier General Custer and his staff stood mounted behind a freshly built clapboard fence. It had probably been rebuilt from the last time the Yankees had come south to burn Southern infrastructure and cripple their ability to make war. While the day had started with a great victory, he'd been driven away from Trevilian Station, his lines stabilized near Netherland Tavern. More or less he'd ended up almost where the day began, only with more compacted lines.

His perimeter had shrunk considerably to accommodate the pressure from the rebels to the north and west. He'd consolidated a significant portion of Hampton's wagon train and sent it to safety along with his own wagon train, giving his troopers space to operate freely to any sorties from enemy troops. They'd already repulsed two charges from the north.

Captain Pennington sat mounted with Custer's staff. The lanky artillery captain made a long target for rebel sharpshooters. His kepi rested low over his eyes and he nervously spied one way and then the other. His guns had been unlimbered in multiple positions, wherever the fighting was the toughest to stiffen up the defense.

Two faced north, another on the western flank, another on a small hill behind them that gave them reliable coverage on the western perimeter. Most of Pennington's guns were 3-inch Ordnance Rifles, but he also had a battery of 12-pound brass smoothbore guns under his command.

The Ordnance Rifle was capable of accurately shooting a shell over a mile away, and with Pennington at the helm, they could hit within a few feet of what they aimed at. Custer would be willing to wager his friend Rosser fifty dollars Pennington's crew could put a shell within two feet of where they aimed. In fact, next time they met, he might see if Rosser would take the bet.

To his right, railroad tracks rose on a cut through the land vital to the rebel war effort. He spied down the prone ladder-like locomotive route toward Pennington's guns. *God bless that man.* He had been wise to have the horse artillery close to the front of his column during the march. They paid huge dividends, holding sizable sections of the field under their deadly watch.

Another one of Pennington's other guns boomed a few hundred yards from the rear. They targeted the road to the north, keeping the rebels from amassing for another charge upon the 5th Michigan. *Where is Alger?* That man better not have gotten himself killed, but the possibility greatly unnerved Custer. To lose a friend was an ugly thought. A pang of worry fluttered in his gut for Rosser. Although the man was a rival in an enemy uniform, he was still his friend. While they would continue to try to best each other with men, bullets, and blades, he never once wanted to think of the man as a cold corpse.

A rider galloped to him and stopped. "I have a message from Colonel Stagg." Sweat poured down the man's stubbly cheeks, his wavy hair stuck to his head beneath his forage cap.

"I assume he will be arriving with all due haste?"

"He is as quick as he can."

The 7th Michigan had already piled into the perimeter, and Custer had been forced to use them to reinforce his battered lines. That left the 1st Michigan as his only unengaged regiment despite having skirmished with the rising sun.

"And?"

"The 1st is heavily engaged along Gordonsville Road."

"Engaged?" Custer turned, looking back from where they'd come from. "To our rear?"

The courier glanced that way nervously. "Yes, sir, to the east."

"By who?"

"Appears to be Lomax and Wickham."

"Fitz Lee's boys." Custer massaged his mustache.

His field of battle just became even smaller, and his escape route had all but disappeared. It was some of the worst news he'd received all day. "Damn it all." He removed his hat and wiped his brow. He shook his head, staring up at the sky. The sun had won its contest against the clouds, the hot ball of flame beating down on his men without mercy. It had already burnt away the morning mists, drying out every drop of morning dew. It was as if the sun wanted to burn them into ash while the rebels tried to ground them into dust. The day had begun with an easy victory and now it would be hard fought to just come out on top.

"Anything else?" Custer asked.

The young man looked away. "The baggage train is gone."

"What do you mean gone?"

"We were unable to recover it. It was last seen riding straight into the rebels." The courier peered at the ground with renewed interest.

Heat rose to the surface of Custer's cheeks, battering his pride. Victory slipped through his fingers with every passing minute. The whole reason to hold his position and strip Hampton of his supplies and horses meant nothing if it was back safely in their hands. He peered behind him then back at his men holding a tight perimeter. He was at a loss finding the words to say to the junior officer. "Tell Stagg to hurry into our perimeter."

"I will, sir" the aide said and tugged his reins back around.

Custer didn't bother to watch him ride. The enemy was all around him. He peered north past Netherland Tavern. *They will break through and link with us. We only need to buy time. Hunker down and give as good as we receive.*

The clapboard fence in front cracked as a bullet struck it. Wood fragments spilled into the air, and Custer jerked his head away. His horse sidestepped. "Where in the hell?" *That shot came from behind.*

Whoops and hoots carried closer from the rear. The crew surrounding the battery half broke out in a run for Custer's lines. Horsemen appeared on the hilltop, their riders' pistols blazing. A man fought them with a rammer, swinging it wildly, then jabbing it like a spear. Another used a handspike to clumsily deflect saber blows, its true purpose to shift the cannon to the left or the right with leverage. Custer puffed his mustache.

"Sir, they're taking one of Pennington's guns," shouted Granger, peering in that direction.

"By God they will." He pointed at men using the fence as cover. "Lieutenant, I need you mounted up and be quick about it."

Chapter 22

Mid-Morning, June 11, 1864
Near Trevilian Station, Virginia

As General Custer issued orders, Wolf realized it was directed at his men. He jumped into action, shouting as he stood, "1st Platoon with me!" He slung his carbine behind his back as he half-jogged. Sergeant Simpson looked at him from farther along the fence. Wolf shook his head no.

He would have loved to have taken the whole company, but nobody knew when the rebels would charge from their positions across Gordonsville Road. If his men broke anywhere throughout the perimeter, Wolf wasn't sure the brigade would hold. Every fifteen minutes, the lines shuffled either forward or backward but almost exclusively backward, the troopers around them forced closer and closer together. The only positive that came from such narrowly enclosed lines was the ability to switch directions and fight the other way quickly. The negatives more numerous. The enemy could shoot you in the back or the front. Whether they aimed at you or the men behind you didn't matter. They were a herd of pigs in a pen ripe for butchering.

He took the reins from Goffman. Every fourth trooper stood with their horses while they were dismounted, further diminishing their defensive abilities. "Mount up." Wolf said. "We're taking back that gun from those reb bastards."

"Where?"

"Behind us."

Goffman nodded, eyes glaring in that direction before climbing into the saddle.

Custer and his staff halted their horses nearby. He had eight staff members around him including his color bearer. A paltry squad of men at best. Air puffed through his mustache as he scrutinized the battle surrounding the cannon. "Hurry now!"

Wolf's men mounted in a rush. Pistols scraped leather and sabers hissed over metal scabbards then glinted a dull gray in the sun.

"Those boys are trying to run with our gun! And we ain't going to let 'em," Custer yelled at them. Wolf's men responded with a rousing cheer. Their general spun his horse and dashed for the artillery piece. The men spurred their mounts, racing along behind. Custer's locks flowed behind him like a golden guidon leading the way.

The cluster of twenty troopers and their general surged over a field with brown sedge toward the gun. The fleeing gunners cheered them as they galloped past, raising defiant fists in the air. "Get it back, boys!"

Their horses' hooves rumbled the ground with fierce speed. The rebels atop the hill saw them coming now. Gunsmoke puffed from pistols. Four rebels had tied their horses to the gun's trail, lifting it into the air so it wouldn't drag in an attempt to wheel it away.

Custer whooped with glee as they drew near. Every man there had seen bravery on the field of battle, but from a general that level of brashness was unheard. It filled Wolf's belly with pride, and he pushed his horse closer, wanting to match his commander's love for battle. Wind and bullets washed over them, unable to bring them down.

They crested the hilltop at a gallop, dirt tossed in the air behind them, and the melee began in haphazard fashion, as men began to fight in ones and twos. The rebels hadn't expected such a swift response to their assault and hadn't formed a skirmish line.

The men stealing the artillery piece didn't look up as the riders blazed past them. Custer brought down a man leading his horse, and Wolf shot twice before hitting a man trying to force the wheel on the other side.

Two Union privates sat with their hands on their heads as prisoners, blood trickling down their cheeks. One artillerist scrambled on all fours for the sponge staff and started to pummel a skinny long-haired rebel stealing the gun. He clubbed the man until he yielded, thwacking him over and over with the stick. The other private beat a man with a handspike until he stopped moving.

Wolf turned Sarah, and she tossed her head in response. A rebel with a saber slashed at him, a wide-arching swing. Wolf leaned back and the sword breathed death as it passed his face. He pointed his pistol and capped multiple shots into the man's belly, and he cried in pain. His horse carried him away.

As quick as it was fierce, the battle was over, and the rebels decided the gun wasn't worth their effort. Turning tail, they rode down the other side of the hill and into the trees as if they were a rafter of turkeys on the move.

Custer lined up a shot and pulled the trigger on the retreating rebels. After, he stuck his neck out trying to determine if he'd landed a hit. He holstered his weapon and exhaled sharply. "Well done, lads." He faced his staff and Wolf's men. "You boys did well."

Wolf grinned, eyeing his men. "Everyone accounted for?"

Wilhelm silently counted the men. "Yes, sir."

"Good."

Bullets whizzed overhead, breaking up their excitement. The men ducked lower in their saddles. The rebels had decided to send them a parting gift.

"Looks like they won't give up without a fight," Custer said.

Men in gray, tans, and browns, with rifles and carbines, dismounted along the tree line. A few knelt, taking aim, while others stood against trees to steady their shots.

"Must be at least a company," Wilhelm said.

"Impossible to tell with that thick undergrowth," Wolf said.

"I guess we're about to find out." Wilhelm crouched down, shouldering his carbine and the bullets came faster now. A horse reared with a high-pitched shriek, dispatching his rider to the ground.

The hatless cannoneer pointed at his artillery piece. He was a young handsome man with a thick Irish accent. "Get her rear facing."

Custer grinned at the young artillerist. "A grand idea!"

"We'll need some help, but we can get her firing again," the cannoneer said with a fierce nod.

"What's your name, Private?"

"Kennedy, sir."

"And you?" Custer asked. His imperviousness to the enemy coming for them made Wolf's heart race.

"O'Neil."

Wolf's troopers jumped down from their horses. Nelson grasped the gun's trail and hefted with a grunt, veins bulging in his neck. "Come, Polish friend, heave."

Dan took a wheel and lowered his shoulders, driving with his legs. "Yes," he grunted. Wilhelm and Wolf worked the other side and they shifted the cannon to face the other direction.

"Canister should send them running!" Custer said, standing tall.

Kennedy pointed at Adams. "Hold your thumb over the fuse vent." The trooper reluctantly went about his simple task, wrapping his thumb before placing it against the blazing hot metal. In the meantime, Kennedy tossed a rammer to Wolf and ran to the caisson wagon, digging through a compartment. He returned with a canister shell cradled in his hands. He handed the tin-can-looking projectile with a charge bag on the end to O'Neil. Then Kennedy pointed at Wilhelm. "Run that wormer."

"Hurry, lads. They're getting braver," Custer said.

The rebels inched forward from the trees. Every moment dominating firepower wasn't applied to their pressure, their confidence grew. A horse screamed and went down, one of Custer's officers ungracefully toppling from his saddle.

Wilhelm took the corkscrew-looking end and shoved it down the barrel of the gun. He twisted and ripped it out.

"Now sponge it!" Kennedy said with a point at Wolf. Then raced around to the other side.

Wolf grabbed the sponge rammer, dunked it in a nearby bucket of black water and forced it down the barrel.

"Put some bloody back into it!" O'Neil shouted, still holding the shell. He glanced nervously over his shoulder at the advancing rebels. "An ember will send us to our Lord!"

Wolf rammed the gun barrel harder. The rebels emerged from the trees at a walk, firing as they went.

"Now the dry sponge!" O'Neil said to Wilhelm.

The sergeant huffed as he dried the gun barrel. O'Neil shoved the tin shell inside. Pistols popped from a few of the officers.

Kennedy went about preparing the fuse. He glanced up at Wolf. "Carefully push the shell to the end." He gestured madly at a wooden rammer. "That one, Lieutenant!"

"Charge!" yelled a rebel officer, and almost sixty men sprinted for the hill. Their yell was almost inhuman, rising and falling like a banshee in a moonless night. The officer held a saber over his head, his slouch hat madly twirling as he charged. Like a gray and brown avalanche they came, easily taking the gradual slope to the artillery position.

The rebel yell grew louder as they closed. After pushing the shell to the bottom, Wolf tossed the rammer and went for his pistol. *All their goddamn sticks and procedures.* Bullets twanged around them. "Goddamn!" Custer said, shaking his arm.

Wolf's troopers glanced nervously his way then back to the rebels. "Kennedy!" Wolf cried. "Fire the damn thing!" Wolf didn't care what was inside the gun. Anything would do even if it was only to scare the bastards half to death.

"Almost there," Kennedy said hurriedly. He stuck his tongue out as he cranked a hand knob on the side. "Have to make sure we hit 'em."

Wolf lined up his sights and fired away, thumbing the hammer to cock the weapon each time, always adjusting his aim slightly at the mass of men charging the hill.

"We ain't going to last long without that cannon," Wilhelm called. He shoved his carbine to his shoulder and fire blasted from the barrel.

"Surprised I lasted this long," Kent said. He smudged the black powder from his cheeks. He stood hunched, regretting most of his life decisions.

"Stand back!" Kennedy cried.

Wolf's men stepped to the side. A moment later, Kennedy ripped the fuse cord and the cannon exploded with enough fire and smoke to temporarily blind them. The rebel yell was overcome by the dragon's roar spitting forth from the cannon's cruel metal lips. The ground quaked beneath them as though a cattle stampede had been let loose.

The one-inch diameter balls flew from the mouth of the gun with a ferocity not unknown to man, but one that he should never have experienced in his existence on God's earth. They sprayed through the rebel soldiers with violent indifference, cutting through the men in the first rank only to blow holes in the men behind them, showering the air with flesh and red mist.

The officer leading from the front had the top of his head removed, the ball hitting the man behind him in the neck, knocking both off their feet and into the bloody grass. The destruction was as extensive as it was devastating.

Bodies were thrown backward like a violent gust of wind had taken them off their feet. Limbs were tossed into the air as they were forcibly ripped from torsos. A blond-haired rebel had both his legs detached; he grasped at his knees, unknowing which one to scream at. The man to his right went down with a cry as a canister ball sped through his hand, rolling through his flesh and out his elbow, shattering the bone as it went. Only shattered corpses and the cries of the dying remained in its devilish path.

For a moment in Wolf's head, bells rang. No more pistols popped, or carbines cracked. He scanned the silver screen of smoke for more rebels. The smoke tasted akin to rotting eggs on his tongue, so he covered his mouth with the sleeve of his coat. Rebels ran from the field. Most had their arms wrapped around the fallen, dragging them back to the safety of the opposing forest. What remained on the field, different than shooting a man or striking him with a saber, was an appalling reminder of the war they fought. Grotesque and almost inhuman death laid in its wake.

Shreds of gray and brown clothing mixed in with pink flesh and white bone, staining the grass red. Wolf stared at the horrors of war with disgusted interest. The power of artillery was as soul-shaking as it was man-breaking. He was eternally thankful that it wasn't his men on the killing end of the cannon.

He turned back and glanced at Custer. His aides danced around him, inspecting his arm. The general appeared upset and angry, his cheeks red with the heat. "It's nothing." He ripped his arm free from an aide. "It's nothing. A ricochet, nothing more."

"Sir, as grateful as we are for your men's help, we need the crew back," Kennedy said.

"I'll send them back." He turned toward Wolf. "Lieutenant. Do you think your men can support this battery for the time being?"

"We will, sir. I still have a platoon back at the fence."

"You just sit tight up here until we can shift some of the 1st Michigan this way."

"We will make sure the gun is safe."

Custer grinned. "And I'm sure Lieutenant Egan will repay the favor whenever he returns."

Chapter 23

Noon, June 11, 1864
Between Trevilian Station and Louisa Court House, Virginia

Branches plucked at her clothes as she ran. With a rough hand, she yanked her dress back up to crawl over a fallen log covered in vibrant green moss. Her chest heaved with strenuous effort. She ducked behind a tree trying to catch her breath. *Ain't gonna be a slave again. Nope. I'd rather die.*

She clutched two valises, hers and Custer's, the one he hid all his letters to Libbie in. Out of all his splendid belongings—the fancy coats, the neckties, fine leather boots and gloves, elegant swords and saddles—his wife's letters were the most treasured.

The sound of a horse crashing into the undergrowth, snapping twigs and crunching leaves alike, made her suck in her breath, her chest quivering as she held it against its will. *Dumb Johnnies. Ain't got nothing better to do than chase down a poor colored girl.* Soft thumps of hooves digging into the dead leaf covered floor came closer. She let the air pass coolly through her nostrils as slowly as her rattled lungs allowed.

"I seen ya, girl," came a Southern man's voice. It held both parts command and disdain. "Come on out and no one will hurt ya."

She kept as still as possible, not daring to move even a finger. The man walked his horse past where she hid. The horse was a bony creature, ill-fed and the color of mud. The rider didn't appear to have been fed any better.

A brown dented farmer's hat covered his head. His gray jacket was faded.

Perhaps it had started as a black garment. His beard was patchy and brown. He held a pistol in one hand, his reins in the other. His chin stuck out as he scanned the forest for her. "Ain't no use in hiding. We're all over these woods. There be worse men to find ya."

And there be better men too, she thought. Gathering her skirts in her hand, she made a run for it. She scrambled to the left, her feet tossing leaves in her hurry to escape. "I gotcha!" he yelled at her.

She swerved through the trees, trying to pick the worst path for the man to follow on horse. Thin branches from young saplings whipped at her with pliable limbs. Even the pliable pines took swings at her. Hoofbeats echoed nearby, and she darted to the right, using a large maple tree to create separation from him.

Her heart drummed in her chest. *Not today. Not today.* She stumbled to the ground, but was back on her feet in a flash, ignoring her shaking legs. A branch caught her dress, spinning her around, the turn bringing her face-to-face with the man's horse. She raised the bags in defense, and the beast knocked her backward, sprawling her out in a mess. She pushed herself off her back with her hands, the luggage strewn about. The man walked his horse to her, each hoof hitting the ground like hammers on anvils. "I don't want to hurt ya now, girl." He pointed his pistol at her then slowly cocked the hammer. "But no one is gonna miss a Negro neither."

They met eye to eye. Her mother's words rang in her ears as clear as wedding bells. *"You can't do nothin' if you're dead."*

"But mother, what I did before wasn't livin'."

"Just relax now. No need to be scared. What you got in them cases right there?" He pointed with his chin.

"None of your business, Johnny Reb."

The man raised his pistol in the air, taken back by her remark. "Brave girl, aren't we? Nothing that a good beatin' can't fix."

She stood and brushed the dirt and leaves from her dress. "Ain't brave, but ain't stupid neither. I won't make a fuss."

"Let me have your bags there." He gestured with his hand.

"Ain't nothing but a woman's drawers in der."

The rebel licked his lips, his tone becoming stern as if he spoke to a child. "Don't lie now, girl. You hand it over."

She walked forward and lifted her bag. He snatched it from her and rifled through her clothes as if she were rich. "I told you, ain't nothing but a poor colored girl's things." While he dug, she tossed the other bag to the side.

He looked back at her in disgust. "Ain't nothing in here but rags. Give me that other bag."

"What other bag, massa?"

He tilted his head to the side. "Now, I told you not to lie. I ain't afraid to carve a switch and use it on you."

"Ain't got no bag."

His eyes scanned around. "I know I seen it." His eyes settled. "There. Git it!" He pointed his gun at her. She lifted her hands in the air. He gestured at the bag with his pistol. "Git it."

She brought him Custer's valise and handed it up to him. He flipped it open and started thumbing through papers.

"Letter to me ma," Eliza said.

He glanced at her, his eyes squinting in disbelief. "Don't bullshit me like that. I know for damn sure that neither you nor your mama knows how to read." He shook his head in contempt. "Colored folks that can read."

Her mouth clamped shut while her mind raced to find some other explanation. "I asked one of the friendly soldiers to draw it for me."

He aimed down the dark-eyed barrel. "I told you to shut your mouth, girl. Don't need no more talk from you."

"Name's Eliza."

He raised his eyebrows. "No talk." He tugged out a letter and held it near his face. "Dear. Dear. Autie? Now what in the Sam Hill is an Autie? They mean Auntie?"

She kept quiet, looking away.

"I asked you a question."

"What, sir?"

"What's an Autie?"

"A name for me Auntie. But I can't read."

He sighed and shook his head, reading farther along. Then he eyed an envelope. "Custer? These be Custer's papers?"

She studied the canopy of green above. The leaves rested, unmoving, and flat, untouched by the wind. They blocked the hot rays of the sun like a roof made from a living green shade. The bugs weren't so bad during the day and in the heat. Almost peaceful.

"Hey, girl. These be General Custer's papers?"

"Don't know. Can't read."

"Come on."

She walked back to her bag of personal belongings and hurriedly scooped some inside. He led her back to the captured wagon train. The rebels were in the act of robbing everything they could from both Union and rebel wagons even as they drove the captured supplies back toward their men.

Men stuffed their faces with every piece of food they found. Pockets bulged with hardtack and salted meats. Saddle bags overflowed with tack. Bags of flour hung off saddles. Her captor reported to an officer. She'd been around enough now to understand the difference.

This man had a formidable beard similar to a grizzly bear topped by a black slouch hat, three yellow bars on his collar, and faded yellow scrolls embroidered on his sleeves. His unbuttoned coat revealed a red and white checkered shirt.

"Sir, I got some papers here."

The captain eyed the soldier with suspicion. "So?"

"And this slave girl."

"I ain't no slave," she said.

The captain looked at her. "You sound like a goddamn slave and you look like one, but it don't much matter cause your a slave now. Talk again like that, and I'll cut out your tongue and feed it to the dogs."

Eliza shut her mouth. She hadn't seen any dogs, but she'd also been around enough white men, in particular slave owners and their overseeing ilk, to know when a man spoke with such violent certainty, he meant it. And right or wrong, he would fulfill his promise as held by whatever code of honor drove him. She dipped her chin, understanding his words just fine.

"Here," the rebel said, handing the captain one of the letters. The captain read it quickly. "How'd you come about this?"

Her words came out softer than she would have liked. "Found it."

"No, you didn't. Must be some kind of servant. Get this bag and girl back to headquarters. Fitz Lee will want to see it."

"Why yes, sir!" the rebel exclaimed.

It was a two-mile walk to the rear of the rebel lines. She was taken inside a country manor. Officers in gray hustled in and out of the home, so she knew it was someplace of importance. She kept her head down but listened to everything. The men paid her little heed, as much as they would any slave or servant, but she listened. The rebel that brought her stood proudly, removing his hat and nodding to every superior rebel that passed with a dumb grin on his lips. *Grinning fool.* Yet they largely ignored him as well.

Voices came from a room messengers traveled in and out of. Important voices. "Do you think we're right to remove him today of all days?" came one voice.

"You saw the man. We did what needed to be done. I only hope that it wasn't too late," came a stronger voice, the voice of a man in charge.

"This bloody war is bleeding us of all our commanders."

"It is, but you saw him in his tent. He clearly is not well."

"He's contesting his resignation. You know their family is politically connected."

"Dear God, what am I to do? He's not fit to lead. If he would've accepted a leave of absence and taken the appropriate rest, perhaps he could have maintained his position, but I cannot in good conscience leave him in command of the 15th Virginia."

"I understand."

"I will write him an appeasing release letter. It will smooth the dismissal in the records."

Eliza glanced at her captor. The man hadn't paid attention to a single word. He just stood there, mouth open like a good dog waiting for his bone.

An officer stepped out of the room in a fine clean gray uniform. He had a well-shaped thin mustache. "You may see General Lee now."

Eliza gulped, and couldn't tell who was more nervous, herself or her captor. They walked inside the room together, her trailing behind the man. Two men stood near a table. They turned to eye them with increased curiosity.

One man had a long pointed black beard. His eyes had a slight worried slant to them and bugged out, giving him a surprised look. He wasn't tall but had wider than average shoulders. He had the distinct look of a farmer. The other man was taller than him by about three inches. His eyes were set back in his head and barely open a crack. Neither man was the Lee everyone always spoke about, the one men called Granny and who was supposed to have white hair and beard.

"What do you have for us?" said the officer with the pointed beard. His voice had a hurried impatient sound to it. He was clearly the man in charge.

Her captor stood with both hands on the valise, almost dumbstruck. He rocked on his feet rubbing the suitcase's handle as if it were his pet. "Ah."

Eliza nudged him with an elbow. "Go on."

He glared at her in shock then blinked repeatedly, trying to compose himself.

The taller man stretched his neck to give them a closer look. "Do you have something for General Lee?"

"Name's Jacob Rochester, C Company, 2nd Virginia, sir. We've captured Custer's wagon train and what appears to be a part of Hampton's."

Lee blinked and peered past the soldier. "I know that. Who sent you here?"

"Captain Donnell, General Lomax, sir."

"You may depart back to your unit, Private," Lomax said. Both men turned away and looked back at a map on their table.

As if not willing to concede his time in front of his superiors, Jacob spoke louder, "We captured this here colored girl and this case."

Both men turned back to him, surprised he was still there.

Fitz Lee shook his head. "Why do we care about a colored girl and a case?"

"Here." Rochester held out the case.

Fitz Lee gestured to the other officer. "Lomax."

The taller man strode over and took the case from Jacob's hands. He opened it and started to thumb through them. He pulled one out and his deep-set eyes shifted back and forth as he read it. A lecherous grin spread over his face then he chuckled. "Fitz, look here. These are love letters." He showed them to Fitz Lee. Both men chuckled. Lomax dismissed the man with a wave. "Take the girl and go, Private. Thank you. You've given two tired men something to laugh about."

"Was an honor, sir. Truly was." He turned to her, starstruck. "Come on." He placed a hand on her elbow and led her back through the door until Fitz Lee shouted at them from behind. "Wait." They stopped. "Who is she?"

"Colored girl we found with the letters."

"She was carrying these?" Fitz held up a letter, eyes darting as he skimmed it for information.

"Aye, she was. Tried to escape twice already. Real spitfire this one."

Fitz Lee stared at her. "How did you come by these?"

"Found 'em."

"What's your name?"

"Eliza, sir."

His eyes grew harder. "Eliza, don't lie to me again. How did you come by this?" He held the paper in her direction as he would a sword.

She licked her dry lips. She hadn't remembered them being so dry earlier. All eyes fell upon her like a pack of wolves on an old moose. "I's was General Custer's cook."

The two generals exchanged a look. "Really?" Fitz said. "Private, you are dismissed. Thank you."

Jacob bowed his head and then gave a fierce salute that the two generals dismissively returned. He grabbed her by the arm, and Fitz held up a hand. "Leave the girl."

Jacob wrinkled his nose in confusion. "What you want with her?"

"None of your concern. Carry on and return to your regiment."

The private bowed his head again and departed.

The sudden feeling of abandonment took hold of her harder than before. There was an odd sense of safety with Jacob despite him being the enemy.

"You'll cook for me," Fitz said. "You start today."

"Yes, massa," she said.

***

She cooked all afternoon for the generals, keeping her eyes down and providing a service she did willingly for Custer but now under coercion from Fitz Lee and Lomax. For she was now in all regards their slave, a servant without pay. It did not matter how it was labeled. There was no exchange of payment or freedom of movement. While her duties were almost identical, the burden of servitude yoked her like an ox, having been forced back into service after tasting the pastures of freedom. Her quick-witted banter was tossed aside for behavior deemed essential to surviving enslavement. She kept her tongue silent and her eyes on the floor.

She fed the two men lunch. It seemed odd to her that while their men were out in the field engaged with General Custer, these men dined as if it was an average afternoon supper. She took a tray of salted beef sandwiches into the men and set it on the table.

"It's most agreeable to be out of the saddle," Lomax said. He had loosened his collar and unbuttoned his shirt.

"It is." Fitz Lee wiped his mouth with a napkin. "I understand Hampton's rush to prove himself, but it reeks of desperation for status. You'd think a rich man would have better respect for himself."

"Agreed. The man is trying much too hard to gain Marse Robert's favor."

"Favor you'd think his nephew would have." Fitz Lee's face soured. "Damn them for promoting him to major general before me. We wouldn't be in this predicament if I was the senior general."

Lomax shrugged his shoulders, still holding a sandwich in his hand. "The battlefield is a dangerous place. Perhaps a stray bullet will fly his way today and rid us of his parvenu presence."

"I'd have to be too lucky for that." Fitz's eyes narrowed in self-pity.

"If mine and Wickham's men pressure Custer, we can capture the whole brigade before the day's end. Perhaps it will sway Marse Robert to your cause."

Fitz Lee shook his head. "No, all credit would go to Hampton, and besides, the entirety of his division is in a poor position to make any acceptable effort. We'd only be sacrificing more men and horses for no reason. Apply enough pressure to look legitimate, but let's prepare our men to link with Hampton by circumventing Custer."

"Combining the two divisions will make it a more formidable fight."

"Exactly. Hampton should have disengaged and moved to a more defensible position long ago. Then we could join. He left this gap in the line. He knew our commands were exhausted, but I would have closed the gap if he would have asked despite the toll on our men."

The men continued to sup, and she hovered nearby, hands clasped in front of her. "Eliza, I must say that you are a mighty fine cook. General Custer will be sad to see you go."

"Yes, massa."

Fitz didn't look at her but kept his eyes on the food. "You'll find our camp very comfortable. You just keep cooking this delicious food, and we won't have any problems at all." He shifted in his chair, turning his eyes upon her.

"Thank you, massa." She dipped her chin to her chest as the men glanced at her.

"What is Custer like? Can't say I've met him," Fitz said.

"He's kind." *He pays me fair for my work. He takes care of me and shows me respect. I don't have to ask his permission to marry or use the bathroom. No one could put a price on freedom.* She would take harsh freedom to a pampered servitude any day.

"That all?"

"His feet stink."

The two men chuckled at her, dabbing their mouths with napkins. "The man has smelly feet. Well, I must say most men do," Lomax said, grinning.

Fitz regarded her. "It was one of his men that slew Stuart, was it not?"

"That's the rumor, massa. I wasn't der."

Both continued to stare at her.

"It is a shame. I miss him dearly," Lomax said.

Fitz peered at his food, his face twisting in a frown. "I've lost my appetite."

He waved at her to clear their plates, and she complied with haste. He shook his head. "He went charging off with that Captain Payne, one of Hampton's irregular captains. You know the man."

"I do. Brutal man. I must say a bit frightening of a fellow. Queer look in his eye."

"He is. Glad he's fighting for us." Fitz Lee sipped his tea, his eyes staring off vacantly. "Payne was the last man to see Stuart alive before they were ambushed. Makes a man wonder." His words trailed off to silence.

Lomax frowned, his eyes blinking as he tried to understand Fitz Lee's meaning. "You aren't saying that it was on purpose? Are you? They are loyal men to the Cause."

Fitz folded his arms over his chest and sighed. "Hampton is. All of his businesses are tied to the war effort. Payne has much to lose as well. His family is rich. But those South Carolinians, eager as they are, perhaps superseded their station in the conflict."

"I would agree. Virginia is king."

"We've lost so many of our men to friendly fire. Jackson, Longstreet, Stuart to ambush." He shook his head. "If men are one thing, they are ambitious. Let's just say I don't trust Hampton and especially his dog Payne."

"Well said, sir. We should be wary."

"We should, but we must be allied while the Yankees still stand on our soil."

Eliza took their dishes outside to a well. She hauled water then knelt down and took the plates washing them one by one. Horsemen crawled all over the encampment. Wagons creaked as they rolled through. She eyed every single one, looking for a place to hide. Something that could extradite her from here. Keeping her hands scrubbing, she let her eyes scan the camp. The two officers walked outside and mounted their horses. They galloped away without a second glance.

Her hands dunked into the basin again and again as she washed the plates. Another slave came from the house. She knelt down next to Eliza. "You's trying to leave you best go now. We'll be moving agin tonight. Away from dose Yankees."

Eliza stared at her. She did not know this woman. For some godforsaken reason, she could be loyal to her masters. Eliza couldn't fault her for it if that was the case. It was ground into them from birth to be subservient, meek, and submissive. Their overlords had created and maintained an entire system based on control of her people. It took true courage to stand up against that system. One had to be willing to suffer or die to escape bondage and it took an even bolder person to escape from the center of a Confederate cavalry division.

Eliza didn't care if they caught her again. They could whip the skin from her flesh, but now that she'd tasted freedom, true freedom and respect, no, they would never steal it from her again, not in this life or any other. She held the final card in the stacked deck, perhaps a slave's only true card, death itself, for she was worth nothing to them dead. She could provide no service from the grave. And she'd rather pass on to the next life than endure a lifetime under their rotten yoke.

"Place is crawling with 'em."

The woman nodded, helping her stack plates. "Come wit me."

Eliza stood upright, tucking the bin under her arm. They walked quickly. As they neared the edge of the woods, a man emerged from a path. He pulled up his trousers, securing his gun belt around his waist. He folded one end over the other. The two women stopped, thinking they'd been caught. He glanced up from what he was doing. Recognition crossed his eyes and it turned into suspicion.

"What you girls doin' out here?" he said with a thick Southern accent. He tugged on the back of his pants as he walked in their direction. He planted himself in front of them, scratching at his stubbly beard.

"I's showin' Ms. Eliza where to use the latrine."

"Is that so?" he stepped forward and used a hand to lift her chin. "Now I know you wouldn't be lying to me girl, would you?"

"No, sir. Promise on me mother."

Eliza let out a squawk then loudly set down her plates. "Ohh, it's somethin' fierce." She gritted her teeth using both hands to hold her belly. "Oh, please, it's gonna come quick!"

He removed his hand from the other slave's chin and gave her a look of utter disgust. "Christ, woman."

"I can't hold it in," she wailed.

His eyes scrunched together. "Well, hurry along then."

"I's show her," the other slave said to the man.

He shook his head. "Hurry along now."

The two women made for the small path into the woods. Neither woman ran. They only walked, attempting to appear natural, not a rush in their step.

"Now you follow this pat', leads to a creek. Follow the creek to the right." She gestured with her hand. "It'll lead north to the the Billy Yanks. I's heard them talking about it. They be north of here only a few miles," she said with a definitive nod.

Eliza returned her nod fiercely. She reached out and gripped the woman's hands. "Thank you. I don't even know your name."

"Nelly."

"Why don't you come wit' me? Always jobs around camp. Most dem officers treat us well enough."

The woman shook her head. "No, my massa here. My family south. If I run." Emotions ran over her face, bringing tears to the corner of her eyes. "You know how dey be."

Eliza embraced the woman quickly. "I do. God bless you." She released the woman, hiked up her skirts, and jogged along the path. Servitude was the only option for some. She could never hold the woman in contempt. There wasn't room for it, but for her, there was no path for returning to slavery. No space for it. Back to the general. She stopped at a creek and stepped down into the chilly waters that pushed upward around her ankles and waded north.

Chapter 24

Afternoon, June 11, 1864
Near Trevilian Station, Virginia

The air screamed with lead from every direction. It was an unpleasant and unsettling sound like being caught in a hornet's nest and unable to run away. No place within the Michigan Brigade's perimeter was safe. Wolf's men had fought on every single flank and section of the encircled lines. After they'd been relieved by a company of the 1st Michigan on the hilltop, they shifted back through the camp, finding some semblance of cover along the embankment of the Virginia Central Railroad tracks and joined the rest of the 13th Michigan.

Wolf's men traded potshots with rebels in the opposing trees. And for that, he was thankful they had decent cover. He sat with his back to the railroad cut. From his vantage, he could make out pieces of the blue line on his far right and left. The Union lines were squeezed so hard they almost touched. The rebels would take turns pressuring them with charges and flanking maneuvers, but Wolf doubted they could flank a closed triangle. Every single area was facing a foe with no way out.

"We're surrounded, Johannes," Wilhelm said. A bullet twanged as it hit the railroad tracks above them, and both men adjusted their heads. There was always a fear of a bullet fragmentation carving its way into your scalp.

"There has to be a way out."

"The only way out is to die," Nelson said with a grunt at the end. He half-crouched over the earthen cut, and fired his carbine, and dropped back down. "Fuckers won't stay dead."

Custer and his staff were everywhere, riding to whichever section needed the most support.

A squad of Simpson's platoon was lost in the woods, five men total were missing, and four had been wounded, only a single trooper killed. A rebel sharpshooter hit him from afar, square between the eyes, dropping him like a sack of wheat from a hayloft. It was decided that if one had to go, a shot through the eyes wasn't a bad way. Instantaneous and painless. The company's flag had been planted in the ground just on their side of the railroad cut. Jutting above the tracks, it gave the rebels a tempting target to shoot. No one wanted to be the man holding it laying down, and they needed every man facing out, so it stuck in the ground garnering the bullets of the opposing soldiers.

The company guidon flapped in the wind, a defiant black and red with flashes of gold, cut with a swallowtail to meet military standards. The men of F Company had fought to use it as their standard despite it not being officially assigned by the Cavalry Corps.

"I'm bloody hungry," Nelson added before standing to shoot again. The company cook heard him and scrambled with his back bent down the line. Munn smiled at the large trooper and handed him a hardtack.

"There, Private."

"Not so bad for a dog robber." With angry eyes, Nelson took a fierce bite like a starved man.

"Wolfie, when do you think they'll break through?" Nelson said between massive bites.

"Not while we stand."

"I meant our allies. They been fighting to the north of us all day."

"They will. They must recognize our predicament."

Wilhelm stood and fired his gun and then dropped back down. "We can hope, but I wouldn't count on it."

Wolf prepared to take his turn on the firing line. "Where were they?"

"Saw one by the big tree," Nelson said, crumbles in his beard.

"There's one a bit to the left," Wilhelm added. "I'd say about a sixty yards."

Wolf gave him a nod. Placing a foot on the embankment, he crept as high as he dared without exposing himself over the edge. He looked for the great oak looming on the other side. It was an easy landmark. When one was trying to shoot another man without revealing himself for long to enemy fire, he tried to memorize the scene and where potential shooters may have placed themselves.

Smoke oppressed the tree line with an opaque silver coating. It hung in the air like a windy gray snowstorm, refusing to give up the Confederate cavalrymen with ease. The only blessing of it all was it hindered their vision as well.

Wolf blinked, trying to make out a target. Fire burst from beside a tree trunk. His eyes drifted in that direction. Then he saw a gray shadow slowly reveal itself from next to a different tree, and he adjusted his sights back. He let the sights steady then gently moved the trigger with enough force to make sure he let loose a bullet. The shadow jumped and disappeared, and Wolf flipped around to his rear, cocking his Spencer for another shot.

The extra ammunition was paying dividends now. His men were still well-supplied while other troopers scrambled about searching the dead for ammo. "Munn," Wolf called. The cook knelt down next to him.

"Sir." Dust sprayed the air from the top of the cut and Munn flinched.

"I need you to find Moore and see what our orders are."

Munn nodded. "Yes, sir."

"Munn," he said. The cook turned. "And any food and water you can find for the men."

"I'll see what we can scrounge up. Gotta keep the boys fed."

"Yes, we do." Wolf patted him on the shoulder. The company cook would fight, but Wolf knew that some men were better suited for different tasks. He'd seen men keep loading a carbine or rifle over and over again never firing a shot. He didn't think it was general cowardice. He thought it was something innate in a man to have a primal aversion to taking another life. He didn't think it was possible to still have that in this war where the killing was so personal.

For the most part, the Southerners were the same people. They may have had different beliefs toward some issues, but they spoke the same language, served under the same god, were raised in the same nation. For all intents and purposes, they were brethren. Yet killing another human being had become easier. A certain numbness took hold of the thoughts inside a man's head that reviled the act and said, "Don't shoot your brother."

Other men didn't have that aversion. Men like Wolf and Wilhelm killed men. Wolf found the longer he fought, the easier it became. It was a game where only one could reach the end.

Then there were men like Adams and Nelson that seemed to enjoy every aspect of it. Wolf thought of them as cutthroats, and men like that excelled at war. He supposed he excelled as well, not for love of the act, but for the love of the men around him.

The cook jogged from the railroad, his back bent searching for food and water. As Wolf reflected, he realized he hadn't received proper orders for hours, excluding Custer's foray to recapture his guns. All they'd done is fight. Fight and try to stay alive.

Wilhelm nodded to him. "Good choice. Some men are better suited for the front than others."

"If something happens to Munn, whose gonna make us those flapjacks when this is all over?"

His men maintained a consistent fire upon the rebels in the trees. It wasn't clear if it made any real difference on the enemy or vice versa.

The fighting seemed to slacken, the bullets flying slowing. Wolf dared to hope one of the other Union brigades had broken through. Then a shrill noise pierced his ears. It was loud and stabbing like a bayonet to his eardrums and a sucker punch to his gut. He'd heard it over a dozen times in this war. One only got used to the feeling when that sound washed over you like the embodiment of fear itself. It made your hair stand on end. It bubbled fear deep inside your belly, almost enough to rattle your soul. And if it wasn't so damn hot already, it would make you sweat.

It was the sound of a thousand ravenous coyotes racing for the kill, ready to feast upon the blue-uniformed men. Then again, only men made that noise, no matter how savage they may be. Flesh, blood, bone, and souls. Yet the infernal sound was not of this earth.

Wolf exchanged a glance with Wilhelm. Every man in the company knew what this meant. The fight was about to become very intimate. He rolled to his knee and peered over the slope. Down the tree line, mounted rebels burst forth from their cover like galloping canister shots making for the embankment. They had almost fifty yards to cross before they reached the tracks. They would be upon D Company before they had much time to react.

"Simpson!" Wolf called. "Lay down a volley!"

Simpson nodded, turning to his platoon and barking orders. The men all rushed for the lip of the tracks. They unleashed a volley and saddles emptied, but the rebels weren't to be deterred. As one body, the squadron leaned forward over their mounts. They would take the tracks or die trying. They whooped again. Sabers flashed. Pistols puffed smoke.

But the riders knew that the key to victory was crossing the railroad and driving the men from their cover. Once the men were on the run, they were easily ridden down like dogs or wrangled like cattle. Wolf knew. He'd ridden down those militiamen outside of Richmond. Less of a fight and better described as a slaughter.

D Company didn't unleash a volley until it was too late. Most of the men aimed high and then ducked and dove to the sides as the horsemen flooded over the tracks. Then the howling came from the forest in front of Wolf's men. His head darted from D Company's struggle to scanning the trees. *They're coming!*

"Bastards are coming!" he shouted. "Get ready!"

Gunshots blared and men screamed as the rebel riders overtook men from D Company. It mattered in Wolf's mind, but they had their own problem to worry about now. Dismounted men ran from the forest, long Enfield rifles in their hands. They didn't bother to walk in formation like infantry but covered the ground on the double knowing it would lead to victory. The last thing they wanted was a shootout with a bunch of dismounted cavalry behind cover with their seven-shot Spencer carbines.

Simpson's men drifted from cover along Wolf's left flank. Rebel horsemen slashed down with sabers and aimed pistols at the exposed men. One Union trooper swung his carbine at a rider as he passed, missing, and instead catching a saber atop his head. He fell to his hands and knees, his head pouring blood. The man to his side clutched his breast as a pistol shot hit home.

"They gotta hold until we deal with them," Wilhelm said at his side.

The rebels sprinted over the ground. Wild yells came from warlike throats, hard men coming to send them running.

"Ready!" Wolf commanded.

"Aim low, lads. Let's stop 'em in their tracks," Wilhelm said.

"Aim!" Wolf sighted on a bearded man, his hat flapping as he ran. It was a spacious target made diminutive by his sights.

He snarled as he shouted, "Fire!" His men let out a volley, staggering the charging rebels immediately in front of them. Rebels twisted in the air, jerking into contorted positions before they fell. Others dropped onto the field, never to move again. Yet still more came as they let the fallen lay. A bullet whizzed past Wolf's ear. "Fire at will!"

His men sped up their firing tempo on the charging rebels now that they were exposed, becoming running men in gray, butternut, and brown. The Union guns played a loud and brash song filled with exploding snaps and crackles. Gun smoke wrapped Wolf's men in its bitter-scented embrace, and every dozen yards, a rebel stumbled and fell.

Wolf yelled down the line as his men worked like feverish fiends doing the devil's work. "Keep it up!"

Wilhelm's voice rose above the gunfire. "Seven before they reach us."

The gray cloud of men continued their race for the tracks. Wolf's men fired like madmen, the intensity of the shooting ravaging the charging rebels. Wolf shot one, two, three shots before the men sprinted up the bank on the other side. The rebels let loose a piecemeal volley as they closed.

Private Powers screamed as a bullet bit through his chest, misting red out his back, then falling backward down the embankment. He slid in the dirt before coming to a rest in a pile. Herman Scholtz cursed in German over and over, and his pistol blazed at rebels point-blank until the butt of an Enfield struck him down.

Wolf swung his carbine to his back, his hand clutching the knife at his belt. A gray-coated soldier bounded onto the tracks, his rifle held behind his head, ready to swing, and Wolf lunged for him. They met with a meaty smack, the rebel dropping his gun in the struggle to grab Wolf's torso. Wolf's arm and the blade were trapped dangerously between them, and the man tossed him over his hip.

The rebel loomed over Wolf, his hand scratching for his own pistol. Wolf leapt forward with his knife, but the man's chest burst open like a mushroom of uniform and blood, exploding from the middle. Wolf kept his blade pointed at the collapsing soldier. The rebel dropped to his knees and Wilhelm yanked Wolf upright.

"Thanks," Wolf said. He snapped his arm forward, ramming the knife behind Wilhelm into a rebel's chest. The man screamed and Wolf threw him backward off the blade. He rolled down the embankment clutching his wound. "Consider the favor returned."

Wilhelm snarled a guttural response, aiming his pistol at another rebel. "Matters not, boy! Drive the bastards back!"

More rebels reached the tracks. An officer in a wide-brimmed hat stood for a moment, his eyes glued on the flag. "Grab their colors, boys!" Rebels pressed through Wolf's men, driving them down the embankment. Adams tripped a man and shot him in the back. Another rebel swung his rifle into Nelson's arm, and he bellowed, grabbing the man by the throat and taking him into the dirt. Thick hands strangled the life from him, banging his head off the ground.

Wolf drew his six-shot .44 Colt Revolver in his other hand, hobbling for the flag. A bulky rebel in a brown jacket ripped the pole free and let out a loud whoop. Wolf fired his pistol at him. The man flinched, and his battle cry died on his lips. He turned toward Wolf, blood bubbling from his mouth. An enraged bear, he swung the pole like a medieval pole arm. Wolf ducked down and fired again.

The man grunted, and his backswing caught Wolf in the side. Wolf caught it with his arm and the man pressed it into Wolf, trying to take him to the ground. Wolf's bad leg staggered and buckled, and he went crashing into the dirt. The man raised the flag overhead and Wolf shot him again in the belly. The rebel's face twisted in anguish as crimson poured from his belly like a spigot. His shirt continued to change colors from dirty white to a deep red as he dropped to his knees.

He used the flag to prop himself upright, bleeding out, and Wolf stood, pried the guidon from his grip. The rebel stared him in the eyes before teetering over to assume his place in the dirt.

Wolf capped his pistol at a rebel about to club Kent from behind as he wrestled with another man. Wilhelm punched a man in the face and rammed a knife into his belly a moment later as easily as a butcher at work. Blood spilled from the man's gut dousing the sergeant. Wolf's pistol hammer snapped forward with a glaring *click*. Never a sound he wanted to hear. He shoved his empty handgun into his belt and hefted the flag, racing for the tracks.

The guidon whipped behind him. "To the flag, boys! Hold the line!" He charged the slope, boots digging into the dirt until he reached the top. He planted his feet and set his shoulders. He waved the company standard from side to side.

Color bearers had a short life span in the field. But none of that mattered. All that mattered was that the colors stood defiant in the face of capture. All that mattered was that it flew high and free from enemy hands.

Rebels came for him, men with wide eyes filled with glory and bloodlust. Hands grabbed for him. Knives pointed at him. Wolf gripped the standard tighter. He swung it wildly, jabbing at one man and then another to keep them back. He evaded one gunstock only to be knocked with another on his upper back. The blow sent shooting pain back into his neck. His eyesight starred like Fourth of July fireworks. He staggered, trying to keep his feet.

A man grabbed the pole, and they fought over it. Gunfire popped in Wolf's ears. Men screamed around him, the din rising in volume as a summer storm. The flag rippled blood reds and night blacks, the wolf's head snarling as it snapped its jaws.

Wolf did the same, trying to keep his feet as an officer thrust a sword at him. The point narrowly missed his side. Men in blue surrounded him now, and they drove the rebels back. Wolf kept his feet, feeling the warm wetness running down his cheek. *When did I get hit in the head?* Adams dove past him, tackling a retreating rebel. His hand darted in a wide sweeping measure as he slit the man's throat. The rebel gurgled as he died, splayed over the train tracks.

The rebels ran back for the trees, turning to fire often as they withdrew. Wolf's men watched them from the tracks. All that could be heard was the heavy breathing of exhausted cavalrymen, the cries of the wounded, and faint pops from down the line. Wolf's hands cramped with a tight grip on the flagpole, the battle fury beginning to subside.

Lowell's voice trailed the fleeing rebels. "Run, ya bastards!"

"Fuck your mothers!" Nelson bellowed.

The men let out hearty chortles. Forearms were grasped in the warrior's embrace. Backs were slapped.

Gunfire answered from the trees, breaking their revelry, and the men took cover again below the tracks. Lying on their backs, they let the rebels waste their ammunition in the dirt.

"I thought for sure I was a dead man," Kent said, chest heaving.

Wolf planted the flag back in its place. The wounded around them started to call for help. Men in gray and blue reaching for aid, bodies battered and broken. Now they were all part of the same nation, one of humankind.

Grimacing, Wolf said, "Get these men out of here." He wiped his brow, seeing the crimson liquid leaking from his head.

"You okay?" Wilhelm said. His curled mustache was bent.

Wolf's head pounded in rhythm with his heart. "Fine. One of them caught me good."

"Sure did." He dried the blood again. "What do the men look like?"

Rebel horsemen galloped back for the trees. Simpson's platoon appeared to have been shattered. Half of them were simply gone where the rebels had punched through D Company. They'd been enveloped in that struggle while the portion closest to Wolf had been wrapped into that fight.

"Keep your eyes on the trees," Wolf called out. "They may try us again."

Simpson hobbled down the line and spit as he approached Wolf, head down. "Bloody bastard's horse stepped on me foot."

"How's your platoon?"

"We got a few boys missing. I think they'll turn up. Three wounded, two dead. I got thirteen boys on the tracks here."

"Wilhelm."

"We got six wounded, two dead, one missing."

Wolf wiped the side of his head again, flicking away the blood. "Not many left. About twenty of us."

"Appears that way. A few of the wounded boys can still fight."

Wolf peered hard at his haggard line of men. Bodies of the fallen lay among them, both friend and foe. A Union trooper dragged himself toward the center of camp. A wounded rebel lifted his hand in the air, waving a white handkerchief. "We don't have anywhere else to go. We have to hold the line." Wolf eyed Wilhelm and then Simpson. "Make sure the men know it. There is no retreat."

"Pretty sure they understand that," Simpson said.

A distant rumble turned all their heads as it grew in volume. They peered down the road behind them. Gray riders galloped toward them, shrouded in a cloud of dust. They threatened to split what little terrain Wolf's men held in half, separating most of the 13th Michigan from the rest of the brigade. Their line was effectively "in the air" and they would pay for their poor positioning if action was not taken quickly.

"We have to fall back," Wolf said.

"And on the double." Wilhelm raced for the flag and ripped it from the ground.

"Fall back," Wolf shouted. "Fall back."

His men sprinted from the tracks and over the road. The perimeter was turning into a disorganized circle of blue troopers shrinking inward on itself. Wolf grabbed his carbine. "Fall back." Men ran around him. Others limped past.

Wolf raised his Spencer and sighted in on the leading rider. A big man with a black beard howled at them as he galloped. Every moment they swept closer to the 13th Michigan who already had a hole in its center. The far-left flank was about to be obliterated and rolled right into Wolf's men. At least two companies destroyed. Wouldn't leave much of the 13th. Companies started to flee before the incoming rebels. *Have to buy our boys some time to shrink the lines. Look at this huge bastard leading the way. Men always follow a big bastard. Let's send him a message. We will bend but never break.* Wolf squinted an eye before resting his finger on the trigger.

Chapter 25

Afternoon, June 11, 1864
Near Trevilian Station, Virginia

Rosser raised his saber in the air. It reflected the domineering sun with heavenly light. "We got 'em by the balls, boys!" He'd heard Butler's men rushing the Union line, but his men were behind, and they would attack late. It would have to do. The bluebellies teetered on collapse similar to a wobbly bridge with an elephant lumbering across. This would break them.

The Union troopers were not poor soldiers. They knew when to flee, yet sometimes they needed slightly more encouragement. They fled like a retreating ocean wave before his squadron sweeping them off the tracks. Soon there would be nowhere left to run as their force would fold on itself.

Men would look to the rear and see their brothers staring back in a panic. Realization of their defeat would come quick. Then they would raise their hands in surrender or die man by man until it was over.

Surely Fanny loved his men enough to not allow them all to perish for his vanity? Perhaps. Perhaps not. His friend was as bold as he was and not wise on when to retire. Rosser would encourage him to surrender and take his sword as the white flags and handkerchiefs waved in defeat. Maybe one day he would return Custer's sword. He laughed at the thought. Not a chance.

He would hang that weapon over his fireplace, and when his friends came to his house for dinner parties, he would point at it and tell them about how he bested the General with the Golden Locks and captured his entire brigade in one afternoon. He would have Fanny and Libbie over, and he would show his friend, and it would be a continuous reminder of who the better soldier and commander was.

When this was over, the South would be its own nation and there would be peace between the two peoples. The North and South were two brothers forced to do battle like Cain and Abel, except they wouldn't kill the inferior, no, they would best him, force him to acknowledge the error in his ways, and move forward as a separate kin.

His eyes focused on a single soldier standing in the road. Other dismounted Union men flooded around him, dragging their wounded. Once Rosser's men smashed any resistance near the tracks, they would turn on the interior, pressuring the other sides to fall into disorganization. Not an overly complex strategy, but simple plans were easier to adjust and employ.

His men savored the cool taste of victory as if it were a tall glass of lemonade with ice, filled to the brim. They rode harder knowing that the enemy would soon be vanquished, and a congregation of weaponless foes. Yet a single dismounted cavalryman stood in the road, unwavering before his horsemen. *Brave bastard. 'Bout to be a dead bastard.* "Give them the blade!" Gunfire echoed ahead from the desperate blue-coated men. Bullets whizzed around the riders, but not enough to slow the force of his charge.

He sat tall in his saddle and gave a cheer. "Death to the Yanks!" A surreal moment later, immense pain erupted in his knee like a flower opening its petals to the morning sun. His horse didn't falter. It kept pace, but the gait soon became gut-wrenching agony for the rider. Rosser's sword dipped lower. His stirrup kept his foot in place, but his whole leg felt disturbingly loose, refusing to function.

The man ahead limped off the road and into his camp.

"Dear God!" Rosser exclaimed. His horse continued to gallop. His saber hand swept down to his knee. The immediate urgency to hold it in place gripped him. All the muscle and sinew ready to fall apart and drop to the earth without his heavy hand.

"Carry on!" he cried. "Skewer the pigs!" He steered his mount to the tracks, and his aides trailed behind him. The rest of the command galloped toward the blue line.

His aide, Lieutenant Lafayette, stared at him holding his knee in place. "Sir, your leg."

Pain ebbed through his limb, spiderwebbing with alarming speed up his leg. "By God, I know. That bastard on the road shot me."

Lafayette dismounted. A company of his men thundered past with a yell. Rosser grimaced. "Help me down."

His aide grabbed his arm, and another removed his foot from his stirrup as gently as possible yet far too rough for a man in agony. "Help him down."

They helped him with little grace fall to the ground.

"Stretcher," called Lafayette.

His men stared now as they rode past. Their faces clouded with concern. Seeing a beloved leader wounded could break an army, so he kept his voice strong. "To victory, boys! We have them!" He let his head drop back in the dirt. The pain took his breath away, but he forced himself to sit back up. He raised his saber in the air. "Let none live!"

Lafayette loomed near. "You're going to be fine sir." He turned and peered at the other aide, Henry. "Get me that tourniquet." The man took the piece of looped leather, and they lifted his leg and Rosser grunted. No point in showing any weakness now. They dragged the tourniquet above his knee and began twisting a wooden handle. He snarled when the pain escalated with each turn of the handle. "Keep it coming, Henry."

The aide carried on until the constricting pain was fierce, an anaconda squeezing the life out of his limb, then Henry tied it off, leaving only a lingering pain of numbness in its place. His limb began to fade into an excruciating memory.

Rosser gritted his teeth. "Fine job."

"Thank you, sir. You're going to be okay."

"Let me see it," Rosser said. His leg throbbed with the beat of his heart as if they painfully missed one another. Blood had soaked through his pants, turning the gray trousers a dark shade of red. The fabric was frayed on either side where he assumed the bullet had entered and exited clean through. He clenched his teeth, knowing that his leg had been wrecked.

An ambulance rolled down the road at the gallop and Henry waved them to a halt.

"Okay, sir," Lafayette said. "On three. One, two, three." His two aides hefted him between them, carrying him toward the back of the wagon. They set him butt first in the back and he slid backward into the bed, his leg flopping behind him like a fish out of water. "Damn it all." His breath seized in his chest, and he applied pressure to the wound with heavy hands. "Lafayette," he breathed.

His aide looked at him from the back of the wagon. "Grab me my tobacco from my saddle bag."

Lafayette returned with a paper-wrapped plug, a woman in a dress on the packaging, and handed it to him. He smiled at his aide. "You're a good man, Lafayette. Both you and Henry are. Stay in one piece today. Send word to Colonel Dulaney. He's is in charge now." He gave him a nod and took a bite off the plug of compacted dark brown leaves. "Ain't so bad now." His pain softened a touch.

"Sir, do you want me to accompany you?" Lafayette asked. His eyes creased with fear that his commander could die.

"Absolutely not. You remind those boys that we are proper cavalry. We fight from our horses. You tell Dulaney that. You show that dandy Custer over there the true meaning of cavalry."

"We will, sir."

"Then let's be off with it. As soon as the surgeon gets the bleeding stopped, I will return." He spit as if to mark his words as true. Rosser slammed his fist into the wagon bottom. "Let's move!"

The ambulance turned around and traveled back west. He caught sight of Henry and Lafayette watching him as he was driven away. Lafayette wiped his brow and put his hat back on. More riders in gray joined him as they reformed. "That's it, boys! We ain't done yet!" he shouted at him. But they couldn't hear him over the sounds of hooves and gunfire. He let himself lean against the back of the wagon and sat silently. Fate had a cruel way of derailing your plans.

He spit off the side and eyed his leg that had betrayed him. "Goddamn leg. You can hack it off for all I care! I'll be back. You hear me, Fanny?" But the wagon cared not and rolled him farther and farther away from the battle.

***

Brigadier General George Armstrong Custer sat atop his horse in the middle of a beleaguered circle of his men flanked on either side by his two aides, Lieutenants Granger and Stranahan. It was the toughest fight he'd ever seen. His men were almost shoved upon each other's backs. The troopers were on the verge of collapse. His mind fiercely denied that this could be the Michigan Brigade's last stand. "Never," he muttered to himself. He peered north. A road and dense forest filled with enough rebels and enough trees for a man to go in and never come out the other side. Through there lay the reinforcements. Stalled, defeated, hindered, or oblivious, it mattered not because they had not appeared.

He had been everywhere that needed support, firing his pistol in one way then running to help a wounded man. There was no time for anything else, let alone figure a way out of the mess.

His eyes scanned the north again. There was audible fighting in that direction, not along his own line. *Torbert must know we are in dire need of support. He must. But what if he doesn't? What if his men do not hurry or attempt to link with me? Worse, what if they withdraw, leaving us?*

He pointed at a squadron of 7th Michigan cavalry waiting anxiously to get into the fight. "Plug that gap." He gestured toward the Gordonsville Road where Rosser had again made a offensive foray to break through his lines. The man was as stubborn as he was tall, and Custer never expected anything less.

The 13th had fallen back from the northern perimeter. They scrambled to find cover from the men hitting their left flank in an almost complete rout. The 5th Michigan's Spencers popped quickly into the rebel cavalry, but the mass of men was enough to burst through his lines. The 7th Michigan squadron was the last of his reserves, if one could even call them that at this point. They were the only men not currently engaged. Every time they went out, they came back with a few less.

Pennington's guns were in the process of being turned to face the new threat. Between the shifting around and consistent firing upon the enemy, his gun crews neared exhaustion.

A bugle call sounded from the 7th Michigan's bugler, and they charged Rosser's men. The men turned into a hazy dust cloud barreling toward another angry dust cloud. The cavalrymen struck Rosser's with sabers and pistol fire, blunting them and allowing for troopers of the 13th to scramble into the interior.

There wasn't much more to give. Another forty yards and their perimeter would be flat, exposing the 5th and the 7th Michigan from assault to the north. If that happened, it would be a cascading effect as the 6th and the 1st wouldn't be able to hold their positions. Then they would run every which way trying to escape unless they chose to die in the field, holding every dry inch of contested ground to the last man. It would be glorious and their last. Most of them would finish the day as prisoners.

But it didn't have to end like that. Not if what little luck he had held. To what benefit was luck if it couldn't free him from this mess? The pressure from Fitz Lee's Division was only enough to keep his men in place. Torbert continued to sandwich Butler's and Wright's brigades to the north, the rebels unable to throw the entirety of their commands against his brigade or the rest of Torbert's division. And Gregg was out there somewhere too. If they moved with expedience, Custer's men may survive this unfortunate ensnarement.

A bullet whistled as it traveled overhead, a tiny bird moving too fast to identify. His lip twitched. They needed to be relieved now. *But how to reach Torbert when the enemy was between them?* None of his couriers had returned.

He'd sent one northeast. Then northwest. Then straight north. Only a deafening silence answered him, which meant the forest north was crawling with enemy forces. His stand mattered little if Sheridan and Torbert were not aware they had reached a breaking point. He knew one thing: to the north was the rest of his division and he needed to link with them.

This left him two ugly options. The first one was to mass his force as best he could and drive north. With the pressure from every side, he doubted he could do this without sacrificing most of his brigade to capture before they raced for safety. The other option was to send a mounted spear thrust to punch a portion of his command through enemy lines. He sighed. Either way he paid for it in northern blood. His eyes found a banner with a golden wolf's head on it. He knew the answer was there. The one man that would be willing to pay that price. A man with enough daring and guts to succeed.

Custer turned to his aide, Lieutenant Stranahan. The man's mustache twitched as if he had to sneeze while he watched the fighting. "Find me Lieutenant Wolf." Stranahan nodded and ran for where the 13th Michigan reformed into a line.

He continued to watch his brave boys fight. He adjusted his necktie. Checked his pistol. He would not dismount. It was too important to be seen. His aide returned in a few minutes with a bloodied Lieutenant Wolf.

Custer stared down at him for a moment. Wolf had quite a gash on his head. Blood ran over his eyebrow and down his cheek into his beard. "Are you okay, Lieutenant?"

Wolf squinted then wiped blood from the corner of his brow in irritation. "I'd be better if those rebs would take a break."

"Wouldn't we all," he said with a smirk. A bullet whizzed by Custer and he flinched. That one was close. Never really got used to it. Best to just pretend the bastards couldn't hit a barn. "How many men do you have in your company?"

"Twenty-three in the fight, sir."

"Tough day." Custer nodded to himself; he did not want an answer. He already knew it. Wolf peered him with intensity. "Then again, you are used to that, aren't you?"

"I am, sir."

"I want your men mounted. You're a skilled rider?"

"I can hold my own, sir."

"Even with that leg?"

"Even with the bum leg."

"Very good. I want your command to cut through the enemy and ride to Torbert or Sheridan, whoever is closer, and tell them I need them to break through as soon as possible. Bring everyone."

Wolf turned and eyed the north to south running Fredericksburg Road. Gunfire banged from the forest around it like a kettle full of popping corn. "Cut through?"

"You won't be alone. I'm going to send a segment of the 7th to screen for you, but your company will be the ones who make the break. Is that understood? No one stops until you reach friendly lines."

Wolf nodded, his mouth flattened and his jaw clenched. "If it can be done, we will do it."

"It will be done, or you won't have a brigade to come back to." Custer stared him in the eyes. This was no game. This was the life and death of fifteen-hundred men if indeed there were that many of them still alive. Not just his own life but the lives of all command. Survival hinged on it. "We haven't seen heavy engagement from here." He pointed north and east. "If they apply pressure with a brigade or two, they should be able to punch through and link with us. Is that understood?"

"It is, sir. The enemy is weakest to the northeast of our position, and that is where additional forces should be sent to break through."

Custer grinned for a moment. "Then do not tarry. Stranahan, grab Lieutenant Carver of the 7th." He eyed the field. The threat from Rosser faded as his men withdrew to skirmish. He exhaled. His men would do as he ordered. They would come through this. He nodded. "Turn that gun north." He'd have Pennington loosen the rebels in the trees with a few shells before he sent his men on their joyride. *They would make it through. They must.* A sharp pain reverberated in his chest. It knocked the wind from him, and he doubled over in the saddle.

"Sir?" Granger said. He stretched out a hand for Custer's arm.

Custer blinked and coughed. *Dear God, that hurts.* "It's nothing, Granger."

Custer grimaced and blew air through his mustache. The ache was real enough. His eyes watered.

"Sir, have you been hit?"

"Course not." He peered down anyway, fearful of what he might behold. He patted his jacket over the area, emanating the pain. His finger found a hole, and he stuck it through. *Is this the one?* His two wounds earlier had been ricochets or spent bullets having lost enough power to penetrate his flesh. Still hurt like the dickens. His finger graced something metallic. It was hard and hot. He dug it out with two fingers and held it out. "Well, I'll be damned. Another spent round."

Relief washed over Granger's face. "You're lucky, sir."

He rubbed feeling into his chest. "I won't call it luck until we're out of this tight spot. Let's hope Lieutenant Wolf doesn't fail us." His horse stamped and he placed the spent bullet into his pocket to show Libbie when this was through.

Chapter 26

Wolf marched back to his men now taking cover by kneeling in a field. Their only saving grace was that the rebs would have to cross an open road if they truly wanted to drive them back. Since the rebels valued their lives as much as they wanted to take those of their enemies, they hung back in the trees almost two-hundred yards away with the roadway and train tracks serving as deadly crossings between the lines.

"Get those weapons reloaded!" Wilhelm called to the men as Wolf approached. The sergeant's curled mustache twitched with irritation as he glanced at him. "What's happened?"

Wolf examined the distant trees as if he could pick out a way through the murky undergrowth held by the enemy. "Get the men mounted."

Wilhelm stood, rushed to Wolf, and knelt again, his eyes agape as he weighed Wolf's words. "Why? What do you mean?" he hissed, trying to mask his questioning of an officer.

"We're cutting our way out to Torbert."

Wilhelm looked behind them at the battered regiments of the Michigan Brigade besieged on all sides. "All of us?"

"No, an escort of the 7th will cover us then we will spring free, riding like hell."

"Probably a job better suited for a single man."

Wolf kept eyeing the forest, trying to anticipate what horrors and enemies awaited. "Don't matter, those are our orders. Custer's already sent three riders. None have returned. If we all race for it, there's a chance."

Wilhelm reached up and twisted his curled mustache. "Sounds like a way to get us killed."

"Not much to like when you're in a tight spot. Just get the men in the saddle and the flag."

His men pulled back from their position and D Company stretched their line even thinner, falling back twenty yards to tighten their position. All of the regiments were within view of one another.

Wolf's Company mounted. Twenty-three men. Three of the injured deemed themselves able enough to ride. The rest of the wounded capable of being moved from the railroad tracks had been dragged to the center of the brigade's perimeter to be cared for. But without the ambulances from the baggage train, the options were limited.

A company of horsemen congregated not far from Custer. Sergeants barked orders at the men to keep their ranks tight. Their guidon had a 7 for their regiment and a C for their company designation on it. The company was made of over fifty men. A captain with bushy muttonchops sat tall near the front of his men, his sword resting on his shoulder.

Wolf positioned himself at the head of his company. Wilhelm planted himself on the edge of his platoon, Simpson on his. The men positioned themselves in ranks of four, his senior enlisted men forming the flanks of each row.

"Can I carry the guidon?" Goffman asked Wilhelm. The sergeant looked surprised and eyed Wolf for confirmation. Aside from the Kilpatrick raid, Wilhelm had been the only man to bear the standard. The other man, Sergeant Roger Smith, was wounded at Buckland Mills and shipped back to Michigan with one less limb.

"Give it to him. I'll need you ready to take over if something happens to me."

Wilhelm nodded, silently handing off the company standard. Holes and tears ripped through the flag now. Most had come from today. It would need to be patched and sewed in order to return it to its former glory, but that would come later. They needed to survive this day, or it would be a keepsake above a rebel fireplace. It was hardly past noon, the sun high in the sky, and these men had been in a desperate place for what felt like ages.

Wolf raised a hand in the air, turning to call to his men. "We make for Union lines." His words took a somber tone. "We all make it through as best we can together. If you fall, we cannot stop. Your brothers will not aid you." He paused, letting his words sink in. "We've been put to the test today, but I must ask you for a bit more. I ask you to carry the day not just for yourselves or the 13th but for the whole brigade." He glanced at Wilhelm. "Know that it has been my greatest honor leading you men for however short of a time it was."

A few laughs came from the company.

"You bloody well got enough of us killed," Nelson called at him, but there was a glimmer of joy that touched his lips somewhere beneath his beard.

Wolf smiled. It was a morbid jest, but it was unusual for the big man to have any humor at all. "More of you will fall before we're done. Know this. When we were all placed into F Company, it was because we were deemed deficient in some way. Maimed." Eyes went to his leg. "Immigrants. Drunks. Criminals. Orphans. Cowards." He paused as each man reflected upon his weakness. "Now, when the war is at its fiercest, they come to us asking for help. Not because they don't care if we live or die, I assure you they don't really care, but because there's only a few men who can get the job done. A few hard sons of bitches willing to win or die trying."

Pride lit up on smoke-stained faces. Wicked grins and wild eyes. For all their deficiencies, they had proven themselves indispensable to the general. These were the men to get the job done. Wolf was sure of it. "I know you men are good for it. We will succeed or die a soldier's death. Nothing more. Nothing less."

Wilhelm barked at them. "We hold rank as long as we can. Together we are formidable. Apart, we will be ridden down and destroyed."

"Anyone who stands before us gets lead and steel!" Wolf said, venom in his voice.

F Company gave a ragged cheer. Bravery and a steady gallop must carry them through the coming action. "Draw sabers!" Wolf called out. The soft serpent hiss of metal over metal scabbards sounded out. Wolf drew his saber, held it high, and laid it upon his shoulder.

"Wolf's Company!" his men shouted, weapons held in the air.

The allied company ahead of them looked antsy. Their horses shifted nervously, and riders struggled to keep them in close ranks. They would go forward in fours down the road. Every man in the desperate expedition waited for the command. The gunfire continued around them. A man screamed along the left perimeter as a bullet struck him.

The sound of trotting horses turned into Custer, and he steered his horse next to Wolf. He nodded lightly, and Wolf's company's cheers slowly receded. "Your men are a lively bunch."

"Ready to see it through to the end, sir."

"Very good. Any requests?"

"Requests, sir?"

Custer gestured with his chin at the brigade band huddled near the wounded. "I thought our band would send you off right with a noble tune. Men always need a marching tune."

Wolf nodded. *Honoring us as we ride to our deaths.* He supposed in a morbid military point of view, this was an honor.

Custer stared, waiting. "We don't have much time now, Lieutenant."

Wolf turned toward his men. His saddle creaked. "How about it, boys? What would you like to hear as we gallop into the jaws of death?"

Men murmured among themselves. It was an unsettling request. "Yankee Doodle," shouted one man.

"Battle Hymn," came from Dickson. It was the loudest anyone had ever heard him speak. He looked ashamed and dipped his head, his lips moving in silent prayer.

"Garryowen!" said Private Patrick Connors, the company's surviving Irishman.

"Haven't heard it yet," Wolf said.

"The band will know it," Connors said. "Good drinking chantey from me home in Limerick."

Lowell chimed in. "My mum named me after my uncle Garry Owen."

"Sure he did," barked Nelson, but the boulder of a trooper cracked a grin on his craggy face.

Wolf glanced at Wilhelm who shrugged in indifference. He turned to Custer and said, "Garryowen."

Custer cocked his head. "Can't say I know that one. I'll take your men at their word." He turned toward the band, cupped his mouth with a free hand, and shouted. "Sergeant, do you know 'Garryowen'?"

The band sergeant nodded fiercely from atop his white horse, "The man or the song?"

"Song."

"Aye, I do, sir. Fine Irish song."

"Well, let's hear it," Custer said with a commanding gesture.

Gunfire still echoed around them, and the band counted out before they began to play. The song came quick and hard with the drum pounding the beat, and the brass instruments, trumpets, and horns blaring away with the fierceness of an attack.

"That's the tune," Connors said, smiling. Connors picked up the song and sang in a sweet baritone voice:

Let Bacchus' sons be not dismayed,
But join with me each jovial blade;
Come, booze, and sing, and lend your aid
To help me with the chorus:—

Instead of spa we'll drink brown ale,
And pay the reckoning on the nail,
No man for debt shall go to jail
From Garryowen in glory!

"Bloody fine tune, lads!" Custer said with a smile, his eyes alight with excitement. "I must say. It's right up there with 'Yankee Doodle' in my mind." He turned back to the band and circled his finger in the air. "Play it again, lads!"

The band began the song again, and Wolf's men took up the chorus with Connors leading them word for word. The column started at a walk and quickly turned to a trot north toward Fredericksburg Road.

Custer held his place and raised his hand high before calling with conviction. "Godspeed, my brave boys! Do your duty and all will be well."

The company sang as they rode north. The bullets began to fly as the rebels took note of the horsemen. Wolf raised his saber skyward. "To the gallop!" The hoofbeats increased in tempo. They tailed roughly thirty yards behind the company of the 7th Michigan.

Eighty men galloped over the road and crossed the train tracks as they hurried for Fredericksburg Road. Too few seconds of peace passed before gunfire peppered at them from the sides, the zipping sounds of death. But the deadly resistance was light, the rebels surprised by the sudden burst of mounted men from the embattled circle of the brigade.

A man slumped ahead of them, his back rounding forward. Another threw his hands in the air as he toppled from the saddle. Wolf's men guided their mounts around him as he rolled to the side and into the brush. No one would stop for you. No one would take your final letter home. No one would hold your hand while you passed to the afterlife. Wounded or mortal, you were on your own.

"Stay together," Wolf called at his men. The flag rippled above them. The golden wolf on the field of night black below a sky of red. Sabers were on their shoulders, ready to lash at any impeding rebels. Gunfire whistled at them from behind and the sides. Herman gave a shout and held his belly, his horse jostling him harder with his sudden weakness.

Wilhelm threw a hand out, trying to stop him from falling from his saddle. "Hold, Herman!" he shouted at the man. Herman's head bounced as he gritted his teeth.

Gunfire rippled from the forest surrounding them as if the rebels clapped loudly at them as they passed. A mounted company of horsemen watched as the blue-coated troopers burst past them. Their surprise ended quickly, and they whooped, taking up the chase. Wolf's men stayed crouched in their saddles as pistols clamored angrily behind them. There was no option for retreat now. Only forward.

"Forward men!" Wolf shouted. They galloped into a man-made clearing holding a house and fields. Two cannons facing north boomed. Gray-coated men surrounded the battery. Wolf's men followed the 7th into the clearing. The captain from the lead company twirled his sword over his head, shouting orders at his men to wheel in battle lines.

Wolf's throat became an aged parchment as he saw the opposition the 7th rushed to engage. On the far side of the field stood a company of blood-red shirted men on one side. A gray-coated company stood on the other side, represented by a red and white pennant stitched with the words Citadel Cadets.

Two full mounted companies. Wolf's heart dropped into the pit of his stomach. The artillery was hurriedly being turned. The pursuing rebels whooped again behind them, a pack of wolves seeing their prey trapped. If their pace lagged, they would be crushed between the two forces.

But the Red Shirts were there. The company of Wolf's mortal enemy. He scanned the men in red shirts, jackets unbuttoned to show the dreadful color of their wicked band. The company that never dipped below a hundred. Each man selected for his status and prowess. Led by the one man that Wolf knew he would have to kill before the war was done. He tried to make out the figure of the notorious Captain Marshall Payne. He must be there. If he yet lived, he would be there.

Then he saw a man he recognized. He was a large man, larger than most. He sat in the saddle near the Red Shirts, centered between the two companies. Bushy bearded and a long sword in his hand, it was the brute, General Wade Hampton himself.

Wilhelm leaned closer to Wolf. "Remember why we ride. Follow orders."

The 7th slowed as they shifted in rank from rows of four to a line for battle. They could not win this race, so the lead company made good on their orders and went to screen their allies from a force that would surely cut them down. Wolf's men must hope that they held long enough to break them free.

Wolf nodded, his duty clashing with his insatiable hunger for revenge. A revenge that was so close he tasted its sweetness on the tip of his tongue. All he needed to do was lead his men in tandem with the 7th and charge to bloody vengeance. Surely such action would be short-lived. His small company would be flanked from the rear almost immediately.

Revenge wrestled duty in his mind. The chance sat to make Payne pay his debt in flesh and blood—everything else be damned—stood across a field. He had never asked for a command or men to follow him. That had been thrust upon him in leaps and bounds. He eyed the men around him. Would he sacrifice every single one of them to win his revenge? *They'd ridden with me before. Why not again?*

His mind raced. He locked eyes with Wilhelm, and his sergeant nodded with a snarl. Wolf raised his sword overhead, spinning it in the air for all to see. His decision had been made. To hell and back.

Chapter 27

Afternoon, June 11, 1864
Poindexter House, North of Netherland Tavern, Virginia

Hampton's division had been hard-pressed all day long. From dawn until now, it had been a desperate fight to avert disaster. A castaway scratching to stay afloat in a sea of enemy soldiers, he'd raced from place to place throughout both Butler's and Wright's commands issuing orders, dispatching cavalrymen in either direction, trying to withstand the enemy's weight from the north, and applying pressure on the embattled enemy from the south.

The Union troopers caught in the rear were close to annihilation, but with Rosser's wounding and Fitz Lee's tardiness, he was unsure if he could effectively capture Custer's force. *Goddamn that Fitz.* Slow to the battle. Sluggish to push the advantage. He must know we are overburdened, yet he delays meaningful advance. And here all these beautiful South Carolina boys are doing all the dying.

They would have words when this was over. *But who was at fault for letting the enemy materialize in your rear?* That part was done. Now he needed his subordinates to follow his orders to dig themselves out of this mess. He was the senior commander, and although Lee hadn't made it official, he would lead the Cavalry Corps just as JEB Stuart had before him. He would succeed where JEB had failed. Yet those concerns had faded to the recesses of his mind as two companies of Union troopers appeared, cutting through his lines, galloping over the field to directly assault him. Their audacity was palpable.

They barreled off the road toward his staff and threatened Hart's battery. This fire demanded to be put out or risk an uncontrollable conflagration. If he lost Hart's guns, he would be in an even more dire position. The tables would turn on him, and he would be the one surrounded.

On his right stood the Red Shirts. He'd held them back all day, waiting for a hole to fill or more flames to smother. They were a king's personal bodyguard, ready to defend him to the last. He nodded to Lieutenant Fickles, his mustache running along his mouth all the way to his chin. "Ready your men. We send these boys' horses back."

The lieutenant cocked his arm and raised his pistol skyward. Fickles twisted in the saddle to the Red Shirts. With a wicked curve to his lips he shouted, "Let's put these Yanks in the grave." Whoops rose from their mouths, and the majority readied pistols and a few sabers. The men carrying multiple sidearms prepared for quick transitions. Once they'd fired all the bullets in one revolver, the next revolver would be ready.

Elite men required little encouragement. Fickles was a quality leader, but at any point since Yellow Tavern, he would have loved to have had the newly promoted Major Marshall Payne back under his command. The elite veterans would do whatever was necessary to win the war. Under Payne they were the best, under Fickles they were elite.

As a businessman, he always knew that he needed employees and associates willing to do anything for the business. The same held for war. He needed a man that was willing to do anything for victory, a man that was willing to press the boundaries of warfare. Yet Fickles would make do, just like all the men did thrust into higher responsibility. Hampton gave him a nod.

He turned to another company he'd been holding in reserve. Standing on his left, were the Citadel Cadets, F Company, 6th South Carolina. He pointed his sword at their captain, Moses B. Humphrey. He was a Citadel Cadet with broad shoulders, maybe even wider than Hampton's, with a thick mustache and strong arms. Captain Humphrey let out a fierce howl. He swept his saber through the air, urging his men to make their battle cry even louder than the Red Shirts.

Hampton pointed his heavy double-edged straight sword at the charging troopers then back at the Red Shirts. He raised his voice so all could hear him. "War is your blood. You come from a long line of red-blooded patriots, men who shed their blood against tyrants before this war. Now is your time to earn your forebearers' respect." He turned his horse, walking it back and forth, his voice rising in conviction. "Earn my respect by running these boys from the field. What say you? Are you true Sons of the South?"

A cheer to the likes of which he hadn't heard in some time overcame the cannon's roar and rippling rifle fire in the woodland around them, the angry chorus of an army of angels ready to ride down the devil's own legion with savage determination. Every single one of them was his son. All his boys. They would fight with vicious honor. Never back down. He kicked his horse back into rank and was surprised to find his son, Preston, had joined them.

"I need you to run a message to Wright," he said, avoiding his son's eyes, knowing the lie he spoke.

His son shook his head. "Do not deny me this, Father. You're here and you lead this army." The enemy galloped over the field, every one of them the bravest of fools. There was no hope that they could win.

"It's different, son. I have a life to give. This is my war. I fight for your future."

Preston's eyes filled with bold fervor. "It's my war too. This is my cause as much as any man here."

Hampton nodded fiercely. "It is. I won't deny you this." The father in him screamed inside to force the boy back to the rear. To drive him off with some meaningless task. There was pride in him knowing his boy demanded to be respected as a man.

Every father had pride for his sons, but Hampton knew his sons were different. They were special; they would exceed their father in rank and status. He felt it deep in his guts that Preston was meant for great things. So was Preston's brother, Hampton's name sake. The world would be theirs and they would be Princes of the South. All he had to do was win this bloody war.

He couldn't deny this young man the chance to prove himself among his peers. If he sheltered him from the fight, how would Preston learn to win of his own volition? Where would he learn to take up the sword of causes greater than himself? Wars over freedom. Wars for his people's way of life.

Hampton gazed at his son. The young man sported a black mustache, well-kept. He was unable to grow a bushy beard like his father. Yet he was his flesh and bone, every inch a part of Hampton. There was a familiar ferociousness in his eyes, and for a moment, Hampton thought he stared in the mirror, yet this man was not him but his son. For all their shared qualities, he still carried his mother's gift of gab. This young man even reminded him of Frank, his personality enough to tell a tall tale or talk an unsuspecting girl into a kiss or a group of men into following him into a battle. Hampton had these gifts but had always been quiet around his brother, letting the younger man be the star of the show while Hampton ran his business with a sharp mind for it.

"Stay with me then. Keep your eyes open for threats," Hampton commanded him. He then looked at his company commanders. "Come on, lads. Let's treat them to some Southern hospitality." He kicked his horse hard and quickly changed his gait into a gallop. He would show Preston true valor from the front line.

There was no time to build speed. They only had sparing seconds to take their horses to meet the enemy or else feel the lethal shock of their assault. Flags billowed behind him. The Union men had one of their own. Eager fellows from the Red Shirts attempted to beat him. Their mounts were as well-bred as his own and it was almost a race, but at the finish line there would be blood and brutal horror. Their black flag with a crimson star in the center whipped angrily as they charged, embodying their fervent spirit.

He leveled his sword. Snarled his lips. The wind tugged at his hat and beard, and he crashed into the enemy. The sound was loud in his ears like a crashing wave. Horses sped by like rolling thunder. Pistols barked. Smoke quickly surrounded shooters.

He plunged his straight sword into the lead rider's breast. Bushy sideburns lined the captain's face and his lips curled as the point pierced him. The sword's cold steel passed through fabric, skin, and muscle. The force of the blow drove the man backward until he'd almost bent entirely flat on his mount.

A Union rider's saber swung downward, and Hampton twisted his head out of the way. A moment later, he shoved the captain farther backward until he toppled from his horse. Hampton clung to his sword as the man crashed to the earth.

He met his next opponent with a roar. He was a bear, his sword his paws, his pistol his bite. His blood grew hotter with each passing second. They traded blows with sharp clangs of metal on metal. The horses shifted beneath, acting as the men's feet. The man tried to circle him. Preston fired his pistol, and Hampton's opponent slumped.

"Thanks, lad!" he shouted gruffly, turning back to the enemy. He rushed to meet the next trooper. The Citadel Cadets were overwhelming the Union flank, enveloping the entire group of riders, and cutting down men left and right. A blue-coated man took a swipe at him, and Hampton feigned an overhead strike, settling for punching the sword outward. The point ripped through the man's coat and into his shoulder.

"Damn you," he spit at Hampton.

Hampton wrenched his sword clear and the man screamed, his blood a warm red rain in the air.

"Preston!" Frantically, Hampton turned his horse back toward the fray, eyes searching for his son. Gun smoke settled over the fight like a fresh white blanket of fallen snow. The Union men were determined and paid dearly for it. There. He thought he caught a glimpse. He drove his horse back inside the melee, trading blows with another trooper before he led his horse away. "Preston!" he shouted again. His gut panicked for a moment until he laid his eyes upon his son.

His boy turned to look at him. He held his pistol toward the sky. Preston gave him a grin. Hampton urged his mount toward his son. No, his son was a man. A Son of the South, but no doubt a man with a warrior's heart.

"I thought I told you to stay with me!" His horse twisted anxiously beneath him.

"It's battle, Father. Isn't it glorious?"

"No, come. I may like to win, but I don't like the game."

Hampton turned when he caught a man approaching from their flank.

The blue-coated rider was hunched over the top of his mount to assume a smaller target. His pistol leveled as he approached.

Steering his horse, Hampton faced the new threat. The enemy bared his teeth as a wolf would before he brought down a deer. This man had his sights on him. Only God could shield him. For how could this man miss a shot from so close? The creases of the Union man's face gave him pause. *Do I know this man?*

He wore a sergeant's chevrons, his shoulders broad with a lean yet strong build, and a curling mustache on a chiseled face. Hampton knew he must have met the man somewhere. Before the war. *A trader? No, that face. That face.* He recognized the crazed look of a madman. *Gettysburg. The crazed trooper at Gettysburg. The one who wounded me twice in the head. Dear God.* Fear quickly gave way to anger. "We meet again!" Hampton bellowed, eager to repay the man for the wounds.

The Union sergeant cocked his revolver. Preston pointed his pistol, but the hammer clicked on empty. "No, son!" Hampton cried. He pushed his horse in front of Preston's, shielding him. He raised his sword in the air, widening his frame. The wild sergeant's eyes widened in recollection.

"I am here!" Hampton held his sword as if he ruled the other man. "Giddy up!" He spurred his horse at him. But the Union trooper adjusted his aim to the side, squinting down the barrel.

The actions happened more rapidly than comprehension allowed, and yet each moment stuck in his brain like an arrow thrown from a bow. His mount, Butler, was fast but not fast enough to reach the man. Hampton couldn't take his eyes away from the barrel of the gun. It absorbed his every thought. The black hole at the end engulfed him as if he encroached upon a cavern of death which no light could touch. Then it burst with flames as a spear from the tip.

The sound concussed over Hampton. Smoke followed the flames, the last of a locomotive's cars. He didn't spy the bullet, only a gust of air washed over him as it past. His eyes met the other man's and Hampton's jaw dropped. He slowed his horse, unable to decide which way to go. He glanced back over his shoulder. His son no longer smiled. Instead he blinked in bewilderment, twice then three times. He brought his hand to his chest. Fabric was torn in his jacket to the right of a button.

Hampton gulped, staring at his son.

Preston touched his chest, his white-gloved fingers exploring the wound. It found blood. His son's blood was his own. He grimaced, his words eking out. "Father?" Then he fell from his saddle, hitting the ground with a barely audible thump.

Hampton turned back to the Union man, eyes brimming with irate tears. "You may as well finish it."

The man cocked his pistol again and pointed it at Hampton, eye narrowed around the top of the gun.

"You shot my son," Hampton bellowed.

"You killed mine," the sergeant growled.

"How?" the word dripping from his tongue.

"Outside Gettysburg in a field."

Realization flooded over Hampton and he closed his eyes, feeling every mile, every battle, every loss crushing down on his soul at once. "The curly-haired boy in the field." His eyes went downcast then back to his enemy. "It's war. He tried to kill me, and I killed him first."

The sergeant nodded, his eyes angry yet understanding. "It is war. It's taken my pride and joy." He gestured with his chin. "I hope you feel every ounce of pain I've endured over the last year."

Hampton slowly shook his head. "I tried to shield him from this."

The sergeant gulped. The two men were one and the same. They were chiseled from different cloth, yet both were men who'd wanted to spare their family from the rigors of war and failed. "Me as well."

Hampton swallowed the bile racing upward in his throat. "He didn't deserve this."

"Yet he still paid for the sins of his father."

Hampton shook his head. He glanced back at Preston. A bugle was sounding in the background, shrill excited notes. On the ground, Preston's hands held his chest. Blood seeped around them.

"Go to your boy, General. At least you will be there for his final moments. A courtesy I never had." The sergeant spit to the side. Blue riders galloped back across the field.

"I will kill you for this," Hampton said. He looked back for the sergeant, but he was already gone, riding with his retreating men. Hampton raced to his boy and jumped from his saddle. He knelt next to him, feeling the pain in his hip as he did, but nothing numbed the fear channeling through his veins and into his hammering heart.

Preston's face was pale and his eyes tired, almost vacant. His hat had fallen off, revealing sweaty brushed hair. His lips trembled to hold a smile. "I miss home." He gulped, his throat loathe to respond. "I miss Mom." Each phrase shattered a piece of Hampton's insides as a man knocking away errant glass from a broken window. He pressed his hands on his son's chest, trying to keep pressure on the wound.

"You're going to be okay." Hampton stared at his mounted men reforming. The injured men cried out around him. A wounded horse lifted its head and let out a piteous shriek before laying it down again. Hampton's men stared at him, mouths dropped open and eyes wide with shock. He gaped. "Get me an ambulance! Do it now!" Riders peeled off toward the makeshift hospital.

He took his other hand and stroked his boy's head, wiping the hair from his forehead to the side. The wet hair stuck into place. Preston was a boy again, young and joyful, just how Hampton remembered him growing up. But the entirety of that image was shattered by the stink of gun smoke and the sounds of war drumming around him.

Preston was not a small lad being tucked into bed by his father, but a young man with a hole in his chest, dying in the grass. Far from home. His only family by his side, his father, gazing at him in defeated agony.

"Father." He struggled to swallow. "Father."

"Yes, son."

"I don't want to die." His eyes flickered. Fear seized them with death right behind. "Don't let me die. Please." His voice shrank word by word. "Papa. Papa." His mouth shook and his breath rattled from his lips.

Tears streamed down Hampton's cheeks. "I'm here, son. It's okay. Everything is fine."

"Papa." The word was small and savage and cut Hampton deeper than any blade or bullet, shot, or shell ever could. It carved through his soul, forming a never-healing wound.

"I'm here, boy. Just lie still." Hampton gulped and stared at his men. "For the love of God, find me a surgeon." He looked back at his boy. His son was silent and still, the life gone in him. Hampton had seen enough dead men in his day to know that while he appeared to be asleep, he had in fact gone to heaven.

With a wet squish he removed his hand from Preston's chest. Tears trailed from the corners of his eyes, running down his cheeks, and disappearing into his beard. He lowered his forehead to his boy's chest, letting the boy's uniform soak his tears. His voice shook, the words feeble. "I'm so sorry, boy. I am so sorry."

"Sir." Lowndes knelt down next to him, his eyes aggrieved. "The surgeon is here."

"He's gone, Lowndes, he's gone."

"Sir, please let him take a look," Lowndes implored.

Hampton sat upright. "I said he's gone goddamnit."

The surgeon knelt near Preston, examining his chest and neck. With intelligent remorseful eyes, he shook his head. "I'm sorry."

"Let me help you, sir." Lowndes wrapped his hands around Hampton's arm.

Hampton fended him off with a heavy hand. "No." Trembling, he stood on his own. Then he bent low again, scooping his boy in his arms. He was much heavier than the last time he had picked his child up. But he did so nonetheless. His body complained, and he ignored it.

The men parted for him, and he strode down the middle. Angry sad faces stared back, but he couldn't focus on any individual one. He carried the boy to the ambulance wagon and laid him in the back as if he were a child who'd only fallen asleep on Christmas Eve night and needed to be put to bed.

The surgeon patted his arm. "We'll take care of him."

"I want him buried in South Carolina."

"We'll do our best."

"You'll do it." Hampton couldn't take his eyes away from his son's peaceful face.

"We will do it," the surgeon said. He waved a man forward and began to treat the wounded men.

Hampton blinked, turning away from the body. He caught a glimpse of Frank among his men. He was well-aware his brother wasn't really there. *Have you come to guide Preston to the next world?* "Bring me my horse." His burly bay Butler was led to him. He remounted his horse and patted his flank. "This battle's not over."

His business. His brother. His son. The war had taken each one in turn. Chipping away pieces of him blow after blow. He was a granite statue when this war began, now he was being sanded away to dust. And now he must see this through to the end.

Chapter 28

Wolf led his men forward while watching Wilhelm charge the enemy on his own. This struck a strange chord inside him. He couldn't shake the feeling that he had made a mistake and the veteran soldier had the only answer. He hadn't imagined it that way. He envisioned the roles reversed, the act of revenge being taken or dying in the attempt. But Wilhelm galloped across the field, linking with the company from the 7th, and Wolf carried forth with the rest of F Company along the road north.

He found himself torn, but his decision was final. Seeing the Red Shirts in the distance stoked a different fire inside him, one that was fed by their deaths. Their black flag was the same color as their hearts with the blood-red star matching their shirts. Yet there was a new fire that bloomed inside him, and this was one of responsibility to his men.

This day hammered his commitment to the men around him like a blacksmith nails a horseshoe. And while that desire for vengeance burned, so did the responsibility to his men. For this reason, he fed the fire of leadership and let bitter revenge smolder until he was ready to fan its green flames again.

Neither vendetta meant anything if they didn't break through to Sheridan. Death still loomed in the trees ahead, and his choice may still lead them all down a doomed path. Yet over a thousand men relied upon his success. He prayed that on such a day he would drink the sweet elixir of revenge. *Lord if you give me anything, allow me to send that man Captain Marshall Payne to his grave. If it only be the last action I take, I will gladly give my life. But not today.*

"Where's he going?" Adams shouted over the hooves.

"Kill Hampton," Wolf said.

"The general?"

"Aye, killed his son."

The men didn't slow and the riders behind them kept pace. Bullets capped behind them, whistling through the air around his men as if they were hunted by miniature birds of prey.

A stretch of men lined the road ahead of them. Running into resistance was a guarantee, especially if the rebels began to understand their true intent. These men were ready. They formed a line like infantry, dismounted and closed rank, shoulder to shoulder. Determined men prepared to shatter them with a solid volley of stinging lead.

"They got Long Toms," Lowell said, in reference to the Enfield rifles the enemy carried, making them more similar to infantry than cavalry.

"We're going to get cut down," Kent lamented. The man dipped his chin.

"Private Goffman, keep that flag up. Make sure they know who we are." Wolf waited a moment. "Who are we?"

"Wolf's Company!" came a shout.

"Never give up! Never surrender!" Wolf shouted.

The call came again. "Wolf's Company!"

Wolf lifted his saber high in the air. "Those men don't know that we will never yield! Let's send them a message."

He pushed his horse farther in front. "Sorry, girl," he said under his breath. Surely if he fell, she would as well. She was a bigger target, and now they galloped at the head of his command. His men surged around him, racing him, eager to scatter the rebels to the wind.

Goffman pushed forward, holding the flag at an angle, threatening the enemy like a mounted knight. Adams was right behind with his pistol in one hand and his saber in the other. Nelson was there, resembling a boulder atop a horse. They screamed with every ounce of breath in their lungs.

There was no other option when you knowingly ran into the jaws of death.

You either turned tail and escaped as fast as you could, and he'd yet to see a man outrun a bullet, or you faced your end with a snarl on your lips.

Wolf charged into that firestorm, embracing the act for what it was. Your last declaration on this earth. It was one of the only qualities that defined men.

A charge could make legends, or it could be a grave miscalculation. It was certain that this would be the last moments for some of his men. Would they face it bravely? If his men shied, he took no note. Their actions would be judged by God in the end.

It was easier to have courage when others depended on you. Bravery swelled in a man's chest when he was surrounded by his brothers, each man embracing his impending death. They raced like demon horsemen, death-givers, fiends who'd already embraced Death's cold hand a thousand times, and now wished to enlist the men forming a line ahead into Death's forsaken army.

The Confederates brought their rifles to their shoulders. Each man around Wolf spurred his mount like men possessed, the sharp prongs of the spur racking and scraping their mount's flesh repeatedly.

The horses only grasped that they must go faster, and the poor beasts, as battered as the men that rode them, complied. They gave everything they had, muscles rippling throughout their bodies, foam spraying from their mouths, hooves digging into the packed earth for every ounce of speed they could muster. Ignoring the exhaustion in their limbs, they ran with everything they had. Every stride carried them closer to contact with the enemy.

And all of it would be short. Despite his men's efforts, they would never reach the enemy before they loosed a hundred Minié balls in unison. There was too much ground to cover, and the enemy prepared to unleash hell upon them.

A rebel officer in the rear of the line raised a sword. Although Wolf couldn't hear anything over the shouts of his men and the pounding of hooves, the officer's lips formed the words, "Ready."

"Aim." The dismounted rebel cavalrymen squinted as they stared down barrels. They gave no ground. They had the upper hand, and although over twenty horsemen charged them, this meant little for surely this enemy would retreat after a thick volley washed over them like a metal ocean wave.

"Break through!" Wolf shouted.

A second later, gunfire erupted along the line. It came hard and fast, a crashing white cap, gray smoke appearing at about the same time as the bullets hit Wolf's men.

The sound was that of a swarm of bees only heavier and metallic. Then the thump of balls ripped into his men, a heavy drops of rain on a thick canvas tent. Goffman wavered in his saddle next to Wolf but held the banner high. The front rank of horses screamed, throwing riders. Private Dickson flew from his horse, his arms outstretched before he hit the ground and rolled off the side of the road. Connors, with his sweet voice and sharp tongue, fell, pierced through with three bullets. He disappeared from atop his mount, vanishing into the hoof-made dust cloud. Yet somehow, those men still in the saddle continued the charge.

Wolf lunged the sword, point forward, over the top of his mount. His men howled with glee. They'd survived the dueling game of death, and now it was their turn to strike their opponents and make them wail in pain. "Break them!"

Dan Poltorak shouted in Polish behind him. The remaining men drove their way closer to the dismounted rebels. The time had come to avenge their fallen brothers.

The Confederates attempted to reload furiously, and this was their fatal mistake. They should have run for the trees and hoped to squeeze off a second volley into the riders' backs, but they didn't. As stubborn as Wolf's men were in charging them, the rebels returned the favor in standing their ground. The thought must have lingered in their minds and in their bellies that no matter how fast they reloaded, it would never be enough.

Goffman's horse was the first to reach them; it bullied men to the sides followed by Wolf's and Nelson's barreling into the gray and brown uniformed men. With a sickening thwack, Wolf brought his saber into an officer's head, splitting him like the watermelon head of a straw man.

The man's scream was short. Gore splattered from the wound and he dropped to the ground quickly. Wolf's men hacked their way through, their horses doing the brunt of the damage to the gray line. The rebels cried out as they were trampled under, hooves shattering bones and snapping limbs as easy as twigs. Men dove into the underbrush to escape the beasts. A few brave souls stood their ground and swung rifles like clubs.

"Forward!" Wolf called back at his men. They had broken into a disorganized mass of man and horse. They would not hack it out with the rebels. They must keep riding hard and hope that everyone caught back up to the company.

Wolf hunkered down on Sarah's back, bending, and urged her onward with renewed effort. Hoofbeats rumbled around him, but he had no idea how many had made it through.

The road veered to the right and a line of skirmishers stretched over it. *Dear God, another rank.* He glanced back at the fifteen or so men still with him. *We will never make another charge.* He side-eyed the flag bearer. He was bent in his saddle, gripping the guidon with white knuckles. "Can you make another charge?"

"Of course, sir." Goffman's chin bounced, his neck having a hard time keeping it secure.

"Don't stop, men! The brigade rests on us!"

With a whoop, his men made for the skirmishers. They turned around, facing the riders, and fired sporadic shots with wide eyes. Men along the flanks scattered for the forest, revealing a path for Wolf's men. The riders raced past with cheers and yells. Gunshots came from the woods, yet nothing would slow them now.

Horse's hooves ate the dirt ground, propelling them onward. Rebels shot at their backs, but none of his men cried out. Wolf held his hand on Sarah's flank; she was cloaked in sweat. The company continued their charge until a mass of horsemen in battle formation stood in their path.

Wolf sighed with a tired grin. The horseman were dressed in blue uniforms. "Bring it to a halt!" he said. His men slowed and stopped. They breathed in audible gasps. He swung his saber and rested it on his shoulder.

An officer from the other command trotted his horse near them. He had a black beard and dark brown eyes with a friendly smile. "Where on earth did you boys come from?"

Wolf looked at his ragged men forming in a line, clutching wounds, gripping bloodied sabers and hot barreled pistols.

"Custer's brigade. Who're you with?" Wolf breathed.

"Major Wilcox 19th New York, 3rd Brigade, 1st Division. Under Merritt."

Wolf glanced at the sky for a moment. Blue skies and a few plump white fluffy clouds floated overhead in their peacefulness, seemingly unaware that men killed each other below. Yet the heavens above made him turn back to the major with a contented look. "We made it."

Behind him, his men gave exasperated sighs and tired laughter.

Wilcox eyed the battered company behind Wolf. "What the hell were you boys doing charging through there?"

"1st Brigade is surrounded." He pointed back the way they'd come. "We're at risk of being overrun. Can you take me to the general?"

"Of course," the major said. He flagged down an aide, a young man with long hair pushing out beneath his slouch hat. "Take these boys to General Torbert."

Wolf's men sheathed and holstered their weapons, and the aide led them at a trot toward the rear. They passed Union troopers as they shifted and reinforced their lines in companies and squadrons, battling through the forest as much as the rebels.

A mile later, they reached a two-story brick farmhouse. The aide pointed. "General Torbert is in there with Sheridan." He turned his horse and left them there.

The corps's short wagon train rested nearby, a line of light-blue wagons with teams of four or six horses, some with mules. A makeshift hospital had been erected and ambulances rolled to it from the front. A trooper splashed water in the back of a covered ambulance and watery red liquid spilled over the edge. Another soldier refilled a water barrel hanging near the back wheels.

Wolf hopped down from the saddle and addressed the rest of the company. "I'll be as quick as I can. You men get the aid you need." He scanned the ranks looking for a sergeant to look after the men. Simpson was gone. Wilhelm was gone. His eyes fell upon Dan. "You're in charge until I get back."

Dan nodded gravely. "Yes."

Goffman keeled from his horse, taking the guidon with him. The men rushed around him. "Not feeling too chipper, Lieutenant. One of them got me." He removed his hand and revealed the dark crimson blood of a shot to his belly.

"Hold on, Goffman." Wolf pointed at Nelson and Dan. "Take him to a surgeon. Go." They hefted the man between them as if they carried a child, rushing to the field hospital. Wolf bent over and picked up the flagpole. The guidon was shot through and dirty. He wiped it off, standing it upright as if it were its first time flying. It was theirs, paid for in blood. Best to not let it lay in the dirt long.

"I'll take it," said Kent. "Standard bearers run in my family. An unlucky bunch, let me tell you."

"Thank you, Private." He turned toward the few remaining men. "I'll return."

***

Wolf limped along a dirt path to the home. He pushed open a worn white-painted door and removed his hat, walking inside. Two couriers waited on one side of the room away from three men in the middle, who were seated around a table yet crowding over it. Cigar smoke hung in the air with no place to go.

Wolf stood at attention, waiting to be addressed. He recognized Sheridan, a short, black-mustached Irishman with two stars on his shoulders. Then there was General Torbert, Wolf's division commander. He had a bushy beard with a shaved chin in the same vein as Major General Ambrose Burnside. Then there was a taller gentleman with a long patriarchal beard and bugged eyes that he recognized from Gettysburg, General David Mcm. Gregg.

Sheridan puffed on his cigar and draped his arm over the back of his chair in a relaxed fashion. He proceeded to pick up a document and read it. He glanced up then squinted at Wolf, quickly waving him over.

Wolf hobbled to the generals, the floorboards creaking beneath him. Sheridan continued to scan the report. He eyed him again and recognition flashed across his face. "Say, I bloody well know you, don't I?"

"You do, sir. Yellow Tavern, sir."

Sheridan smiled around his cigar. "That's right. You're the enlisted fellow parading around as an officer." He gestured at his comrades. Eyes turned toward him, half-smiles on their lips. "He's the one I told you about. Escaped Libby then kidnapped Stuart's wife. Bamboozled poor Butler into sending him North." The men laughed at that. "He's from your division, Torbert."

Torbert wagged a finger at Wolf. "No, tricks like that here now." Then he gave him a fond grin as he would for a favorite son. "I have a bunch of the devious devils under me." He looked at Sheridan. "Keeps a man on his toes." He faced Wolf again. "Say, what's your name young man?"

Sheridan snapped his fingers. "Don't tell me. You're Roberts?"

Wolf's eyes betrayed him and he gave a terse shake of his head.

"No, some kind of animal. Fox? Bear? No. Buck? Beaver?"

Wolf shifted his weight uncomfortably. "It's Lieutenant Wolf, sir."

Sheridan kicked his head back. "What'd I tell you? Don't tell me."

"Sorry, sir. I come from General Custer."

Torbert gave him a friendly smile. "You came from Custer's Brigade. Why, you men have been missing all morning." He nudged at Gregg with an elbow. "Not like the fellow to miss a scrap, huh, Gregg."

Gregg nodded brusquely.

Wolf had a hard time containing his irritation. These men had no idea Custer's Brigade was close to annihilation. "We have been engaged since dawn, sir. We are surrounded and in dire need of relief."

Torbert gave him a quizzical stare, his nose scrunching. "We are pressuring as far as we dare."

"Sir, I lost a dozen men cutting my way through here."

"Surrounded?" Sheridan said, his cigar dipped on his lip.

"Yes, sir. We're cornered by Rosser from the west, Hampton from the north, and Fitz Lee from the east. We are at risk of being destroyed."

Torbert's friendly grin faded. "You are not to tell us how to run a battlefield, Lieutenant."

Wolf kept his eyes focused on the wall. "Yes, sir. General Custer requests immediate assistance or his brigade will be destroyed down to the last man."

Gregg sat forward in his chair with an uncomfortable look on his face. "Perhaps my cousin's regiment can advance to ascertain the situation?"

Sheridan puffed hard on his cigar, smoke billowing from his mouth. "Surrounded. Hmm. Where would you say?" He gestured at the table.

Wolf stared at the paper. Seeing the topography from above didn't help much. "Where are we, sir?"

Sheridan circled a field north along Fredericksburg Road with his finger. "Here."

"We are near the depot and Netherland Tavern."

Sheridan stood, leaning over the table with some interest and nodded, resting a finger on the map. "If Custer truly is pressed, then Hampton is between us. Perhaps we can wrangle that brute up today."

"Sir, Custer says that the enemy is thinly placed through here." He touched the map. "North and east of his position. A concentrated assault would link our forces and relieve the pressure on his brigade. We cannot disengage without sacrificing whole regiments. I can attest, the entire situation is a hornet's nest squeezed in a vice. I implore you, send everyone you can."

"Lieutenant," Torbert chided, his eyes razor sharp. "Let's leave the planning to us."

Wolf gritted his teeth. "Yes, sir."

Sheridan clapped him on the shoulder. "I trust this young man. He gave me Stuart on a platter, and we served him up like a suckling pig to Grant."

Wolf couldn't contain his disappointment in their lethargy, a tired frown forming on his lips.

"Don't look so downtrodden, son. We will extract the Boy General," Sheridan said.

Gregg stood to attain a better view of the map. He was a tall and lanky man. "I still believe Irvin is well-positioned to penetrate southwest. If the

Lieutenant is correct, he can cut near that creek until he finds Custer's lost brigade."

Sheridan nodded. "I believe you're right. But not alone." He glanced at the other general. "Torbert, you'll send Merritt and Devin forward, keep Hampton and Butler in place. Gregg, let's shift Davies brigade to support. Perhaps we can flip the situation on Hampton or Fitz Lee if they're separated." He gave a quick nod of his chin. "Hurry now, opportunity awaits." He turned to Wolf. "You did well reaching us. Make sure your wounded are treated and your men are fed."

Wolf gave him a swift salute.

Sheridan returned it. "You're quickly becoming one of my favorites, Lieutenant. Make sure you survive this war." He gave Wolf a smart grin laced with confidence.

"I'll do my best, sir."

Hand on his back, Sheridan led him from the house. "Take a break now. There will be more fighting ahead of us."

His words brought little comfort to Wolf. Post-battle exhaustion started to shallow his breathing. "Sir, I'd like to get back to the brigade."

Sheridan peered up at him. "That's a risky proposition."

"If it is possible, we'll link with one of the units to the front."

Sheridan eyed him, weighing his words before nodding. "Can't deny a man a fight. Your request is granted." Sheridan pointed at an officer ducking beneath the doorway. "Colonel Irvin Gregg," he said, waving over a tall slender man with a beard and look similar to that of General David Gregg. "You take this man and his men with you as you go south. Understand?"

"I do, sir," Irvin said. The man was even taller than his cousin David, longer face, eyes that brooded even more. "Yes, sir." He turned toward Wolf, regarding him with fiercely observant eyes. "You lead those Michigan boys through enemy lines?"

"Yes, sir."

"Bloody fine work."

"Bloody," Wolf said.

Irvin's eyes were swift calculators, able to read a man and situation alike.

"Get your men saddled and formed. We depart in twenty."

Wolf nodded and took a breath. "Thank you, sir."

"Off with you, Lieutenant," Sheridan said.

Chapter 29

Mid-Afternoon, June 11, 1864
Near Trevilian Station, Virginia

An hour after he'd sent the two companies northward to link with Torbert, the pressure began to wane off his command. Starting with Hampton's men from the north, the hostilities slowed to a dull roar. Less gunfire at his men. An occasional pop, but nothing of substance. The engagement along his eastern perimeter dampened as Fitz Lee's men pulled back like beaten thieves in the night. Even Rosser's wild men had appeared to have taken a step back, fading toward the west.

A nasty rumor abounded that Rosser had been wounded. The severity was unknown, and it brought him no joy to know that his friend may be dead and gone. He took a gloved finger and pressed it through the hole in his jacket just to the side of the heart. The spent lead round, misshapen and bent, kept in his pocket to show Libbie. The third such occurrence of the day. As bad as it had been, his luck had held. More often than not, all a war-ridden man had was his luck, so he would take it as a magnanimous omen that they would make it through this.

Then finally he let himself begin to relax when it was reported Yankees trudged through the woods from the northeast toward his position. His men breathed sighs of relief and treated their wounded.

However, he didn't have relaxation on the mind. No, relaxation was only temporary as vengeful feelings bubbled in his belly and grew in his chest.

Those bastards had his wagons and his camp servants. He turned to Stranahan. "Get me the 1st Michigan." They held the distinction of the senior regiment and were the least bloodied this day. Venerable lads all around. Always ready for a fight.

He mounted his only remaining horse, Harry, a tall bay. The beast had served him well today. The rest of his spare mounts were with his captured baggage train. His mind sped in anger, his pride as battered as his personal battle flag. "Took my horses, took Eliza, took my letters from Libbie, and I'm not going to stand for it," he said to himself, solidifying his righteous anger. The letters stung the worst of all. His personal correspondence with his beautiful wife was meant for him and him only, not for some poor sheep farmer from the mountains of Virginia.

"Forward, men." He waved to a waiting captain with bushy sideburns and a mustache, and he led the squadron east. They passed bodies in the forest. Most were facedown, shot in the back as they ran. Both blue and gray men, but too many men were Union troopers, and he knew they were his boys. The sight made his mouth tighten and his need to exact vengeance greater.

They came upon the place where the wagon train had been ransacked. An abundance of abandoned wagons on either side of the road had been plundered for anything of value. A few were tipped on their sides, ripped bags and tossed trash left by the thieving rebels. Others lay teetering on three wheels, axles broken on the rough terrain. An ambulance with wounded enemy soldiers still inside rested in the shade of the trees.

A man with a bloody sling holding his arm waved them down with his free hand. His voice cracked with raspy dryness. "Please."

Custer slowed down and gave quick orders. "Send it back to camp." The men would die incapacitated on the side of the road without aid. A squad of troopers peeled off to assist the abandoned wagon. "Hurry!" Custer called to the men of the 1st, and they proceeded in silent determination, pistols in hand prepared for a fight.

After a two-mile trek, they came across a company of Fitz Lee's men trying to hurry the captured train along. They hadn't gotten as far as he'd suspected. They lacked either proper initiative or clear orders. Either way, they would pay for their lethargy in ferreting away his belongings.

He continued to eye the hurrying men. "Captain, prepare your squadron for a charge. I want those wagons."

The captain sat on his horse and nervously gulped. "Sir, isn't this how we got in this mess?"

Custer cocked his head to the side, unable to believe the man's arrogance. "You can stay behind if you lack the courage to do your duty. I'll lead them."

The captain shook his head in the negative. "I will lead them." He barked at his bugler. Bugles sounded.

Custer drew his sword, a fine double-sided straight blade. "At the gallop!" he shouted, and the squadron made hard at the train rushing to escape. It was a short fight. Fitz Lee's Virginians scurried away down the forested road within a minute of contact. Where it should have been his men tired of the fight, it was the opposite.

Drivers held their hands in the air, exhausted by the forced marches between the two armies. He trotted down the baggage train until he spied a once fine carriage appropriated from a southern planter earlier in the war. Now it had been banged, battered, and leaned slightly to the right as it drove, and behind that, his personal wagon carting around his belongings.

He spurred his horse to it. The team of horses stood still, hooves nervously stamping the ground, tails swishing flies away. No teamster or driver sat on the rear draft horse, nor did any wait nearby.

He climbed down from his saddle, reaching out to pat the lead horse. "Whoa, there. Everything's fine." Walking down the side, he let his hand run along its flank and walked to the rear of the wagon. With his pistol, he flipped back the white canvas flap.

"Eliza?" he called out. His eyes scanned every nook and cranny as if they played hide-and-seek with him. "Johnny Cisco?" The back of the wagon was empty. A few papers lay unmolested, but all of his other belongings had been removed. "Treacherous bastards." He holstered his pistol. His heart leapt for a moment with the renewed understanding that his personal letters had been taken. He muttered, his heart sinking, "Probably some dirty scoundrel reading them."

A courier from the 1st stopped nearby. "Sir, we've recaptured some of Pennington's caissons, but we've met stiff resistance farther up the road."

Custer waved him back, any chance at true vengeance lost along with his personal belongings. "Do not pursue. Reform and ensure that our link with Torbert and Gregg is unmolested." He glanced back inside his personal wagon. Nothing. Those grubby bastards had left him with nothing. He'd rather be shot a dozen times than be subjected to such humiliation. Not to mention the terrible public assault Libbie would undergo for writing such things. He sighed and straightened his necktie.

He patted Harry's flanks as if the horse needed comforting. His men guided the recaptured wagons backward. "Harry, it's a damn cruel world out there." The horse eyed him with big dark orbs. Custer nodded at his mount. "I assure you; it is."

"Ginnel?" came a soft voice from the trees.

He spun on his heel, his hand flying to his sidearm. With a scrape of leather, the pistol was in his palm. He peered into the thick undergrowth, searching for the person it belonged to.

"Dat you, Ginnel?" came louder. Leaves rustled and Custer squinted, his finger running along the trigger like a lost lover. It was a female voice, but who knew what kind of devilry the Southern populace was willing to engage in.

"Ginnel Custer?"

He cocked his head to the side, pistol lifting skyward. "Eliza?" he said at a shadowy form in the trees.

Leaves shuddered and the undergrowth shifted and crumpled beneath her feet as she emerged. Her dress was ripped along the hem. She lifted her chin. "I been looking for you, Ginnel."

Custer chuckled out loud. This was the first opportune event to happen to him all day. His luck was starting to shine through the cruel world again. He gave her a broad grin. "Come here, my girl." He reached out and wrapped his arms around her. "I thought we lost you."

Eliza pushed herself away. "That Reb Ginnel tried to make me his slave girl. And I told him I'd never be no slave again. They laughed at me, Ginnel.

Laughed. So I snuck off when they wasn't looking. I told 'em I wouldn't be. Told 'em true."

He held her at an arm's length. "Yes, you did, my dear Eliza. What of Johnny?"

She shook her head and her eyes watered. "I's try to hide, but dey took him away. Only a boy and they be treatin' him like a man." Her mouth set in anger.

Custer lifted his chin high in the air. "We'll secure his freedom. He's a good lad. He'll be fine." He extended his hand, and she took it as a woman would at a grand ball. "Let's get you back to camp." He helped her into the dilapidated carriage.

Custer flagged down a teamster. "You're going to drive my wagon."

"Sir? My wagon's back there."

"You're in charge of this one. That's an order now."

The man stared at Eliza seated in the back. "What's she? The Queen of Sheba?"

"As a matter of fact, she is," Custer said with a general happiness in his voice. He tied Harry to the rear of the carriage and took a seat on the bench. "That is just the reason I'm going to drive her."

The man scratched his head. "Yes, sir. Ain't never seen royalty."

"First time for everything, my good man."

Custer flicked the reins on the back of the two horses. "You ever been driven by a General?" Custer asked Eliza over his shoulder.

"Can't say so, Ginnel. It's a mighty fine honor."

He glanced over his shoulder. "And given as free as rain." His pride was battered, but the blow a little less so with the recovery of his trusted cook.

***

Night brought about an exhausted slumber for his men. Most of the Confederates had retreated south and west with the pressure from the north. Those that hadn't found themselves in their own last stand. Over five hundred rebels had been rounded up before nightfall, many wounded.

He leaned on a post of the Netherland Tavern's doorway. It was a simple overhang with a few steps leading to the ground. A swinging seat creaked with the breeze. Custer peered over his quiet encampment. His losses would be even greater. Almost half the 5th was being labeled as casualties, most plain missing and assumedly captured.

Fitz Lee's men had disappeared. Rumor around camp was that Hampton had retreated back to the Army of Northern Virginia, leaving the route to General Hunter's men open and all but assuring Union victory. But Custer knew different. He knew Hampton wouldn't give way that easily. That wasn't in his stubborn nature.

Loud boisterous voices of the commanders of the Union Cavalry Corps, resonated from inside the tavern barroom, and he tried to tune them out. As admirably as his men had fought this day, everything had hung on the edge of a precipice and they had been hauled out at the last possible moment. His brigade was battered in both man and mount. One in four men had been a casualty, maybe even higher. Too many men. *Yet we survived. That has to count for something.*

Campfires smoldered throughout the field they'd fought and died on for most of the day. Men slept so sound it was difficult to tell the fallen from the exhausted. Men in a makeshift hospital cried. The campfires didn't look right. There should be more. *Could I have prevented this? Could we have done this differently?* He blinked back his thoughts. No. He had his orders.

He had seized the initiative and struck a grievous blow when the moment presented itself. When the enemy revealed themselves to be in all directions, he directed his men with fierce conviction, not showing either fear or yield. He'd done right, but something inside shook to the core. It had been a close fought match.

His thoughts shifted to his friend, Thomas Rosser. That man would charge a barn that stood in his way and then bet the man next to him that he would be the first one through the doors.

The sound of his name broke his contemplation. "Autie!" came a voice.

A congregation of officers walked their horses toward him. The man in front waved his hand, taking off his hat and circling it in the air. "Autie!" he called again.

Custer shook his head. "Russell Alger. I'll be damned. I thought you were dead and gone."

The black-bearded handsome colonel of the 5th Michigan dismounted, handing off his reins to an aide. He kept his hat off as he approached. He stopped at the bottom step, and his joy of finding a friend faded away as the sun retreated beneath the horizon. "My boys and I took a beating today."

Most of the brigade's casualties came from the 5th and the 13th Michigan regiments. Until now, both regimental commanders were missing in action. "We did. Where have you been?"

"Just about captured, Autie." He turned and waved down the road. "We got cut off a few miles that way. Were forced to take to the trees. Rebs all around us. Every which way you looked, there were more of the bastards." He let his hat fall back to his side. "Thought we were going to have to ride all the way to Washington."

Custer stuck his hand out and gripped the colonel's, pulling him in. "Don't give your pal a scare like that again. You hear? Dear God, we had a day."

After a moment, Alger took a step back. "We're going to need rest and a refit." He turned, surveying the camp, and after a few seconds, he turned back. "It was a pardonable zeal, wasn't it?"

Custer nodded slowly. Any commander needed to be assured that the sacrifice of his men was necessary and honest and that he'd given the right orders. It was a blunder that could plague a man for the rest of his life and keep him awake in the cold night, yet the sweat would still form on his brow. *Had it been the right decision?* "It was. Who could not reach for such a noble prize if it was within their grasp?"

"God himself would try."

"He would try. Come, Alger. Let's confer with the other officers and see what tomorrow shall bring." He wrapped an arm around his friend's shoulders. "Perhaps we'll get another go of it."

Alger wavered his head to the side. "Maybe a day of rest between the two."

The two men entered the tavern. It was really a single two-story clapboard home that had another house exactly the same built alongside it, turning it into a ten-room inn for travelers of the railroad. They stepped inside a crowded barroom.

General Sheridan smoked and joked with his subordinate officers. He glanced up as Custer and Alger walked inside. "Good to see you men in one piece."

Eyes all shifted toward the two newcomers. The officers there knew it had been a hard day for the Michigan Brigade. There was sympathy and concern but also hints of pride that they withstood the beating.

"Happy to be in one piece," Custer said.

Sheridan nodded. "Let's talk about how we're going to scatter them right off the map tomorrow."

Custer and Alger took their spots among the officers. Custer silently watched, wary of the part that he still may play.

Chapter 30

Late Afternoon, June 12, 1864
Netherland Tavern, Virginia

By 4 p.m. of June 12th, the fighting at Trevilian Station came to an ignoble close. Hampton had rejoined with Fitz Lee in the night and built entrenchments along Gordonsville Road, the route to reach General Hunter's army. Sheridan had thrown his brigades into action against the dug in rebels leading to a costly and inconclusive fight.

Custer had directed his battered brigade with as much gusto as a weary commander could muster. He sent the 1st Michigan toward the barricades on the train tracks, and when they shied before the determined efforts of the enemy, he attacked in name only.

They exchanged long-range fire, supporting the other less exhausted brigades. He'd already lost four captains and six lieutenants. His men didn't have the stomach for another demanding fight. He didn't blame them either. They needed respite. They'd done their finest the day before, and he could ask nothing further without risking a complete mutiny.

Despite breaks here and there, this culminated over a month of campaigning almost non-stop. Almost half of Custer's brigade was incapacitated in both man and horse. The entire command was shackled with fatigue. They bordered upon combat ineffectiveness. Against a well-armed foe, they could put forth no real effort aside from harassment.

This day it was Merritt's and Devin's brigades turn to suffer greatly. They were beaten at the "Bloody Angle," a smaller version of what had taken place near Spotsylvania Court House. Men from both armies died over the entrenchments and close hand-to-hand fighting. He'd never expected Hampton to roll over in the fight, but the rebel stand was commendable.

That late afternoon, Custer moved to Netherland Tavern to dine with Sheridan. Custer's body was bruised and stiff from the day prior, but he was alive and that was good enough. His boots thumped the four steps leading to the tavern door and he went inside.

The scene inside the barroom was the opposite of the previous night. None of the officers laughed or joked. All were quiet and demure, mirroring their commander's mood. The room was devoid of rich cigar and pipe smoke, only a dank musty scent of damp wood prevailed.

Sheridan sat at a table with David McM. Gregg. Both men sipped tea and ate toast in hushed discussion. Custer approached and saluted. Sheridan regarded him in a dejected manner and returned his salute. He was a balloon with no air that gestured with an almost limp hand. "Take a seat, George."

Custer pulled a scarred rickety chair out and gently eased his sore body into it. Both his arms were bruised along with his chest. "Toast? Or Tea?" Sheridan asked.

"No, thank you, sir. Had some coffee and two rashers earlier."

"Very well." Sheridan sipped his tea. "I've been discussing with David our withdrawal."

Custer grimaced a fraction and listened. Not the kind of words a general wanted to hear from his commander after only two days of battle. "I'm going to pen a letter today to Grant telling him I've failed to complete any of his requested actions." He shook his head in tiny waves. "This is a bitter tea to swallow," he said softly. It was clear he wasn't referring to the tea inside his cup.

"I will say, sir, the men and the horses do need a break. My brigade has been severely battered."

There was no joviality in Sheridan's voice. "I understand, General. We will do what we can." He set down his cup and quickly took out a cigar and lit it. "It's been a game of chess except we use sledgehammers and the pieces are men, shattered and blown away with a sharp gust of wind, leaving us with nothing." He paused, glancing at Custer, his bright eyes having lost their luster. "We haven't joined with Hunter. The railroad is largely intact between the critical junctions."

"Resistance has been formidable, and we've deprived Lee of his eyes and ears," Gregg said. He took a drink of his tea as if it made his argument stronger.

"Yet we have not met our objectives. We must trek back to Grant and do so in haste for we've stripped the land of any forage, the people are hostile giving no succor, and I have hundreds of wounded, prisoners, and contraband so no considerable speed can be made. What would you suggest we do?" Both Gregg and Sheridan turned toward Custer.

"We should pack as many of the wounded as we can into wagons to ensure they get the proper care they need."

"Prisoners?" Sheridan asked.

"Marched on the double with our column."

Sheridan puffed hard on his cigar. "How will you forage? The land is stripped bare. We must travel quickly as to avoid killing the horses. We cannot handle both."

The realization of why Sheridan had asked Custer specifically dawned on him. A disproportionate amount of the casualties came from the Michigan Brigade. Custer read his eyes, understanding him. His wounded men had been deemed a collateral that the two divisions couldn't manage, so he said the only fair declaration in the face of their abandonment. "Then we should leave surgeons and medicines behind to give them care."

Sheridan nodded. "Fine idea." He sounded like he wanted to spit. There was doubt in his voice that the rebels would let the medicines be used for Union troops. They would also be sentencing any surgeon left behind to imprisonment, and in many cases, it would mean death. Sheridan waved an orderly to his side and gave the orders. "Next, what to do with the contraband?"

"Allow them to trail along as fast as they can," Custer said. He believed in giving a man a chance.

Sheridan's face tightened. "Do not go slower because they call for your help. Our responsibility is to keep our divisions in the best possible condition for Grant."

"Surely Hampton will move to intercept us again," Gregg said. His eyes bugged out and his beard held a dusting of crumbs.

Sheridan puffed angrily on his cigar. "Then we will whip him back to whatever hell he came from. His men must be as fatigued as ours. He can't be looking for a fight."

"I wouldn't count on it, sir," Custer said.

"Damn him." Sheridan nodded with a frown. "We must give ourselves a head start. I want your commands to leave your campfires burning. I want the rebs to think we're still here." He eyed Custer. "Don't bury the dead." Another grievous blow to his men's morale. As if losing their comrades weren't enough, now they were going to abandon the dead for the crows.

Custer blinked it back. "Sir, they deserve burial."

"They do, but we can't afford it. This command must reach the safety of our main lines. We're going to have to travel back north of the North Anna River. We can't risk running into the rest of Lee's army."

"Yes, sir."

"Tell your men to take care of any wounded and loose ends they may have. We march at midnight. You are dismissed, General." He gave a silent wave to a civilian waiting in the next room, who was wearing a checkered vest, a black bowtie, and a white button-down shirt. A derby hat was perched high on his head. Sheridan's voice embraced a lighter tone. "Come on in here, Nathaniel. Let me give you a briefing for the newspapers."

Custer gave a terse nod, shutting the door as he left. Sheridan's voice trailed behind him. "We've destroyed almost a hundred miles of enemy tracks, driven them from the field of battle. The contest was hard fought, but I can assure you of our victory here."

The door latched and Custer traveled back to his exhausted command. Campfires billowed smoke into the air. Quiet, tired men surrounded the flames. There was little joy and revelry coming from his men, no laughter or singing, only deadened existence. It would only become worse when he gave the orders to abandon the severely injured. Orders he must give. Yet these were the lucky ones. Still intact. Still in the fight. Or were the lucky ones dead and gone?

***

Wolf sat in exhaustion near a campfire feeling like a spent percussion cap, used and burnt up, frayed around the edges. His company was in worse shape. They'd been scattered and broken, barely a dozen men left and able to fight. Five or six would eventually return to duty after recovering from their wounds. Another few could go either way. They would muster out or end up with a long train ride home. The godforsaken missing men were likely dead or would die in a rebel prison in the deep South with little chance for rescue. Rumor was that Andersonville was worse than Libby and Belle Isle combined. Wolf couldn't fathom it, but in this war, Death played the fiddle and armies danced to his tune.

The flames rippled and gave off a soft glow; he found comfort in the warmth. The killed mounts were dragged into piles and set ablaze, causing the stench of burning horseflesh to pervade the camp. The only other alternative was to let them rest as the stink could lay a man low, make him gag, and upset a horde of flies mid-feast. Either way, it paid to burn them quick.

A shadow approached from the camp and stopped at a distance. The soldier stood silent, watching him. Wolf stared back. In the darkness, the man was obscured, but he was familiar with his build and his stance. The light of the fire flickered over the man. As he stepped closer, the shadow became Wilhelm.

Joy leapt in Wolf's heart. He'd thought his friend and mentor had been lost, but anger flirted around the edges, all tossed together to brew in the cauldron of his gut. A sense of wariness shrouded Wolf as if something had changed and this man deserved caution now. "Sergeant."

"Lieutenant." Wilhelm's eyes told a story of anguish. "You made it through," he said with a nod.

Wolf studied him. *Was this the same man?* "We did. You left us when we needed you."

263

Wilhelm chewed his words with a slight nod. He turned away from Wolf and his question, reaching into his saddle bags. He removed his pipe and loaded it with shredded tobacco. He struck a match, the flame brightening his hardened face as if he were a statue. He took a moment to puff on his pipe as it lit. He walked his horse over to the other mounts and tied him along the line then returned with a gesture at the campfire. "May I?"

"Go ahead, Sergeant, but you must tell me why you did it."

Wilhelm sat down, puffing hard on his pipe. "I made a choice."

"The men needed you."

Wilhelm puffed. "I will make my amends. They will understand."

The two men stared at one another. He understood a man with a vendetta.

"Did you get it? Did you find your revenge?" Wolf asked.

"I did."

The relief of closure relaxed Wolf, and yet a great yearning remained to have his own. He glanced downward then back at the sergeant. "Franz deserved it."

Wilhelm puffed harder, a blue cloud forming around him. "This country had a lot more to offer him than loose soil to bury his bones." He spit to the side and the two men sat in silence for a moment, both reflecting upon Franz and his death.

"You see Payne?"

"I didn't." Wilhelm inhaled the smoke into his mouth; it escaped in tiny wisps as he spoke. "His men were there. It was chaotic."

"Battles tend to be." Anger wrestled the control from the joy of seeing his friend alive. A sense of having been duped and cheated shrouded his mind. "Now don't tell me how your situation was different. You told me to stick with the mission and watch out for my men while you rode for revenge. I should have been there and gotten mine. I deserve as much."

"You do deserve as much. I deserve as much. Our situations are not different." His steely eyes searched Wolf for a response.

"Enlighten me."

Wilhelm dipped his chin for a moment then spoke. "This is war. No man knows how long he'll grace this earth, men in war doubly so." He continued after a moment. "There was one thing I promised myself I'd do and that was make that man who took my son feel that pain. To make him hurt like I do. To make him feel it deep in his bones. To make him know that his son, that precious creature that he's raised from a babe to a lad to a soldier is gone before him. It's a wound that will never heal, Johannes." His lips tightened around his pipe as he relived his triumph. "And that look in Hampton's eyes. That recognition of another damaged soul. The realization of the pain that is going to plague him the rest of his life. It felt good."

Wolf's words came on sharp lashes of a whip. "Yet you told me to think of the men and follow orders. I could have been there with you."

"I did. You had the chance to do the right thing and you did it. For the greater good. You're a better man than me."

"I'm no better," Wolf spat. "I want the same thing you do. Vengeance for the injustice that's been done."

Wilhelm shrugged his shoulders. "No man, no matter how grounded, is perfect." He turned to Wolf and stared him in the eyes. "As gratifying as it felt to take that boy's life and to see the pain in his father's eyes, I immediately regretted it." His eyes watered, but no tears would grace his cheeks. "Perhaps I could have spared a man that ungodly pain. Maybe I should have stayed my hand. Yet the dark part of my heart pulled that trigger and sang with joy when that boy clutched his breast." He sucked in a breath. "And now that this is over, I don't feel any better than I did two weeks ago. No better than I did after Franz died." He looked away in distaste. "All joy faded to ash in my mouth a moment after Hampton's son cried out." He paused. "You remember something. Any man who stares the wraith of revenge in the eye and lets him pass unacknowledged is a man who is superior to all who embrace its touch."

Wolf nodded slowly, eyeing the man. "That man deserves that pain. He made a choice. He didn't have to kill Franz, yet he did."

Wilhelm glared at him in anger. "Don't you see, boy? Can't you see what I'm telling you? It wasn't worth it. Let those feelings die with the dead. They will only consume you and burn you up from the inside. I'm no better than I was yesterday. In fact, I feel worse." His eyes glinted hard in the firelight.

"Do you see?" He pointed at him with his pipe. "Answer me, Lieutenant."

"I see just fine."

Wilhelm's face relaxed a fraction. "Do not repeat my mistakes." He clamped down on his pipe, jaw clenching.

"I'm my own man. I'll make my own way."

Wilhelm raised his chin. "As a man should, but remember what I told you."

"I'll worry about that if we survive the rest of the war."

"Leave the fires lit," came a voice. Both men turned toward the newcomer. A messenger drove his horse through the camp. "Boots and saddles, lads. We be moving soon."

Wolf stood slowly, addressing the rider. "We're mightily used up. We got wounded."

"You don't think I'm tired, Lieutenant? Orders are to move out soon. Keep the fires going."

Wilhelm watched the rider go. "We withdraw back to the safety of the main army."

Wolf sighed. "All this madness for a retreat?"

"Appears so."

Wolf shook his head. His inherited company was barely enough to be considered a platoon. Men were missing. Men were wounded. Men dead and gone. And for what? To tear up a few miles of track? To run their horses into the ground? He knew why they fought, but this battle, this sacrifice, surely hadn't furthered the cause. He spit and gave Lowell a kick with his boot. "Get up."

Lowell shot upward on his elbows with a heavy groan. "What? Why? No more, Sarge." His eyes narrowed at Wolf. "Poor form, Lieutenant."

"Ain't a joke. Everyone up. We move in thirty," Wolf growled. He walked down the line, kicking boots and rousing his men.

Chapter 31

Night, June 12, 1864
Near the Bloody Angle entrenchments, Virginia

Hampton stared into wrinkling flames of the campfire. He hardly noticed the dirt and grime caking his clothes and skin. There was gore mixed in there too. He threw his gloves into the fire, disgusted with the stain left by his dead son's blood. The glove fingers slowly curled as the fire ate them away until they were crumpled ash.

He had elected to stay with the men as every local house and building were filled with both Union and Confederate wounded. His men held the field at the close of the second day, and they crawled from the breastworks made of fence rails and logs. The grisly sight of the numerous Union dead, left where they'd fallen, were now buried in a mass grave. Seven times the Union troopers charged his fortified position. Seven times they were thrown back like a pack of hungry dogs until they fled in the dying daylight. Even Fitz Lee had followed orders, flanking the Yankees with an excellent counterattack.

"Who would have thought my Fanny was such a lover boy," Rosser said from his seated position near the fire. His leg was supported by a splint and propped in the air. He refused to leave the field, so he languished in misery masked by copious amounts of alcohol to numb the pain, refusing anything stronger.

After a day of drinking, the libations began to take their toll even on the big officer. Words slipped off his tongue in a slur, and he tapped the note with his free hand. "This is good stuff." He then reached over and grabbed a bottle and took a quick swig. Then he cleared his throat and read for all to hear in his loud Texan accent. "I cannot wait to ride with you again for you are the finest." The burly officer grinned. "Unbelievable." He handed the letter to Butler, who appeared almost a skeleton compared to the well-built officer. He took it and silently read.

"I feel inappropriate for indulging in such a private conversation," Butler said with a joyful smirk. He deserved to have some delectation. His men performed incredibly deadly work early in the day. The Enfield rifles had had a devastating effect.

Colonel Gilbert J. Wright leaned forward, his spread-out eyes and dark beard giving him the appearance of a fiery preacher. "I don't even want to read that Yankee profanity." He shook his head gravely. "I must say they show the length and magnitude of Northern depravity. Godless. Immigrants and miscreants. They mustn't be allowed to run rampant through our God-fearing country."

"We sent them running like whipped dogs," Rosser said, sloshing a bottle in the air.

"Amen, brother," Wright said with a nod of respect.

"We have his spurs," Butler said. He held them in the air, and they clinked together with soft metallic whispers. He reached over and handed them to Rosser. "You two are friends. Perhaps when this is over."

"I will never understand your kinship with such a creature," Wright said darkly.

Rosser spit, pointing a finger at the man. "You shut your goddamn mouth."

Wright peered away into the darkness.

Rosser continued to stare at the other commander with violence and liquor in his eyes. His breathing settled. "I'll wear them until then. Bloody fine piece of craftsmanship. We should have had that Golden Boy right by the short hairs."

Hampton glanced vacantly from the dancing flames. Their words were mere background noise to a misery ringing in his ears. "You'll do no such thing."

All three of his brigade commanders turned his way. They were well aware of his grief and treaded lightly before it. Wary eyes stared at him, meaning it must have been some time since he'd last spoken. He had no idea how long it had been. And it didn't matter.

"I'm sending you to Gordonsville for treatment."

Rosser's blood was filled with enough whiskey to loosen a grizzly bear's tongue. "By God, you will. I'm staying with my men. We got some Yankees to whip."

"You will not," Hampton's voice became louder with every word. "Now that is a goddamn order."

Rosser's eyes grew wider. They'd seen him mad, but never as much so as he was against one of them. Hampton pointed an angry finger. "I will not sit by while your leg becomes swollen with pus and you die. You're leaving now."

"You can't." Rosser peered at him, dumbstruck.

"I can and I will. Lowndes," he said. His aide stood. His eyes were worried. Even injured, the belligerent officer was dangerous to escort. "Get me an ambulance and a surgeon. Take the general to Gordonsville for recovery."

Lowndes visibly exhaled and didn't ask any questions as he slipped off into the night.

Rosser shook his head. "Wade, you need me. Leg'll be fine."

"What are you going to do? Ride to battle in the back of an ambulance? You leave now." He eyed all his subordinates. The rest of them knew better than to make a case for Rosser to stay.

The entire group was composed of battered and scarred commanders, each one having been severely injured during the war. Hell, Butler didn't have a foot for Chrissake. Sinewy scarred holes where they'd been shot and hit with shrapnel lined their bodies beneath their clothes. Tiny bits of metal were embedded in their flesh, waiting to be pushed free later in life. Limbs hung useless at sides. Limps and uneven gaits showed from shattered hips and broken bones. And they were the ones that were still here. So many others had gone before. His mouth turned to ash and formed a bitter frown. "You men did well." He stood and walked away. None of his subordinates rose to follow him. They respected his desire to be left alone.

He crossed through the campfires and tents of his men. Picketed horses grazed on whatever grass they found. Most of his soldiers slept the sleep of the dead. Others ate stolen rations until they passed out, thankful to be fed and alive. General enervation smothered them, and yet the men still had hope that he did not share.

His war had become a barren place. He dreaded the letter he would have to pen to his wife relaying the tragedy of the day's events. Although she was not Preston's mother, she would wail in anguish. He gulped down a dry throat, unable to reconcile the death of Preston in his mind. Men died by his command every day, yet he never thought he would order the death of his own son.

His footsteps padded softly as he reached the graves of the men who had been killed that day as if he were afraid he may wake them. A makeshift cemetery had been made for the rebel dead. Freshly dug mounds rested in long rows in a farmer's field. *Ogg's Farm?* His mind was still addled by yesterday's events.

It was as if he'd lost an arm, a piece of him gone with no way to find it again. He could fill that void with drink, whores, or expensive watches and horses. Even if he hunted down every single bear from here to the Mississippi River, all those things would only be a wooden prosthetic limb where it had once been flesh, blood, and bone. He was sure of it.

His only comforting thought was that his men still needed him. They may not need him the same way his son did. *What happens when you sacrifice all of them?* He was the farmer and he cut them down one by one like stalks of wheat and fed them back into the earth as fertilizer for a spring planting. *What happens when there are none left? Only a farmer staring out at a dead field. What will we reap then?* Then the war would be over and whoever still lived would rule the day and the embers of a broken nation. And that pitiful fool would stand victorious on a pile of graves from Virginia to the heavens. And for what? Everything.

Everything was at stake, every bit of business he conducted was related in some fashion to slaves. He owned several hundred. Treated them fine. Gave them Sundays off. Made sure they were clothed and fed. What more could a man in servitude ask for? *If I would have known the sacrifice at hand from the beginning, would I have joined the fight? Knowing that it would take my brother and my son. Knowing my businesses would be burnt down and my body battered and filled with lead.* He sighed, a tired sound, and removed his hat and took a knee.

There had been no other option. He did what he must. He'd done what his father and grandfather would have done. Stood in the face of a tyrannical enemy. They just wanted to be left alone and live their lives. There was just no sitting this war out. And if it were his neighbors, friends, and family going to fight then he would be with them. It was the American way. Perhaps this whole affair could have been avoided, but those calmer people and cooler heads were a distant memory. Now he sat next to the grave of his son, nineteen-years-old, hardly even graced the earth as a man. Put to rest far from his family's home cemetery. In this alien place. He'd once demanded that his body be sent to South Carolina, but if he was to make his enemy pay, then Virginia soil would have to do.

Bugs, crickets, and frogs sang in the night. He ignored the few winged creatures buzzing around his ears. "I'm proud of you. You died a free man on free soil. Most men can't say that." His words came out fractured, mimicking the same state as his soul. "I only wish I could have taken that bullet instead of you. That you would stand over your father's grave. But we have a cruel God." He glanced at the moon. "That is certain." He sighed again, wiping a tear from his cheek. "We will meet again. Give your mother my love."

He lifted a knee upright, gathering his weight carefully as to not exacerbate the pain in his hip then moved to standing. He peered at the silent mound, rubbing his hat brim between his fingers. There was still more to say. "While there's still breath in me, I will carry on our fight," he said with a nod. Even with this loss, they'd turned back the Yankee cavalry. With a bit more luck and sacrifice, they would prevail. *But more fathers' boys will be put into the ground. It is something they will all have to accept. Just as I have.*

He waited for a response but knew one would never come. He placed his hat on his head and strode back to his men, a piece of him gone and buried, the long war still on the horizon.

Chapter 32

Custer sat in the saddle watching the flatboats ferrying across wagons and ambulances. Blue-uniformed horsemen waited to be ferried next. There was a general air of battered existence clouding over the Union command. Men called to one another as they rowed hard, oars dipping into the brown waters of the short crossing.

The Northern and Southern newspapers had quickly picked up on Sheridan's words of a great victory, but the questions that followed rang the bell of fabrication to his claims. Custer felt it too. He'd been battered, his men thrashed.

The entire command felt it. Gregg's Division had nearly collapsed the day before at Samaria Church. The cluster of near routs all but solidified the public's perception of a raid gone bad. Six of Hampton's rebel brigades viciously assaulted Gregg's two. Yet Gregg proved his steadiness as a commander, and his men covered Sheridan's flank to their own detriment, staving off an assault that could have crippled the Cavalry Corps with the capture of Sheridan's wagon train. The general had come close to capture himself tending a fellow officer, unaware that the rebels prepared to charge his position.

The battle reeked similarly of Custer's bloody stand at Trevilian Station. The only difference between their situations was Gregg had been able to retreat when the pressure became too great whereas Custer had been forced to hunker down. He had no doubt that Gregg would receive a promotion for his stand. *All I've received is the ill looks of my men.*

Exhausted skin-and-bone mounts mimicked their riders depressive state, heads down. And those were the poor beasts that had survived the journey. The rest were rotting carcasses on the sides of unnamed roads. He estimated over a thousand of them had been destroyed as they marched back toward the Army of the Potomac.

Men with arms in slings, heads bandaged, and legs wrapped rode and walked along in whatever they could find. But many of his men were just plain gone, missing or captured. The missing men that should be around him tugged at his heart. Their faces made his jaw grind and his teeth ache.

Most of his regiments had lost numerous junior officers further multiplying the impact of the losses. Colonel Moore simply vanished with the wagon train. He kept his chin level. It would mean something. It had too. Fresh faces would now attend his brigade staff meetings. It was a never-ending rotation of new officers in new posts, none were new to the war, only command itself.

I should write to Libbie. I wonder how she is. She surely is missing me. Yes, my love, I yearn for your comfort. He pulled at his red necktie. His uniform was soiled with enough dust for him to be mistaken for a rebel in gray.

Not that he had a choice in the matter. The rebels had left him with nothing but the clothes on his back. An extra pair of drawers would be a luxury. No, his toothbrush better. Yet he had neither. His mounts were gone, probably serving some poor horseman. At least he had Eliza back, but young Johnny Cisco was gone. He'd see the boy returned. He was only a boy; he didn't deserve the harsh reality of a rebel prison. No one really did.

He pursed his lips, feeling the bristles of his mustache. The heat was still unbearable. He'd led charge after charge. He'd been right beside his men in every danger they had faced. He would never ask them to go where he wouldn't lead. His men were battered, but they were Michigan boys, hearty stock, and would bounce back.

Yet this was the first time his faith had been shaken. The first time he'd seen the end in sight. He felt similar to a young boy climbing a tree with the courage of youthful invincibility, only to fall, breaking his arm, the cruel ground revealing to him the fragility of his own precious existence.

The entire thought was almost foreign. Surreal. But he had been there. The bodies of his men, bullets cutting them down like giant scythes of lead and steel. He knew that he had been lucky. A divine intervention. Could a man maintain his own luck? Seven horses shot out from beneath him and he had received nothing worse than a scratch and a bruise. It paid to have a short memory, but did it? He straightened his necktie again and wiped his cheek. He needed to see Libbie. That was it. God, that woman could warm a man's soul.

He gestured to one of his aides. "Granger," he said, pulling out a letter from his pocket. "I need you to go to the nearest telegraph office and send for Libbie. By the fastest means, I want her to meet us."

Granger looked uncomfortable, his eyes darting. "Sir, if I may speak frankly."

"You may if it's quick."

"We are still in danger here."

Custer dismissed him with a wave. "This raid is over. My men aren't doing anything except resting and refitting from here on out."

"Sir?"

He pushed the letter into his aide's hands. "Send for her. Fastest means possible. Train. Riverboat. I don't care."

Granger gave him a quick nod, flicked his reins, and galloped away.

Custer licked his lips with a half-smile. Now that would solve his problems right there. To see his bride and express his love for her would make the losses seem trivial. He sat a bit straighter in the saddle, his whole mood taking a swing for the better. *All is not lost on this war.*

A rider trotted toward him and gave him a quick salute. *I'm not following any orders that do not involve at least a week of rest.*

"General Custer, sir," the man said, shifting through a bag on his saddle. Removing a letter and a small wrapped package, he held it out timidly.

"What is this?" Custer said, regarding him with suspicion.

"Came through the lines, sir. I came straight here."

Custer frowned taking the package and note. He ran a finger along the envelope, opening it.

Dear Fanny,

I've come across a few of your belongings and correspondence, and I must say Libbie sounds like a wonderful treat. If I would have known she so enjoyed such a vigorous ride, maybe I would have courted her before you. Well done, my friend.

Custer felt the fires of anger burn away any doubt about the war. He continued reading.

Thought you might need a pair of your old drawers to replace the ones you were wearing at Trevilian Station.

- Tex

Custer snorted in amused disgust. "Tex, you son of a bitch." He shook his head, the anger simmering into a friendly spite. "I'll best you before this is done. We'll find out who is the better general." The thought of ill luck had all but disappeared. He took the letter and bent it in half, tucking the drawers in his pocket next to the spent bullet to show Libbie.

The sting of defeat whisked away. When one was bested in a fight, he stood back up, wiped his lip, and carried on a little wiser, a little better, and with the idea to give as good as you got. And repaying the favor to Thomas Rosser seemed as respectable an endeavor as any.

He'd see to it that big Texan met his match. Custer shook his head thinking of his old friend. *How much better would it have been, friend, if we fought some other poor sons of bitches instead of each other?*

Surely with Custer's performance at West Point, he would have been lucky to have received a commission in some other conflict. But in this one, they needed every single officer they could find. Many said he earned his stars only because of this war.

Lucky enough to have a war break out just as he was nearing graduation. Lucky enough to fall under the right rising commanders. Lucky enough to be promoted over other ambitious men. Lucky enough to have survived his last stand unscathed.

It may have been luck that he hadn't been wounded or killed so far in this war, but a little luck was better than no luck at all. One thing better than a little luck was a lot of luck and his luck hadn't run out yet.

Chapter 33

Wolf and Adams stood adjacent to the James River, lazily watching a steamship dock. His jacket was unbuttoned and his black hat shoved high on his forehead. A pistol and knife adorned his belt. No sword or carbine. He was as relaxed as he'd let himself be in as long as he could remember.

For days, Wolf's men had camped near Light House Point, a fingerlike sliver of land jutting out into the brown river. A white-sided lighthouse with a red capped roof stood sentinel on the shore alongside a small harbor and docks. It served as a docking station for supplies to Meade's coffers, and the men had taken full advantage of their close access. Morale for the Michigan Brigade slowly edged upward as the men healed in both body and mind, the emotional toil of the botched raid fading on the surface.

A broad sidewheel steamship named the *River Queen* was moored in the dock. Sailors onboard worked a gangplank into place while eager men waited below.

"Say isn't the *River Queen* the president's personal yacht?" Wolf asked.

Adams gave him a grin. "You think Old Abe came down to check in on us?" He didn't bother to wear his jacket, just a long-sleeved shirt rolled up to the elbows and trousers. No weapon save a knife on his belt.

Wolf snorted a laugh. "I think not." He squinted as a small troop of women lined the edge of the ship. "There's women onboard."

Both men scrutinized the ship even harder.

"You think they brought them down for us?" Adams said with a wink.

"Don't really care why they're here," Wolf said.

As one, the men on the dock surged forward as the females began to descend the gangplank like debutantes at their very first reveal. Caps and hats were removed. Men bowed and grinned doggedly. The women were smartly dressed in uniforms made for the fairer sex. Long dresses with braided long-sleeve tops, capped by kepis and satchels of nursing equipment.

"Come to nurse us back to health," said Adams.

"We are in sore need of some tender care."

"Apparently the general more so than most," Adams pointed out another woman and finely dressed gentleman walking down the gangplank from the ship. "If I ain't mistaken, the general's Mrs. came for a visit."

Wolf couldn't help but smile even if it was laced with sadness. He wondered if he would find love somewhere. Not the kind Roberts had found with his camp girl but true and respectable love. Remembering the way his friend spoke of his camp girl, maybe it was love? Who was he to say what true love was? Maybe he could find it long enough to enjoy it before a rebel bullet stole his life. He daydreamed of a foreign life without war and with the accompaniment of a lady.

Adams clapped his back, bringing him back to reality. "Well, Wolfie. They tend to not like it when you stare."

Wolf frowned at him and adjusted his jacket. "I wasn't."

"You were. Like a castaway seeing land for the first time."

"I dunno about that."

"Let's go talk to them." Adams gave him a mischievous glance.

Wolf returned it. It would be enjoyable to talk to some ladies. "Better than talking to you lot."

"You echoed my thoughts exactly." The two made their way through the camp toward the docks, but they were flagged down by Lieutenant Granger, his face red from the heat. He stopped them and did a double take at Wolf's leg then said, "Are you Lieutenant Wolf?"

Wolf and Adams eyed him suspiciously before Wolf spoke. An officer looking for you seldom was for a congenial reason. "I am."

"The general wants to see you now."

Adams clapped his back, quickly stepping away. "I'll be off on my own then." Adams had a keen instinct of when to make himself scarce. He tipped his hat and dipped away.

"Are we sure this can't wait?" Wolf said. He glanced over Granger's shoulder. Men removed their caps and gave the women support staff bows and charming smiles. The ladies responded in kind with broad smiles and an air of general happiness followed them. Even the scene from afar made Wolf's heart long for a woman to spend time with even if it was just a short conversation. That window of opportunity appeared to be closing with each second.

Granger peered over his shoulder at the growing congregation. "Sorry, chap," he said, his eyes softening. "He said as soon as possible." He peered at the ladies again. "They can wait."

Wolf gave him a slight nod. He supposed the women could wait. The congregation started to move toward the hospitals. More men stepped from their tents to wave or at least catch a friendly glimpse of the fairer sex.

"I suppose they can."

He tailed Granger and they weaved through the camp toward a dusty road. Men smoked and ate, slept, played cards, and wrote letters home. Very few did anything remotely soldierly. The only military duty was assigned to rotating pickets set far to the west, but even that task lacked any real threat. Most rebel forces operated south and west near Petersburg.

Wagons rolled down the street, moving supplies and goods from ships. A carriage creaked past. A platoon of troopers from the 1st Michigan walked their horses on by, their carbines resting on their hips. Even the men returning from picket duty appeared relaxed. They were living the easy soldier's life. Some may even consider it the boring soldier's life, but no man appeared to care much.

Granger led him to a small cottage-style house near the water. A man, his hair long and golden, sat on a porch swing with a short woman who laid her head on his shoulder. Custer's boots were kicked up on the railing, gently rocking the swing.

"Sir," Granger said. "Sorry to interrupt."

Custer gave him a grin. "You should be. Do you know how long it has been since I've seen my wife?"

"I do not, sir, but you requested that Lieutenant Wolf be led to you as soon as possible."

"That was earlier," Custer said, gesturing to his wife with his chin. "This is now."

Granger frowned, looking for a way to exit. "Yes, sir." He looked at Wolf with apologetic eyes.

Custer removed his feet from the railing and stood, giving his pants a tug with a free hand. "Don't fuss, Lieutenant. You may depart." Custer walked to the edge of the porch, looking out at the water. Granger gave him a slight nod and quickly departed, leaving the three of them.

The woman eyed Wolf with interest, her mouth curving in a sultry manner. Wolf gulped under her gaze and faced his superior. "Sir?" he asked Custer.

The general stared at the flowing brown waters. "Could be pleasant if the mosquitos weren't so bad."

Wolf followed his look. "Agreed, sir."

"Autie," Libbie said. "I don't think you've introduced me to your man here."

Custer glanced back at her, his eyes returning into focus. "You're right." He gestured at Wolf. "This is Lieutenant Johannes Wolf, 13th Michigan Cavalry."

Libbie stood, sauntering her way to the handrail. She was petite and pretty. She held out a hand with elegance for him to make her acquaintance. Wolf took it, clumsily unsure what to do as it was not a man's handshake. She eyed him with mirth, softly removing her hand. Her fingertip lingered for a moment then disappeared. "It is a pleasure to meet you, Lieutenant," she said, her eyes sparkling as a fresh snow on a sunny day.

Custer grinned at them both. "Rose through the ranks this one." He nodded. "One of my bravest. Reminds me of myself at a younger age. More guts than brains. But who needs brains when you got guts?"

Although unsure if Custer paid him a true compliment, he said, "Thank you, sir."

"He is a handsome lad," Libbie said with a smirk. "Surely he belongs to someone."

Heat surfaced in Wolf's cheeks. "I do not, Mrs. Custer."

She hmphed to herself. "You keep Autie in good company, Lieutenant, and I will see what I can do for you. There are plenty of women back home waiting for courtship from eligible bachelors such as yourself."

Wolf bowed his head to hide his embarrassment. "Thank you."

She lifted her chin. "But you have to promise to keep my Autie in one piece until the end."

A promise he could never keep. "I'll do my best."

She gave him a commanding nod and a simper. "That will have to be enough."

Custer leaned forward, his blue eyes alight with cheerfulness. "She's good for it too. She knows everyone. My eyes and ears that one. I would offer you a drink." His eyes darted to the side. "But not today."

Wolf nodded. "Of course, sir."

"I understand that your regiment took the brunt of the fighting at Trevilian Station."

"We did. My company has been through the mill."

Custer eyed the waters for a moment then glanced back at Wolf. "Too bad. The battle developed quicker than I would have liked."

"It did, sir. Was a difficult first day in command of a company." He could hardly call F Company a company now. Barely twenty men remained. Even fewer men than from the beginning of their enlistment.

"And Colonel Moore has unfortunately been captured. We received news from Richmond requesting exchange."

Wolf couldn't hide his lack of empathy for his commanding officer. The man was a coward and blowhard, deserving neither respect nor command. His eyes narrowed at the mention of his name. "That is unfortunate. Are they going to start exchanging prisoners again?"

"Time will tell. Although I am not saddened by the loss," Custer said. "I am happy to be rid of him, and I suspect you are too."

Wolf nodded. "There are better officers in this army."

Custer studied him and gave him a nod. "There are. A Major Bucklin from headquarters staff is rotating out into the field to take his place. Not a true Michigan lad, I believe he hails from Indiana, but he's been itching to find his way into the field for much too long. You captains will do well under his guidance."

"I'm sure they will."

Custer grinned at him again. "While the toll has been high, we are blessed to have able men in our brigade. Courageous men willing to go above and beyond." He eyed Wolf curiously as if he expected him to say thank you. "Congratulations, Johannes Wolf, you're a captain."

Libbie clapped from the porch, sounding the same as delicate rain drops on a rooftop. "Bravo, dear Captain."

Custer gave her a nod. "Yes, a well-deserved promotion for one of my best."

Wolf let out an exasperated sigh. Shaking his head, he said, "There must be someone else. Half my men were casualties. I'm not sure that shows true leadership potential."

Custer stuck out his hand. "Shows more than that, Captain. It shows you're the right man for the job."

Wolf took his hand, and Custer gave it a firm shake. "You'll have some men return to your company over the next few weeks. Wounded men and the such. If your company is still too thin, we'll shift over a platoon from a less affected command. Either way, I want you as one of my captains. Had half a mind to place you on my staff." He eyed him for a moment, trying to judge if he'd made a mistake. "But I'm not sure you'd be happy there."

Wolf nodded. "You're right, sir. I prefer to be with the men in the field."

"As do I. As do I." He glanced back at Libbie. "I hope you don't mind if I cut this celebration short. I have some business to attend to." With a friendly hand, he guided Wolf away from this cottage. "Rest up, Captain. I'm sure we will be back in the saddle before it's too late."

"I have no doubts."

"I'll put in the proper paperwork for the promotion." He tugged a letter from his pocket. "And take these orders to pick up your jacket with the proper insignia on it. Brigade's quartermaster." He handed Wolf a piece of paper. "Godspeed, Captain." He patted Wolf on the back and Wolf limped back toward the camp, eyes wider than normal as he comprehended his good fortune.

He unfolded the letter, silently reading. *Please outfit Captain Wolf with the proper insignia. Respectfully, Brigadier General G.A. Custer.*

Dumbfounded, he made his way to Sutler's Row where the quartermaster operated a large depot in a cluster of warehouses. The door was open, and he walked inside. The stench was dank with the mixture of leather and dried meat. The Michigan Brigade's quartermaster sat at a desk. He stopped scribbling on a page, and he peered at Wolf with narrow eyes and a rounded chin.

Damn. It was the same one he'd tricked a few weeks earlier. Wolf composed himself and marched toward him. "Good day." He slid the paper over the desktop to the man then stood straight, avoiding the man's eyes.

The quartermaster captain eyed him, his lids narrowing before he glanced at the paper then back at Wolf. He sucked his teeth after a moment. "Say, do I know you?"

"Can't say I know you. I'm Captain Wolf."

The man scrunched his nose. "No, can't be right." His close-set eyes narrowed. "You're the new quartermaster sergeant for the 7th Company D. I remember everything."

Wolf gave a quiet shake of his head. "I'm sorry. You must be mistaken." He nodded at the letter. "I am Captain Johannes Wolf, F Company 13th Michigan."

The quartermaster captain frowned. "I'm sorry, sir." His face twisted in consternation. "An oversight on my part. You must forgive me. There was a sergeant who looked just like you."

Wolf leaned over. "A lot of boys in this army. Bound to be one that looks like me."

The man sat back in his chair then slowly nodded. "Yes, of course. Let me check to see if I can find new insignia for you." He stood and disappeared into a back room.

Wolf let out a sigh. *All I need is this guy turning me in for stealing right after I've been promoted.* He put on a false smile as the man returned. "Here you go, Captain. Congratulations."

"Promotions are easy to come by nowadays. Good day, Captain."

"Good afternoon," the quartermaster said while taking a seat.

Wolf walked toward the door, each step easing his concerns over being caught.

"Wait a minute, Captain."

Wolf stopped and glanced at the ceiling in irritation. He turned around. "Yes?"

The quartermaster captain pointed. "Your knee brace."

That's it. This buffoon knows that I tricked him. He thought about punching him as he got closer, but that was only a short-term fix to his present situation. "What about it?"

The quartermaster captain smiled at him. "Here's some oil for the hinges." He bent down and rubbed an oiled rag on the hinges. Then stood. "Keep that corrosion down." He glanced at Wolf, his eyes friendly. "Far too many lads need new limbs."

"Agreed. Thank you, Captain."

"My pleasure."

Wolf walked back to his campsite, the knee brace mobile and less grinding. He found Wilhelm lounging near a campfire. He looked up at Wolf with a pipe in his mouth and nodded. "Lieutenant."

Wolf grinned. "Well, Sergeant, not anymore."

Wilhelm raised his eyebrows. "No?"

"Captain."

"Few men could deserve it more," Wilhelm said with a satisfactory grin beneath his curled mustache.

"I'm not sure about that. It was more a process of elimination."

Wilhelm puffed on his pipe, grayish-blue smoke billowing from the top. "Those boys gave us a hell of a run for it. No doubt about it."

"They did."

Removing the pipe from his mouth, Wilhelm said, "Got some fight in 'em still."

Wolf's eyes found the company guidon planted proudly in the ground nearby. Ripped and torn, battered and blooded, just like the company. Yet it still stood ready for the next battle. "They do."

"But so do we," Wilhelm said and placed the pipe back in his mouth to settle the point.

"Enough to finish this war."

Historical and Personal Note

The Battle of Trevilian Station was in some ways much like the Battle of the Wilderness for the cavalry. It was marked with hot dry weather, confusion, large swings in battle momentum, and a general chaos multiplied in intensity by the terrain. It also resulted in numerous casualties amongst the officer corps of each army. Sheridan lost six regimental commanders and numerous junior officers at Trevilian Station and Samaria Church (St. Mary's Church). This seems to have been brought on by the quickly moving forces of both Sheridan and Hampton.

The breakout of hostilities at Trevilian Station appears to have been a surprise to Sheridan and, to a lesser extent, Hampton. Sheridan was unaware that a credible rebel force had positioned itself to block his connection with Hunter. While Hampton was well aware of Sheridan's movements, he was caught off guard when an enemy brigade galloped into the rear of his command.

If Custer would have left a bit sooner than he had in the morning of June 11, 1864, he would have run smack into Wright's brigade shifting in position to support Butler near the opening of the battle. Who knows if this would have changed the outcome. For one thing, the 5th Michigan and Custer's Brigade as a whole would have most likely not ended up in temporary possession of Hampton's train and subsequently would not have been surrounded and forced into a "last stand" situation.

Custer's flanking movement to Trevilian Station was likely the result of poor intelligence by Sheridan. This poor intelligence almost led to a lucky break. Capturing Hampton's wagon train would have crippled his corps's effectiveness, not to mention the fact that a sizable enemy operated in Hampton's rear, potentially spelling an early defeat for rebel forces.

The gap between the parts of Hampton's division and Fitz Lee's division almost cost them both dearly. Some blame can be put on Fitz Lee for not linking with Hampton sooner. His men marched much slower and behind Hampton's in the rush to get ahead of the Union cavalry. His delay in closing the gap had a detrimental effect on Hampton as he scrambled to respond early in the battle with the rear flanking threat. Yet some blame does go upon Hampton for not forcing Lee to link and not recognizing he was so exposed.

Once Hampton realized he was in a bind, he operated quickly to change his situation, urging his forces to surround the enemy brigade. Custer's position was a triangle with Butler and Wright to the north, Rosser to the west, and Fitz Lee to the east.

Custer surely felt the chaos within the first hour of the battle when the tides shifted from capturing the enemy's wagon train to missing both Alger and Kidd, two of his four regimental commanders. Quickly the situation became even worse as he was surrounded and almost annihilated. Then his pride was battered with the capture of not only his prize but his personal luggage and servants, especially the love letters from Libbie. The pressure was so fierce on his command he hid the brigade's flag under his coat. Knowing of Custer's demise in the west, the battle eventually became known as Custer's "First Last Stand." But some historians argue there were two other "last stands" before Trevilian Station indicating a pattern of reckless behavior.

The battle itself is marked by much confusion by the men who wrote about it later. The fight swung back and forth throughout the day. There is some source material putting regiments in unlikely positions during the day. This probably has to do with the densely forested terrain. Units were separated from one another, isolated, and generally lost through portions of the battle. Men were held prisoner one moment, then freed the next, then captured again. There was even an instance where a squadron of Kidd's men were chasing fleeing rebels, then the next moment fleeing themselves, only to turn around and chase the rebels again.

The landmarks of the battlefield added to the confusion as men labeled Netherland Tavern as the "depot" or Trevilian Station, which was in fact farther to the west. Even today there is debate as to where Trevilian Station actually stood during the battle. The original structure is gone. Much of the fighting stretched over the length of the two structures, and to the north, this may have been confusing to the men in their reports and to historians deciphering the battle later. This made the timeline of events difficult to hammer down, but also left some literary wiggle room to craft an entertaining story.

A few things were clear. Custer's men deemed the that nowhere was safe. There were countless desperate engagements over the course of this battle. Hampton lost his baggage train early, increasing the intensity of the whole affair. After he realized the vulnerability of the enemy force(Custer's Brigade), the tempo of the conflict grew even more heated. For Custer, but a lesser extent Hampton, being surrounded and almost knocked out of the war added even higher stakes. For large segments of the battle there was no place for brigades to retreat, leading to an even more committed fight.

This novel largely glosses over the second day of Trevilian Station. This is only because of the focus of the story itself. The second day was as hard fought by both armies as the first. Hampton took the initiative to block Sheridan's path on June 12, 1864, but this time had a defensive entrenched position.

Sheridan threw his men at Hampton's position all afternoon before he retired. There is debate as to the indecisiveness shown by Sheridan. He may have been attempting to withdraw after the first day then thought better of it. If so, he sent one of his divisions in the wrong direction. Torbert claimed he was sent to conduct reconnaissance on the enemy, yet when he found them, he deployed his brigades and attacked. After the fact, Sheridan claimed he sent Torbert's division to attack Hampton. Either way the Union commander's orders showed a lack of proper coordination between his divisions, but the fact remains, Hampton's men held them off, forcing a withdrawal beneath the moonlight.

Claiming great victory in name only, Sheridan left the field and marched back toward Grant, neither linking with Hunter, destroying the railroad, or destroying Hampton's Corps. He conflicted himself in subsequent reporting, rewriting the narrative and his mission priorities. What remains true is that the sacrifice was immense. The Michigan Brigade would never be the same. They sustained almost 500 casualties, over 700 after 6 weeks of campaigning. Sheridan's divisions lost thousands of mounts. He temporarily crippled the Cavalry Corps without much to show for it. It would take time to remount and bring the corps back up to strength.

The players and narrative of the novel are largely based in historical fact. Some scenes depicted may appear fictional but are fact. Colonel Alger went missing early in the attack on Hampton's baggage train and was almost captured several times. Much of Alger's command, the 5th Michigan, was not that lucky and were prisoners by the end of the day.

Major Kidd had traded mounts with another officer "to take the ginger out of him," and his new mount went wild during the attack on the baggage train. He was captured and then freed, and captured his captors taking the finest mount from the rebels.

Custer was everywhere during the battle, propping up his besieged force. At one point, he led a charge to recapture a cannon. His servant Eliza Brown was captured and escaped back to Union lines. Johnny Cisco, his other young servant, was captured and his whereabouts unknown after the battle. The only information I could find about Johnny's fate was that he followed Custer to the West after the war where Custer secured him a position as a messenger for Wells Fargo. Later Johnny was killed by Indians, unrelated to any of Custer's Indian campaigns.

I took some license with the positioning of units and the timeline of the battle itself, so if you do fact-check the work, please remember that this has been fictionalized for the purpose of creating a compelling tale. I always try to come clean in this note so you have a better understanding of the reality. Here are some of the major fictionalized events.

While communication was scarce between Custer's command and his division commander, elements of Torbert and Gregg's divisions could make out fierce fighting by the Wolverine Brigade. Both Torbert and Custer struggled all day linking lines of communication, and it wasn't until the afternoon that Captain Amasa Dana from Torbert's staff was able to reach Custer. This precipitated a breakthrough from Merritt's Regulars, who were eager to help their Michigan comrades in danger. Yet it was still some time before the Michigan Brigade would be fully relieved, and communication issues continued to plague Torbert and Custer for the entire day.

Preston Hampton was killed at the Battle of Boydton Plank Road or Burgess Mill and not Trevilian Station. I took literary license here for the series and character arcs/plot. I also changed the timeline for the linking between Custer and Torbert, putting the Charge of the Citadel Cadets at a more pivotal moment in the novel. This was all done for story purposes although the intensity remains the same.

The number of Union forces appears to be disputed between historians. The number in Sheridan's command ranged from 6000-9,300 men. This is significant as 6,000 makes the opposing forces close to equal in size while 9,300 basically gives the Union the superiority of an entire division (however understrength) over Hampton. I speculate that it must be somewhere closer to the 8,000 mark for Union forces based on the knowledge that he only traveled with two divisions, the third under Wilson staying with the main army. It can be speculated that there is confusion as the 9,300 number would have been the forces on paper, but as we now know, and in particular during the Civil War, the forces on paper were never that large due to illness, injury, desertion, and probably, most importantly, access to mounts.

If Sheridan started the toward Yellow Tavern with roughly 10,000 troopers in early May, then surely he would have less than 9,300 after continuous campaigning for the month. At the Battle of Yellow Tavern alone, he lost almost 700 men. This doesn't take into consideration any of the engagements after Yellow Tavern, which includes Haw's Shop and Cold Harbor. But what needs to be taken into consideration more than available fighting men is the available horses as there was limited opportunity for remount.

The amount of riding and raiding done had drastically diminished the health of the Union Cavalry Corps mounts. They were further depleted in number by employing the tactic of shooting any mounts injured along the way to keep a potential horse from Southern hands. Some sources report that between going to Trevilian Station and back, there were almost 2,000 slain horses from the journey alone. Sheridan himself, after the war, claimed to have only roughly 6,000 men, but it is inferred he did this to soften the blow of his failure. I read numerous sources and came across the numbers 10,000; 9,300; 8,000; and 6,000. I chose one number in the middle—8,000—and moved forward from there.

These next few fictions are quite trivial, but I thought they should be mentioned.

Confederate Brigadier General Thomas Rosser was shot in the leg as his forces were linking with Butler's, not leading a charge upon Custer's Brigade.

Colonel Russell Alger was on sick leave in Washington for the Battle of Haw's Shop.

The song "Garryowen" was a fun historical piece from Custer's lore. It is unknown when and where he first heard the song. We do know that it became one of Custer's favorites and was subsequently adopted by the U.S. 7th Cavalry after the Civil War as their marching song. The song was said to have been brought to the 7th Cavalry by Myles Walter Keogh, who served in the Civil War under Buford and Stoneman. Then later in the west, he died with Custer at Little Bighorn. However, the song was known throughout the army during the war having been introduced by the many Irish soldiers serving in the ranks.

Custer's charge to reclaim his wagon train near the close of June 11th was in actuality the 7th Michigan and not the 1st Michigan. That night he stayed at the nearby Trevilian plantation home, but only used the front porch as the daughter was sick with typhoid fever the night of June 11, 1864. I made the decision to switch his HQ to the Netherland Tavern because the setting was already established instead of introducing a new one.

While this novel is a piece of historical fiction, you may be interested in more detailed information on the history itself. I would encourage you to read *Glory Enough for All* by Eric J. Wittenburg or *Trevilian Station, June 11-12, 1864* by Joseph W. McKinney. Both provide an excellent portrayal and interesting analysis of the largest all-cavalry battle of the Civil War.

Thank you for reading, and I cannot wait to share the next installment of the Northern Wolf Series with you.

Best,

Daniel Greene
September 15, 2020

Extras

Thank you for accompanying us on this historical adventure! The fourth novel of the Northern Wolf Series ended with a brutal stand for Wolf and his company. However, the war is grinding to a close. The nation will never be the same. The final book in the series is coming your way soon! Pick up *Northern Shadows* **Book 5 of the Northern Wolf Series here!**

The Greene Army Newsletter: Want exclusive updates on new work, contests, patches, artwork, and events where you can meet up with Daniel? An elite few will get a chance to join **Greene's Recon Team**: a crack unit of talented readers ready and able to review advance copies of his books anytime, anywhere with killer precision. Sign up for spam-free Greene Army Newsletter here: http://www.danielgreenebooks.com/?page_id=7741

Reviews: If you have the time, please consider writing a review. Reviews are important tools that I use to hone my craft. If you do take the time to write a review, I would like to thank you personally for your feedback and support. Don't be afraid to reach out. I love meeting new readers!

You can find me anywhere below.

Facebook Fan Club: *The Greene Army - Daniel Greene Fan Club*
Facebook: *Daniel Greene Books*
Instagram: *Daniel Greene Instagram*

Website: *DanielGreeneBooks.com*
Email: *DanielGreeneBooks@gmail.com*

A special thanks to all those who've contributed to the creation of this novel. A novel is a huge feat and would remain as a file cluttering my desktop without the contributions of so many wonderfully supportive people. This includes my dedicated Alpha Readers, Greene's Recon Team (GRT), the Greene Army, my editor Lisa, my cover artist Tim, Polgarus formatters, and especially my readers. Without readers, this is an unheard/unread tale. I can't wait to share more stories with you in the future.

About the Author

Daniel Greene is the award-winning author of the growing apocalyptic thriller series The End Time Saga and the historical fiction Northern Wolf series. He is an avid traveler and physical fitness enthusiast with a deep passion for history. He is inspired by the works of George R.R. Martin, Steven Pressfield, Bernard Cornwell, Robert Jordan, and George Romero. Although a Midwesterner for life, he's lived long enough in Virginia to call it home.

Books by Daniel Greene

The End Time Saga

End Time

The Breaking

The Rising

The Departing

The Holding

The Standing (Coming Soon)

The Gun (Origin Short Story)

Northern Wolf Series

Northern Wolf

Northern Hunt

Northern Blood

Northern Dawn

Northern Shadows (2021)

WITHDRAWN

Printed in Great Britain
by Amazon